Forsaken Beauty and the Etherbeast

Kelsey Josephson

Edited by Jeanne De Vita and Kristi O'Meara

Proofreading by Jeanne De Vita, Kristi O'Meara, and Stephanie Fung

Formatted by Michael Lee

Cover designed by Deranged Doctor Designs

Steampunk Publications

ISBNs:

Print trade paperback: 979-8-9879210-2-9

Print hardcover: 979-8-9879210-3-6

A NOTE FROM KELSEY

Welcome to Nuzaran, a world with steam-powered airships, sentient automatons, and slow-burn romance! A quick note before you dive into this steampunk fairy tale: Forsaken Beauty and the Etherbeast was previously published as a weekly serial on several online platforms. This book contains the complete epic story. Happy reading!

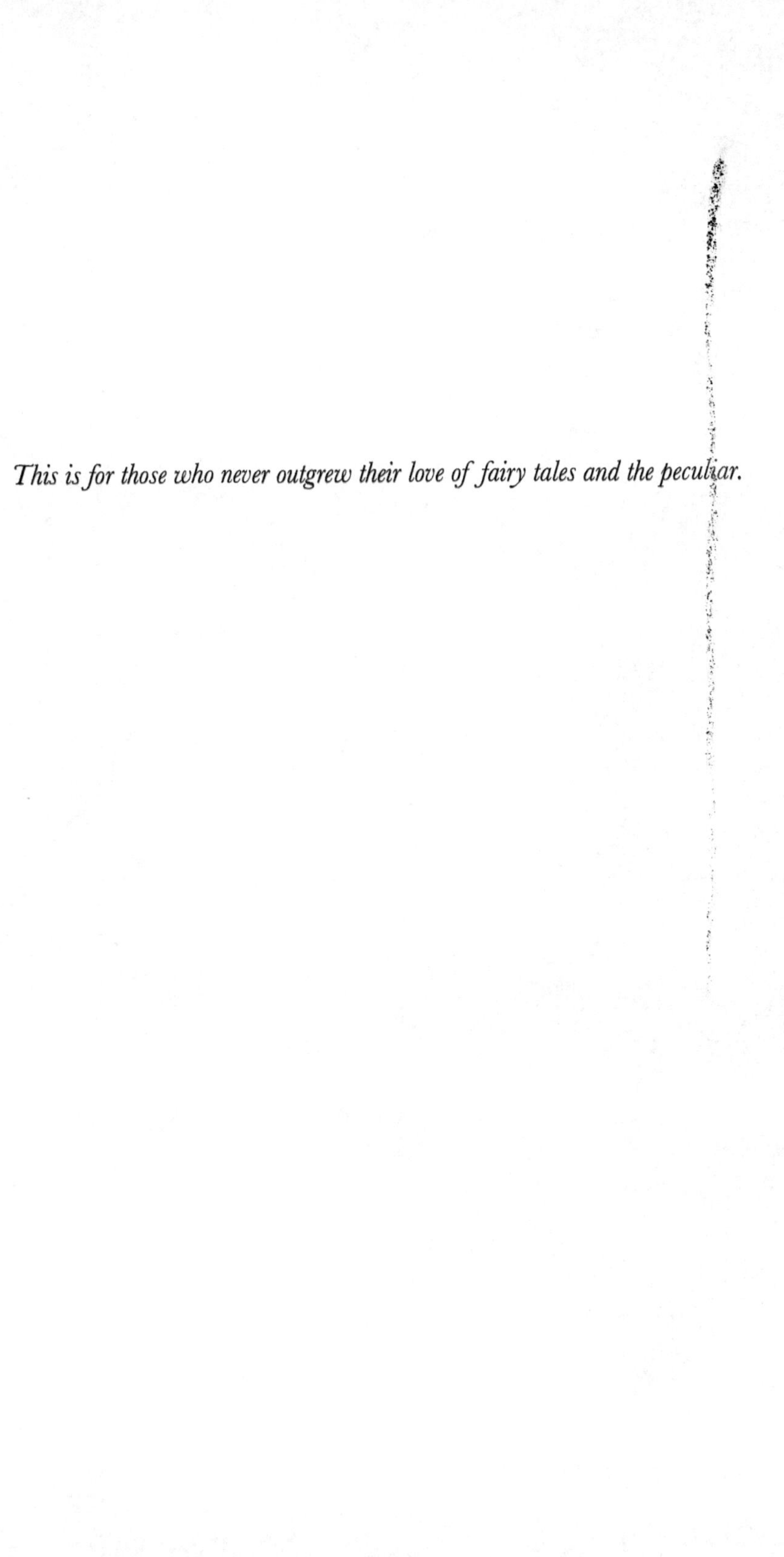

This is for those who never outgrew their love of fairy tales and the peculiar.

CHAPTER ONE

The Circus Illume billed their strongwoman as "Belle" to mock her. Her dull charcoal hair matched the soot-filled sky of Aetherbourne, the miserable mining town she had called home before she was bought for a meager sack of silver coins.

No one would call her a beauty. Blue veins snaked beneath her almost translucent skin. She towered over the tallest patron at every show. Audiences whispered that there had to be something wild and unnatural in her blood to give her such height and strength. The truth was far more simple. Belle wasn't the first child born with ether-poison deformities, but hers were the most striking.

The ether that fueled airships and powered cities was mined from volatile ore deep within Nuzaran's caves. Both of Belle's parents had labored in the mines since they were old enough to operate the tools. By six years old, she was already working alongside her father when her mother succumbed to the airborne ether-poisoning.

On the day her mother was buried, Belle's grief and rage culminated in her first and last childhood tantrum. She'd grabbed a loaded minecart barehanded and derailed it, smashing the cart into the ore body and terrifying the other workers. Whispers of the child's uncanny strength spread far and wide from Aetherbourne.

When the Ringmaster of the Circus Illume heard about the young girl of massive stature and supernatural power, he showed up at their crooked shack with coins and false promises. Belle tried not to hate her father for putting his trust in the showman. He had looked so desperate and frail.

"It will be better than the mines." Her father hugged Belle goodbye, the money still clutched in his hands.

It'd been ten years since she'd seen him. Belle wondered if the poison had taken him, too.

In the distance, the Ringmaster barked out orders to his crew as they set up portable heaters for the circus' caravan, bringing Belle out of her morose recollections. The Circus Illume should've been on the road heading south, but winter had come early. A hurricane had ravaged the next city they were due to perform in. If Minport flooded, the circus' light show and steam-powered props couldn't go on.

The Ringmaster decided to set up camp halfway to Minport until the storm blew over. Belle's shabby trailer was parked at the edge of the forest. Farther into the clearing, other performers laughed around their fire.

The copper ankle bracelet—a constant reminder of her status—would send a nasty shock through Belle's body if she strayed too far. But she should have been safe to travel within eyesight of her trailer in any direction, so Belle settled in a secluded picturesque spot where the birch trees gave her enough privacy that she could pretend she was alone.

A fallen log served as her bench. Belle admired the falling snow as she sipped hot mulled cider by her cozy fire, courtesy of the meager supplies she was allowed to keep in her trailer. Tension melted as her belly warmed.

But her good mood vanished when she heard twigs snapping. Belle stood, peering into the woods.

Low, rumbling growls followed more snapping twigs, closer this time.

A bear, its hazy silhouette visible through the smoke, emerged from the thicket behind Belle's campfire.

As Belle debated whether or not she could reach a weapon

without triggering her shock anklet, the creature stood on its hind legs. Transfixed, Belle immediately realized it was not a bear. The beast stalked closer. Delicate but deadly antlers crowned his head. His lean body was covered in silver fur, with specks of black reminiscent of the birch trees' patterned bark behind him. His paws ended in long wicked claws that reached toward her.

There was a hungry gleam in his owlish yellow eyes. Belle thought she also saw pain and loneliness, but wondered if it was a trick of the light or her own foolish hope. She reached into her pouch for jerky and held out several pieces for her uninvited guest.

Perhaps the beast would take it and leave—or devour her whole. Belle supposed she should have cared more about the latter.

"Go on. You can have some." Belle waited while he considered her offering.

Then the beast snatched the jerky and fled into the night, leaving Belle relieved and oddly bereft. Her cider had grown cold, but she finished it before turning in for the night.

Dawn revealed another blanket of snow that had fallen on the caravan. The Ringmaster put Belle to work chopping more firewood for the camp. She didn't breathe a word about her visitor, not wanting to be responsible for another unwilling act joining the show. But still, she scanned the trees as she finished her tasks. The day was disappointingly mundane.

As the sun set, Belle's muscles burned. She considered either going straight to bed, or burning precious fuel in her lantern to read a book from the secret cache hidden under her cot. But instead, she felt compelled to stay by the fire a little longer, sipping cider again. When the moon was high, a familiar rustling sounded in the thicket.

The beast appeared, slowly approaching as if he was trying not to spook her. When he was by Belle's side, he held out his paws, a plump apple in each.

Belle's sparse brows rose. "Fresh apples in winter? Where on earth did you find them?"

The beast opened his mouth, speaking in a low, indecipherable growl. Shaking his head, he shrugged.

"Thank you." Belle patted his paw.

He nudged her to eat, pushing one of the apples closer.

As Belle took the apple, distant raucous laughter reminded her that they weren't alone. "If you keep coming here, they'll catch you," she warned, pointing to her chafing ankle bracelet.

The beast huffed as he bit into his apple. After wiping the last bits of juice off his snout, he stalked into the woods without glancing back at her.

Belle was morose the next day. In the circus, she had no true allies. She had forgotten what it was like to have someone who wanted to see her for herself, not for a performance. Though Belle knew sending the beast away was for the best, she'd not felt so alone in a long time.

So even though she knew better, Belle once more waited by the campfire as night came, the wind failing to bite through the thick wool cloak she'd bundled up in. Laying out extra jerky and cider in a second steaming ceramic mug, Belle hoped she wasn't making a horrible mistake.

When the moon was high, the beast emerged once again, his silver fur tangled and covered in burs. He clutched a single white rose between his claws, ducking his head at Belle's puzzled scrutiny.

"Are you hurt?" Belle asked, gently touching the scratches on his forearm.

The beast nodded once as he handed her the flower.

"Thank you. Let me help you." Belle coaxed him to sit by her. She tucked the rose, its thorns pulled off, behind her ear as he padded closer.

The beast was tense, perching on the log bench. After murmuring reassurances, she plucked burs and detangled his fur with her fingers. As she delicately separated a matted section, Belle bit back a gasp when she noticed a patchwork of smooth skin and scars running the length of his forearm that suspiciously resembled stitches healed up long ago.

"Who did this to you?"

The beast gave her a despondent shrug.

"I'm sorry you have so many scars."

The beast growled, but there was no menace to it. He huffed, wrinkling his snout in disgust.

To distract him, Belle talked about life in the circus. When he seemed agitated by her story, she switched to describing the fantastical places the caravan toured.

As she spoke, the comfortable heat radiating from the fire and the beast's rapt attention lulled Belle into a dreamlike state. She told him about the time the electric fence malfunctioned and she'd escaped, choosing to spend the day marveling at an orrery in the capital city, Onyxmark. The model sun was twice her height. Watching the hypnotic orbit of the surrounding planets had been the most enchanting experience of her life. When she'd been discovered, her heart had shattered, but the memory sustained her on her worst days.

"Find a friend?" The familiar mocking voice startled Belle into the present. The Ringmaster brandished shock sticks as he stood across from the fire, flanked by two cronies.

"Run," Belle choked out.

Hackles raised, the beast roared at the men, displaying crooked canine teeth.

"Run!" Belle repeated, adrenaline thrumming through her as she swung her fist at the Ringmaster.

It was too late.

Shock sticks crackled as they connected with Belle's torso, burning her skin. She twitched as she collapsed, gasping. The beast fell next, hitting the ground with a resounding thud.

"What a fine addition you'll make once I've broken you," the Ringmaster said, his lips curling.

In a guttural rasp, the beast uttered a single word to Belle. "Help."

CHAPTER TWO

The beast did not break easily. When dawn broke, he was still bellowing.

The night before, after the beast had been dragged off, Belle was tossed into her trailer and dumped onto her thin cot. She had agonized all night over how to free the beast. Her copper ankle bracelet seemed even heavier than usual, its glowing crimson orb an ever-present reminder of her captive status.

Belle knew it should have frightened her to encounter such a strange creature. A sentient, antlered bear was not the norm for beasts in Nuzaran, but something found only within the fiction she consumed right under the Ringmaster's nose. However, ether often had mystifying effects. The few times that Belle had been able to sneak a newspaper, she'd read about bioluminescent sparrows and other oddities. Her own translucent skin was proof enough of the effects of undiluted ether, so she reasoned that a creature such as the beast wasn't impossible. Only unexpected.

Giving up on rest, Belle resolved to see the beast. When she finally reached the scene of the chaos, her bloodshot eyes couldn't believe what they were seeing. The Ringmaster had imprisoned the beast in the old tiger enclosure behind the storage trailers. An anklet identical to the one Belle wore cut into the beast's hind leg, though his looked as if the dented band had weakened—the orb flickering pale red.

The beast snarled, baring his sharp teeth at the Ringmaster and one of his lackeys who cowered behind the grappling pair. Pinned under the beast's massive paws, the Ringmaster barked orders, too preoccupied to notice Belle's presence.

Belle's knuckles turned white, and her jagged fingernails bit into her palms as she clenched her fists. Fresh burns from the shock sticks stung underneath the loose-fitting blouse she wore to cover the faded scars crisscrossing her torso. Last night was the first time she had attempted to strike the Ringmaster in years. Despite her strength, Belle rarely engaged in violence, always afraid of her power and the consequences.

Belle helplessly watched a few feet away from the scuffle. The beast gained ground, shoving the Ringmaster against the bars with a clang.

The hapless lackey shrieked, catching the beast's attention. With a low growl, the beast charged at him.

Belle stepped on a twig, snapping it.

Looking toward Belle, the beast halted, his antlers narrowly avoiding gouging the lackey. Bloodshot yellow eyes met her brown ones. His brows drew together in a deep frown. He stopped growling, ducking his head as he turned away from her.

The Ringmaster stood, dusting the straw off his long red duster, his blond plait frazzled. His makeup had been smeared, revealing the faded, jagged scars disfiguring his left cheek. "What's this?" he asked, looking between Belle and the beast.

He smirked when he saw Belle standing near the enclosure. "I see. And here I thought the beast was finally cowed under my methods, but I see his weakness is clearly your…charms." The Ringmaster pursed his thin lips as his eyes traveled from Belle's tangled charcoal hair to her flimsy muddy boots.

Angry heat flushed Belle's face. Trembling, she tried to keep her words guarded, but her control slipped. "Why are you doing this? He could be dangerous."

The Ringmaster's hazel eyes glittered. "Don't you realize how many people will flock to the Circus Illume when they hear about our one-of-a-kind exotic beast?"

"What good will it do if he rips off someone's arm?" Belle pinched the bridge of her nose, the beginnings of a migraine forming in the center of her forehead. A wave of nausea washed over her.

Belle couldn't believe the sheer ego behind the Ringmaster's scheme. She supposed nothing was beyond his shallow pool of morals, especially considering all the years he'd kept her—a bag of silver shouldn't have covered a lifetime of servitude. Even the cage the Ringmaster now stood in was a damning piece of evidence of his past misdeeds with a creature he couldn't control. Belle had failed to save the tiger. She hoped she wouldn't fail the beast.

The Ringmaster's smile was cold. "You're worried about him hurting someone?" He shrugged. "Don't worry. If the beast knows what's good for him, he'll cooperate. He responds to you. And if he doesn't, there are alternatives."

"What do you mean?" Belle asked, her gaze flicking over to the beast's hunched form. He was curled up in his cage, ignoring the exchange. He hadn't uttered a single word since his cry for help. Belle wondered if she'd imagined him speaking last night or if the beast had enough sense to keep quiet in front of the Ringmaster. Belle wished she could do the same.

"Simple," replied the Ringmaster. "If the beast doesn't comply, we'll dispose of him and find a taxidermist. I'll either sell his corpse or display it myself. Charging separate admission, of course. Either way, I'll make a tidy profit." The Ringmaster scoffed at the tears pooling in Belle's eyes.

"What do you need me to do?" Belle hated herself for asking, but the Ringmaster would make good on his promise if she didn't choose her words wisely.

Belle felt delusional, thinking she could help the beast. She would have escaped by now if she'd had an inkling of a successful escape plan.

"He's going to be your co-star for a new act to debut in Minport. I want you to convince our new guest to participate." A malevolent light sparked in the Ringmaster's eyes. "What a fine pair you'll make."

"That doesn't give us a lot of time to prepare."

The Ringmaster pointed a gloved finger at Belle. "Since when are you so talkative? Have you forgotten your place? If it weren't for me, you'd be wasting away in the ether-mines." His eyes flicked down to her ankle bracelet. "Or do you need another reminder?"

Belle stepped back, her gaze downcast. "No."

Internally, Belle wanted to scream. She'd never talked this much while with the circus, especially to the Ringmaster. Every interaction she'd ever had with him was fraught with peril. His mercurial nature was grating and dangerous. Belle never knew if she had overstepped his ever-shifting boundaries until it was too late.

"Then it's settled," said the Ringmaster, lifting his arms in benediction. "We'll have a wonderful new act. I'll tell you all the details later. That damnable hurricane has blessed us in the end." His too-white teeth shined in the dawn's pale light. "Report back around lunchtime. I don't suppose you know what this beast eats?"

Belle blinked. "He ate an apple and some of my jerky."

"Outstanding." The Ringmaster motioned with his hands, and soon his sniveling lackey dashed off, likely to fetch breakfast for the beast. The Ringmaster let out an exaggerated yawn. "Now, if you'll excuse me, I'm going to get my beauty sleep and finalize my plans for the new act."

The Ringmaster left with a flourish of his red duster, leaving Belle alone with the beast.

Swallowing hard, Belle took a few tentative steps forward until she was at the edge of the cage, fresh tears stinging her sensitive eyes. "I am sorry, you know. I should have turned you away when you returned again and not let my guard down." Belle took a shuddering breath. "I'm a fool."

The beast didn't turn around or even huff with annoyance. Instead, he curled tighter into himself, not unlike a sleeping cat. A bittersweet memory of the old tiger sleeping in the same cage five winters ago came unbidden to Belle's conscience. Another wave of nausea hit her, though it had little to do with her pounding migraine.

Before leaving, Belle placed her hand on the enclosure's tight bars. "I'm not asking for your forgiveness. I don't deserve it, but I will make this right."

The beast huffed but didn't stir.

With a lump in her throat, Belle left the enclosure, more worried than ever that the Ringmaster's cruel streak would find another victim in the beast.

Belle meandered to the makeshift cafeteria, her headache now a dull, constant pain. The outside of the trailer featured a large open window with a worn wooden counter, packed with a basket of fruit, a jug of water, and mugs of cider. The scent of fresh bread was enough to make her stomach rumble and almost forget her queasiness.

Cook's silver curls were in rollers when she poked her head out the window and gave Belle a toothy grin. "I thought I heard you out here. It's a little early, but no matter. Look what I have for you! Some breakfast reading." She beamed as she handed Belle a tray with bread, cheese, bacon, and a steaming mug of cider. A dark-blue pocket-sized book dotted with silver stars on its cover was placed on the tray.

"Thank you. I appreciate it." Belle mustered a smile as she accepted the tray.

"It'll be our secret." Cook put a finger to her painted lips. "It's what the Maker would want."

Belle's smile faded as she took her breakfast back to her cramped trailer. She didn't know what the Maker wanted, but hoped the omnipresent deity would want her free instead of a captive performer, reduced to accepting illicit books.

It was sweet that the grandmotherly Cook smuggled Belle books. But it would have been better if she helped her escape or at least did something to the Ringmaster's food to make him indisposed. Belle didn't want to be ungrateful because she knew there was only so much Cook could do, but it hurt that even those with freedom never challenged the Ringmaster.

Unhurried snowflakes dusted the camp in a powdery coat as Belle made her way back to the beast's cage. In her absence, someone had erected a green tent over it. She brushed the snowflakes off her faded blue cloak as she entered the tent. Inside, the beast was forlorn, despite being outside of his cage. When she drew closer, the reason was immediately clear: ether-laced chains kept him tethered on a short leash.

The Ringmaster, or more likely one of his cronies, had dressed the beast in a dramatic emerald-green velvet cloak and tattered black pants, and placed an evergreen wreath over his horns. It made the creature appear as if he were from a classical painting—only instead of a regal forest king, the beast looked disgusted, wrinkling his snout at the ridiculous costume. It was such a human expression that Belle's breath hitched at the realization.

She kept her mouth shut, though. If the beast had chosen to hide from everyone else that he could speak, she wasn't about to further betray his trust. She'd have to talk to him in private about it later.

"Glad you could join us." The Ringmaster's cream-colored sleeves were rolled up to his elbows and the laces of his shirt were untied. He led a mechanical unicorn into the center of the tent. His makeup was back in place, concealing his raised scars.

Despite her terror and revulsion with the Ringmaster's actions, Belle was enchanted by the machine. Delicate movements and occasional wisps of steam rose from its nostrils, giving the mechanical unicorn a convincing likeness to the mythical creature.

"Impressive, no?" The Ringmaster preened as he pressed a button on the back of the neck that was concealed by a translucent fiber mane. Small lights covering the unicorn's entire body glowed electric blue and violet. The mane shone like starlight as the machine took a few graceful steps forward.

Belle reached to pet the mechanical unicorn, enchanted by the light show. But as if wounded by the very same display that drew Belle to the unicorn, the beast let out a pained roar that brought her back to reality. When she looked to see what was wrong, the beast was covering his eyes and growling.

"Stupid creature!" the Ringmaster spat, striding toward the beast. "You will do your part. We'll see if you're more inclined to perform after you've missed a meal or two."

The beast wasn't just covering his face. His eyes were squinted shut, his large claws and hairy paws not even capable of blocking out the brightness streaming from the mechanical creature. He snarled, but Belle detected a note of pain. She remembered his owl-like eyes and winced. All the times he'd come to her campfire were after sunset. Perhaps he was a nocturnal creature. If so, the bright light would be far too much for him.

"You'll look at me when I'm talking to you." The Ringmaster glowered, reaching for his shock sticks.

The beast lunged at the mechanical unicorn, tackling it to the ground and yelping when his chain yanked him back. A few of the bulbs shattered. Claws extended, the beast slashed at the artificial creature.

The Ringmaster loomed closer, his shock sticks sparking.

Belle dove for the beast. "Stop!" She gently grabbed his arm, all too aware that her shirt would do nothing to prevent him from ripping through her thin skin.

The beast bared his teeth. But astonishingly, he stopped his destruction of the mechanical unicorn. Squinting his eyes, he shrank back from the lights.

"Fascinating. It looks like this might work after all." The Ringmaster hovered behind them, his shock sticks dormant in their holster. He pointed to the broken machine. "You go fix this while the beast spends some time alone. I think he'll come around. If not, I'll fetch a taxidermist."

Belle grimaced as she stood. She wanted to pat the beast's arm but felt she had already done too much. Instead, she left.

Back in her trailer, Belle's stomach churned with guilt and worry as she replaced the broken bulbs on the mechanical mount. Images of the beast being tormented haunted her thoughts as she tested the circuit, flicking the switch after replacing each bulb. As blue and violet light bathed her, the beginning of an idea formed. It was beautiful and terrible and scared Belle to her core.

But it felt right.

After fixing the machine and making a quick detour to pick up her contraband book, Belle made her way to the beast's enclosure. Remembering his eye sensitivity, she didn't dare turn on her lantern. "Hello?" Belle called out. "I wanted to check on you. May I turn on my lantern?"

He grunted, and Belle took that as a yes.

Belle switched on the lantern, its light casting long shadows in the oppressive darkness. The beast peered at her between the bars. He was close enough that she could see scratches etched into his antlers.

"I'm so sorry this happened to you." Belle swallowed hard. "I don't expect you to forgive me, but I will do everything in my power to free you."

The beast snorted, sending puffs of condensation out of his nostrils, making him resemble a fuzzy dragon. He turned back around and curled into his cape.

Belle snapped, "I meant what I said. I'll do my best to get you out of here, but if you don't at least try to stay out of trouble, I can't help you! Don't you want to live?"

The beast shrugged.

Belle leaned in close. "Look, I know you have no reason to trust me, but the Ringmaster always means what he says. If he says he'll display your pelt if you don't cooperate, he'll do it."

Snarling, the beast turned back toward her. Condensation from his hot breath coated the bars of the cage. "I'm aware."

Belle wrinkled her nose at the proximity of the beast's rank smell. "Then can you please at least pretend to go along with the act? I need time to come up with a plan. I've only got the beginnings of one."

The beast looked pointedly at her anklet, then met her gaze. "You failed before." His voice was gravelly, softening to almost a whisper as he finished speaking.

Heat rose in Belle's cheeks, and she clenched her lantern tighter. "I won't get caught this time."

The beast stared her down. When Belle didn't blink, he sighed, sending more puffs of condensation out like smoke, and slumped to the floor of his prison.

Belle wondered if it was difficult for him to speak. He seemed to speak only a few words before fading into grunts the more he talked. Despite her curiosity, she didn't want to ask because she didn't have the right to do so. So instead, she said, "If you don't object to having company, I thought I'd read to you a bit." She held up the book of fairy tales containing stories set amongst the stars in a distant future she dreamed of.

The beast nodded gruffly and sat next to the edge of the cage, peering over Belle's shoulder as she read from the contraband book.

The Ringmaster always punished Belle with hard labor when he caught her with books.

She was determined not to let him know about this one; it was becoming one of her favorites.

The beast seemed to agree, at least partially. His body relaxed as he hung on to her every word. When Belle couldn't keep her eyes open anymore, she closed the book and told the beast, "If you'd like, I can come back every night and read to you some more, either until we finish the book or escape. Whichever comes first." Belle gave him a brave smile, despite her trembling nerves.

The beast nodded. "Thank you."

When Belle left for her trailer, a nervous knot twisted in her stomach as she realized the beast never agreed to pretend to go along with the Ringmaster's act. Belle worried about what tomorrow would bring. She needed a plan, fast.

CHAPTER THREE

Steam released from the caravan train as it transformed back into a campsite, the metal trailers groaning and creaking as they automatically decoupled on the grounds of Cacophony Hippodrome. The circular stone building had been home to a bloody arena in Nuzaran's early days, but now it was the Circus Illume's southern base in Minport.

The crew pulling Belle's trailer to its lot was barely visible from her foggy porthole window. She braced against a support beam as the trailer hit a bumpy patch. The crew swore and screeched as the trailer's wheels drenched them in mud. Underneath Belle's cot, her false-bottom trunk rattled, thumping against the frame so hard she thought it was going to loosen its bolts.

Then finally, the chaos ended.

Belle winced as she rubbed her stiff neck and yawned. She lumbered to the window and peered out at the greenery lit by the pale sunrise. It had been a year since the circus had returned to the coastal city of Minport. She was relieved to see the hurricane's damage had been minimal. Only a few branches were strewn about the otherwise manicured grounds. In the distance, the electric fence crackled with life as smoke billowed from the chimneys of the squat building housing Cacophony Hippodrome's massive steam-powered generator.

Belle wrinkled her nose at the sight.

Since the caravan left four days ago, Belle had barely been able to speak to the beast. The Ringmaster had begun practicing with him after finding that tinted goggles dimmed the stage lights, making him more compliant. But a crowd would still be too much for the poor creature. The best Belle could hope for was that the beast would cooperate while she formed an escape plan. But the trouble was that she still didn't know how to get past the electric fence.

Loud banging on her battered door halted any scheming. Belle rubbed her temples before opening the door. She knew what the Ringmaster's hired hand wanted even before he opened his toad-like lips. "You want me to help unload?" Belle asked, raising her eyebrows.

The spindly man sneered. "Perhaps the Ringmaster should have hired you for fortune telling," he scoffed. "Yes, you're to unload the props for your show with his new pet."

Despite his mocking tone, Belle perked up. She had spent most of the tedious ride south improving the mechanical unicorn for the new act. It now galloped as smoothly as a real horse and had a switch to toggle the lights and increase its speed. She'd even included an autonomous mode that allowed the mount to move of its own volition.

The Ringmaster had praised her ingenuity but didn't know Belle's mind was on freedom. The mechanical unicorn wasn't an ideal getaway vehicle, but it was an option.

In the meantime, Belle had taken to smuggling food and supplies under her trunk's false bottom in case an opportunity to escape arose. There was far less room for her contraband books now, but she reasoned that she could always find more books later. However, Belle did keep the fairy tales. Before the caravan had left, the beast made her promise to keep it, and so that book remained snug among the stockpile.

Smuggling supplies distracted Belle from the fact that she had taken to thinking of the beast as Beast. Guilt gnawed at her for never asking him what his name was and, worse, assuming he didn't have a name to begin with. Next time they were alone, she would ask him.

"Hello?" The lackey scowled. "You have a job to do."

Belle shook herself. "Yes, sorry. I'll be on my way."

But the Ringmaster intercepted Belle before she could reach the storage trailers. "There's been a change of plan. Go to wardrobe. You're going into town to advertise." The Ringmaster wore his silk dressing robe, but his presence was still domineering.

"What about unloading?" Belle asked, rubbing the sleep out of her eyes.

"I have a crew for that." The Ringmaster sniffed. "All you need to worry about is dazzling customers. You have a new act to sell."

Belle swallowed hard as her voice caught. She didn't want to call the creature Beast in front of him. "Is he coming with me?"

The Ringmaster waved her off. "No. The beast's first appearance will be on the season's opening day. Now, report to wardrobe."

Belle's knees shook as she headed to wardrobe's indigo trailer. Lately, her interactions with the Ringmaster had become more frequent than they'd ever been in her ten years with the circus.

She could happily do without more.

Luckily, her fitting was painless, and the seamstress dressed her at breakneck speed. After a whirlwind of burgundy fabrics and a splash of glittery makeup, Belle was performance-ready. The dusting of silver flecks across the bridge of her nose and cheekbones highlighted the dark blue veins crisscrossing her skin, giving her an otherworldly appearance. Belle's brows were exaggerated into thick slants, and pearl powder coated her eyelids. Her rosebud lips were tinted a berry color, giving her face a pop of color.

After wardrobe was finished, Belle tightened her cloak over her sleeveless costume to keep the morning chill away, and reported to the steam-powered omnibus the cast would ride into town. The elaborate vehicle was a marvel to behold, its entire exterior wired for a light show timed to play in sync with an automaton band, wearing mismatched uniforms, performing on its upper deck.

The Ringmaster tapped his jeweled walking stick. "You're the last one here. Come here so we can leave." His lip curled as he twirled the key to Belle's anklet.

Once Belle stood before him, the Ringmaster kneeled with a mocking bow. The crimson light on the anklet's orb turned a lurid green, allowing Belle to pass through the circus fence without suffering electrocution. As if reading her thoughts, the Ringmaster said, "I almost left you behind, but then you wouldn't be earning your price. Let's go."

Belle seethed as she took her seat on the omnibus.

"None of that. Or do I need to execute my override?" The Ringmaster tapped his walking stick against her seat, a reminder of the button underneath its handle that allowed him to send a shock through her. There would be no escaping in town. Not that she was planning on leaving without Beast, but it was still disheartening.

"No," Belle said, averting her gaze and noting the other passengers.

A trio of clowns whispered amongst themselves in the back of the omnibus, no doubt planning a prank. Belle had been fond of them until she became a victim of one of their crueler tricks. She avoided the clowns out of habit now, as did the juggler sisters, who kept to themselves. Behind the jugglers sat the trio of acrobats, the star performer tucking her golden curls under her tiara as she chatted with the bald fire-breathing stuntwoman.

The omnibus's engine rumbled as the driver shifted gears, drowning out the conversations around her. Belle kept herself occupied by studying the streets as they departed, hoping to memorize possible escape routes. Her fingers itched for a pen and paper to keep notes, but she couldn't raise anyone's suspicions, especially with the Ringmaster only a few rows ahead of her.

Minport was a mismatch of architectural styles: old-fashioned stone buildings mixed with modern brick structures and whimsical scrolling artwork decorating the windows. Peppering its skyline were recently constructed skyscrapers—towering buildings with private airship docks. Minport boasted of having the busiest docks in Nuzaran, even bigger than Onyxmark's. Airships dotted the sky, coming and going at a steady rate. Belle was dizzy from watching all the activity.

At last, the omnibus reached the city plaza. It was midmorning, and the streets were bustling with pedestrians.

"Smiles, everyone. We've arrived." The Ringmaster flashed his dazzling showman smile before disembarking.

A crowd gathered around the city plaza, drawn in by the flashing lights and the automatons' merry calliope tune. Belle wiped her palms off before removing her cloak and striding off the omnibus, grabbing her weights and props from the overhead storage along the way.

The small circus wowed the audience. The stuntwoman blew fire, and the clowns caused chaos while the Ringmaster admonished them for show. Meanwhile, the sisters juggled increasingly ridiculous objects until they were throwing spanners back and forth between them, much to the dismay of the parents, but to the delight of the children in the audience.

Everyone in the audience gasped when Belle waltzed with all three acrobats balanced delicately on her arms in time with the automatons' melody. She assisted the leader with a standing flip trick that made the nervous members of the audience cry out. When the leader flipped gracefully to the ground, Belle kissed her hand and the crowd squealed with delight.

The show was a smashing success. As the sun sank below the horizon, the lights of the omnibus shone brighter. Soon, they'd be packing up. Belle's muscles ached from the extended performance, but she loved seeing the children's smiles as she broke chains and wielded her weights with ease.

The Ringmaster bade the circus members give their final bows. Belle's back ached, but she did as he said, knowing she'd rest soon.

As the crowd dispersed and Belle packed up her props, she noticed a folded newspaper caught underneath her weights. She almost discarded it, but something compelled her to peek at its contents. Belle stared when a thick brochure fell out containing a map of Minport, complete with a timetable for the public airship dock.

It was as if all the oxygen had left Belle's lungs. With this in her possession, she wouldn't have to memorize the route back to the city from the circus. A wild, mad idea wormed its way into her consciousness. She had half an escape plan in her hands, but only if she didn't get caught with the brochure.

With that sobering thought, Belle stashed the brochure inside her costume lest the Ringmaster or one of the gossipy performers noticed anything amiss.

On the way back to camp, Belle thought she'd explode from her inner turmoil. The contraband brochure was safely tucked away, but the knowledge of its existence on her person made her skin feel as if it were burning.

Self-doubt whispered into her hopeful heart. So what if she had a map and a timetable for the airships? She still had the anklet and no concrete plans for escaping the circus with Beast. Worse, she didn't have airfare. The idea of starting a new life felt both impossibly far and close at the same time.

When the omnibus parked inside Cacophony Hippodrome's garage, before Belle could disembark, the Ringmaster blocked her path. At her confused expression, the Ringmaster tsked. "Don't think that I've forgotten to turn my security back on." He used his key to reactivate Belle's copper anklet. In her exhaustion, she had forgotten all about it.

When the light on the anklet glowed crimson again, the Ringmaster cackled, "You'll always belong here."

Belle tersely nodded as she stormed off to her trailer, her trembling fists concealed by her cloak.

Her resolve hardened as she cleaned off her makeup. Bits of glitter still stubbornly clung to her face as she dressed in her own clothes. Concealing the brochure within her cloak, Belle headed for Beast's tent.

When she arrived, it was too quiet. Even if Beast was sleeping, she couldn't hear him breathing. With growing trepidation, she lifted her lantern. The cage was empty, its door wide open.

Did he escape on his own? Belle's heart beat wildly against her ribcage. Before she could investigate further, Beast's familiar roar sounded from within the camp, followed by panicked shouts.

Belle didn't stop to think, racing toward the sound of Beast's distressed roars. She didn't know what she would do when she reached him but hoped she wasn't too late.

When the roaring died down, Belle panicked. She bolted in the direction where she'd heard Beast's roar. The brochure chafed horribly underneath her linen blouse, but the adrenaline kept her going. More shouting resumed as a moaning howl carried on the wind. Belle sprinted harder, gasping for breath as she neared the source of the racket.

Running in the dark, Belle didn't notice the crude cloth hanging between tree branches and ran face-first into the makeshift partition. The sound of her struggling echoed throughout the camp as she became hopelessly entangled in the sheet.

One of the Ringmaster's seasonal workers pulled the cloth off her, a bemused expression on his face. "What now?" His coveralls were soaked, and soap bubbles clung to his thinning hair.

Movement behind him caught Belle's eye. She peered over his shoulder, and her jaw dropped. Three workers were pinning Beast down as they scrubbed the filth off him in an oversized metal tub, a relic from the Ringmaster's failed attempt to tame the tiger. By the lights haphazardly hung nearby, Belle could see one worker's arms covered in fresh scratch marks. Meanwhile, another worker narrowly avoided being gouged by Beast's antlers.

Belle blinked. "Beast?"

He stopped thrashing as his baleful yellow eyes met her gaze. His dingy silver fur stuck up at odd angles, with bubbles clinging between his claws.

The workers stared at Belle. "I don't know why you're here, but since you calm him down, you bathe him." The worker closest to her spat on the ground. "Let's go, boys. I need dry clothes."

Before Belle could respond, the workers departed, sending wary glances over their shoulders at Beast. She knew she should be thankful he wasn't in a worse condition—and her brochure was secure—but she seethed at their predicament.

Matters were made more awkward by how humanoid Beast looked with his wet fur clinging to his body. She could make out the outline of his calves and a man's waist before she buried her face in her hands and turned around. The poor creature deserved basic dignity.

After collecting her thoughts, Belle lowered her hands. Over her shoulder, taking care not to stare directly at him, she asked, "Beast, can you give yourself a bath?"

He grumbled, "Yes. The water's cold."

"I can fix it." Belle kept her eyes trained on the ground as she approached the tub. Unfortunately, the poor lighting obscured the rock in her path, and she tripped, stumbling into the tub. Belle was caught by strong, soaking arms wrapping around her waist. Both her outfit and her dignity were done for. Flames of embarrassment burned her cheeks as she stuttered her apologetic thanks.

Beast grunted as he righted her, releasing Belle after she was back on solid ground.

Taking care to keep her gaze downcast, Belle pointed at the twin knobs on the far end of the tub. "This should warm up the water." With a quick twist of the knob, heat immediately radiated from the bath. Plumes of steam rose, and Beast enthusiastically leaned back in the tub, splashing the ground.

Belle kept her back to him as she asked, "I trust you can take it from here?"

"Yes," Beast said, his gravelly voice low and contented.

A shaky laugh escaped from Belle's lips. "I'm sorry. After years of enduring petty cruelty from the Ringmaster and his lackeys, I'm glad I could finally undo something he's done."

Beast grew quiet, then muttered, "I'm sorry."

"Thank you." Belle took a deep breath, then plunged ahead. "I'm glad we have a moment to talk. I found something today that might help us escape."

There was a startled splash from the tub. "Really?" Beast's voice was equal parts hope and skepticism.

"I found a map of Minport with a timetable for the airships."
Belle held up the contraband brochure over her shoulder, hoping he
could see the map without causing water damage.

"Oh."

"I know it's not much, but we can at least navigate the city. All
we need now is a plan, and we're out of here." Belle clenched the
map tighter in her fist.

"You have no plan," Beast said flatly as he stood up in the tub.

"I'm working on it. Do you have any bright ideas?"

"No. Head's too foggy."

Belle blinked at the admission. "I'm sorry I don't have more, but
I will figure something out. In the meantime, can you please do your
best not to cause a scene? I don't want them hurting you, and it'd be
easier to escape if the Ringmaster wasn't constantly putting three or
four workers on you for a bath."

Beast grumbled as he shook his fur dry, causing a few droplets to
land on Belle. When the commotion stopped, she allowed herself to
face him, choking back a hysterical chuckle at the sight of the
massive beast with damp fur and a raggedy towel wrapped clumsily
around his waist.

"I will try," he huffed. "But hurry."

"Thank you." The tension in Belle's shoulders softened. "I know
I'm asking too much. You don't even know me." She hesitated, then
asked, "Do you have a name?"

He shrugged. "I don't know."

Belle averted her eyes as the towel dipped further. "What should
I call you?"

"Beast."

Belle gave a small smile. "Beast it is, then. I'll see you tomorrow.
I hope you rest well."

"Are you done?"

Startled, Belle snapped her head in the direction of the voice.
The worker was back, scowling at them both and smelling of cheap
whiskey and tobacco.

Belle's stomach plummeted. How long had he been lurking
around? Did he hear them discussing escape plans? With a

hammering heart, she said, "I just finished. Is there something else I can help you with?"

"No. Go back to your trailer and sleep. You'll need it for opening day." The worker cuffed Beast, forgetting his earlier fear. "Come on, you too. Off to sleep, the both of you."

As the worker led Beast away, Belle turned from him, blinking back hot tears.

As Belle sat on her wretched cot in her trailer, despondent, she stared at the ankle bracelet, crossing her legs to study it better. It didn't look complex, just a simple copper anklet with a glowing orb. She leaned closer, frowning as she realized the plates surrounding the keyhole were loose. The Ringmaster had been careless over the years, sometimes turning the key the wrong way. Maybe doing so had damaged it enough for her to take it apart.

With trembling fingers, Belle loosened the cap housing the orb on the anklet's outer plate. Mid-turn, it caught on a wire. She held her breath; it was stuck halfway on. Stunned at her progress, Belle retrieved the few tools she kept hidden in the false bottom of her trunk and pried the cap off with small rusty pliers, exposing the wiring of her anklet. The orb glowed the steady crimson it always did when it was set.

Belle bit her lip, steadying her breathing as she studied the circuit. It was crude. She clamped a hand over her mouth at the obvious, poor choice that had been made with the board. If she followed the wiring correctly, she could easily switch the wire to show crimson even after turning off the electrical fence sensor. The wiring in the mechanical unicorn she'd worked on had been more complicated than this shoddy work. Belle only needed to use a delicate touch, and the anklet would be bypassed.

As an experiment, she switched the wiring for the fence. Everything seemed fine until the orb no longer glowed crimson but instead bathed the entire trailer in blue with its warning light.

"Shit!" Belle worked to put the wire back in place.

Nothing changed.

Hyperventilating, Belle tested out different wiring combinations. The circuit had looked so simple. What happened?

Pounding on the door made Belle's heart sink. "Open up! Delivery!"

Belle let out another string of expletives. The glowing anklet wouldn't close.

CHAPTER FOUR

The warning light from Belle's copper anklet shone throughout the trailer, illuminating everything in a serene shade of blue while she muttered obscenities, scrambling to change it back.

Outside, the insistent knocking grew louder.

Inexplicably, the anklet's orb went dark. The clasp creaked open and fell with a clatter.

Wild-eyed, Belle slapped the anklet back on, but the clasps wouldn't stay closed. Frantically, she pushed on the orb, trying to light it up.

"Open up! It's wardrobe!" The thick trailer door muffled the seamstress's throaty voice.

"One moment, please!" Panic and bile rose in Belle as she attempted to reattach the clasps with shaking hands. Why wouldn't the orb light up? She had been so careful not to short any wires.

Doubt gnawed at Belle as she inspected the anklet. Nothing seemed to be amiss, except the orb was clearly off. When the trailer's door handle clicked open, Belle sharply inhaled as she slammed the pieces together and threw a blanket over her legs. Whatever happened, at least the room wasn't still lit blue.

A woman Belle had never seen before propped up a steamer

trunk in the doorway. She was not the circus' seamstress from wardrobe. "What are you doing?" asked the stranger, cocking a pale lavender eyebrow dyed to match her hair. She wore too much rouge, distorting her face comically as she gave Belle a skeptical look.

"I fell asleep." Belle inwardly cringed. She was never a gifted liar, and now it seemed she kept having to do so. Before the woman could ask more questions, Belle had one of her own. "Who are you?"

The stranger harrumphed as she set the trunk on its side in the middle of the cramped trailer, opening it to reveal an elaborate pearl-colored costume. "Your boss contracted your costume for tomorrow from my shop, Delilah's. Try it on. He shouldn't have waited until the last minute for a custom job. Doesn't leave much time for alterations."

With growing trepidation, Belle untangled her legs from the flimsy blanket. It took all of her willpower not to glance down at the anklet to see if it was functioning. Faking nonchalance, she prayed the seamstress wouldn't notice anything amiss.

Delilah tapped her foot. "Come on. That damn beast wasted enough of my time caterwauling during his fitting."

Belle quickly changed out of her trousers and blouse, grimacing when the pant leg caught on the anklet.

The seamstress tutted as Belle struggled to put on the new costume. The iridescent costume's corseted bodice suffocated her until Delilah loosened its stays, then fussed with the dress's translucent, cascading skirt. Lastly, she helped Belle put on impractical lace-covered boots and adorned her messy hair with a simple silver circlet, completing the costume.

"It's a shame about the anklet. The boots would look better without it." Delilah wrinkled her nose and shook her head. "The Ringmaster has no fashion sense."

For a moment, Belle panicked at the mention of the anklet, but the seamstress moved on, making small adjustments to the costume as she checked the fit.

"Everything seems in order. Be careful with the fabric. It was expensive." Delilah wagged her finger as she left the trailer, closing the door behind her.

Belle immediately examined the anklet, finding the orb once again glowing a steady crimson. She sank to her bed and sighed as the skirt's fabric crinkled. She'd have to straighten it in the morning.

As her breathing rate slowly returned to normal, a wild idea took root. Belle toyed with the anklet. Maybe she only needed better tools to finish the job.

After changing out of her new costume, Belle donned her own clothes, throwing her cloak on and pocketing her meager tools as she left the dark trailer. The moon was high overhead as she snuck to the squat power building. If the distant raucous laughter from the crew's trailers were any indication, no one would be on guard duty at this hour. By now, they were likely deep into a card game and their cups.

As she neared the Ringmaster's elaborate red and gold trailer, Belle held her breath, hiding behind a massive oak tree. She peeked around the trunk to see if his light was on.

All was quiet.

Beyond his trailer, only a muddy, grassy field lay between her and the power building. If the Ringmaster looked out his window, there'd be nowhere for her to hide.

Belle crept across the field, keeping one eye on the Ringmaster's trailer. But she should have watched her step. Wincing at the sharp pain in her thigh, Belle rubbed the sore spot where she'd collided with the building's doorknob.

The door was locked, but Belle came prepared. Using the thinnest screwdriver in her pocket, she tinkered with the simple lock. It clicked, and the door opened with a low creak.

Inside the windowless building, it was pitch black. The noise of the steam-powered generator's whirring drowned out all other sounds. Belle grumbled under her breath as she fumbled for the light switch. Grasping in the darkness, she despaired that she'd come so far only to be foiled by her lack of a lantern.

Finally, Belle's fingers brushed against the switch. Before turning it on, she softly kicked the door closed, thankful for her long legs.

When the lights flickered on, Belle squinted as her eyes adjusted. The power building's interior was filled with pipes, wires, and at the center of it all, the biggest generator she had ever laid eyes on. Belle had once contemplated sabotaging the generator to escape, but seeing it in person, it looked impenetrable.

Belle turned her attention to the crooked desk against the opposite wall. It was covered with teetering stacks of papers, spare parts, and multiple toolboxes. There didn't seem to be any method of organization, so she rifled through toolboxes until she found the delicate tools used for repairing and replacing the smallest of lights on the omnibus.

Sitting down on a high stool, Belle propped her leg up on the desk as best she could. Gritting her teeth, she unclasped the anklet and placed it on the desk. Leaning over it, she contemplated how to rewire it without triggering the blue warning light again.

The overhead light caught on a round piece of glass sitting on a stack of old schematics. Belle picked up the glass and inspected what appeared to be a jeweler's lens. She held it over her eye and adjusted it, gasping when she zoomed in on the anklet's circuit. Now having the clarity needed to fine-tune the wiring job, Belle could see where it had been shorted earlier—she'd crossed the wires in a narrow section.

Several tense minutes passed as Belle worked to rewire the anklet. It was nerve-wracking working with her back to the door, the noise of the generator drowning out any outside noises. Belle worked as quickly and carefully as she could since there was no way of knowing if anyone was approaching.

At last, the wires were reattached, and the orb still glowed crimson. Belle put the anklet back on and waited to see whether or not the orb turned blue again.

Nothing changed.

Belle released a shaky breath as she pushed damp strands of hair out of her face.

There was only one thing left to do. Belle needed to test it and see if she could really get past the electric fence.

With a hammering heart, Belle walked to the humming electric fence as if in a dreamlike trance. The orbs on the fence's copper posts were lit crimson, matching her anklet's orb.

After several deep breaths, Belle stepped across the barrier, squeezing her eyes shut. What if she was wrong? She'd be electrocuted and likely rendered unconscious. Worse, the Ringmaster would find out what she'd done. Would Beast be punished, too?

When the anticipated shock never came, Belle opened her eyes.

Nothing had changed. Belle was still in the same woods surrounding Cacophony Hippodrome, the fence behind her humming the same whine as always. The orb on her anklet glowed crimson. Her wiring job had worked.

Blinking back tears, Belle took a few more steps forward until branches obscured the lights of the circus.

Standing in the starlit forest, a lump caught in Belle's throat as she took gulping breaths. This was the furthest she had ever been on her own in a decade. She could leave right now and never look back. The lights of Minport glowed warmly in the distance.

Belle breathed in the petrichor. The electric fence hummed in the distance as she contemplated leaving for Minport. No one from the circus had noticed she'd been missing for the last hour. Her cloak billowed as a cool breeze rattled tree branches and far-off thunder rumbled. The springtime rain in this region was infamous for bursts of torrential downpours. One good soak and her tracks would be washed away.

The glittering city lay ahead, beckoning her. She could leave right now.

Belle took a few lumbering steps closer, the mud squelching beneath her boots, until she was at the forest's edge. A cobblestone road stretched before her, lit by gas street lamps casting twisting shadows over the path, mimicking the ominous clouds gathering overhead.

Belle stepped back, retreating into the woods.

Beast was still in his cage. She couldn't abandon him to the Ringmaster. If she left now, she wouldn't be able to live with herself.

With a sinking heart, Belle stalked back to the other side of the fence.

By the time Belle reached Beast's enclosure, the clouds concealed the stars over Cacophony Hippodrome. Beast's snores echoed around the musty tent. Belle held up the gas lantern she'd pilfered from the power building, its light reflecting off the formidable new lock the Ringmaster installed after his last tussle with Beast.

The lock came from Onyxmark's master smith, and an internal clockwork mechanism changed its tumblers every five minutes. Picking it was well above Belle's skill level, though not for lack of trying.

She took tentative steps toward Beast's cage but stopped short of leaning against the thick bars.

"Beast?" A crack of thunder drowned out her whisper.

Beast snored again. He was curled into himself, his cloak acting as a blanket. Careful not to shine the light directly into his sensitive eyes, Belle tried again.

"Beast! I know how to get past the fence."

He slowly opened his eyes, shining yellow in the dim lantern light. "You what?" he asked, sleep distorting his voice, his words blending together.

Belle's gaze softened. "I found a bypass for my anklet. I crossed the fence."

Beast bolted up, eyes fully alert. "You have a plan?"

"Yes, but you'll hate it."

Beast let out a long-suffering sigh. "Fine. Tell me."

Belle grinned.

The next morning arrived too soon. Somehow, Belle had managed a few hours of sleep. But after sneaking out to check on their travel bags one last time, her heart rate took ages to recover, making it impossible to drift off.

Glittery makeup disguised the bags under Belle's eyes. Her skin was scrubbed pink, clashing horribly with her dark veins. Powder and pasty makeup barely concealed the purple bruises on her knees, damaged while climbing the scaffolding inside the great circus dome.

Thank goodness her costume included gloves. Belle's hands were ruined, stained with grease, and dotted with little nicks from when she'd slipped with the wiring tools during her exhausting retooling of Beast's anklet.

Belle fought the impulse to rub the sleep out of her eyes lest she further incur Delilah's wrath. The seamstress was already furious about the crinkles in her costume's flimsy skirt. Belle didn't want to give her any more reasons to scold her.

At least if the plan worked, Belle would never have to worry about rumpled clothing again. But for now, any extra attention could spell doom for both her and Beast. Belle prayed to whoever listened that the last-minute modifications she made to the automaton unicorn would hold—along with Beast's temper.

Backstage, Belle could hear the crowd roaring as the Ringmaster riled them up. Last night's rain was still falling, pelting the dome's tin roof, but the crescendo of the automaton band's lively tune mingling with the cheering audience camouflaged the noise. In the center ring, acrobats performed aerial stunts, flinging themselves through rainbow-lit hoops as the crowd gasped.

The scent of roasted chestnuts made Belle's stomach growl. Under normal circumstances, she would persuade Cook to sneak her a bag, but there was little time to find Beast before they were on next.

Belle didn't have to go far to find him. A grizzled handler was next to Beast, giving him suspicious glances. Beast sat stoically, the blue-tinted goggles shielding his eyes from the brightest lights as he ostensibly watched the acrobats twirl in the air.

"Everything okay?" Belle asked as she approached them.

The handler jabbed a thumb in Beast's direction. "He's being quiet today. It's odd."

Belle shrugged. "It's the goggles. Without the bright lights bothering him, he's fine."

"If you say so." The handler narrowed his rheumy eyes. "I've got other duties."

Belle sighed with relief as the handler left. She hadn't yet thought of what to say to make him go away so she could talk to Beast alone. At least that was one less lie she'd have to tell.

While the stagehands readied the massive props for the next act, Belle leaned into Beast, close enough that his fur tickled her nose. "Everything's ready," she whispered.

Beast turned sharply to face her. "It's happening?" he whispered back, his scratchy voice rumbling in her ear.

"Yes. Just hang on to the unicorn when it's time." Impulsively, Belle pecked his cheek.

Beast sat up straighter, surveying the hubbub backstage. "There are too many people here."

"I know. I'm counting on the chaos."

The stage director raced up to them. "You two are on."

Belle smiled genuinely for the first time before a performance, causing the director to blink. "Let's break a leg."

The music swelled to a crescendo as the Ringmaster announced, "Here they are, Beauty and the Beast!"

Beast was already on stage, posed dramatically in an artificial tree, which was lit by the colorful light bulbs making up the tree's faux leaves and flowers. His path was lit from below him, making his figure even more imposing as he stalked the branches.

The spotlight then trained on Belle's entrance as artificial mist rose from steaming fog machines. Sitting atop the lit mechanical unicorn, Belle absentmindedly patted its neck as she guided it to a trot on stage—its body lit a violet hue to match Beast's cloak. Belle's soft white costume was ethereal underneath the light. It was almost a shame the outfit would be ruined before dawn.

Beast stuck to the script, leaping from branch to branch on the tree, descending its height until he dropped in front of Belle. He snarled and growled, sending the audience into a frenzied delight.

Belle reached out her gloved hand, her shimmering body reflected in Beast's dark goggles. He glowered, and for a horrifying moment, she thought he would really attack. But then he gave the slightest shake of his head, the light catching his antlers.

"Peace," Belle said, and with her other hand, she pressed the concealed remote. Colorful smoke bombs exploded across the stage, swirling thick in hues of blues, pinks, and purples. She hit the switch for the mechanical unicorn, and its lights shut off.

It was a race against the clock now.

"Let's go," Belle hissed.

Wordlessly, Beast mounted the mechanical unicorn, and together they charged for the dimly lit exit sign.

The crowd couldn't see anything, only colorful smoke and lights dancing. Belle'd had a difficult time rigging the spectacle up, but the dazzling distraction was working. She knew the Ringmaster would know there was a problem, but the delighted crowd thought it was all part of the show.

For once, luck seemed to shine on Belle. No guards or workers idled by the exit. Good. Maybe the Ringmaster wouldn't realize it was an escape plan yet. Perhaps he thought it was only a technical malfunction—stranger things had happened than this.

In her heart, Belle knew it wouldn't be long before the Ringmaster caught on and gave chase. But for now, as the mechanical unicorn galloped through the exit, Belle let hope guide her, praying no one would catch up to them.

Beast clung to Belle's back as she urged the mechanical unicorn onward. They burst through Cacophony Hippodrome's loading dock entrance into unexpectedly bright sunlight.

Belle blinked rapidly, wishing she had tinted goggles like Beast's as she adjusted to the harsh light. It was a shame the downpour had ended abruptly. She'd hoped the rain would make it harder to follow their tracks.

Thundering applause reverberated throughout the grounds from inside the arena.

The mechanical unicorn's gears groaned in protest at the extreme speed. Steam hissed and rose in dramatic billows surrounding them, obscuring their figures. Belle hoped that between Beast's cloak and the steam, passersby on the road wouldn't notice his monstrous form. Although, they'd probably be too busy staring at the galloping mechanical unicorn to notice.

With that sobering thought, Belle squeezed the levers tighter on the mechanical mount and kicked up the speed, wincing as the body of the metal unicorn grew hot to the touch, her gauzy costume offering no protection from the heat.

They were nearing the edge of the grounds, where the electric fence bordering the woods emitted a low hum. Belle spotted the tree hollow where she'd smuggled their supplies last night.

"Our bags are in the tree ahead. I'll dismount and—damn!"

The roar of the Ringmaster's automobile sounded in the distance. The mechanical unicorn was fast, but the automobile could easily outpace it.

"New plan," Beast's voice rumbled, his fur tickling Belle's ear before he dismounted from the charging unicorn. He ducked and rolled effortlessly over to the ancient, gnarled tree. Reaching inside the hollow, he tossed both heavy packs over his back and bounded toward Belle as she gaped at him.

Beast was nearly back at the mechanical unicorn when the clamoring engine grew louder. Belle peered over her shoulder, eyes wild with fear. She couldn't yet see the atrocious yellow automobile, but it wouldn't be long before they were discovered.

"Come on!" Belle slowed the mechanical unicorn to a trot, the hydraulic bearings groaning and creaking in protest.

A spring snapped. Belle hoped it wasn't an important part.

Beast leaped through the air, landing on the back of the mount with a semi-controlled crash, face-first into Belle's back. She could feel the bruises already forming, but at least he hadn't landed antler-first. By the time this was over, she'd be all black and blue.

"Sorry," Beast apologized, his voice muffled as he struggled to right himself.

Belle blinked back tears as they approached the fence. "I'm fine," she lied. "Do you have both bags?"

"Yes."

"Good. Moment of truth time." Belle kicked the overheating unicorn back into a gallop. With a flying jump, they cleared the low fence. Despite knowing she had disarmed their anklets and tested her own last night, she still squeezed her eyes shut, bracing herself for the inevitable electric shock.

A decade of pain made old habits hard to forget. But this time, the jolt never came.

"Look out!"

Beast's panicked growl shook Belle. She opened her eyes to see the forest thinning out to a clearing bordering the cobbled road to Minport. They were moments away from running headlong into one of the gas street lamps lining the road. Belle jerked the reins hard to the left, grazing the street lamp's metal base.

"Sorry," she said.

"We're fine."

The pursuing automobile engine thundered closer. Belle looked toward the noise. Farther down the cobbled road, a dot of yellow—trailed by a cloud of thick smoke—raced behind the line of trees.

"Less talking. More running." Belle leaned in like a jockey and pulled the lever to the mechanical unicorn's maximum speed. "Hang on!"

The skyline of Minport loomed overhead as they dashed at breakneck speed. It wasn't long before they were at the city's edge, but now there was traffic to deal with.

Omnibus and automobile drivers gaped at the steam-covered mount darting between lanes. The fishing docks were ahead on the other side of the bay, over which a series of bridges led into the city. The bustle near the marina was at a fever pitch as fishers brought in their haul, and cargo ships loaded and unloaded. Belle noted the activity with interest in case the airship docks proved impenetrable.

"He's gaining!" Beast's low rumble cut through the noise.

Belle chanced a glance over her shoulder.

The Ringmaster's hideous automobile sped closer. He blared its horn and revved its engine, sending clouds of steam around the open-top vehicle. Lackeys armed with stun sticks were crammed into the automobile with the Ringmaster. Sunlight glinted off a rifle in the hands of a stout lackey sitting in the passenger seat.

The color drained from Belle's face as she looked back to the road. Beast tightened his hold around her waist, claws nipping through her paper-thin costume.

Tires and brakes screeched as the Ringmaster plowed through traffic. Belle weaved her mount between vehicles. She ignored the shouts and curses from drivers, their voices muffled by the hisses of the mechanical mount's overworked engine.

"Almost there." Belle patted the unicorn's hot metal neck with sweaty hands as she steadied her labored breathing. Smoke and steam mingled in the air, burning her nose.

They neared a bridge closed for repairs. Construction vehicles and machines were parked on the road, blocking the path of larger automobiles.

"We're here. Get ready!"

Belle pressed the red button concealed underneath the mechanical unicorn's mane before charging the mount past the machines and over the rails straight into the waiting sea.

They dismounted midair, tucking and rolling into the water, hidden from the Ringmaster's sight by the bridge.

The unicorn's legs kept running as it tumbled through the air. Just before reaching the water, it exploded into a fiery ball as it crashed into the bay.

When the Ringmaster pulled up with his lackeys, it was too late. What remained of the mechanical unicorn had already sunk beneath the choppy waves. Only the blood-stained, torn skirt from Belle's costume remained, floating on the sea foam.

CHAPTER FIVE

Belle found out almost too late that Beast couldn't swim.

It hadn't occurred to her to ask whether he could swim when they'd discussed the plan. Belle herself wasn't the best swimmer, but the circus had stopped often enough by lakes and riversides that she'd been able to teach herself and, unfortunately, had discovered that her anklet was waterproof, even against deep submersions.

Still, Beast should have said something when she'd told him the plan was to jump off a bridge into the ocean. The only objection he had raised was when she'd told him to rip the skirt off her costume.

"Why?" he'd asked, looking equal parts scandalized and horrified.

"They need something to see in the water that's ours. It'll add to the effect. Trust me."

Beast had reluctantly agreed and performed his part admirably.

Now, Belle anxiously scanned the waves, looking for any signs of him. But the sea was calm. Her clammy hands trembled as she balled her fists.

Faint bubbles appeared on the ocean's surface.

Belle plunged into the sea, diving farther than she'd ever gone before. She found Beast thrashing deep beneath the waves. She slid his powerful arms over her shoulders and strained to swim to the surface, far away from the bridge.

When they finally made it to shore, Belle dragged Beast's waterlogged body onto a secluded beach. Outcroppings of rocks and dunes shielded them from any would-be onlookers on the road above. But Belle still kept her eyes on the horizon as she checked Beast for a pulse.

He began coughing up water.

Startled, Belle looked down. Aside from the fact that his blue-tinted goggles were askew and his eyes remained closed, he appeared otherwise unharmed. After Beast expelled the last of the water from his body, he blinked his eyes open and winced, still clinging to their supply bags, holding them close.

When his gaze focused, Belle fixed him with a glare.

"Why didn't you tell me you couldn't swim?" Belle asked, her hands on her hips as she towered over him.

"You wanted to escape. Drowning was preferable to staying in the cage."

Belle offered him a small smile. "Hard to argue that, but I would have come up with a less dangerous plan had you told me."

Beast shrugged. "I survived."

Belle was tempted to crack another joke, but the Ringmaster's shouting in the distance put her back on high alert. "Can you stand? We need to keep moving."

Beast's legs shook as he stood, but he managed, even with the packs slung over his back. Belle offered to take the bags, but he waved her off. "Lead the way."

Belle gulped as they trekked into the woods. They needed to make it to nightfall, or else the whole plan would fall apart.

Sunset seemed to take forever to arrive. Worse, there were several tense moments where Belle and Beast had to stop their trek through the woods to listen, thinking they'd heard the rumble of the Ringmaster's automobile or his sonorous voice.

Every snapped twig and branch that creaked in the breeze set Belle on edge, causing her to look over her shoulder, expecting the Ringmaster to be behind her. Each time was a false alarm, but after years of imprisonment, it was hard to accept that she was free at last.

Thankfully, the waterproof lining of the knapsacks held up, despite their plunge into the ocean. Other than a few damp pens and tools in the bag's outer pockets, everything else was intact.

After changing into dry clothes, Belle and Beast slept in shifts. Although when it was Belle's turn to rest, she spent most of the time tossing and turning. But eventually, exhaustion won out, and she fell into a dreamless sleep.

At dusk, they headed toward the airship docks via the meandering path they'd memorized from the brochure map. They timed it so they'd be near the docks once the sun set. Belle didn't want to be creeping about in the woods after dark and run into a tree or something worse.

Beast led the way. He was happier traveling at night—his tinted goggles shoved into his trouser pocket. Belle suspected he truly had owl eyes considering the ease with which he guided them to the airship dock.

Once they made it to the dock, Belle's heart sank. It was teeming with activity. She had naively thought the dock wouldn't be active at night, and all they'd have to do was sneak aboard an airship and wait for it to take off in the morning. But she had forgotten something vital: Minport was a city that never slept.

Steam-powered cranes airlifted cargo under gas lanterns. The docks were built as platforms, rising higher and higher on each level. Belle had to crane her neck to see the top docks level with the twin moons in the hazy sky, the stars obscured by steam and clouds. A flash of white lightning flickered, too far away for thunder.

They hid at the edge of the woods, watching the airship dock with horrified fascination.

"Now what?" rumbled Beast in Belle's ear. His arms were

crossed, cloak pulled in tightly around his chest. The hood concealed his antlers, but only barely.

The two of them stood out too much, Belle reflected grimly. Even with her hood up, if anyone looked directly into her face, they'd see the dark veins running through her translucent skin. Between her skin and height, it wouldn't take much for a stranger to figure out where she'd come from.

"Give me a moment to think," Belle said, chewing her lip absently as she studied the motion of the dock. "I'm working on it." The cranes seemed to move in sync to a rhythm. Everything moved like clockwork, from sea level to sky level.

Wait, Belle thought. *The cranes move like clockwork.* "Beast, how good are your eyes in the dark?"

"I can see the flecks of starlight in your eyes," he responded.

"What?" Belle blinked and shook her head. "Can you see anyone operating the cranes?"

Beast stared at the cranes, studying each one. "From this angle, no. No one is operating them."

"What about the platforms?" Belle held her breath, not daring to hope.

"Only a few dock workers per ship. Some don't have workers, though." Beast pointed. "Look."

A medium-sized airship was docked but seemed to have no crew taking in the massive shipping crates. Instead, an autonomous crane loaded the cargo onto the airship's deck while a mechanized track pulled the shipping crates below deck, presumably into the cargo hold.

"That's our ticket out of here," breathed Belle. She felt hysterical laughter bubbling up inside her but resisted the urge. This wasn't over yet. "There could be a crew inside, so we'll need to be careful, but a ship that size shouldn't be too crowded. It'll work."

"Something feels off," snarled Beast.

"I know, but what else can we do?" she asked, gesturing around them.

"I don't know."

"Then let's find a crate to sneak into. There has to be one around here that they haven't loaded yet."

Beast sighed as he scanned the horizon. "I should have let the sea take me."

Inside one of the cramped wooden crates, Belle held her breath and willed herself not to sneeze as Beast's fur irritated her nose.

The crate they had snuck into was loaded with medical supplies that shifted painfully into her ribcage as the platform beneath them moved.

Belle hoped Beast could refrain from roaring in frustration. She could feel his hackles rising like an overgrown, annoyed cat. His shoulders tensed beneath his cloak, the hood drawn tightly over his head, barely covering his antlers. What little light slipped in between the slits in the crate gave him a distorted silhouette as he hunched to fit in the tight space.

Tentatively, Belle reached to pat Beast's back in what she hoped was a soothing manner. But his knotted muscles tensed under her touch.

"There, there," she murmured. "We're almost there. Then we're on our way out."

Beast's shoulders drooped as his back muscles relaxed. He let out an irritated sniff but otherwise remained silent.

Belle was sure they'd gotten through the worst, until the automated crane dumped their crate into the waiting airship. The crate rocked precariously, slamming Belle into Beast. Equipment collided with her elbow, and she bit her lip to keep from screaming —a thin line of blood pooling on her chin.

To distract herself, Belle peered between the crate's thick slats. But she couldn't discern anything about the airship besides that its name was the *Figment*, which was painted in ornate letters on the starboard side.

Belle's stomach roiled at the thought of being miles high in the air for the first time. But it was too late to worry about that now. There were more pressing issues to deal with, like how they were going to sneak off the ship once it docked again.

Beast had asked Belle what her plan was, but she didn't have a concrete one.

The best idea she could come up with sounded flimsier by the second. They would wait until the room was empty, then find somewhere on the ship to hide once it was in flight. After the airship arrived at the next dock—wherever that was—they'd wait for the cover of darkness to disembark and hope for the best.

Belle cringed at her flawed plan, but it was the best one she could come up with, given the circumstances. Wherever they landed, she hoped it would be far enough away that news of the circus escape hadn't reached there yet.

The sound of heavy boots approaching made Belle recoil away from the side of the crate. She landed with a soft thump in Beast's arms, narrowly brushing up against their packs of supplies resting by his feet.

Belle clamped her mouth shut, tasting copper.

When they'd been deciding on an airship, at first glance, Belle had dismissed the *Figment* as a viable option because it wasn't getting as much cargo as the other ships. But then Beast had pointed out that a crane was occasionally loading large wooden boxes on board, and Belle jumped at the chance. They'd chosen the *Figment* because it wasn't lit as brightly as the other ships, and they hadn't seen dock workers on it.

But now, looking between the slats of the crate, Belle could count six pairs of boots.

She hoped they were only dock workers and not crew.

The workers traded verbal barbs with each other for what seemed like an eternity as they worked, none the wiser to the stowaways in one of the crates as they strapped it into place before moving on to other cargo.

"Next ship's ready to load!" shouted an authoritative voice cutting through the noise.

Dock workers, after all.

The chatter faded away, and the cargo door slammed shut, hissing steam as it sealed.

Beast's claws dug into Belle's aching shoulders as the airship's steam engine roared to life. The engine had been a steady hum as it burned to get up to speed, but now it was working overtime. If it weren't for Belle's thick cloak and shirt, the skin on her shoulders would have been in tatters from Beast's wicked claws. Belle bit her lip, thankful that at least he was being quiet.

Metal parts groaned and creaked as the airship's stays were cast off. When it rose with a jerky motion, Belle squeezed her eyes shut, not ready for her first flight.

Traveling inside the crate was not fun, but it could have been worse. The dock workers' sturdy knots held, so the crate didn't slide as Belle feared it might. However, her stomach was acutely aware of the change in height as the airship took off.

They hit turbulence as the airship ascended. Beast and Belle clung to each other as their cramped crate shook violently.

Less secure cargo slammed into the walls and each other. Belle heard a few wooden boxes crack open, spilling their contents, adding to the chaos as supplies crashed to the floor and scattered.

At last, the shaking stopped, and the airship settled into a steady clip. The noises died down, an eerie calm descending on the cargo hold.

Beast held Belle close, as a child might hold a security blanket. Gently, she rested her hands on top of his paws while listening for any crew members coming to inspect the cargo.

After several minutes of silence, Belle whispered, "I'm going to see if I can find us somewhere else to hide. We don't want to be here when the airship docks. We'll have to sneak off later."

Beast held her tighter. "What if you get caught?"

"I don't hear anyone. I'll be fine," she promised, willing herself not to gulp. Belle knew she was lying through her teeth, but it wouldn't do to panic him.

"Be careful." Beast slowly released her shoulders.

"I'll be back as soon as I can."

Belle was relieved that the side of the crate easily slid off when she pushed against it. Climbing out, she loosely put the panel back in case she needed to return in a hurry.

The lighting was dim in the cargo hold. Gas lanterns were lit low, casting eerie shadows among the crates. Belle furrowed her brow. She had no experience with airships but expected to find more cargo than this for all the work the dock workers had done. But only about a dozen crates were in the hold, leaving plenty of room to spare.

Belle crept along the wooden floor, praying none of the boards creaked. As loud as the steam engine and pistons working to keep the airship airborne were, she shouldn't have worried, but everything had her on edge.

Just as Belle reached a dusty cleaning closet that made for a promising hiding spot, distant meowing pierced through the loud rumbling of the engine.

Belle whipped her head toward the sound, realizing it had come from the direction of Beast's crate. Having made little distance in her slow creep to find cover, Belle could still see his crate but not the source of the sound. She ran as quietly as she could toward the mewing.

When she reached the crate, Belle found a diminutive gray cat scratching at the crate's opening, meowing plaintively. It startled as Belle approached, its green eyes wide with curiosity.

Belle reached out a hand timidly. "Nice kitty…"

The cat touched its heart-shaped nose to her finger, purring gently.

Belle sighed, her shoulders slumping.

The cat turned around, scratching again at the opening. The side of the crate clattered to the floor, the noise echoing around the spacious room.

Frightened by the noise, the cat zoomed away, running out of the cargo hold.

Inside the crate, Beast was mortified.

Belle's heart raced as she scrambled to right the side of the crate. "Maybe it'll be okay," she muttered. "It's a cat. We'll be fine."

A piercing, scraping sound behind Belle made the hairs on the back of her neck stand up.

"Turn around. Slowly," commanded an alto voice that boomed throughout the cargo hold.

Belle did as instructed, wincing as she turned around.

A woman wearing a leather duster over a billowing,

mismatched, asymmetrical shirt and skirt pointed her saber level with Belle's throat.

"What are you doing on my ship?" The woman's thick brows arched as she glared. Red indentations formed rings around her eyes, likely from the goggles pushed up onto her short copper curls.

The cat padded back into the cargo hold, purring. Curling its tail around one of the woman's knee-high boots, it looked up curiously at Belle as it cleaned its paws.

"I—uh." Belle's mouth ran dry as she fumbled for any excuse. She gulped.

Suddenly, the gray cat darted inside the open crate.

The woman lowered her saber a fraction. "Cinders!"

Inside the crate, Cinders hissed.

The woman turned her attention back to Belle, pointing the saber at Belle's heart. "Who are you? What's in the crate?" Her gloved hand squeezed the hilt, a crackling blue current electrifying the saber. "Are you Delphine's spy?"

Beads of sweat dripped down Belle's back as she stared down the crackling electric saber, the blood rushing in her ears drowning out the noise of the airship's steam engine. Gas lamps on the walls flickered as minor turbulence rocked the ship, but the stranger wielding the saber didn't flinch.

"Start talking." The woman pushed the sparking saber closer.

Belle winced at the heat radiating from the saber's proximity. "We're stowaways," she said, meeting the woman's gaze and straightening her stiff shoulders. Belle towered over the stranger as she did nearly everyone she'd ever met. But unlike most people, this woman wasn't intimidated in the slightest.

The woman narrowed her wintry eyes. "What do you mean *we're*?" She sidestepped to the left, maneuvering around Belle's massive frame to peer into the open crate behind Belle.

Belle choked on her words but recovered in time to plant her feet wide, blocking the woman's path.

The cat's hissing grew silent.

"Let me pass!" Terror and anger flashed in the woman's eyes as she pushed past Belle, the electric saber slipping. "Cinders!"

Belle ducked low, kicking out her foot. She caught the woman's ankle and knocked her flat on her back with a thud. The electric saber clattered to the wooden floor, flickering off as soon as it left its owner's hand.

"Maker's moldy knickers!" the woman groaned, pushing herself off the ground and reaching for the saber.

Belle was faster. She pinned the woman's shoulder with her boot, exerting the minimal pressure needed to keep her down and hoping the shoulder wasn't broken or dislocated. "Sorry, I can't let you do that."

With a grunt, the woman strained to look up at Belle. "Your friend better not hurt Cinders, or I'll gut you both."

Belle swallowed hard. She didn't think Beast would hurt the cat, but the lack of sound coming from the crate was disquieting. Only the steady hum of the engine and the occasional creak of the airship adjusting course filled the stretching silence. "I'm sure your cat is fine. Look, we just need a ride—"

Loud, contented purring and heavy footsteps sounded behind Belle, leaving the rest of her plea to die on her lips.

"What the blazes is that?" asked the woman struggling beneath Belle's boot.

Belle cringed as she pressed down harder on the woman's shoulder, her leather boot creaking. She burned with curiosity, dying to turn around, but had no desire to get stabbed.

Beast stepped into view, holding Cinders. His hood was down, revealing his curled antlers. The cat snuggled into Beast's dingy fur, happily purring.

"Hello, sweetheart," Beast said to the content cat. "Who's a good girl?"

Belle's mouth went dry. Heat flushed her face when she realized Beast was staring at the diminutive gray cat with the devotion of an indulgent parent cooing over their baby. Once she recovered from the shock, Belle said, "I see you made a new friend."

Beast gave Cinders' chin scratches. "We came to an understanding."

"Traitorous cat," the woman snorted, grasping at Belle's leg to no avail. Defeated, she laid back down with a sigh. "Who the hell are you people?" The woman jerked her head toward Beast. "And seriously, what the hell is he? Is he going to eat my Cinders?"

"Never," Beast rumbled as he cradled Cinders. He scowled at the woman, baring his teeth before turning his attention back to the cat, who nuzzled her head against his powerful forearms.

Belle tore her eyes away from the strange display of affection and looked down at the pinned woman. "We're only stowaways. As you can see, our options for transportation are limited." She pulled down her cloak's hood, revealing the blue-black veins running through her translucent skin.

The woman blinked. "That would have been much more shocking if your companion didn't have a full set of antlers coming out of his head." She gave Belle a crooked smile. "You're from the circus, aren't you? I've seen you on the posters."

Belle blanched. She tried hard to forget about the tacky posters plastered around Minport. Under the direction of the Ringmaster, the painter had exaggerated Belle's scowl to the point where she'd looked bestial compared to the angelic acrobats balanced on her shoulders.

The cargo hold rattled, likely from more turbulence, bringing Belle back to the present. "Ah, yes. We are." Belle's gaze darted to Beast as she rubbed the back of her neck. "The circus became too dangerous for him. We had to leave by any means possible." She took a deep breath. "I'm sorry to impose on you, but if I release you, can we please have a lift? We'll stay out of the way. We brought our own supplies."

The woman tilted her head, squinting at Belle. "And if I say no?"

Belle's shoulders sagged. "Then we'll have to do whatever it takes. Though I'd rather go the peaceful route."

The woman snorted, raising her eyebrows. "Would you even know how to fly this ship?"

"We'd figure it out."

The woman guffawed. "Let me up. I'm Captain Darling Charity, and this is my ship. You can both stay, but you'll have to earn your keep."

Belle lifted her boot off the woman, keeping a wary eye on the dormant saber.

The captain caught Belle's stare and laughed as she brushed off her duster before picking up the saber and sheathing it. "Don't make me regret my decision. If I find out that you were Delphine's spies all along, I'll run you through."

Belle's eyes widened as she stepped back. "What? We're not spies. I've never even heard that name before."

Captain Charity's brows rose. "You don't know who Delphine Wyerstone is?"

Behind the captain, Beast glowered, grinding his teeth.

Belle caught herself staring and fumbled her response to the captain. "My father sold me to the circus when I was a girl. I don't get out much."

Captain Charity's mouth opened and closed. "Your father…sold you?"

"Yes." Belle's mouth twisted into a crooked grimace as she shrugged. "We're not spies. I mean, look at us." She gestured to herself and Beast.

"Alright, I believe you." Captain Charity shook her head. "You'd make terrible spies—both of you stick out too much."

"Thank you…I think." Belle smiled, warmth blooming in her chest. Maybe this wasn't such a terrible plan after all. "I'm Belle, and this is Beast."

The captain shot Beast a sideways look. "Of course he is." She hesitated before saying, "My pilot doesn't enjoy meeting new people, so the two of you will have to rest on the observation deck. After we land, I'll have a quick job for you to do before I send you on your merry way."

Belle beamed. "Thank you."

"Follow me."

Captain Charity only took two steps forward before the airship rocked. Everyone lost their balance as the crates shuddered against their restraints.

"Turbulence?" Beast asked, still holding Cinders.

"No." Captain Charity's brows furrowed. "That was different."

A crackling noise filled the cargo hold as a tinny voice emitted from a speaker overhead. "Captain, we have a problem! We're being boarded. I saw green and gold balloons on their ship."

"Shit." The captain ran to the cargo wall and pressed a black button Belle hadn't noticed before. "We also have a stowaway situation, but they're temporary crew now." She glanced over her shoulder at Beast and Belle. "I'll go man the cannons."

"Aye, Captain. Hurry!" The voice crackled, then faded away.

Captain Charity pointed at Belle and Beast. "You two are earning your keep early. Don't let them through the hatch. If we're breached, keep them away from the cargo. Got it?"

Belle gaped at the captain. Cinders meowed, pawing at Beast's cloak.

The captain grunted, shaking her head. "Come on, you feckless cat. Get to safety."

Without further ado, Cinders hopped out of Beast's arms and trotted past her mistress, tail aloft, as she exited the cargo hold.

"Right. Help me brace the hatch. I need to get to the cannons." The captain's mouth was set in a firm line as she strode to the massive hatch.

Belle and Beast followed her, exchanging uneasy glances.

The hatch was a little wider than Beast, plated with thick, impenetrable metal. Captain Charity pointed to an enormous turning mechanism in the center of the hatch door. "Beast, check the lock. Belle, help me barricade the hatch. There are beams against the wall you can use."

Belle loaded up wooden beams, then braced the hatch while Beast tightened the turning mechanism.

As Belle went back for another plank, she wondered what would scare the unflappable Captain Charity, who had so quickly gotten over her fright of Beast.

"Belle!"

Beast's anxious voice cut through Belle's thoughts. She whipped her head toward him. His nostrils were flared, and his eyes were wide, wild with fright.

"Something doesn't smell right," he rumbled. "Get back."

The three of them listened, waiting in silence. The sound of claws raking across the outside of the heavy metal hatch pierced through the silence.

Three booming knocks followed.

"Shit. I need to get to the cannons! Stall them!" Captain Charity dropped the beam she was holding and raced out of the cargo hold, leaving Belle and Beast to their fate.

CHAPTER SIX

The claws scraping against the metal hatch sent shivers up Belle's back.

The cargo hold felt claustrophobic. There was only one door to the rest of the airship, several feet behind Belle.

On Belle's right, Beast snarled as he pulled his tinted goggles over his owl-like eyes. His hackles raised, causing his cloak to stick up at odd angles around his shoulders and back.

The tempo of the scratching sped up, transforming into frenetic clawing, scraping, and pounding on the door. Belle covered her ears, but it wasn't enough to block out the horrible noise.

Beast bellowed, pressing his paws against his ears as well.

Belle squeezed her eyes shut, the sensory overload too much.

As quickly as it began, everything went silent. The only noise was Belle and Beast's labored breathing and the engine's steady hum.

Belle opened her eyes, slowly lowering her hands to wipe the sweat off her brow.

Beast sniffed the air, then wrinkled his nose and yelped. The horrified expression on his face terrified Belle more than the quiet.

"What is it?"

"Something smells unnatural. Stand back." Beast shielded Belle, sweeping his left arm in front of her.

Belle opened her mouth to ask what he meant when a wave of pungent odor hit her. Coughing and hacking, Belle doubled over as nausea overwhelmed her senses.

Peculiar hissing and popping sounds came from the other side of the hatch.

"Something's burning," Beast grunted, covering his nose with the tattered end of his cloak.

Following his lead, Belle weakly grasped the edge of her cloak, covering her nose and mouth. But it did little to dull the overpowering scent.

The hatch opened with a grinding screech, the beams bracing the door clattering to the floor. Gusts of wind whistled through the new opening. Backlit by the pale dawn light, abominations were revealed—creatures beyond what even Belle's vivid imagination could conjure.

Three furry humanoid creatures crowded into the entrance, each wearing a leather gas mask covering their head. They wore militant green uniforms with golden buttons, and gold and green collars adorned their thick necks. Behind them, a bridge connected another airship to the *Figment*.

The middle creature ripped its mask off, revealing a canine head. It tossed an empty flask off the bridge and growled, snapping its powerful jaws. The other two creatures howled and bayed as they discarded their masks.

"Hounds," Beast growled, crouching into a defensive position.

Belle wanted to ask Beast how he knew what the creatures were called but didn't get the chance. The Hounds bayed and growled, their howls carrying over the wind. Belle flinched, tripping over something solid—one of the wooden beams had landed by her feet.

Inspiration struck. Wielding the beam like a lance, Belle rushed the pack of Hounds.

A yell ripped from Belle's throat as she slammed her makeshift weapon into the creatures, sweeping the beam side to side. The Hounds cried out as they were knocked back onto the narrow wooden bridge precariously hooked to the *Figment*. Unable to keep their balance, the Hounds fell off the bridge.

One tried to grab onto Belle's beam and pull her down with it. But the creature missed.

Belle's stomach churned, and bile burned in her throat as she tried not to think of the miles-long drop from the rickety bridge. Putting on a brave face, Belle turned to look at Beast. "Well, that went better than I planned."

"Behind you!" Beast lumbered forward on all four paws.

Belle turned around in time to see that more Hounds had spilled out of the gold and green airship and were practically on top of her. She swung the beam but met resistance. A wolfish gray Hound, towering over the others, latched onto the other end of the plank. Growling, the Hound pulled on the beam, throwing Belle off balance.

The tip of Belle's boot caught on an acid hole burnt into the wooden bridge. She tumbled forward, teetering on the edge of the bridge. Her vision swam as the dark forest below came into focus.

The beam was wrenched out of Belle's hands as powerful arms pulled her back inside the *Figment*.

"Thank you," Belle panted, unable to catch her breath.

Beast patted her shoulder before stepping protectively in front of her. He widened his stance, lowered his head, and bellowed before charging at the Hounds.

Belle strained to see what was happening on the bridge, but it was all fur, teeth, claws, and antlers.

Grabbing another wooden plank, Belle carried it to the doorway. She jumped into the fight, taking advantage of any openings to knock more Hounds off the bridge.

Beast became locked in a grapple with a wrinkle-faced Hound who made up for its shorter stature with hulking shoulders. Neither seemed able to gain the advantage.

"Beast, duck!" Belle yelled, hoping her voice carried over the wind.

Beast released the Hound, crouching low.

Belle swung the beam, grazing past Beast's antlers and

connecting solidly with the Hound. The doomed creature bayed as it tumbled off the bridge.

Wiser now, Belle didn't stop to celebrate. She eyed the much larger enemy airship, where Hounds continued to barrel out of the cargo doors.

Belle's muscles burned. There were too many Hounds to fight.

She stepped back, evaluating.

Beneath her boots, the board closest to the *Figment* was crooked, with one partially melted hook resting at an odd angle. The bridge's connection was falling apart.

"Get back inside!" Belle shouted.

Beast's brows furrowed, but he retreated. He was nearly inside when the *Figment* shifted hard to the left. Beast crashed into Belle, and they tumbled into the hold. Belle scrambled to a crouching position as she tugged on one of the hooks lodged in the edge of the *Figment's* hatch.

Her short nails chipped and her fingers bled as she worked to remove the embedded hook. Belle grunted as she attempted to pull up the hook, holding her breath as it shifted marginally.

The Hounds rushed the bridge. They shoved past Belle as she worked, charging into the *Figment*, their claws scratching her up and tearing her cloak.

Groaning, Belle turned to see four Hounds making a dash for the crates, gnawing at the ropes tying down the cargo.

"Beast! The crates!"

Beast rushed the Hounds, bellowing as he threw them off the ropes.

Belle returned to her work. But the hook refused to budge, despite her best efforts. She tried her best to tune out the sound of Beast's battle so she could think.

Loosened boards on the bridge caught Belle's eye. One board was completely missing on the bridge. Maybe if she tore out a few more boards, the hook wouldn't matter anymore.

With grim determination, Belle reached for a board next to the gap.

The *Figment* shook, falling into a rapid descent.

Belle was thrown forward, almost falling through the gap.

Staring down at the quickly approaching ground, Belle was too petrified to stand while the ship appeared to be freefalling. Joints and connecting pieces on the bridge snapped and popped. Panicked, Belle crawled on her stomach toward the *Figment*.

Belle made it back inside just as the bridge ripped in half, splintering boards and breaking chains. She slid inside the cargo hold, careful to keep a low profile.

The *Figment* suddenly stopped its rapid freefall.

Over the sound of the Hounds' growling and Beast's roar, the tinny voice came back on the intercom. "Hope you're still with us, bonus crew. I'm engaging in evasive maneuvers until the cannon is charged."

Captain Charity's voice cut in over the speaker. "Damek! I need a few more seconds. No more descents—it threw calibrations off. I have to start over!"

"Aye, Captain. Hang on, bonus crew."

The intercom went silent. Belle blinked.

A pained bellow grabbed her attention.

She looked to find three Hounds biting down on Beast's limbs. Two of them had their teeth sunk into his arms, clamping down with powerful, locking jaws, while a wolfish Hound worried Beast's leg like a dog with a bone.

Belle grabbed a plank and charged. She cracked the board down on the closest Hound, hitting it repeatedly until it slumped to the floor. The other two Hounds shook their heads, biting down even harder.

Beast roared, struggling to kick and pull off his attackers with his freed bloody arm.

Belle swung again, connecting the board with the side of another Hound's head. It collapsed with a whine.

All that remained was the wolfish Hound chomping on Beast's leg. Belle brought the plank down as hard as she could.

The Hound crumpled.

After making sure all the Hounds were motionless, Belle turned to Beast and asked, "Will you be alright?" She reached for his torn forearm.

"Thank you," Beast muttered weakly. Behind cracked tinted goggles, his eyes fluttered closed, and he collapsed into her arms.

"Stay with me!" Belle pleaded, gently laying him on the floor away from the unconscious Hounds.

His eyes opened. "I'm here."

"Good. I need to clean up. Then I'll patch you up." Belle brushed his temple before beginning the unpleasant task of dragging the Hounds to the hatch.

With a grunt, Belle shoved all three bodies out of the exit. She stood in the hatch for a moment, puzzling over the nightmarish attack. Despite the ruined bridge, the other airship still followed too closely.

A great shudder rocked the *Figment*, and Belle braced herself against the doorway. Blue electricity crackled through the air, coming from the *Figment*, heading toward the enemy airship. Electricity enveloped it.

Belle shielded her eyes as the airship exploded into brilliant white and green lights reminiscent of fireworks. Stumbling to get inside the cargo hold, Belle closed the broken hatch as best she could.

"Direct hit!" Captain Charity said over the intercom, sounding out of breath. "How's the cargo?"

Belle went over to the black button and pressed it just as she had watched the captain do earlier. "Beast is injured, but the cargo's safe. The creatures are gone."

"Excellent! I'll get the med kit and—"

"Don't celebrate yet," the pilot's voice cut in. "The cockpit has been breached! Hurry!" Cinders yowled and hissed over the intercom. A menacing growl responded.

The speaker went silent.

"Damek!" Captain Charity's panicked voice rang out.

Hearing Beast struggling to sit upright, Belle turned to face him.

"Go help the pilot," Beast said, sinking back down. "I'll be fine."

Hot tears stung Belle's eyes as she nodded. "I'll be right back." With a lump in her throat, Belle raced to the cockpit.

The *Figment* rocked violently, sending Belle crashing into the galley wall. Her burning muscles screamed in protest as she braced herself against the porthole, praying the shaking would stop so she could reach the pilot before the ship crashed.

Captain Charity was presumably on her way, but where was the rest of the crew? Belle hadn't encountered a single soul on her journey to the cockpit. Though there were plenty of signs of the Hound.

Blood spatters, bits of fur, and scratch marks were everywhere. Belle followed the trail, her stomach churning at the thought of encountering more carnage.

It seemed the Hound had gotten lost. The creature's trail often led Belle to a dead end, forcing her to circle back, her sense of dread mounting. She feared that by the time she found her way to the cockpit, it'd be too late.

At last, Belle found herself in the main corridor: a long hallway with several doors on each side. She ignored the other rooms and headed for the front of the airship, logically thinking that would be where the pilot was flying the ship. But she was mistaken.

The front of the ship was a gunner station. Walled in by curved windows, only a lone cannon and a chair furnished the room.

Where the blazes was the cockpit?

Heart pounding, Belle went back into the corridor. She studied the doors again. One in the center of the hallway was cracked open just enough to let light shine through.

Slowly, Belle opened the door all the way, revealing stairs.

Scratches on the railing confirmed her suspicion. She bolted up the stairs.

The cockpit door was already open. Inside the room, the battered Hound menaced over Captain Charity, who wielded her electric saber. It crackled, sparking on the creature's fur.

The captain slashed at the Hound. The air filled with the scent of burnt fur mingled with coppery blood.

Belle heaved, steadying herself against the wall.

Captain Charity thrust her saber at the Hound.

Belle turned her head to the side, not wanting to see the Hound get skewered.

"Captain!" yelled the pilot, his modulated voice weak.

Belle looked back at the captain. Unfortunately, Captain Charity had missed the Hound. The creature lunged for the captain's arm, knocking her off balance. The saber clattered to the ground, falling underneath the cabinets.

The Hound tossed the captain to the side. Hard. She slammed into the doorframe of the cockpit, slumping to the floor.

Finished with the captain, the Hound leaped at the pilot.

Belle raced after the Hound, her eyes burning with rage and pain.

The creature chomped down on the pilot's arm.

Belle took a sharp intake of breath. The pilot wasn't screaming or crying out in pain. Was she too late?

"Get off of me, fleabag!" yelled the pilot, his voice just as metallic as it was over the speaker. Belle had assumed the sound quality of his voice was because of the intercom. But she didn't have time to wonder about the strangeness of it now.

As the Hound worried the pilot's arm, Belle slammed her fist into the back of the creature's head.

Unfortunately, her punch only enraged the creature. It turned to face Belle, snarling as it bared its blood- and oil-slicked teeth. It lunged forward at her, but Belle was faster. She ducked, and the Hound stumbled forward.

With a hammer blow, Belle's fist connected with the Hound's temple. The creature crumpled to the floor.

With the Hound out of the way, Belle was finally able to get a good look at the pilot. "What?" was all she could think to say as she gaped at the metal man slumped in the pilot's seat.

The mechanical pilot turned to face her. "My savior! Thank the Maker for bonus crew. I'm Damek Wraithe, pilot extraordinaire."

Belle had thought nothing else could shock her after meeting Beast and then fighting the Hounds. But apparently, the universe wasn't done surprising her.

Damek was an automaton that shouldn't exist. While the Circus

Illume had their own musical automatons, they were more like novelty machines with no independent thought or actions, everything perfectly programmed and coordinated.

Damek was different.

The automaton's metal lips were set in a grimace as he cradled his bent left arm. He wore loose clothing over his mismatched mechanical body that, at some point, had been painted to look as if he were wearing a black uniform. Visible wear covered every inch of him, revealing bits of copper, bronze, silver, and even gold on the tip of his little finger. Where Damek's arm had been broken, clear tubes carrying silver and black liquid were visible. The tubes were akin to Belle's dark veins, making her realize that the substance was ether in its liquid state. She couldn't tear her eyes away.

"I'm Belle," she finally said.

"I'd shake your hand, but I'm losing too much fluid. At least the airship's…" The pilot was mid-sentence when his voice trailed off, and he blinked. He inclined his head toward Belle. "Are you going to deal with that or…"

"What?"

Hot breath on Belle's ear made the baby-fine hairs on the back of her neck stand on end. Something wet splashed on her shoulder. A low, menacing growl rumbled behind her.

In Belle's peripheral vision, she could see the Hound was back on its feet, ready for revenge.

"Duck!" Captain Charity's voice rang out.

Belle ducked, covering her head with her arms.

Even Damek slid down in his chair with his good arm still on the steering mechanism.

Captain Charity swung her electric saber at the Hound. Sparks flew as she sliced into its forearm.

The Hound bellowed, swiping at the captain's face.

Tiny angry hisses from the ground made Belle uncover her face so she could confirm her suspicions.

Belle was right. The cat was back, scratching furiously at the Hound's legs.

"Cinders, no!" yelled Captain Charity, glancing down at the tiny gray cat.

The Hound took advantage of the captain's distraction, swatting her saber away.

Belle rose, pulling the Hound back as it lurched at Cinders. The two wrestled in the cramped cockpit, bumping into walls and cabinets. The Hound snapped at Belle, coming dangerously close to ripping out chunks of her face. Belle's muscles strained while she kept the Hound at bay.

"Damek!"

Captain Charity's anguished cry distracted both Belle and the Hound. While they'd been busy grappling, the captain had moved to the pilot's side, Cinders ensconced in her arms. Damek was now half-fallen out of his seat, the lights in his working eye dim.

The ship took a hard turn right, then down.

Swearing, the captain took control of the steering. "Finish the Hound! I need you to pilot!" Captain Charity's voice was panicked, her eyes darting glances at the ailing automaton.

Belle wiped a trickle of blood off her lip. It seared with white-hot pain. The Hound had gotten in a lucky scratch. "Working on it," Belle said before her brain caught up. "Wait, you want me to do what?"

"You heard me. Hurry."

Belle dodged the Hound, feeling its hot breath on her skin as she ducked. "Then give me your sword. I'm unarmed." Her knuckles were raw, but she threw another punch into the side of the Hound's jaw.

"No way in hell."

"Then you'll have to be patient," Belle grunted as the Hound lunged for her. She caught it in a grapple, but the Hound forced her back against the wall.

Belle winced as something hard jabbed into her lower back: a door knob. Hope blossomed in her chest. "Does this door lead to where I think it does?"

"Yes," Captain Charity responded, leveling out the airship so they were finally flying smoothly.

Belle twisted the door handle with her free hand, praying she could keep the Hound at bay a few moments longer.

Yowling from below caught both the Hound and Belle's attention.

Free from her mistress's clutches, Cinders was back, hissing and clawing at the Hound's hind legs.

Belle's stomach twisted. "Get back, kitty!" she yelled, her voice breaking. She didn't want to harm the cat, but the choice had to be made. She opened the door.

The Hound stretched out its claws to snatch the cat, but amazingly, Cinders listened. The Hound caught only air as Cinders darted away to safety.

The wind whipped Belle's stringy hair and stung her eyes as she grabbed the Hound and threw the creature out of the emergency exit. After slamming the door shut, Belle was hit by a wave of exhaustion and slumped to the floor.

Cinders trotted back to her and rubbed her head against Belle's bruised and bloodied knuckles. "You are a good girl," Belle said, patting the cat weakly. She hoped Beast was stable. As soon as she gathered her strength, she'd check on him.

"Take over. Hurry!" yelled Captain Charity.

Belle groaned as she stood and staggered to the captain.

Captain Charity gestured at the steering mechanism. "You need to fly. Now! Or Damek won't make it."

Belle blanched. "I thought you were joking."

"I'd never joke about that. Look at him!"

Damek clutched his broken arm, black fluid leaking all over, soaking his gray coat. His one functional eye flickered on and off.

"I don't know how to fly!" Guilt gnawed at Belle. "I have to check on Beast. He could be dead."

Captain Charity drew herself up. Though the top of her head barely reached Belle's collarbone, the captain still cut an intimidating figure. "Listen, you can check on Beast with the intercom while you steer. Damek will die if I don't fix him right now. Understood?"

"Maybe I should repair Damek, then check on Beast," Belle suggested, despite every instinct in her screaming to leave the cockpit and go straight to Beast. "I've never flown before, but I'm good at fixing things."

"You're not touching Damek. You either take the wheel or join the Hounds." All traces of amusement were gone from the captain's eyes. "My ship, my rules."

"I'll try not to crash."

"Just keep us steady. The gauge on your right will tell you what you need to know. The black button is the intercom." Without giving any further instructions, Captain Charity set to work on Damek, laying him down carefully on the floor.

The tense silence that followed was peppered with occasional swearing from the captain, the sound of tubes being tightened and reattached, and Damek's metal bits clanging together.

Belle eyed the controls warily. "Are you sure you trust me with this? I'd have more faith in myself as a mechanic than a pilot."

"I love the *Figment*, but there are hundreds of other airships. There's only one Damek Wraithe. Fly!"

Belle sat down in the slightly-too-small pilot's seat. There was a dizzying array of buttons, switches, and levers.

Nothing was labeled.

Hesitantly, Belle grabbed the steering wheel with her left hand. A gauge resembling a level told her if the airship needed correcting. After a moment's struggle, Belle found a position that kept the steering mechanism stable.

With her free hand, Belle pressed the intercom button. "Beast? The last Hound is gone. The pilot's hurt, so I have to fly. I'll tell you about it later if I don't crash." She swallowed hard. "Are you okay?"

Silence greeted her.

Belle's stomach churned as she took a deep breath. She told herself that there were many reasons why Beast might not be answering. He might have succumbed to exhaustion or couldn't figure out how to work the intercom. But worry permeated all her thoughts. "Beast! Are you there?"

Static popped and fizzled on the intercom.

Belle's heart hammered. "Please, answer me."

Finally, a low and familiar rumble sounded on the intercom. "I'm alive. Hurt, but here."

"I'll come to you as soon as I can. Hold on!"

"You can go now." Captain Charity's voice startled Belle.

"Damek's stable enough until we make port. Med kit is in the bottom right cabinet. Get your friend patched up enough to walk, and then we can take him to the med bay."

"Thank you," Damek piped up, both eyes glowing steadily.

Belle nodded curtly to the automaton and the captain. "I'm coming now. Hang on," she said to Beast. Belle snatched the med kit from the cabinet before sprinting all the way to the cargo hold, barely registering Cinders' light footsteps behind her as she opened the door.

"Beast!" Belle cried.

He was propped up next to the intercom button. A trail of blood stained the floor where he had dragged himself to the wall.

"Hello," Beast said, opening one bloodshot eye.

"Why didn't you say how bad it was?" Belle asked as she closed the gap between them, tearing into the med kit and pulling out bandages by the fistful.

"Didn't want you to worry." Beast closed his eye, and his breathing slowed.

Cinders darted toward Beast, nudging her head against his side, purring.

"Please stay with me." Belle gulped. "We'll be at port soon."

But only Cinders' purrs answered her.

CHAPTER SEVEN

Belle's swollen, bruised fingers, were slick with blood and slipped as she bandaged the bite on Beast's forearm. The pungent odor of the tonic stung her nose long after she applied the salve to the worst of his puncture wounds. In the nearby corner of the cargo hold, Cinders crouched down, watching as Belle performed her ministrations on the unconscious Beast.

Grimacing, Belle wiped her sore, messy hands on her tattered cloak before loosely tying bandages around her much-abused knuckles. Tending to her own wounds one-handed was even more difficult than administering first aid to Beast, but his shallow breathing spurred her on.

Belle swore when she dropped a bandage and again as she leaned in to examine Beast's injuries. His limbs were completely covered in bites and scratches. Splashes of pink and red tinged his dingy silver fur. Everything seemed to catch up with her at once as she leaned over Beast to examine his other arm. Swaying, she slumped forward and fell against his chest. Belle closed her eyes as she felt his heartbeat. The siren's call of sleep lured her into a drowsy state as she listened to the reassuring rhythm thrumming against her cheek.

Soon, she drifted off and dreamed that she was floating amongst the stars, far away and above her terrestrial problems. The scene morphed into Hounds pulling Beast down with their teeth, but Belle could only watch helplessly as her dream self was ensnared by thorns that wrapped around her limbs.

Her eyes snapped open and she let out a shuddering gasp.

"Hello?" Captain Charity's voice crackled over the intercom. "Is everything alright?"

Belle's legs had fallen asleep underneath her. She felt as if a thousand needles pricked her wobbly legs as she stood. She trudged to the black intercom button, cringing with each step.

"Beast has lost too much blood and is covered in bite marks. I did my best to bandage him, but he's lost consciousness, and I don't know if I've seen the worst of his injuries." Belle's ragged voice cracked.

"Blast it all." Static popped over the intercom. "Damek? Can you keep us in the air for a while?"

The automaton's voice echoed faintly in the hold. "As long as we don't hit turbulence, I'll be fine. I need you to land, though."

"Thank you." Louder, Captain Charity added, "I'm on my way. Hang on."

Belle sniffled as the intercom clicked off. She was relieved that the automaton was safe, but she never should have left Beast's side. A twinge of guilt twisted in her gut like a knife as soon as the thought crossed her mind. The memory of Damek's grateful expression haunted her conscience.

Belle chased away her uncomfortable thoughts by throwing herself into mending Beast's wounds. The work kept her hands busy, but her pain was excruciating. She had barely finished bandaging up his right arm when the captain's voice startled her.

"Is he going to live?"

The clinical, matter-of-fact tone the captain used made Belle's blood boil. Rage coursed through her as she remembered all the indignities Beast had suffered since that fateful night by the campfire. She turned to see Captain Charity peering at Beast. The gas light sconces cast shadows over her inscrutable expression.

Belle straightened, looming over the other woman. "I don't know." Her voice was quiet as she seethed. "But if he doesn't live, it'll be on your head. I told you he was hurt. I needed to go back to him. It wasn't enough that we put our lives on the line to protect your precious cargo so you can continue your smuggling ring."

Ugly purple and red splotches bloomed on Captain Charity's freckled cheeks. "I didn't invite you aboard my ship. You two made the choice to stow away." She punctuated her sentences by jabbing her index finger into Belle's chest with each word.

Belle glared at the offending finger. "Yes, to escape a fate worse than death. I'm sorry we inconvenienced you. What would you have done if we weren't here to fight the Hounds? Where is the rest of the crew? Or did you cast them aside for profit?"

"You dare…" The rest of Captain Charity's sentence died as Belle knocked her arm away.

"Don't touch me." Belle pushed the captain against the wall, her scabbard clanging against the metal support beam.

"I'm not a smuggler!" The splotches on the captain's cheeks darkened. "Well, I am a smuggler, but not the kind you're thinking of."

"Quiet." Beast's grumbling drew both of their attention. Groaning, he shifted on the bloodstained floor to look at them. "My head hurts."

Belle released the captain and rushed to Beast's side. "What do you need?"

"Sleep. Medicine, probably." He weakly gestured to the bandages on his arms. "Thank you." He frowned as he looked pointedly at the loose wrappings slipping on Belle's scraped knuckles. "You need help, too."

"I know." Belle's voice caught at the sudden intensity of Beast's gaze as he stretched his less injured arm to tuck the stray strands of charcoal hair behind her ear. His paw lingered a moment before he dropped it to his side, wincing at the movement.

Belle cleared her throat and turned her attention back to the captain, who was leaning against the wall, arms crossed, averting her eyes as she shifted her weight. "Can you please help me finish bandaging him? As soon as we make port, we'll be out of your way."

Captain Charity sighed. "Yes, let me do it."

The cargo hold was silent as the captain set about bandaging Beast while Belle propped him upright, practically in her lap, as she braced herself against the chilly wall. Occasionally, Beast growled if a bandage was too tight. Movement in Belle's hands was becoming increasingly difficult as the swelling in her joints increased, but she gently stroked the uninjured parts of his arms that she could reach. She hoped the gesture was soothing and not dehumanizing.

Captain Charity glanced at Belle's battered hands. "I have something for swelling. Hang on."

With that, the captain sprang up with far more energy than either Beast or Belle had and left the cargo hold. Cinders came out of hiding to trot behind her mistress, tail high in the air.

When they were alone, Beast looked back at Belle. "You don't have to keep holding me. You need rest."

Belle gave him a crooked smile. "I have the wall holding me up. I'll be fine."

He narrowed his eyes and shook his head. "You've overdone it. Come here." Without waiting for a response, Beast groaned as he shifted to sit up.

"What are you doing?" She tilted her head, her stomach inexplicably fluttering as she watched Beast.

"You heard me." Propping himself against the wall, Beast carefully pulled her against his chest.

Comfortable heat radiated from Beast as he covered them both with his cloak. The tension in Belle's neck and shoulders abated, but she worried her lower lip.

"Thank you, but isn't this too much for you?" She frowned as she listened to his shallow breathing.

"Compared to jumping off the bridge, I'm fine. Rest." Beast squeezed Belle's shoulder.

It didn't take long for Belle's eyes to flutter closed. She nestled against Beast's chest and let exhaustion take her.

They woke to Damek's cheerful voice over the intercom. "Captain, we're twenty minutes away from port. Landing preparations need to start."

Belle rubbed her eyes. She was bereft and couldn't figure out why until she realized she was lying alone on a stiff cot. They had been moved into a sterile room with cabinets thrown open, revealing the remains of hastily opened med kit packaging.

Her hands felt heavy. She looked down to see someone had expertly bandaged her hands. Beneath the wrappings, a soothing balm had been applied. Bumpy linen packs of chilled rice were tied around her hands, relieving some of her pain.

Belle smiled at the gesture until panic seized her heart. She looked wildly around the room, until she saw Beast was lying on a long cart meant for cargo, surrounded by mismatched pillows and blankets.

A small cough drew Belle's attention.

Captain Charity stood in the doorway, looking as if she had run a marathon. Her short copper curls were in disarray and sweat drenched her billowy clothes.

"You two are difficult to move, even with the dolly." The captain dabbed her brow with a crumpled handkerchief. "We'll be landing at a hospital soon. We can't risk being docked too long, but a doctor owes me a favor. She'll look at your injuries."

"What about the job you mentioned earlier? Before the attack?" Belle sat up, wincing at the numbness in her calves and feet. Her legs dangled off the edge of the too-short cot.

Captain Charity shook her head, bouncing her curls. "Neither of you are in any state to help. Focus on healing, then you can pay me back later. There'll be other opportunities."

"Thank you." Belle nodded. Her thoughts were in turmoil as she couldn't reconcile the same woman who'd held her at saber-point as the same person who'd gone out of her way to look after injured stowaways.

After the captain left, Beast rumbled, "Can we trust her? What kind of job would she have for circus runaways?"

Belle settled down on the uncomfortable cot. "I don't know. Hopefully, not fighting more Hounds." As she closed her eyes, a lingering question came back to her. She bolted upright. "How did you know what those creatures were?"

Beast grimaced. "Ask me another time. It's a painful story. I hurt enough."

"Fair enough."

Silence stretched between them, a thousand questions swirling in Belle's mind before the gentle swaying of the airship rocked her to sleep.

Violent shaking jolted Belle awake. Her heels hit the edge of the too-short cot, but the leather belt strapped around her waist prevented her from completely falling off. Vials of elixirs tumbled out of the med bay's mismatched cabinets. Something deep within the *Figment* shuddered as the airship lurched forward with a screech.

Beast bellowed as his cart-turned-makeshift-bed slid wildly in the cramped room, crashing into cabinets. The blankets fell off and tangled in the squeaking wheels. He held himself up by the cart's handle as it shifted again. Giving up on remaining upright, he dropped down on the cart, digging his claws into its wooden base as he held on.

Belle fumbled with the strap around her waist, fingers slipping as she tried to unbuckle it. Her hands were better since Captain Charity applied the salve and cold packs, but her stiff, swollen fingers were still far from healed. Finally, she unhooked the belt, staggering off the cot as the airship rocked again, throwing her into the corner of a cabinet. Wincing at the jabbing pain in her thigh, she braced herself for another collision.

Captain Charity's overly bright voice carried over the chaos via the sputtering intercom. "Good afternoon, bonus crew! We are approaching Ichorfell. It might be a bumpy ride, as some of the landing gear appears to be malfunctioning. Please stay seated as we land."

The intercom fizzled off.

"Might be a bumpy ride?" Belle shook her head. A pained growl from Beast silenced any further quips. She lunged for the runaway cart, perilously close to crashing.

"I've got you." With a grunt, Belle caught the cart by the handle barely before it could run over her bare feet.

"Thank you." Beast's breathing was labored as he righted himself.

Belle's stiff muscles groaned as she pushed the overladen cart against the wall, wedging it between the cot and the cabinets. Between the airship's tremors, she tethered the cart with the cot's leather strap.

"Hopefully, this will work." She was immediately knocked to the floor, knees first, as the *Figment* made its descent.

Beast leaned over the edge of the cart, his matted fur sticking up at odd angles, as he narrowed his eyes. His goggles were missing. "Belle?"

"I'll be fine." Belle gritted her teeth. She pulled herself off the floor and onto the cart to sit next to Beast, bracing her feet against the cold floor. Everything in the *Figment* rattled as it landed. Even Belle's teeth chattered as she clung to the cart, her knuckles turning white. A piercing, groaning screech echoed throughout the airship. Beast slammed pillows over his ears.

Finally, all the commotion stopped.

The intercom crackled on. "Welcome to Ichorfell! How are you doing, bonus crew?" Captain Charity's breathless voice still managed to sound peppy.

Spying the call button across the room, Belle groaned as she lumbered over to press it.

"Battered, but still here. Beast's cart tried to kill us both."

Captain Charity let loose a string of expletives. "I'm so sorry. I was in too much of a hurry getting you guys to the med bay. On the positive side, there are more bandages in the cabinet."

"Thank you. Anything for bruises?"

"Probably. I'm going to contact the local hospital and get the doctor on board before unloading cargo. She'll do a much better job than I can. Stay put."

Belle flopped down on the cot and groaned. "As if I'm running after all that. I feel like I could hibernate for a week, minimum. How about you?"

"Sleep sounds wonderful." Beast's voice was muffled as he covered his face with a pillow.

It wasn't long before they were joined by Captain Charity and a grizzled stranger with a steel-gray bun, wearing a black apron over her crisply ironed gray suit. The captain flipped a switch on the wall and the bright overhead lights built into the curved ceiling made Belle flinch.

"This is Dr. Brownlow. She owes me a favor, so she'll be taking care of you two. Don't worry, she's discreet." Captain Charity ribbed the doctor, whose frown deepened.

"Why is your face in the pillow? I wasn't aware of any facial injuries." Dr. Brownlow's clipped steps across the room matched her staccato cadence.

The doctor lifted the pillow from Beast's face, revealing his sharp, twisting antlers, fur-covered body, and squinting yellow eyes as he peered back at her.

"Maker! What is that? I'm a doctor, not a veterinarian." Doctor Brownlow stepped back, away from the annoyed Beast.

"He speaks, you know, and probably would love to tell you his origin story if he weren't so injured." Belle's nerves were in tatters, and the doctor's flippant attitude toward Beast grated on her last intact nerve.

"My apologies. Still, if he's not human, then—"

Captain Charity slung her arm around Dr. Brownlow's bony shoulders. "Remember, you owe me. I'm trusting you to get them patched up while I unload the supplies. You've got this."

"Yes, but I—"

The captain left, whistling a merry tune as she waved goodbye.

Dr. Brownlow scowled at the captain's retreat. "You can't stay long. Patrols are increasing in frequency."

"I know!" Captain Charity's voice echoed from the corridor. "I'll unload and get the *Figment* airworthy. It'll be quick!"

The doctor shook her head and turned her attention to her patients. "Well, let's see what I'm working with here." She pursed her thin lips.

Belle squirmed, hating the scrutiny. Would this doctor turn them in to the circus? Ichorfell was such a small town that the Circus Illume never stopped there, but there was a chance that the doctor traveled to the larger cities.

Dr. Brownlow examined Belle's hands, tsking at her swollen,

bruised knuckles. Her tiny round glasses slid down her crooked nose as she met Belle's gaze.

"How are your ether-poisoning symptoms?"

Belle blinked. No one ever asked her about her symptoms. In the circus, it was always about her strength and unnatural appearance, not how she was feeling or if her migraines were back. "Fine, thank you. Beast needs more attention than I do, especially if we're short on time."

"Let me change your dressings, then I'll get to your friend."

Dr. Brownlow set her worn medical bag on the counter and set to work removing Belle's bandages, stained dark red. Cool relief washed through her as the doctor applied a translucent green salve on her battered hands before redressing her wounds.

"Thank you so much." Belle flexed her fingers experimentally.

The doctor smirked. "You remind me of her. Be careful brawling, or you're going to end up with permanent damage. Rest your hands."

Belle flushed. "I'll keep that in mind, thank you." Her brow furrowed. "Sorry, but I remind you of who?"

Dr. Brownlow bent low to examine Beast. He gave the doctor a wary look but otherwise cooperated with the examination of his bitten limbs. "Captain Charity, or whatever she's calling herself these days. She's always getting into trouble, but her heart's in the right place. Without her, our hospital wouldn't have the supplies we need."

The doctor removed Beast's bandages and applied salve to his wounds. He huffed but was uncharacteristically quiet as she worked.

"Why are supplies so scarce?" Belle leaned forward, resting her palms on her knees.

"Someone keeps buying up medicine at a premium and hoarding it." Dr. Brownlow bent closer to Beast's arm, a deep frown etched into her features. "Whoever it is, they're certainly not a hospital. The problem is widespread. Captain Charity thinks it might be Delphine Wyerstone, the inventor. But that makes little sense."

"Why would that be?" Belle burned with curiosity as she watched the doctor.

Dr. Brownlow sighed. "Wyerstone owns the factories that produce the medicine. She wouldn't need to hoard anything. Besides, she's wealthy enough to create medical supplies beyond the ordinary ones we use at the hospital. The captain holds a grudge against her over the automaton, but don't ask her about it unless you want an earful."

Belle desperately wanted to ask more, but a gasp from Dr. Brownlow interrupted her train of thought.

"What happened to you?" The doctor adjusted her glasses with trembling fingers as she stared at Beast.

"I was bitten." Beast slouched against the wall behind him.

"I know that. I mean, these scars. They're everywhere. You look like you've been vivisected. You shouldn't be alive. What are you?"

"I don't know."

"But—" Dr. Brownlow opened and closed her mouth before shaking her head. "I need to disinfect these bites and change the bandages. You're lucky you don't need a blood transfusion."

"Will I heal?" Beast's tone was flat, but Belle thought she saw a flash of worry in his tired eyes.

"Your outlook looks positive, but..." Dr. Brownlow held up the bandage to the light.

Beast tried to follow the movement but ended up squinting at the bright light. "What is it?"

"Your blood is laced with...gold? What is that?" Dr. Brownlow lowered the bandage and pointedly stared at Beast's antlers. "I suppose that isn't the strangest part of your physiology. I have so many questions."

Belle frowned. The metallic blood made her think of her own condition, but her blood was darkened by the ether-poisoning.

"As do I." Beast's gaze was downcast.

Damek's panicked voice cracked over the intercom. "We're about to have company! The *Curator* spotted a patrol ship heading this way and sent us a warning message."

Belle reached the intercom first. "Is the captain back?"

"I can see her running up the dock now. The dock workers are trying to close the hangar, but it's damaged. We're going to be spotted!"

Dr. Brownlow rushed to finish cleaning up Beast. As she checked over her work, she said, "You and Beast should come with me. The patrol ship wouldn't be looking for you two. I can find somewhere for you to hide."

"Thank you, we'll—"

Beast's low rumble interrupted. "They might be looking for me."

The doctor's offer was tempting, but there was only one choice Belle could make. "Thank you, Dr. Brownlow, but we'll take it from here. Return to the hospital. It's about to get rough."

Belle guided the doctor to the med bay door by her elbow.

"But what are you going to do? You're not healed yet." The doctor's voice wavered.

"We'll be fine." Belle watched Doctor Brownlow leave with a heavy heart. She scooped up her boots by the exit before returning to press the intercom button. "Does the cannon still work?"

Static sizzled, muffling Damek. "Yes."

"I'll buy us some time until the captain gets us airborne."

Beast stared as she slipped her boots on.

"Buckle up." Belle patted his shoulder. She left before he could protest. With a hammering heart, she headed to the gunner station.

Belle's footsteps thundered through the corridor as she sprinted for the gunner station that she had stumbled upon hours ago during the Hound attack. After getting lost once in the uniform passages, she threw open the door to the station, wincing as the crooked, unhinged door squeaked. She reached for the switch and illuminated the room in cool light, which was supplemented by the sunlight streaming through the bubble-dome glass window.

The heavily insulated cannon dominated the sparsely furnished room, extending outside the dome window through a hole cut just big enough to accommodate the protruding cannon. How was she supposed to aim if the glass kept it stationary?

Her knees creaked and her back protested as she sat down on

the rust-colored, high-backed seat next to the gigantic cannon. Sound-dampening earmuffs were suspended on a rope next to the seat. Before her, faint crosshairs were visible on the dome window, which gave a 360-degree view of Ichorfell's open-air hangar. Her stomach dropped as she realized the glass dome extended all the way to the floor, ending only a few feet in front of the cannon's base. She wasn't looking forward to the illusion of only sky beneath her feet when the *Figment* took off.

If they took off. The engine sputtered again, rumbling and echoing inside the airship.

Outside, dock workers frantically waved bold, colorful flags at the three other airships on the small dock to coordinate departures. Orderlies ran carrying medical supplies, sometimes two to a crate, into the run-down, sickly green hospital loading bay. Above the chaos, more dock workers attempted to close the hangar's roof, but the great geared turning mechanism jammed as three workers turned its crank. One of the hanger's walls was crumpled, as if something had crashed into it. The gap in the wall revealed foamy ocean waves far below the dock.

Belle's brow furrowed. For an obscure middle-of-nowhere town, Ichorfell's dock was buzzing with activity.

Two sharp, staccato whistles from the dock's air control tower snapped Belle out of her contemplation. Off in the distance, the sleek outline of the patrol ship came into view. Belle shook herself and looked down at the cannon. A messy array of buttons and switches greeted her, somehow even more complex than the cockpit's dashboard.

"How do I turn this thing on?" She leaned forward, swearing violently when her tender knee smashed into the console. A warning buzzer sounded, ending when she repositioned her throbbing knee.

Damek's voice filled the room. "Captain's back. I've been instructed to tell you how to turn on the cannon. Ready?"

Belle startled, bumping her other knee against the bottom of the console. Groaning, she reached for the intercom button. "Yes, please."

"Red switch, silver toggle, brass knob, light bulb button. Got it?"

Static popped and fizzed as Belle searched for the silver toggle. At last, she spotted it at the left edge of the array.

"Got it!" Her bruised fingers ached and her bandages caught a few times as she pushed the red button, flipped the silver toggle, turned the brass knob, and hit the light bulb button.

Nothing happened.

"Damek? It's not doing anything." Belle fought the rising panic in her stomach as she watched the horizon. The patrol ship would be here within fifteen minutes.

"Turn the brass knob counterclockwise." Captain Charity's breathy voice crackled over the intercom.

Too panicked to grumble about vague instructions or aching hands, Belle ran the sequence again. Nearly every light on the cannon flickered on with a low hum, save for the biggest crimson button, labeled with a black skull and lightning bolt.

"It's humming! Now what?"

"Wait for the skull button to light up, then aim and fire!"

Belle experimentally turned the square handles flanking the console. Even with her loose grip, the cannon moved faster than she expected. Much to her surprise, the glass dome moved with the cannon, acting as a shield.

"At least that part won't be difficult. Come on, hurry." Belle tapped the side of the console, waiting for the button to light.

"We have a problem. The fuel is low. The ship doesn't have enough power to take off and fire the cannon." The captain's voice was grim. "There's another tank of ether in the engine room, but I can't leave. Damek's too injured for takeoff."

"Think I can handle it?" Beast's gravelly voice over the intercom startled Belle into nearly falling off her too-small seat.

"Maybe? Can you open a container and pour it into the tank?"

"Probably. Where is it?"

Belle tuned out, her thoughts plagued by Beast's injuries. As much as she hurt, she couldn't imagine how much pain he was in from the bite wounds and scratches covering his limbs. She was amazed he was even able to stand and use the intercom.

Beast grunted, the sound amplified by the glass dome. "I'm on my way."

Steadying her breath, Belle's voice caught as she replied. "Be careful! Watch your bandages."

"I'll be as careful as you are." The intercom shut off with a resolute click.

Belle blinked. Was that venom in Beast's voice? Her hand hovered over the button to reply, but movement in her peripheral vision caught her attention. The last of the other airships took off, blowing dust across the hangar as the workers scurried closer to the hospital. Only the *Figment* remained as the patrol ship loomed closer.

Belle pressed the button again. "What kind of range does the cannon have?"

Captain Charity sounded anxious, her tense words coming too fast. "Your target is within reach. As soon as the button is lit, fire."

"Oh, good." Belle shifted on the seat, staring at the ominous skull button.

"Make it count. There's a cool-down period between each shot." Damek's voice cut in.

"And put on the sound dampener!"

"Right." Belle gulped, remembering how long it had taken between shots against the Hounds' airship. She grabbed the padded earmuffs, clutching them as she waited for the power to kick in.

"Done," Beast rumbled over the intercom.

The huge red fire button lit up, giving the black skull and lightning bolt on it an eerie halo. Belle put on the sound dampeners. She prayed her aim was steady as she lined up the crosshairs with the patrol ship, sunlight reflecting off its ether-silver paint.

Bile churned in her stomach as Belle pressed the crimson button, wondering if the patrol ship's crew even knew what was coming for it. Thunder sounded within the cannon, sending tremors through her seat. Even with the sound dampeners on, the noise was engulfing.

Electricity arced from the *Figment* to the patrol ship.

The other ship dropped like a rock, crashing into the sea miles below.

The gunner station reeked of burnt ozone, stinging Belle's eyes and nose. She took off the sound dampeners and sank on the seat, cradling her forehead with her hands. Guilt ate away any feelings of victory at the thought of the lives lost beneath the waves.

"Nice shot!" Captain Charity's triumphant yell was punctuated by loud crackles. "Buckle up, we're taking off. Once we're airborne and stable, let's meet on the observation deck. I want to speak to you both about an opportunity. Damek can cover us for a while."

Belle sat up straighter. "Will do."

The *Figment* rocked as the engine grew louder, its rhythm like a mechanical heart.

Belle scrambled as she buckled in and hoped Beast had found somewhere safe to sit as the airship shakily lifted off the dock. Just as she feared, the front-facing seat gave her too much of a view of the rocky island-city of Ichorfell growing smaller as The *Figment* ascended. The last thing she saw before squeezing her eyes shut was a rescue boat speeding through choppy waves to the wreckage of the half-sunken patrol ship.

Belle hoped the other crew was safe, but she was relieved that they wouldn't be following the *Figment*. Tormented by her conflicting emotions, she let her mind wander as she puzzled over the captain's proposal and waited for the airship's rattling to settle down.

CHAPTER EIGHT

Belle made her way through the corridors of the *Figment* to the enclosed observation deck. She was surprised to find she was the first to arrive, but happily took advantage of the solitude to explore. Cozy pillows, blankets, and couches furnished the room, along with a long, sturdy table decorated with a gas-lit candelabra centerpiece, surrounded by mismatched chairs. The spacious, warm room was a welcome relief after the stark gunner station.

A glass dome surrounded the entire observation deck, with mechanical shades to block out the sun. Belle imagined the view would be spectacular at night, with nothing to obstruct the view of the stars as the *Figment* flew over the clouds.

All romantic notions of stargazing screeched to a halt when the door opened with a bang.

Belle jumped as Beast stalked in, Cinders following close behind. The diminutive gray cat darted past Belle to a comfortable perch near the window, where she promptly curled up and fell asleep.

As Belle's breathing slowed back to normal, she pointed a shaking finger at the scowling Beast. "You scared me!"

"You're one to talk," Beast huffed, crossing his bandaged arms.

Belle was relieved that his dressings were intact and clean, but his tone grated on her fragile nerves. Every fiber of her being was exhausted, and her stiff muscles ached. Beast's belligerent stare sent her over the edge.

"What is your problem? We made it out of Ichorfell." Belle crossed her arms, glaring back at him.

"You took off without a second thought. What if the patrol ship shot at this ship's cannon first?"

Belle pinched the bridge of her nose. "I miss when you didn't talk so much. There wasn't time to plan. Unless there's more crew hiding somewhere, there wasn't anyone else who could man the cannon. The pilot is injured. Neither of us knows how to fly the airship, and you were knocked out for a while, in case you forgot. I had to do something."

"Your hands are still swollen and bruised. Look at them." Beast reached for Belle's free hand.

"Hey! What are you—"

If she hadn't felt the slightest brush of fur, Belle would have sworn she imagined Beast caressing her tender hand before abruptly dropping his paw to his side. "You need to be more careful."

Belle's mouth formed a tiny "o" as realization hit her. All the anger deflated, her shoulders slumped. "I couldn't afford to be careful. It was act or die." Her gaze met Beast's bloodshot eyes. "I could say the same about you. What were you thinking, dashing off to the fuel tank?"

"I had to do something." Beast's hackles lowered as his scowl vanished.

"So, we're even?" Belle smirked.

"I suppose." His sullen grumble was back. "Please don't go running headlong into danger again."

Belle shook her head, tipping up on her toes to smooth Beast's ruffled fur behind his ears. "I wasn't always like this. Maybe it's your fault I'm always sprinting toward trouble now."

Beast leaned in, huffing with righteous indignation. His hot breath tickled Belle's nose.

Whatever scathing reply he might have had was interrupted by a polite cough from Captain Charity, who stood in the doorway in a fresh change of clothes. Her billowy patchwork blouse was hastily tucked into leather trousers, and her electric saber was sheathed on a belt looped twice around her waist. She held a full bag made of repurposed flour sacks in one hand and a bottle of wine in the other. A savory, mouth-watering scent wafted from the bag.

At the audible grumbling of both their stomachs, Belle flushed while Beast looked down, scratching the back of his neck.

"Sorry, I hope you all didn't have trouble finding the room. I forgot I hadn't had time to give you a tour." The captain looked between Belle and Beast, raising her brows at their tense expressions. "I'm glad you both made it. Let's eat, and I'll tell you my idea."

Captain Charity led them to the table, where she unloaded the sack, revealing individual piping-hot shepherd's pies, cheese cubes, a fluffy loaf of bread, and mismatched tableware.

At Belle's bemused expression, the captain grinned. "The hospital had extra food on hand and gave us a meal as thanks. Sorry it's late for lunch, but I kept the pies in the galley's warmer while I finished unloading. The wine is from my stores. Nothing fancy, but after our exceptional getaway, I think it'll be celebratory enough."

"Thank you." Belle felt faint. The meager jerky from their supplies had barely fueled their escape. When was the last time they'd eaten? Her stomach growled again in answer. She immediately turned crimson, burying her face in her hands.

Laughing, Captain Charity handed Belle her shepherd's pie first, along with an ornate golden fork. "Don't stand on ceremony. Please, help yourself."

"I truly appreciate it." Belle took a bite and closed her eyes. The meat practically melted in her mouth, and she let out a contented moan. When she opened her eyes, Beast gawked at her, his goldenrod eyes round and glittering. Belle wondered if spontaneous combustion via embarrassment was possible.

Mercifully, the captain ignored the exchange as she handed Beast his meal.

They ate in silence as Captain Charity uncorked the wine with a pop and produced glasses as if by magic. She poured three servings, then pouted for a moment as she split the contents of the third glass between the other two as Belle and Beast stared, nonplussed.

"Alas, Damek needs me functional in case of an emergency, so no wine for me today." Captain Charity shook her head before giving Beast a thoughtful look. "I suppose I should have asked. Do you drink wine? Should I give you raw meat instead?"

"I don't know if I've ever had wine. Thank you for the meal." Beast's mouth was full as he spoke. Bits of potatoes escaped as he talked.

Belle and the captain exchanged an amused glance.

Captain Charity poured half of Beast's wine into the other full glass before giving it to him. "If this is your first time, I don't want you to overdo it."

The captain then handed Belle the full glass. She took a cautious sip, wrinkling her nose at the heady flavor. She missed Cook's cider—the only part of circus life she'd ever miss.

As they ate, Captain Charity steepled her fingers. "Now that you have some food in your belly, to business. I have a proposition for you both. Well, it's more of an opportunity."

Belle sat up straighter in her seat as Beast's ears perked up.

"Under different circumstances, I'd offer you places on my crew, but the *Figment* is going to be out of commission for some time with repairs. Damek's reconstruction is going to take a while, too. If I don't do some serious sweet-talking, fixing my ship is going to be expensive. As you might imagine, the kinds of jobs I take on are not the most lucrative. Back-water hospitals aren't exactly wealthy, but the food is great." The captain shrugged.

Belle furrowed her brows. "Wouldn't repairing Damek be more expensive? Since he's one of a kind?"

Captain Charity pointed an index finger at her. "I like you. You're smart. I wish I could keep you aboard." The captain's short copper curls bounced as she nodded. "Damek's repairs are trickier, but I know his creator. She's going to be cross with me, but she'll fix him up as a matter of personal responsibility. If she doesn't kill me first."

"Are you in danger?" Beast lowered his glass, revealing his red wine-stained muzzle.

Captain Charity guffawed. "No, I mean Maureen's going to cuss me out." The captain's expression sobered. "Speaking of Maureen, that's where you two come in. See, she's the mayor of Duchollow, and I think she might help you."

"A town? With people?" Belle blurted. She looked pointedly at Beast and back at the captain. "Won't someone turn us in?"

"Duchollow is a small town, and it's a…unique community." Captain Charity shifted in her seat. "Let's just say the citizens have no problem letting someone like me dock there whenever I need. It's also off major trade routes, so you're not likely to run into the circus there." She popped a bite of cheese into her mouth before continuing. "I take it you've never heard of Duchollow before today?"

"No," Belle and Beast answered in unison.

Captain Charity's gaze softened. "The mayor is the smartest, fairest woman I've ever met. She studied all kinds of sciences at Onyxmark University, before devoting her life to helping people. I think she could help with your ether-poisoning and maybe figure out what happened to Beast."

"What's the catch?" Beast's voice grumbled.

"Maureen doesn't like outsiders coming into Duchollow. She's had too many run-ins with the Hounds and Delphine's spies. She and Delphine are mortal enemies." The captain leaned back in her chair. "The mayor is going to be furious with me for bringing you into town."

"Why bring her up then? It sounds hopeless." Belle furrowed her brows.

"Maureen might agree since you saved Damek, me, and the hospital cargo. If she agrees to let you stay, she'll more than likely put you to work because she's always looking for help."

Belle burned with anger. "I'm done being someone's kept workhorse."

Captain Charity lifted her hands up in surrender. "I don't mean you'd be working for free. It'd be paid work, and you'd be able to leave whenever it suited you. I mean, Duchollow's a community and everyone's expected to pitch in. That's all."

"Would this community welcome someone like me?" Beast huffed, gesturing to his antlers.

"I'm sure your sunny disposition will win them over." Captain

Charity grinned, but it faded at his glare. "It might take time, but I wouldn't rule it out. Where else would you two go? Or were you planning on shacking up in the woods?"

"No. We only agreed to help each other escape. Having done that, we're free to part ways." Belle's eyes bulged as she realized how crass she sounded. The wine must have been stronger than she thought. Mortified, she covered her discomfort by stuffing a piece of bread into her mouth.

Hurt flashed in Beast's eyes as he ducked his head, feigning newfound interest in his dinner.

Captain Charity covered her agape mouth with her hand. "I'm sorry. I assumed..." She looked back and forth between them, clicking her tongue. "Never mind. Well, you don't have to decide tonight. We're taking the long route to Duchollow in case the patrol ship sent a distress signal."

The captain rose, clearing her plate. "Enjoy the rest of your meal. I put your things in here last night, next to the pallets. The water closet is down the hall and to the left. If you need anything, I'll be in the cockpit checking on Damek. Good evening."

Belle and Beast murmured their goodbyes as the captain left.

They both startled when Cinders yowled, leaping off her perch. The cat stretched and promptly scampered out the door after her mistress. The sun set, bathing the room in golden light.

Belle fidgeted in her seat as she ate. She and Beast had never talked about where they were going to go after escaping from the Circus Illume. Until recently, freedom had only been an idea. They'd never got around to discussing the future. It's not like there was any real reason for them to stay together. It might be safer for them to split up between Belle's notoriety from the circus poster and Beast's appearance.

The thought didn't bring her comfort.

As she sat her fork down, Belle felt Beast watching her, his expression inscrutable.

"Is there something on my face?" She dabbed her mouth with a faded cloth napkin.

He shook his head. "Thinking."

Belle placed the napkin in her lap. "I see."

The seconds ticked by painfully slowly.

Beast broke the silence. "Are you going to Duchollow?"

"I think so. It doesn't sound like the mayor is keen on outsiders, but I have no other ideas. I didn't think I'd make it this far." Belle tried to act casual as she gulped the last of the sweet wine. The delicate curve of the wineglass felt wrong in her calloused, bruised hand. "What about you?"

"Do you think they'd accept me there?" The gas-lit candelabra reflected in Beast's wide anxious eyes.

"Honestly? I'm not sure that they'll welcome any strangers, clawed or otherwise. But from what Captain Charity said, it sounds like there's a chance. What do you want to do?"

"I'd prefer to stay with you." Beast's rumbly voice was barely audible over the din of the steam engine running in the distance.

Tears prickled in the corners of her eyes. Startled by how much his words affected her, she cracked a watery smile. "Why's that? Haven't had enough running for your life?"

"We have done a lot of that, but I feel safer with you. Even with the near-drowning."

Belle's cheeks burned. "Why?"

"Your eyes."

"Huh?" Belle snorted. Her tired brown eyes were not the stuff of sonnets.

Beast tentatively reached his paw forward to brush a strand of charcoal hair out of her face and tuck it behind her ear. "Your eyes. They're kind. They're the first to look at me without fear or disgust. How you were not horrified when you first saw me, I'll never know, but I count myself lucky you didn't scream."

Belle stammered. "We-well, if I would have screamed, and you ran, maybe the Ringmaster wouldn't have caught you. You'd be free in the woods."

"I don't belong in the woods. Never have, as far as I can tell."

"Oh."

"So, if it's all the same to you, I'd like to stay together. We make a good team."

Belle blinked back tears. "Together then."

They ate the rest of their meal in amiable silence. After dinner, they discovered the two cozy pallets laid out for them in the center of the observation deck. Thick jewel-tone blankets and pillows were piled high on each of the makeshift beds.

Their battered packs lay next to the pallets. After ducking out to wash away the grime and change clothes in the water closet, Belle returned to her knapsack and found the fairy tale book Beast had asked her to keep.

"Should I read before we sleep?" Her stomach fluttered as she waited for his answer.

"Yes, please."

Starlight streamed through the crystalline glass dome, the view even more beautiful than Belle imagined it would be. She read to Beast by gaslight until he fell asleep, snoring gently. After she covered him up as best she could with his blankets, she padded across the room to shut off the lights. She drifted off, her belly full for the first time in days, and allowed herself to hope, dreaming of the wonders of Duchollow. Would they finally find a new home, or would the mayor throw them out?

The *Figment's* intercom crackled to life with a static pop echoing in the enclosed observation deck. Belle startled awake from the most restful sleep of her life, yelping as she nearly gouged her eyes on the wicked pointed ends of Beast's curved antlers. She flinched, scooting back, only to realize quickly that one of his bandaged arms was wrapped securely around her waist, pinning her beneath their combined tangled blankets.

Captain Charity spoke over the intercom. "Good morning, bonus crew! We're about twenty minutes from Duchollow. Have you decided what you're doing? I need to message their dock soon so they can expect us."

Belle's heart hammered. Before last night, it wouldn't have fazed her to wake up next to the slumbering Beast. Many times since he first stumbled into her camp, they'd been forced to be in close quarters. Logically, she knew the cold overnight temperature caused them to gravitate to one another off their individual pallets in their sleep.

She could even see them being subconsciously drawn to each other for comfort after everything they'd been through together. It was the first night that Belle had slept without fear of the Ringmaster or discovery.

And yet...

Last night, when Beast asked to stay together, something shifted between them. Unbidden, his words came back to her.

"So, if it's all the same to you, I'd like to stay together. We make a good team."

She shook her head. Even if he were a man, it wasn't exactly a declaration. She shouldn't make anything more out of his words. It couldn't be. After all, he was a beast.

With the soft light streaming in through the tempered glass, it was very apparent how not-human Beast was, between his deadly antlers and bearlike build. His mouth was more of a long muzzle, and he was completely covered in dingy silver fur. However, with the blankets tucked around him, it was almost too easy for Belle to imagine he was human.

"What are you yelping about now?" Beast's voice was hoarse as he blinked away the remnants of sleep.

Determined to not let her runaway thoughts get the best of her, Belle steeled herself.

"Sorry, the intercom scared me. The captain wants to know our decision. Are you certain about Duchollow?"

He yawned and stretched, rolling his neck. "Yes."

"Okay. Then we'll go."

Beast looked at Belle, staring intently at her. She smiled softly.

The crackling of the intercom shattered the tender moment. "Bonus crew? Are you awake?" Captain Charity's amusement was palpable.

"I better answer her." Belle tapped Beast's arm lightly, mindful of his healing wounds. "Can you let me up?"

"Sure." He slowly removed his paw, staring intently at her.

Cheeks burning, Belle untangled her legs from the twisted blankets and lumbered to the intercom.

"Sorry for the delay. We're awake." Belle cleared her throat, tucking her unruly hair back. "We'd both like to see if we can make Duchollow our home."

"I hoped that would be the case." Belle could almost hear the captain's smirk. "I figured you two would stay together. I was going to wake you up earlier when I brought breakfast in, but you both looked so…comfortable."

Mortified, Belle pinched the bridge of her nose. While attempting to formulate a non-humiliating response, she spotted breakfast. Generous selections of cheese cubes, apples, and scones were on the table, along with a pitcher of water and a carafe smelling of rich coffee. Her stomach growled.

"Thank you for breakfast and for letting us sleep." Belle scratched the back of her neck.

Captain Charity poorly disguised her laughter with a cough. "You're welcome. We're about fifteen minutes away from landing, so I'll leave you to get ready. There're safety harnesses built into the couches underneath the cushions. Do put the pitcher and the carafe in their cupboard once you've had breakfast. It'll be a mess if you don't. Cupboard is on the wall closest to the door."

"Will do. Thank you again."

"My pleasure. See you in Duchollow."

With that, the intercom clicked off.

Belle turned around to see Beast returning to the room. She blinked. She hadn't heard him leave.

"I washed up." He shrugged.

They stood awkwardly, looking at each other.

"I see," Belle finally said. "I suppose I'll go do the same. The captain left breakfast on the table and we're landing soon."

Beast nodded. "I heard. Thank you." He stepped out of the way, letting Belle pass.

In the washroom, Belle splashed warm water on her face and steadied her breathing. She had to control her emotions, especially before they met this Maureen person, if they were to have any hope of staying in Duchollow.

She grimaced. It probably wouldn't do if the mayor thought she was mooning after…

Belle violently shook her head as she cleared her thoughts. It wouldn't do to continue this line of thought, because nothing good would come of it. She was lucky to even have the beginning of something that looked like friendship with Beast, as unconventional as it was. No need to complicate things, especially since he might not even be human.

His arm around your waist felt human, a traitorous thought whispered in the back of her mind.

Belle pinched the bridge of her nose again. Clearly, she had been too sheltered in some ways in the circus. The prolonged loneliness had done its damage. The contraband fairy tale books with their enchanted princes and princesses probably didn't help either. Whatever Beast was, those old scars and stitches revealed a tortured past. He didn't need her misguided…whatever this was. They both needed healing.

She took another calming breath, then returned to the observation deck to find Beast had already plated breakfast for her and poured her a steaming mug of coffee. All the leftovers, the pitcher, and the carafe had been put away, without a single crumb left on the table.

"I wanted to make sure you had time to eat before we land." Beast sat on the overstuffed couch, struggling with the harness.

"Thank you." Belle smiled.

"Could you help me with this? It's difficult with these." He gestured to the harness with his paws.

"Yes, of course." Belle quickly crossed the room to him. She leaned down and carefully strapped him in—the harness fortunately large enough to fit around Beast's broad shoulders. She clicked the front buckle. "There, that should do it."

"Thank—" Beast's thanks were interrupted by the *Figment* lurching. Belle fell forward, into the seated Beast.

His arms shot out to catch her.

When the shaking stopped, Belle was firmly in Beast's arms, halfway on his lap and narrowly missing the plate next to him on the sofa. Their foreheads were inches from touching. Beast's eyes were round and alarmed.

"Are you okay?"

Belle gulped, finding herself unable to speak.

Captain Charity's voice over the intercom cut in. "It's landing time! Buckle up, it's going to be a bumpy ride!"

Belle and Beast's eyes met, and they burst into laughter. Mirth twinkled in Beast's eyes.

All the twisted emotions brewing in Belle's fragile heart evaporated. They were going to be okay, whatever happened next.

"Better grab your breakfast." Beast released Belle, offering a paw to help her up.

Belle retrieved her food and carefully buckled in. It was a tight squeeze on the couch, but it didn't feel uncomfortable as they ate, occasionally holding on for dear life as the *Figment* descended.

The bumps and groans of the airship made her stomach churn, but the nervous anticipation and excitement of seeing Duchollow was nearly enough for her to forget her fear. To distract herself from the bumpy landing, Belle looked out the window. Below the *Figment*, a forest stretched out for miles.

"I don't see a town. Do you?" For a paranoid moment, Belle wondered if the captain was setting them up in an elaborate trap. Maybe she was some kind of bounty hunter, and she was taking them to the Ringmaster?

Beast leaned in closer, smelling like smoky, wild woods mixed with a salty sea breeze. "Over there," he said, pointing at something just outside the glass dome window.

At first, Belle couldn't see what he was pointing to. But then the trees thinned out as the airship descended, revealing a picturesque town nestled in a secluded valley. With its colorful collage of disparate buildings, the town looked like something out of a fairy tale. Greenhouses dotted the surrounding fields, and shepherds tended sheep. Trees on the town's edge held houses with enclosed sky bridges between them and plenty of automated elevators to give residents access to the upper levels. The ground-level buildings were older but given new life by thoughtful renovations. Paved streets surrounded them, traversed by automobiles and automated bicycles, alongside wide sidewalks where pedestrians purchased food from street vendors.

Though the bustling town wasn't as busy as Minport, it charmed Belle.

As the airship drew closer to the raised docks on the edge of the town, Belle noted some buildings looked abandoned but not completely derelict, and a small crew was hard at work fixing up the broken siding of one. The dock itself was considerably less hectic than the one in Ichorfell, housing only a handful of docked airships. The *Figment* wobbled as it landed, knocking Belle into Beast. She landed with her ear pressed against his chest, allowing her to hear his heart hammering, even under his thick fur and his soft linen shirt. Her eyes fluttered closed.

Damek's chipper voice broke the silence. "Captain's informed me we've officially landed in Duchollow. She insists on exiting the *Figment* first and alone because, quote, 'Maureen's upset enough.' She says you can relax in the observation deck, but you should be ready for the mayor in case she comes aboard to meet you."

Static crackled and fizzed over the intercom.

Dazed, Belle barely remembered to unbuckle first before rising to press the intercom button.

"Thank you, Damek. We appreciate it."

The pilot answered, "You're welcome. If it makes any difference, I hope Maureen says yes. Everyone deserves a chance at happiness."

Belle's heart was full. "Thank you, Damek."

"You're welcome." Static fizzled over the intercom. "If you'll excuse me, I must attend to my injuries. I need to be presentable, at least as much as possible, before Maureen comes aboard."

Belle gulped, remembering what Captain Charity had said of the mayor and her displeasure over the automaton's condition. "Good luck," she told him, and she meant it.

When Belle turned back, Beast was also unbuckled. He stood by the glass dome window, watching the dock workers secure the hole-riddled remains of the *Figment's* boarding bridge.

"We're lucky the whole ship didn't break." His amused voice was laced with worry.

"I agree. I think I've had enough of flying." Belle crossed her arms over her chest as she joined him at the window.

"Parts of it weren't so bad." Beast gave Belle a sidelong glance before going back to studying the dock workers.

Belle's eyebrows rose. "I suppose having a comfortable place to rest and having good food for a change helped. Reading under the stars was nice." She looked down, feigning fascination with the scuffing on her worn boots.

"It was nice," Beast's voice rumbled pleasantly. "I enjoyed waking up with you."

Belle froze. "You what?"

"After waking up in the cage alone day after day, and before that, on the run in unfamiliar forests for so long, getting to wake up to a friendly face was a privilege." Beast's eyes were shimmering, though whether it was tears or the lighting, it was impossible to tell.

Belle's voice was barely above a whisper. "I think I get it. I was alone in the circus. Even with other people there, it still was a quiet, lonesome existence."

They fell into an amiable silence, peering at the visible slice of Duchollow outside the window.

Their serene people-watching was interrupted by thundering footsteps coming down the corridor.

"Wait! I need to tell you about them first." Captain Charity's voice sounded more panicked than it did when the *Figment* was overrun with Hounds.

"You're not telling me anything after what you've done to your ship. I need to see what you've brought into my town. Honestly, Darling, what's gotten into you?" A low voice, like honeyed venom, resounded in the room.

The observation deck door opened with a bang. In the entryway, a regal woman gazed imperiously at them over thin silver-wire, octagon-shaped glasses that slid down her nose. Her black hair was plaited in dozens of tight braids, pulled into an elaborate updo and decorated with delicate brass beads. Her brocaded indigo blouse, studded with brass buttons, would have been the envy of the Circus Illume's costumer.

"Maureen, wait—" Captain Charity finally caught up to the mayor. She halted, put her hands on her knees, and panted.

"Darling, what have you brought to Duchollow?" Maureen's icy tone made the fine baby hair on the back of Belle's neck stand on end.

"Let me explain." Captain Charity lifted her index finger.

"No, I think I want to hear it from them first. Wait." Maureen's eyes narrowed as she adjusted her glasses, pushing them up the bridge of her nose. Her eyes widened and her voice raised as she pointed at Beast. "What in the Maker's name did you bring to my town?"

Belle's heart sank. They should have known it would not be easy convincing the mayor. With growing dread, she stood protectively in front of Beast, waiting for the mayor's next move.

CHAPTER NINE

Darling Ethel Charity, I'm going to ask one more time. What did you bring to my town?" Maureen jabbed her finger in Beast's direction.

"Ouch, if you're going to full-name me, at least add the 'Captain.'" The contrite airship captain looped her fingers in her belt, shifting her weight from side to side. At the mayor's pointed glare, she added, "They're refugees."

Belle's heart hammered as her eyes locked with Maureen's. What if the mayor sent for guards to take Beast away? Or worse, ordered him killed? She had to tread carefully.

"We're on the run from the Circus Illume." Belle lifted her hands in surrender, palms up. "We don't mean any harm, we just need somewhere we can be free to live our own lives."

"Running away from the circus?" Maureen snorted. "That's a new one." She looked Belle and Beast up and down. "And just how did you know to come to Duchollow?"

"We barely had a plan when we left."

Under his breath, Beast muttered, "That's an understatement."

Belle cut her eyes at Beast. "We were lucky to make it out alive. When we snuck aboard the *Figment*, we knew nothing about it. We were only trying to put distance between us and the Ringmaster."

Maureen narrowed her eyes. "What was the rush?"

"I was sold into the circus, and Beast was captured against his will. The Ringmaster threatened to kill him and have a taxidermist prepare him for display."

Something flashed in Maureen's eyes akin to sympathy. Hope bloomed in Belle's chest until the mayor shook her head.

"I'm truly sorry for your plight, but something isn't adding up. Why does your friend look like Delphine's handiwork? I've seen her Hounds more times than I care to remember. How do I know this isn't some elaborate setup to infiltrate Duchollow? She's been wanting to get her hands on my research for years. You can't tell me it's a coincidence that I'm on the cusp of a breakthrough and you two show up." Maureen put her hands on her hips.

"No offense intended, but I don't know who you are. I was only a child when I was sold to the circus. I've only been free a few days." Belle pointed to the dark veins crisscrossing her translucent face. "I stand out too much to be a spy." She pointed to Beast. "So does he."

Maureen huffed. "Yes, but this is exactly the sort of scheme Delphine would plot. She knows me better than most people."

Captain Charity scoffed, tapping her foot indignantly.

Maureen ignored her and continued. "She knows how much of a bleeding heart I am. Not to mention my tendency to be curious about anything…unusual." She gave Beast a sidelong glance.

Belle stammered. "But—"

Captain Charity tapped the mayor on the shoulder. "They saved me and Damek from the Hounds when we were boarded. That's what I was trying to tell you. If they wanted to sabotage your research, they would have had plenty of chances."

Maureen lifted her eyebrows. "Did you really?"

Beast nodded. "Yes. The Hounds tried to turn me into a chew toy." He lifted his arms, revealing the layers of bandages covering them.

Maureen's eyes widened. "I see." She pursed her lips.

"Please, we won't cause any trouble. All we want is some peace. I don't want to keep running and fighting." Belle clasped her hands together, praying the mayor would show them mercy.

Captain Charity added, "And if you needed a bodyguard, you should see her in action. She threw a Hound off Damek!"

Maureen sighed. "Okay, here's what I can do. You can stay on probation until your wounds heal up, then we'll go from there."

Belle was about to express her heartfelt gratitude when Maureen furrowed her brow and pointed at the captain. "What was that about a Hound on Damek? What did you do to him?"

"I did nothing to Damek! The Hound got into the cockpit and —" Captain Charity gasped as Maureen sprinted past her, dashing out of the observation deck.

"Damek? I'm coming for you!" Maureen's panicked voice echoed through the corridor.

Captain Charity face-palmed. "Maker's moldy knickers."

Without another word, the captain took off after the mayor.

Belle and Beast stared after them, nonplussed.

"What just happened?" Belle scratched the back of her head.

"No idea," Beast huffed.

Outside the observation deck's dome window, the dock workers were laughing and joking with each other, finished with their duties. One brought steaming mugs of coffee to cheers from their coworkers. They huddled together, leaning against a stack of huge freight crates ready for the next airship as they enjoyed their drinks. Belle was envious of their easy camaraderie. They looked so happy and relaxed.

Quietly, she asked, "Do you think we'll still get to stay?"

Beast shrugged. "I hope so. I've been thinking. This Delphine they keep mentioning sounds like my tormentor."

Belle's eyes widened. "What makes you say that?"

Beast pulled back the fur on his neck, revealing faded scar tissue crisscrossing his skin. "Someone did this to me. I don't know if I began life as a man or beast. Before I found you, I was on the run."

Belle took a sharp intake of breath. This was the most he'd ever talked about himself.

"There was a woman, and a room filled with vials. I remember nothing before the pain, but when I woke up, I was horrified to see this." Beast gestured to his bearlike visage and curved antlers.

"Whatever I was before she came into my life is long gone. Maybe I can find some answers here."

"I hope you can, too." Belle couldn't believe he'd finally confided in her. "How did you escape?"

Beast's voice grew sober. "I poisoned her."

Her jaw dropped. "You did what?"

Before Beast could explain, Maureen and Captain Charity returned. The captain was looking repentant, or at least doing a good impression of it, while the mayor's panicked rage had cooled to mere annoyance.

"If you two want to stay, get your things. We'll head to my office and sort out housing while you recover." Maureen gave the captain an exasperated look. "Luckily for you, Damek had nothing but good things to say about you all. Even you, Darling."

"Gee, thanks." Captain Charity rolled her eyes, but the slightest smile played on her lips.

"Thank you so much." Belle resisted the urge to throw her arms around the mayor, not wanting to press her luck.

Still, she couldn't help but wonder about Beast's escape from his captor. What would a beast know about poison?

"Would you like me to carry our bags?" Beast gestured to their packs lying by their pallets, pulling Belle out of her morbid thoughts.

"I'll get them. Your arms are still healing." Belle shook her head. Whatever choice Beast had made to make his escape, she was certain he'd had his reasons.

With budding excitement, Belle followed the mayor and the captain to the *Figment's* exit. She was ready to see Duchollow up close. She hoped the residents wouldn't stare too much.

"I'm not cargo." Damek Wraithe's voice echoed in the *Figment's* cargo hold as he fixed Maureen with a baleful stare. Belle held the wooden cart steady while Beast and Captain Charity lowered the protesting automaton pilot onto it.

The captain must have scrubbed the blood off the floors while Belle and Beast had slept, but jagged scratch marks remained as evidence of the Hounds' brutal attack. Belle wondered if she didn't want to make the mayor worry more than she already did, as Maureen was clucking over Damek like a mother hen, fussing over his loose joints while strapping him to the makeshift gurney.

The mayor looked down at the grumpy automaton, adjusting her octagon-shaped glasses as she gave him a stern glare of her own. "It's for your own good. You're barely holding on by a few pieces of tubing and cogs—and not much else."

"Yes, Mother." Damek's eyes flickered, simulating an eye roll. Something deep within his frame whirred and whistled as shimmery black fluid leaked from one of his shoulder-joint hoses onto the handkerchief tourniquet tied around it. The automaton's voice took on a fuzzy quality as he spoke. "I suppose I need repairs."

Belle swore she saw Damek smile, but a horrible screeching noise drew her attention.

Captain Charity stood by the hatch, wincing as she turned its handle. "Sorry, the hatch is sticking."

"Wait." Beast sat his pack down on the suspiciously clean floor and rifled through its contents, wincing when his bandages caught on the bag's contents.

Belle furrowed her brows. "What is it?"

"What's the holdup?" Captain Charity paused opening the hatch, tilting her head at Beast.

Beast fished his tattered cloak out of his pack and fastened it around his neck. Though it was ripped in places, it concealed some of his features. He donned the hood, which disguised his antlers to a degree, but unfortunately, the antlers created odd bumps under the thin material, giving him a peculiar silhouette.

"I don't want to scare anyone." He shrugged his massive shoulders.

Belle pursed her lips. "I almost wonder if it'd be less noticeable if we cut slits for your antlers in the hood and make it look like your antlers are decorative?"

"Maybe?" Beast looked skeptical. "I'd still stand out."

"True." Belle pointed to the visible dark veins on her neck and face. "Maybe I should wear mine, too."

"Unless you're cold, it won't be necessary." The mayor dusted off her brocade blouse as she rose from adjusting Damek's tubing. "People in Duchollow have seen ether-poisoning before. You'll be fine."

Doubt flickered in Belle's eyes. "People are still going to stare, though. Combine my height, build, and condition, and I'm a walking circus act."

"Well, it won't be a problem today. I brought my truck with me. You won't have to talk to anyone on the way to my office." Maureen smiled genuinely. "Let's get you both healed, then you can worry about frightening the townspeople later."

Cinders bounded up from wherever she'd been hiding from the commotion and purred, rubbing her head against Captain Charity's boots.

The captain leaned down for scratches. "You need to stay here for now, kitty. I'm sorry."

Cinders slinked away to lie against the cargo hold's wall, watching her mistress with narrowed eyes.

Maureen pointed at the exit. Shall we?"

"Yes, please." Captain Charity swung open the hatch, flinching as it creaked open to a hole-riddled boarding bridge. "Ugh, watch your step. And your eyes!"

Wincing at the bright sunlight, Beast promptly put his tinted goggles on.

Belle squinted. Weren't his goggles cracked? No, the lenses were different, darker than the ones he had in the circus. A new wave of gratitude for Captain Charity washed over her, though she wondered how the captain had thought of repairing the goggles amid everything else going on.

With the hatch fully open, Belle lifted her free arm above her face to shield her eyes from the sunlight streaming down on them. After her eyes adjusted, she gasped when she saw the dock. She'd been to shipping docks before, but this one was a technological marvel, balancing aesthetic and function.

Dock workers relaxed against the shipping crates with their

coffees, while behind them, a crane machine with a clockwork conveyor belt sorted cargo into their destination with steady precision. A few curious workers looked up as the five departed the *Figment*, the cart carrying Damek catching on to the holes riddled on the boarding bridge. As the captain closed the hatch behind them, Belle heard Cinders yowl plaintively before the door shut.

"Damek!" Maureen cried out as the cart's wheel caught on another hole in the bridge and her hand slipped. The cart careened forward, threatening to tumble and crash.

Belle dashed forward, catching the runaway cart by the handle in the nick of time. Her swollen, bruised hands throbbed, and she bit her lip to keep from screaming in pain.

Damek looked up from the cart, wide-eyed. "Thank you."

Something glitched in the automaton's eyes, and they were lit by a rainbow array of colors all at once before settling back to their usual shade of silvery blue.

"You're welcome." Belle gritted her teeth as she steadied the wayward cart. Beast came around to the front of the cart, and together they half-carried, half-pushed it down the bridge.

Maureen caught up with them on the dock. "Thank you so much. I was so eager to get Damek off the ship that I forgot the bridge was blown to pieces." She peered over her octagon-shaped glasses at Belle's bandaged fingers. "Are you going to be okay? That looks horrible."

Belle nodded. "I'll be fine."

Captain Charity bounded up to them. "Everyone still with us?" She glanced down at the automaton and patted his dislocated shoulder. "There's my pilot."

Damek gave her a lopsided grin. "It'd take more than a bumpy landing to get rid of me."

Beast warily eyed the dock workers and tightened his hood. "Can we get moving?"

"Yes, let's." Maureen led the way, taking over pushing the wobbly cart.

Belle linked her arm around Beast's, mindful of his bandaged injuries. His tense posture softened, and he nodded at her before they followed the captain and the mayor.

Captain Charity stopped by the workers on break and dropped a small bag of coins on the crate next to them.

"Keep an eye on the *Figment* for me? She's been through the wringer." The captain gave the group her most winning smile.

The worker closest to the captain weighed the bag in his hefty palm.

"You have a deal." His bushy mustache partially concealed his grin.

The worker on his left, a stout woman with graying curls, cracked a smile. "But when hasn't the *Figment* gotten into one scrape or another?" At the captain's indignant look, the woman guffawed. "We have you covered, Captain. Go on, Maureen and your guests are waiting for you."

To Belle's amazement, the woman merely waved at their odd group and went back to sipping from her mug. She'd been certain the woman would ask more questions. Judging by the tight grip of Beast's paw loosening a fraction on her upper arm, she wasn't the only one surprised.

When Beast caught Belle's concerned glance, he mouthed, "Sorry."

Belle shook her head and smiled, patting his paw lightly.

"Come on, Darling. We don't have all day." The mayor was already several steps ahead of them, waiting with her hands on her hips. "No one is going to steal your ship. It looks ready to come apart at the seams. You have to go easier on her."

Captain Charity scowled, the tips of her ears turning a shade of pink that clashed terribly with her copper hair. "My occupation isn't exactly a safe one, you know. These things happen."

Belle and Beast followed as the captain caught up to the mayor.

Though it was barely audible over the noise of the cargo machine, Belle heard the captain mutter, "You know, if you made me an honest woman, maybe I wouldn't get into so many scrapes."

Maureen scoffed as she maneuvered the cart over an uneven plank. "I tried to give you a job, but you're not interested in being honest."

Captain Charity tutted. "You know what I mean."

From his prone position, Damek complained, "I'm going to power myself down if you two are going to bicker."

Maureen shook her head and kept walking past the dock to the brick parking lot.

Belle tilted her head at the trio's antics; they almost seemed like a family. Beast tapped her arm, pulling her away from her speculations. She turned to look at him, her eyebrows raised.

Beast pointed at her overstuffed pack. "Want me to carry your bag?"

She shook her head. "We're almost there. Besides, you're the one with injured arms. You need to be careful about overdoing it. Thank you, though."

"If you say so." Beast looked skeptical.

"I do. Look, we're here."

The sea-glass green truck was a little worn but looked well-maintained. A boxy canvas covered the bed of the truck, with its back left open. The cab was roomy, with an extra bench behind the front seats, but there was no way they would all fit inside. Maureen and the captain lifted Damek off the cart and laid him across the cab's bench.

The mayor stepped around from the driver's side to Belle and Beast. She looked apologetic as she gestured to the truck. "Can you two ride in the back? We're short on space. I'll drive slow."

Belle nodded. "Thank you. That'll be fine."

Beast hummed his approval. "The cover will be nice."

"Good. We'll be at my office soon." Maureen eyed the cart, pursing her lips. "Darling won't like it, but I'll send for someone to retrieve the cart later. I'd like to get moving."

As the mayor entered the driver's side, Belle walked around to the back of the truck. Beast was already in the truck bed, crouched down at its end.

"Need help?" Beast extended his paw.

Belle smiled at the gesture. She didn't really need assistance, but the offer was sweet. She took his paw. "Thank you."

Her heart was warmed when Beast delicately pulled her into the back of the truck, careful not to squeeze her tender hands. Once inside, she immediately realized it was going to be a cozy ride to the mayor's office. The cover made the truck look bigger than it actually was. Beast moved farther back, closer to the cab.

"Does that leave you enough room? There's a stack of crates behind me or I'd move more." His soft fur brushed against her cheek when he leaned in.

"Thank you, yes."

The truck's steam engine rumbled on with a loud hiss, startling them both.

Beast wrapped his bandaged arm around Belle, drawing her closer.

From the cab, Maureen yelled over the engine, "Hope you're both seated! Hang on."

Facing the back of the truck, Belle smiled contently as she watched the *Figment* grow smaller. She was still concerned about Beast's past, and she was tempted to ask about it now that they were alone, but as protective as he was of her, she doubted he'd ever endanger her. For now, she was happy to see Duchollow up close, even if it meant being cramped in the covered truck bed. The open back gave them both a good view of the city, while the canvas kept them concealed.

There were more people here than Belle would have expected in a small town in a mostly forgotten valley. At least the town wouldn't be one the Ringmaster would bother with, as the heavily forested mountains would be impossible for his caravan to traverse. The realization made her breathe easier.

The scent of fresh-baked bread coming from the cozy bakery nearby wafted on the breeze. Street vendors hawked their wares, selling them to happy patrons. Belle's stomach rumbled. As good as her breakfast was, it had been a rushed affair. She dearly wished she could stop for lunch, but she steeled herself. *Housing first, then see about lunch*, she told herself forcefully. She knew there was still jerky in her pack, but if she could go the rest of her life without having the bland dried meat again, she'd be happy.

As the truck stopped at an intersection, Belle was plagued by a troublesome thought. Why weren't the dock workers more frightened by their appearance? While she was happy to not be scrutinized, it was unnerving. She desperately wanted to ask why no one at the docks had been curious about Beast or had recognized her from the circus. Surely some of the townspeople traveled to the bigger cities.

Beast tapped on Belle's shoulder.

"Look over there." His breath tickled her neck.

She squinted, wondering what he was trying to show her.

Her eyes widened as she spotted a couple strolling close enough behind the stopped truck that Belle could make out their features. The woman's skin was pale, and visible light-blue veins crisscrossed her skin in a pattern similar to Belle's, but the shade of blue was significantly lighter. It looked like faded ether-poisoning. The woman's companion had similar features, his veins making pale dashes along his cheekbones and forehead.

Belle's breath caught. She'd never heard of ether-poisoning clearing up. Captain Charity had mentioned that Maureen might help with her condition, but she hadn't taken it to heart. Now her head buzzed with questions. Did the mayor have a cure? If so, did everyone know about it, or was it a hidden Duchollow secret?

It was not like Belle'd had many opportunities to keep up with current events after she was sold to the Ringmaster. News of the world outside the circus was limited, especially as she'd been expressly forbidden from reading newspapers. She'd never set foot in Aetherbourne again after that fateful day, nor had she heard another word from her father.

She didn't even know if he was still alive. A lump formed in her throat and hot tears stung her eyes.

As if Beast sensed her distress, he patted her back. "Did you see them, too?"

Belle nodded. When she could finally trust her voice not to break, she said, "Those people looked like they've been healed of ether-poisoning. I've never seen that before."

"Maybe there's a cure?"

Belle sniffed. "A cure might be too much to hope for. Let's start with finding out if we can stay longer than probation."

The truck started moving again, and soon they were near a great plaza with a gorgeous clockwork tower in the center. It chimed twelve times, and a soothing music box melody played from inside the celestial clock. Silver stars and jewel-tone planets swirled around each other to the music on the top half of the clock face. On its bottom half, painted clouds moved over the sky, finally revealing clear, blue skies when the song finished.

"Beautiful," Belle whispered.

Beast murmured in agreement, but when she looked back at him, he was looking at her. Their eyes met briefly until Beast shifted his gaze to the clock tower.

Belle knew Maureen said their stay in Duchollow might be temporary, but her heart ached for the life she and Beast might have in the town. She wanted nothing more than to try the street food and find a bench in the plaza to listen to the clock tower's song again.

Shaking her head to keep her imagination from getting the best of her, Belle was startled to find the truck was parked with the engine turned off.

Maureen appeared at the back of the truck. "We've arrived! Sorry about the crates. I forgot those were in here." She scratched the back of her neck. "Come on down. I'll unlock the door."

The mayor disappeared as quickly as she'd come.

Remembering Beast's kindness earlier, Belle turned around to offer her hand to help him. He struggled, but they both got out of the truck bed and found themselves in front of a cozy two-level building. Rose bushes lined the entrance while wild vines covered the gray stonework all the way to the second floor, where a curved compass window jutted out above the doorway.

"Welcome to my lab." Maureen grimaced. "And the official mayoral office. Let's get your paperwork sorted, shall we? I think I have a house on the edge of town you two can use, as long as you behave yourselves."

Belle could scarcely speak as her pulse quickened. "Really?"

The mayor nodded. "Damek and Darling spent the entire ride pleading your case." She took a breath before the rest of her words came out in a rush. "If you'd like, I can try to ease your ether-poisoning."

Hope swelled in Belle's chest. "Is there a cure?"

"Yes. And there's more." Maureen clasped her hands together.

"Darling told me a bit about your background. I don't know what lies have been fed to you over the years, but that Ringmaster has kept too much from you. You never should have had to live like that. The practice of people ether-mining has been over for at least nine years. I've had plenty of time to perfect a cure for ether-poisoning since then."

Belle's vision swam. "Nine years?"

Her father. He could have gone to get her.

No.

It couldn't be, could it?

Beast caught Belle as she faltered, stumbling backward.

Maureen's earnest expression morphed into concern. "Let's get you help right now."

The news about ether-mining and a cure should have elated Belle, but all she could think about was her father. He could have come for her at the circus, but he didn't. Yes, he'd sold her to the Ringmaster, but couldn't her father have made a new arrangement with him? Or at least come to apologize to her?

Maybe it was too late, and her father had succumbed to ether-poisoning. Or perhaps he knew he couldn't afford to buy her back.

Belle's lower lip trembled.

"Coming?" Maureen called, poking her head out from behind the open cobalt-blue door.

Belle plastered a fake smile on her face. "Yes, sorry."

The pitying looks from both Beast and Maureen told her she wasn't fooling anyone.

The feeble excuses died on Belle's lips as Captain Charity swore violently behind her. Belle turned to see the captain struggling to lift Damek out of the back seat of the truck.

Remembering how much both the automaton and the captain had helped her and Beast, Belle's heart swelled with gratitude as she jogged back to the truck. Belle tapped the struggling captain on the shoulder. "I can take him."

"Are you sure?" Captain Charity brushed her curls out of her face and smeared the oily black-silver liquid leaking from Damek's hoses across her forehead. Her billowy clothes were stained from the fluid and torn where bits of broken metal had caught on the delicate fabric.

"I'd be happy to take him." After the captain stepped back, Belle reached into the cab and lifted the battered automaton out. She cradled Damek close, mindful of his injuries.

"Thank you, I didn't think I was ever going to get out of here." Damek's droll voice contrasted with his chaotic appearance. The tubes were looking worse for wear, and the lights making up his irises flickered intermittently.

"It's the least I could do after you two helped with the mayor. Thank you." Belle fought to keep her voice from cracking with emotion, and nearly succeeded until Captain Charity smiled at her.

"Don't mention it. We're all outcasts here. You'll see what I mean soon enough." The captain jabbed her thumb back at Town Hall. "We should get moving."

Before Belle could reply, Beast was at her side. "Should you be carrying him right now?" He pointed at her bandages, now darkening with the automaton's leaking fluid.

"I'll be fine. Your arms are in much worse shape."

"I don't want to nag, but my secretary's out to lunch. I'd like to get this done before he's back. He scares easily," Maureen called.

"Coming!" Captain Charity led the way, with Belle walking more slowly as she carried Damek. Beast trailed behind her, huffing and stomping.

The interior of Town Hall was beautiful and cozy. It looked like the building had formerly been a stately residential address but was now converted into an office. The repurposed foyer reception area had plush sofas lining the walls and a silver tank housing luminescent fish swimming between the leaves of aquatic plants. In the center of the back wall, there was an elegant mahogany desk with fastidiously organized paperwork and a name plaque that read "Arthur Cadwell." Behind the desk was a mail sorter, with documents neatly stacked in their slots.

Maureen and Captain Charity led them to a doorway on the

right of the foyer with Belle following close behind, teetering as she carried Damek. His weight was nothing, but trying to keep a grip on the slippery automaton was proving to be more difficult than she'd anticipated.

"My office is this way."

Belle grunted, shifting her weight as she adjusted her grip on Damek for the sixth time. Her bandages were slick with the dark liquid leaking from the automaton's tubes.

"Are you sure you don't want me to take him?" Beast was at her elbow.

"I've got him." Belle gritted her teeth as pain seared her swollen fingers.

"I'm right here, thank you," Damek grumbled. "I'm fine, but I would appreciate it if I were banged around less."

"Sorry." Belle switched arms and slung Damek over her shoulder. "Better?"

"If by better, you mean everything is upside down, then yes." The automaton's tinny voice was tinged with annoyance.

"Let's get you inside." Captain Charity shook her head at Damek.

Maureen pushed on the heavy, carved wooden door leading to her office. A black plaque with gold embossed letters read "Mayor Maureen Dawkins."

Unlike the secretary's workspace, Maureen's office was pure chaos. There were two chairs in front of her massive writing desk for guests to sit in, but aside from the seats, every surface was covered in books, journals, schematics, and bits of metal prototype parts from some type of complex machinery.

"Sorry for the mess. I'm close to a breakthrough in my research and when that happens, well..." Maureen gestured to the teetering stacks of papers and spare parts.

"It looks more like a breakdown than a breakthrough," Captain Charity piped up.

"Yes, thank you, Darling." Maureen's voice was dry as she added, "Why don't you take Damek to my lab while I get their paperwork sorted out?"

"You're no fun anymore." Captain Charity pouted as she

pivoted toward Belle.

The captain held out her arms. Belle raised her eyebrows.

"I'll take him."

Belle hesitated. "He almost looks bigger than you."

"I've had to carry him more times than I can count. I just couldn't get a good angle to get him out of the truck. It'll be fine." Captain Charity beamed.

"If you say so."

Slowly, Belle transferred Damek to the captain's waiting arms. She thought for sure the captain would collapse under the weight of the automaton, but she managed better than Belle thought she would.

After Captain Charity shuffled out of the room with Damek slung over her shoulder, Maureen sat down at her desk. "If you give me a moment, I'll have the forms we need." Her voice trailed off as she searched through the files.

Beast sat on the edge of his seat, acting as if he thought his armchair would turn into matchsticks under his weight.

"There we are." Maureen held up three papers triumphantly. At Belle and Beast's blank stares, she explained, "I keep basic records of residents. The third form is the agreement to let you two take possession of the house I mentioned. It's isolated—perfect for your recovery."

Butterflies fluttered in Belle's stomach. The idea of having official paperwork made her break out in a cold sweat. She crossed her arms. "What do you need to know from us?"

"Nothing too invasive, only the basics." Maureen cleared a spot in front of her chair and retrieved a pen. "I think I'll start with you, Belle, since there's probably going to be gaps in Beast's information, if I had to guess."

"Fair enough. Though I have to warn you, I might not be much better off than Beast on some of my background." Belle tucked a stray hair behind her ear.

Maureen twirled her pen. "Well, we'll fill it out as best we can. If all else fails, you can always make up answers." The mayor snorted. "You wouldn't be the first."

Something about the mayor's smile gave Belle the feeling she was talking about Captain Charity. "Sounds like a plan." She settled into her too-small chair.

"First things first: name?" Maureen peered over her octagon-shaped spectacles, fountain pen poised to write.

"Belle. It's not my birth name, but I've used it for so long that anything else would feel odd." The former strongwoman fidgeted, adjusting her weight on the uncomfortable seat. "It's a little embarrassing not remembering my actual name," Belle lied, "but I suppose it'd feel even stranger using it."

Maureen hummed in agreement. "Family name?"

Belle blanched as she lied again. "I don't know."

She remembered her full name, but she'd rather die than use it after her father sold her. The phrase "family name" left a sour taste in her mouth.

"We'll leave it blank." The mayor turned her attention to Beast. "What about you?"

Beast gave her an exasperated look, gesturing to his curved antlers and long crooked canines. "I'm Beast."

Maureen poorly concealed her grin by ducking her head down as she wrote. "No worries." When the mayor regained composure, she pointed at Belle. "Age and birthday?"

"I'll be twenty years old this spring." Belle shrugged, shaking her head. "I'm iffy on the exact date, since it was never celebrated in the circus, and even before then, my parents didn't make a fuss about it. I was nearing eleven years of being under the Ringmaster's thumb before we escaped." Feeling suddenly exposed by the admission, she crossed her arms.

"You don't have to explain anything you don't want to." Maureen was about to ask another question when the door opened with a bang.

Belle looked up expecting Captain Charity, but instead she saw a stranger. A gentleman with the fanciest, most stylized mustache she had ever seen, and pomaded dark hair that grayed at the temples, stood in the doorway, panting as he rested his hands on the knees of his impeccably pressed suit.

"Sorry for the interruption, Mayor Dawkins, but have you heard the lunchtime broadcast?" The man's eyes darted from the bulky wooden radio behind the desk to Belle and Beast. His brown eyes widened as he gaped at Beast. "Goodness, gracious. The broadcast was right."

"Call me *Maureen*, Mr. Cadwell, I keep telling you…" Maureen closed her eyes briefly and rubbed her temples. "What's so important about the news that you came back early from lunch?"

"I believe it concerns your guests." Mr. Cadwell nodded at Belle and Beast.

Maureen sighed and turned on the radio, static and garbled music filling the office. As she adjusted the tuning knob, the static gave way to a cheerful announcer's voice.

"And now for the recap of this hour's news. A reward of one thousand silver pieces has been offered for the return of the Circus Illume's Beast, wanted dead or alive. The creature allegedly has taken their strongwoman, Belle, captive. The reward money will be doubled if she is found as well. A description of the fugitive Beast and endangered Belle will be made available at all national post offices. You can send reports by telegraphing—"

Maureen shut off the radio with a forceful twist.

Belle froze, her nails digging into the armrests as she sat shell-shocked. "All those dock workers saw us," Belle whispered. "We have to leave now."

Beast bolted up from his seat, sending it crashing to the floor as he slung his pack over his shoulder. "Let's go." He kept his eyes trained on the door, watching the secretary.

Mr. Cadwell gulped, cowering under Beast's glowering stare.

Belle nodded, a lump in her throat. She wanted to stay, but two thousand silver pieces would be a lot of money to turn down. It could be life-changing money, for all she knew.

There would be no haven in Duchollow for them.

Maureen's cluttered office blurred as a wave of dizziness washed over Belle. Shaking her head, she took a steadying breath before retrieving her pack from the back of the guest chair. She winced as her bandaged fingers slipped.

"Wait!" Maureen bolted from her chair, sending papers flying everywhere across her desk and onto the vacant seats. "Where do you think you're going?"

Belle's mouth was set in a grim line. "We're not waiting for someone to turn us in. We can't go back."

"No one in Duchollow is going to turn you in. Not even for that kind of money." Maureen wrung her hands. "Most people here either have something they're running from or come from a hard life. All I need is a chance to tell your story to the townspeople, and all will be well." She inclined her head at the secretary. "Isn't that right, Mr. Cadwell?"

The nervous man quaked under the scrutiny. His eyes darted between Beast and Belle. "Yes, of course. Wouldn't dream of handing anyone over."

"See?" Maureen gave Mr. Cadwell a tight-lipped smile. "Please return to your post and make sure our meeting isn't interrupted. We need to strategize."

"Gladly."

The secretary dashed out of the room, slamming the door behind him. Belle and Beast exchanged uneasy looks as they stood awkwardly in the center of the crowded office.

The mayor cleared her throat. "I know you have no reason to trust me yet, but when I say I want to help, I mean it. Especially with your ether-poisoning. There's no need for you to keep living life like this."

Maureen turned her attention to Beast. "And I want to help you with your condition, whatever it is. I honestly can't tell if you're a man or beast. Fascinating." The mayor pursed her lips as she studied his antlers. "I'd love to help you find out who did this to you and why."

Beast hung onto Maureen's every word, and when she was done, he looked back at Belle. His tinted goggles were pushed up, revealing his pleading eyes.

Belle's heart ached. There was something earnest in Maureen's manner that made her desperate to believe the mayor, but she doubted that anyone would be this benevolent. "Why?"

Maureen's expression grew haunted as her voice cracked. "It's my way of making amends."

Belle opened her mouth to ask what the mayor meant, but instead she yelped at the familiar sound of an intercom speaker crackling on, the static muffled by the stacks of schematics partially burying it.

Mr. Cadwell's faint voice sounded from the covered speakers. "Mayor Dawkins, Mr. Windlass is here for his appointment and insisting he sees you now."

"Maker's grace." The mayor lifted an agenda, covered by spare parts, off her desk. After frantically flipping through its pages, she swore under her breath before looking back at Belle and Beast, who were still halfway to the exit. Maureen held up her hand, beckoning them to come closer as she pressed the intercom button with her other hand. "Tell Mr. Windlass I need a few minutes to ready my office."

"Yes, ma'am."

As the intercom shut off, Belle and Beast shuffled a few inches closer to the mayor's desk.

Maureen's voice was quiet but urgent as she leaned forward. "If you can trust me, Captain Charity can take you to the house. It's safe, on the outskirts of town. You'll have no neighbors. We can discreetly send you food and supplies until this dies down. Otherwise, you can walk out that door and take your chances on your own. What do you say?"

Belle turned to Beast. "Between the two of us, you have the most to lose. Your choice."

Beast's eyes were overly bright as his expression softened. "I'll go wherever you go."

Flustered by Beast's words, it took Belle a moment to respond. "Let's take a chance and stay." She fixed the mayor with a pointed look. "First sign of trouble, we're gone."

Maureen nodded, a small smile playing at her lips. "You have a deal. Let's get you out of here."

She walked to the wooden panels behind her desk, clutching documents close to her chest. With her free hand, she felt along the seam where the panels met. A section of the wall swung inward, revealing a secret door.

"Hurry." The mayor ushered them through the narrow passage to a spacious laboratory, marginally cleaner than her office.

Inside the lab, Captain Charity looked up from checking over

Damek, who reclined on a cushioned work table, reading from a book suspended within arm's reach via a mechanical holder. He turned the pages with his good arm, waving before returning to his book.

Maureen crossed the room at a clip, Belle and Beast scrambling to follow her without tripping over the large mechanical prototypes, gears, and cogs strewn across the stone floor.

"Here's their documentation and keys. Sneak them over. There's been a complication." The mayor thrust the paperwork and keys into Captain Charity's arms.

The usual traces of mirth in the captain's expression vanished. Her expression was stony as she pocketed the keys. "I'll get them to safety."

"Thanks, Darling." Maureen grimaced. "Gotta run. I have an appointment with Mr. Windlass. Completely forgot. Poor Cadwell is stalling."

"I could chase him off," Captain Charity offered, her smile returning.

"No, I'll handle it." Maureen nodded curtly. To Belle and Beast, she said, "Good luck. I'll be in touch when I can. Don't worry, Darling will get you where you need to go."

Without another word, the mayor disappeared back through the passage. When the door closed, it looked like the overstuffed bookcase lining the entire laboratory wall had never moved. There were no traces of the door, only trinkets, jars, and thick tomes lining its shelves.

Captain Charity muttered to herself as she read over the papers. Idly, Belle noticed that the captain was cleaned up, dressed in a fresh change of her trademark billowy clothes—all traces of the dark stains covering her forehead earlier now gone. Belle marveled at the captain's wardrobe change, a little envious, as she wished she'd at least had the chance to change her filthy bandages.

When Captain Charity finished reading the papers, she folded the paperwork and tucked it under her arm. "Here's the plan," she whispered. "I'm going to bring Maureen's truck around back, where there's a covered loading bay. The good news is your house is on the edge of town, so the chances of being seen are slim."

"That's a relief." Belle blinked at the phrase "your house." She'd never had a house of her own, only a trailer in the caravan.

Beast and Belle's stomachs rumbled, and Captain Charity chuckled. "We'll get food on the way. Just trust me for the next, oh, twenty-to-forty minutes, and I'll get you home."

"Thank you." Weariness hit Belle all at once. It felt like they were always on the run, and their brief respite on the observation deck seemed like a distant dream.

The captain pointed to a closed door to their right. "Best if you hide in the supply closet. Keep your voices down. The walls are thick, but I don't want to risk it. I'll knock when I'm back with the truck. It'll be less suspicious if I walk out through the main door and pull the truck around."

Belle eyed the closet dubiously. It looked only a little bigger than the cleaning closet she'd stumbled into on the *Figment*. "Will we fit in there?"

Captain Charity stroked her chin. "I think so. It'll be cozy, but it's only for a few minutes." She flashed them a dazzling smile. "Let's get going, shall we?"

Beast let out a long-suffering sigh as he made his way to the supply closet. Belle followed suit, her heart still pounding.

"I'll be back soon." Captain Charity closed the door, plunging Belle and Beast into darkness.

Belle stumbled back, tripping over something on the floor. She collided into Beast's chest.

His arms instantly wrapped around her, the rough bandages tickling her arms.

"Easy," he murmured into her hair.

Belle was grateful for the darkness because she could feel heat prickling from her collarbone up. At least Beast wouldn't be able to see her blush. She hissed when her tender hands caught on the wall of the closet.

"Are you okay?" His voice was anxious.

"Yeah. My hands are hurting again, that's all."

"I'm sorry," Beast huffed. "You should have let me carry the pilot."

Belle tensed at his change in tone. "I thought I'd be okay.

Finding out about what happened to the ether mines shattered me. Helping someone else was a good distraction. I just needed to feel something."

"You needed to feel something?" Beast drew out every word slowly.

The closet suddenly seemed far too small.

"Well, yes. My entire world crashed down on me." Belle took a shuddering breath. "I didn't realize the extent of my abandonment until today."

In the dark, Beast shifted closer, ducking down until his forehead touched hers, his fur brushing against her skin.

"Belle, you don't have to punish yourself. You can mourn for what you lost. Just don't spend all your time dwelling in the past." Beast's hot breath sent shivers down Belle's arms.

Belle could hardly speak. Her heart hammered so loudly she wondered if Beast could hear it. She finally managed a feeble, "Oh."

After a few moments passed, Beast spoke again.

"Thank you."

"What for?" Belle felt breathless.

"Everything. I know I gave you a hard time about the escape plan, but you've done everything in your power to help me. Thank you." Beast lingered, wrapping his bandaged arms around her.

"Oh. Um, you're welcome." Belle closed her eyes and leaned closer, enjoying his touch more than she cared to admit. "It's nice to have a moment to breathe."

There was a brief knock on the supply closet door before it was flung open.

"Sorry to interrupt." Captain's Charity's smirk contradicted her words. "I have the truck around back. Are you decent?"

Belle and Beast scrambled to exit the closet, only to collide with each other. Belle caught Beast as he stumbled forward into her arms.

"Never better." Belle winced, hoping Maureen's guest hadn't heard the racket.

Captain Charity snorted. "Let's go."

CHAPTER TEN

Belle's footsteps were wooden as she followed Captain Charity to the back of the lab. Her skin prickled with heat and her dark hair clung to her face, damp with sweat. As she tucked a wayward strand back, she noticed Beast's silver fur had shed on her sleeves. She brushed the bits of fluff off a little more forcefully than warranted.

What had she been thinking?

Beast's pack bumped Belle's arm as he adjusted its shoulder straps. His goggles were pushed up near the base of his antlers, revealing a mischievous glint in his eyes as he nodded at her.

"Sorry." Beast gave her a lopsided grin.

She froze when their eyes met. Belatedly, she attempted to return his smile, but it was too late. The moment had passed. Beast ducked his head down, shoulders hunched as he shuffled behind the captain.

Belle stared at the floor as she followed, staying a safe distance behind them. Deflated, Belle's shoulders slumped and she kept her eyes on the floor. Rejection was the last thing on her mind. She just couldn't figure out what they were doing in the supply closet. When they embraced, it was as if her every nerve ending came to life. She had confided in Beast about needing to feel something. Now she felt too much.

Belle didn't regret the tender moment, but her emotions were a tumultuous mess. Why did the captain have to open the door at the wrong time? Captain Charity had said she'd only be gone a few minutes. Couldn't the captain have hurried back faster, before everything became complicated with Beast?

Or arrived a few minutes later…

Clenching her fists until her nails bit into her palms, Belle quashed her traitorous thoughts. She needed to focus. They were going to be hiding out together under the same roof indefinitely unless they were betrayed for the reward money. Both of them were still healing from trauma. This was a bad idea.

But Beast started it when he leaned in.

Belle shook her head. They'd need to talk sooner rather than later so they could go back to their comfortable companionship.

"Here we are!" Captain Charity's overly bright voice jolted Belle out of her spiraling thoughts, saving her from colliding with Beast's back when he stopped in front of the open door.

On the other side of the door was a covered porch, converted into a private loading bay with metal and wooden shipping crates stacked almost as tall as Belle. Maureen's truck was parked with its bed facing the door. Puffs of steam rose from the vehicle's engine as it idled, shrouding the loading area in a haze.

"See? No one's going to spot you. You two stay in the back and everything will be fine." Captain Charity's calm demeanor eased Belle's fragile nerves.

Both Belle and Beast grimaced as they again loaded into the cramped truck, scooting back as far as possible in the covered bed. Belle's leg brushed against a folded tarp on top of a crate. Inspiration struck, and she unfolded it, using it as a makeshift curtain over the precariously stacked crates neighboring her and Beast. Her fingers slipped as she tucked the tarp between crates in the dim lighting.

"What are you doing?" The bristly fur on Beast's muzzle tickled her ear.

For the first time, she wished she had his night vision so she could see his face more clearly. At least he sounded like his usual self. Maybe he realized it was only a misunderstanding?

"I thought we could use this in case someone gets nosy when the truck is stopped." Belle gestured at the tarp.

"I see." Beast shifted behind her and reached over her shoulder.

In the low light, Belle strained to see what he was doing.

"It's slipping. Fixed it."

The truck shifted gears and lurched forward. Loose cobblestones crunched under the tires as Captain Charity peeled out of the lot, sending Belle crashing into Beast. As if it were a habit now, Beast caught her in his arms. The ride was much bumpier this time. The crates shook violently. More than once, Belle thought the cargo was going to crash down on them, but eventually the truck drove at a steady pace.

When her heart rate settled, she muttered, "I guess airships are easier for the captain than terrestrial vehicles."

Beast chuckled, his low voice rumbling. Belle joined in, and for a moment, she forgot all about the awkwardness between them.

When the laughter died down, Beast withdrew his arm, carefully releasing her. "Are you okay?"

"Yes, I think so. I'm sorry about earlier. I mean, not about the closet. I'm sorry about afterwards. Finding out about the ether-miners and my father was too much." Belle clamped a hand over her mouth. She'd spent years lonely and now she was in danger of ruining her first real friendship by spontaneously turning into a blundering fool.

Beast guffawed, his laughter amplified in the cramped space. "I meant from the terrible driving, but I'm glad to know where you stand."

"Oh." She fidgeted in a vain attempt to find a more comfortable position. "I'm fine, unless the captain shifts gears again."

They spent the next several minutes in silence, with the muffled noises of the town and the rumbling engine the only distractions. Belle wished she could pull back the tarp so she could see more of Duchollow, but she didn't want to risk it. She felt lucky that earlier, no one had seemed to care to look in the back of Maureen's truck on the way to the mayor's office.

Was no one in Duchollow curious? Even the dock workers had been nonchalant when they'd disembarked the *Figment*. Now she wondered if the dock workers were already on their way to collect the Ringmaster's reward money.

She still couldn't believe the Ringmaster, as stingy as he was, had offered a reward for them. He must have been banking on their new act to bring in a lot of revenue. Belle smiled grimly at the thought of making the Ringmaster's deep pockets lighter. Her good mood soured as she remembered Beast's reward said either dead or alive.

When the truck stopped, Belle tensed. They were still within the town limits as far as she could tell from the sounds of laughter and automobiles driving by. The smell of something delicious permeated the canvas. Her shoulders relaxed slightly as she remembered the captain mentioning that she'd get them food on the way to the house.

Still, she couldn't help wondering if Captain Charity had changed her mind and planned to collect the reward. Beast must have been having similar thoughts. He clasped Belle's shoulder protectively.

"Don't worry. I think she's getting us lunch." Belle patted the paw that held her a little too tightly. "At least, I hope she is."

"Are you feeling any better?" Beast released his death grip on her shoulder.

"Processing," Belle whispered back. Without the engine running, it was impossible to tell if anyone could overhear them. She doubted that any pedestrians were close enough to pay attention, but she preferred playing it safe. "I'm still in shock. I don't know why my father didn't come get me after the mining practices were outlawed. Maybe he died, or perhaps he didn't want to deal with me anymore."

"I'm sorry." Beast clumsily patted her back in the cramped quarters.

They were both quiet and contemplative when the truck started up again, its steam engine hissing as it warmed up enough to run.

After they were on the road for a few minutes, Beast spoke again. "Maybe your father was too ashamed."

"I don't think there was any part of him left that could feel shame." Belle shook her head. "He sold me to the Ringmaster, willingly, when I was a girl, and tried to tell me it was for the best. While he might have been right in that it was better than furthering my exposure to ether and backbreaking work, it was not…" The words died on Belle's lips as she struggled to articulate the horrors of the last ten years. "Well, you know what it was like in the circus."

"I do." Beast hesitated before saying, "What I mean is, I'm sure your father knew what he did was wrong. Maybe he didn't have the strength to face you after that? How could he? He sold his own daughter."

Belle shook her head. "It's been so long, I don't even know what I'd expect out of him."

"Would you want to see him now?"

"I—" Belle's voice caught. She shook her head. "I don't know if I'd want to face him. I'd want to know if he was safe, and I'd like him to know what he did caused me so much damage." She took a shuddering breath. "I have so many old scars. I wish he knew about that." Her eyes misted. "Does it make me a bad person if I want him to know how much I hurt?"

Beast wrapped his arms around her. "No. You're the best person I know."

Belle snorted, wiping away her tears. "Aren't I one of the only people you know?"

"Yes, but I know your heart."

"Thank you." Belle snuggled closer to Beast, her stomach fluttering. For whatever reason, she felt safe with him, and he seemed to feel the same pull toward her. A little voice niggled at the back of her mind that it was entirely possible he started off his life as a literal beast, but she shushed it.

The way Beast looked at her lately seemed far too human for that to be true. She refused to examine the implications of that last thought.

Belle gulped when the truck came to a stop.

Captain Charity pulled back the canvas covering the back of the truck bed, beaming as she held up an overflowing bag filled with bundles of wrapped food. Sweet and spicy scents mingled in a mouth-watering aroma.

"We're here! I got your lunch. Wanna eat and explore your new place?"

"Yes, please!" Belle scrambled out of the truck, Beast following close behind her.

"Welcome home!" Balancing the bag of takeaway on her hip, Captain Charity gestured with her free hand to a magnificent stonework cottage nestled between ancient, towering birch trees. It looked like a scene straight out of one of Belle's fairy tale books.

The house was beautiful, but it looked as if it had been many years since it had a caretaker. Vines grew unchecked along the stonework. An inviting covered porch that wrapped around to the back of the property needed posts replaced. The arched dark green roof was missing several shingles, but the two chimneys jutting out of it were intact.

"We're staying here?" Mouth agape, Belle couldn't tear her eyes away from the cottage. The imperfections didn't bother her in the slightest. Truthfully, she thought the mayor meant for Beast and her to hide out in a tiny shack. She never dreamed it would be something so spacious and cozy.

"Let's eat outside. I doubt there's furniture inside, and even if there is, it's probably filthy." Captain Charity adjusted her bag as it slipped, catching it before disaster struck. "I saw a gazebo around the back when I pulled up. Maybe it has a table?"

Too entranced with the cottage, Belle didn't register anything the captain said.

"Belle?" Beast tapped her arm. Sunlight glinted off his tinted goggle lenses, obscuring his expression.

"Oh! Yes, sorry. Let's go." She blushed faintly.

Captain Charity snickered as she led them to the crooked wooden fence surrounding the property. The rusted gate squeaked as they passed through it. Behind the house, there was a gazebo, but to Belle's surprise, the yard stretched back for a couple of acres, much farther than she would have imagined.

A dense forest surrounded the far edges of the fence, and in several sections, brush overtook the buckling wooden planks. A once elegant greenhouse bordered by wild rose bushes sat forlornly in the center of the backyard, its glass panes partially covered by ivy. A few panels were missing or broken. Inside, plants had grown unchecked, lining the interior with all kinds of greenery.

Several feet away, unruly vegetation and weeds overtook what once might have been a thriving garden next to a complex well system. It appeared as if the well once had automations for pumping water, but it was unlikely the machinery was still functional. Weeds overtook the mechanism's misaligned gears. Belle knew nothing about gardening, but seeing all the potential made her want to learn. Even in its neglected state, the grounds held a romantic charm.

The gazebo was intact, though it needed a fresh coat of white paint. Beneath it was an antique ironwork table with chipped green paint, along with mercifully sturdy seats and a bench that could support Beast's weight. Captain Charity set her bounty on the round table as they all sat down.

Belle's mouth watered as the captain unpacked the bag. Soon, three mugs, a carafe of coffee, two steaming trays of barbecued chicken on sticks, rice balls, and pomegranates were spread out on the table.

Captain Charity caught Belle staring at the food. "I wasn't sure what you'd like, so I got a little of everything."

"This looks amazing. Thank you." She was overwhelmed by the generosity. "I've had nothing like this before."

"Well, go ahead before it gets cold." The captain smirked.

Beast didn't need told twice. He popped the rice balls in his mouth whole and guzzled his coffee.

Belle thought it was endearing and chuckled before trying her own food. Everything was better than it looked. She closed her eyes while savoring bites of chicken off the skewer. When she opened them again, Beast was staring at her. She flushed crimson from her collarbone up, remembering the oil stains from carrying Damek that had made a mess of her outfit. Under the bright sunlight, it was obvious her clothes were ruined.

The captain covered her smile with her mug as she took a deep drink.

When Belle and Beast were finished eating, Captain Charity handed Belle a weighty metal keyring with four elaborate keys of varying sizes.

"If you don't mind, I'll come in with you so I can make sure it's livable. If it's not, we can find somewhere else for you two to recover." The captain rose, tidying up the packaging left from the street food.

"That'd be great, thank you." Belle held onto the keys like a lucky talisman, clasping them close to her chest. The prospect of going inside their home made her giddy with anticipation. Theirs. Her heart thudded as she gave Beast a sidelong glance. She wondered how he felt about sharing a roof.

Captain Charity led them to the front of the cottage. Lost in thought, Belle missed the loose stone on the path leading to the chipped violet door. Beast caught her in his arms just before she hit the ground, in a fluid motion akin to a dancer's dramatic dip.

"Careful." His breath caressed her neck as he steadied her.

Belle trembled at the proximity. "Thank you."

"Coming?" Captain Charity called. "You have the keys."

"Right. Sorry!" Scrambling to the porch, she tried each key until the third one opened the front door with a satisfying click.

Inside the cottage was completely dark. Trying her luck, Belle groped along the wall until she found a light switch. She was surprised that the abandoned home had power, but the overhead lights emitted warm light, soft enough for Beast to remove his goggles.

The light revealed that they were standing in a small foyer connected to an open great room, with a large stone fireplace dominating the right-side wall. Built-in bookshelves lined the other walls, though Bell was disappointed that no books remained. Next to the great room was a sizeable kitchen. Grime clung to the counters and built-in cabinets. The only furniture the previous occupant had left behind was a sturdy wooden table and chairs in the great room.

"Wow," Belle breathed. "It's huge!"

Beast nodded, eyeing the kitchen thoughtfully.

"I'm glad you like it. If you two decide to stay longer, this looks like it has a lot of potential." The captain beamed.

Belle stifled a gasp by covering her hand with her mouth. When she could trust her voice to not shake, she lowered her hand. "I thought Maureen was only letting us stay temporarily?"

Captain Charity shook her head and retrieved the rolled-up papers from the mayor's office from her trouser pocket. "It said in the papers she's going to transfer the deed to you two."

Belle's mouth hung open. When she recovered, she blurted, "But why?"

Captain Charity shrugged. "It's not my story to tell, but Maureen meant what she said about making amends."

"What did she do?" Beast's brows furrowed.

"Beast's right. This sounds too good to be true." Belle hoped she was wrong, but this was too generous. There had to be a catch.

The captain sighed. "You're not going to let this go, are you?"

Belle and Beast shook their heads. Belle's pulse thrummed. What could the mayor have done that she felt she had to go to such lengths to make amends to strangers?

Captain Charity ran her fingers through her wild hair, chewing on her lip as she thought. Sighing again, she met their curious gazes. "Maureen's always been an inventor first, mayor second. One of her biggest successes was the ether-mining machine, because it eliminated the risk of ether-poisoning. All of her inventions are amazing, but this was the first one that got national attention."

Belle frowned. "How's that a bad thing? I would have been relieved."

Captain Charity held up a finger. "The mining companies couldn't get enough of her machine. More orders came in than she could keep up with, so she had to commission as many factories as possible to make them. She had plans to hire former miners to manufacture her machines because the assembly of her invention was far less hazardous than mining, but…"

"What happened?" Belle's heart ached. If this had happened a little sooner, maybe her parents would have had safer, steadier work, and she never would have had to endure the mines or the circus.

"Her rival, Delphine Wyerstone, that's what." Captain Charity practically spat the words. "The trouble with Maureen's machine was that it took longer than what the companies were willing to wait for, even though she did her best to keep up with demand while maintaining safety practices. The barons were hungry for faster results. Maureen's invention worked four times as efficiently as a full team of human miners. Delphine offered her own version of the machine, claiming it could be built for a fraction of the cost and half the wait time. Many companies reneged on their deals with Maureen."

"Oh." Belle pursed her lips. "I thought Delphine was in the natural sciences because of the Hounds."

When Delphine's name was mentioned, Beast's nostrils flared and his eyes narrowed.

Captain Charity smiled bitterly. "She's a bit like Maureen in the sense that she's gifted in multiple fields." She scowled. "But Delphine doesn't let morality get in her way. Anyway, her machine became irresistible to these companies. Though there were reports of injuries in her factories and whispers of worse, nothing was done about it. Maureen's orders dried up and she couldn't commission factories anymore. As a result of Delphine's version of the machine, many workers found themselves out of work without warning. There were no jobs for them when the machines took over, especially in the smaller mining towns."

"That's horrible. But why does Maureen feel responsible?" Belle tilted her head.

"She feels like all those mining families were displaced because of her." Captain Charity's voice grew quiet.

"What does any of that have to do with me or Beast?" Belle wasn't expecting a history lesson from the captain, but now she had more questions than answers.

The captain gave them a rueful smile. "I'm afraid I've already said too much. It's Maureen's story to tell, not mine."

"It's still odd." Belle didn't know what to think.

"I know, and I wish I had more time to explain, or better, have Maureen speak for herself, but I have to leave soon." Captain

Charity jabbed her thumb in the direction of the unexplored hallway. "Can I do a quick run-through before I go?"

Unease gnawed at Belle as she turned to Beast. "Still want to stay?"

"Yes. Maybe we'll finally get answers when things settle down." Beast's intense gaze focused on the captain.

Belle nodded. "We're grateful for everything, but I hope you can understand our confusion."

"I'm sorry things are this way. We should get moving, though." Captain Charity led them to the hall, where there were four doors. "According to the floor plan, there's supposed to be three bedrooms and a bathroom over here." She riffled through the papers again, holding them close to her face. The lighting over here wasn't as good as in the great room. "The primary suite is over there and has its own fireplace and water closet."

Belle blinked. "Maureen was generous in giving us such a big place."

"That's how Maureen is. However, I don't want to get your hopes up. There might be good reasons this cottage sat for so long without her moving a family in." The captain gave her a crooked smile as she shrugged. "Sorry, I don't want to take away from your gratitude. I just want to be as honest as I can about the situation, so your dreams aren't dashed. Should we see what's behind door number one?"

Belle nodded, a lump in her throat. Despite the captain's words, she was grateful for the roof over their head, even if the circumstances were strange. Both the mayor and the captain were doing their best to keep her and Beast safe, despite being strangers. Though their actions defied logic, they warmed her heart.

The captain opened the first door and a wave of dust hit the group. As Belle hacked and coughed, with watery eyes, she could make out the sunlight streaming in from several places on the roof.

"Looks like this room's not habitable yet," the captain sputtered.

After the dust settled, the three of them crowded inside. Beast grimaced, though Belle couldn't tell whether it was the dust clinging to his fur or the bright light bothering him more. Captain Charity pulled out a small notebook and a pen from her pocket and began taking notes. She narrowed her eyes at the places where the warped wooden floor boards were stained dark.

"Water damage?" Beast asked.

"I'm afraid so. Do you all see anything else wrong in here or that needs fixing? I'm taking notes for the contractors."

Belle startled. "Won't the contractors be curious about us? I thought we were in hiding?"

"You're right. You're lying low for now, but after you've healed and Maureen can work her magic with the townspeople, she'll call in help to fix up this mess."

"Huh?" Belle wanted to ask more questions, but the captain was already off to the next room.

As Captain Charity opened the door to the water closet, Belle was half expecting burst pipes and rotten floorboards, but, miraculously, the small room was mostly fine. After a few seconds of rust-stained water, the tap, which must have connected to a well nearby, flowed clear.

Satisfied, the captain wrote a note. "I'd let it run for a while before using any of the water, but I think this will be okay. Two more to go!"

The roof was mercifully fine, but the window glass was cracked —badly—and the wood around the sill showed signs of rot. "It's not as bad as it could be, but I hope the last room is better. It'll get freezing cold in here."

"I can manage it." Beast pointed at his fur.

"That won't stop you from being a blanket hog," Belle muttered without thinking.

She flushed crimson at the incredulous look Captain Charity gave her.

"I just meant, on the observation deck, in your sleep, you rolled over and took some of my covers."

"Let's go check the other room." Captain Charity unsuccessfully disguised her laughter with a cough.

As the trio went back through the main room, Beast murmured in Belle's ear, "As I recall, you curled into me as well."

Belle stammered, "I, uh…"

She was saved by Captain Charity poking her head out of the master bedroom.

"Good news! This room is fine. You'll still need furniture, but at least you'll be able to get one bed in here, maybe two?"

Belle's heart hammered. How on earth would she be able to live with Beast if they kept having these oh-so awkward moments?

"Wonderful." Beast's expression was unreadable.

Captain Charity hooked her thumbs through her belt loops. "I'll get in touch with Maureen when she's free. Someone will bring you supplies later."

"Thank you for everything." Belle was sorely tempted to hug the captain, but she didn't want to push her luck.

"Yes, thank you." Beast nodded, looking deep in thought.

"You're welcome. Have a good afternoon and try to stay out of trouble. I'll see you again, probably."

With that, Captain Charity left after breezily waving them goodbye, leaving Belle and Beast gaping at the closed door.

Outside, Maureen's truck rumbled to life before the sounds of crunching gravel and the engine hissing faded away. They were truly alone now.

Belle fidgeted awkwardly with her bag. "Should we unpack?" Suddenly, the large cottage felt claustrophobic.

Before Beast could answer, there was a brisk, insistent knock at the door. It was far too soon for Captain Charity to be back, and it couldn't possibly have been Maureen.

"Hide," Belle hissed, putting herself between Beast and the front door. The knocking grew louder. "Why aren't you hiding?" The veins in her neck throbbed as she shooed him away.

"I'm not leaving you," he growled as he flexed his wicked claws. He padded to her side, crouching in a defensive position.

Belle pinched the bridge of her nose. "You're wanted dead or alive, Beast. You need better survival instincts."

"Is my life really worth living if I leave you to your fate?"

Sighing, Belle relented. "Fine, find something to barricade the door," she whispered, her eyes darting to the meager furniture in the great room.

The knocking ceased. A muffled, trembling voice called from the other side of the door, "Please let me in. I'm Secretary Cadwell. I've a delivery from Mayor Dawkins and I can't carry it much longer."

"Mayor Dawkins?" mouthed Beast.

"Maureen," Belle whispered back, remembering the plaque in Town Hall.

"Should we let him in?" Beast cast a wary glance at the door.

"I don't know. How'd he get here so fast?" Belle's tension headache spread, threatening to turn into a full-blown migraine.

Beast tilted his head, giving her a sidelong glance. "You could break him in half if he gets out of line."

Grimacing, Belle shook her head. "I don't want to fight more if I don't have to."

"Didn't stop you with the Hounds."

Belle huffed impatiently. "That was different." She lifted her bandaged hands. "And I'm still healing."

An amused glint appeared in Beast's eyes as he smirked. "Fine. I'll huff and puff and blow him away if he causes trouble."

"Very funny, Beast."

Mr. Cadwell's muted voice piped up hesitantly. "You know I can hear you, right?"

Belle raised her brows at Beast, who nodded back. She cracked the door open a sliver, prepared to slam it in Mr. Cadwell's face if this was a trap. Through the narrow opening, she could see the harried secretary place something heavy and boxy on their porch before lifting his empty hands in surrender.

"Please, let me just bring in the supplies and I'll leave. I can't stay long. Maureen's expecting me to report back."

Stiffly, Belle opened the door wider, peering over Mr. Cadwell's shoulder. He was alone, save for a sleek black automobile still running out front. Her eyes lowered to the porch, where next to the secretary's high-shine polished shoes were a radio, similar to the one in the mayor's office, and a full burlap sack.

"Be our guest." Belle swept her hand toward the dusty great room, keeping her gaze firmly locked on Mr. Cadwell.

"Thank you." Panting, the secretary pointed to the supplies. "A little help, please?"

Wordlessly, Belle lifted the bulky radio onto the wooden kitchen table. Beast stepped forward, stalking past the cringing secretary, picked up the bag, and placed it next to the radio.

Mr. Cadwell briskly crossed the threshold, closing the door behind him, and stood by the table, retrieving an envelope from his black knee-length frock coat. He handed the envelope to Belle.

"The mayor sent this for you. There are water canteens and a few other miscellaneous items in the bag to tide you over until more can be brought here. Everything else you need to know is in the envelope." Mr. Cadwell gave them a curt nod and turned to leave. "Good day."

"Wait!" Belle reached for the secretary with her free hand, grabbing his shoulder. "Can't you tell us anything else? We're thankful for all that Maureen's done for us, but we're confused."

A visible vein on Mr. Cadwell's forehead throbbed as he stepped out of her loose hold and shook his head. "I'm afraid I'm not at liberty to discuss the mayor's plans." He glanced down at the specks of debris clinging to his elegant coat, wrinkling his nose as he dusted it off.

"Why not?" Beast pulled himself to his full height, glowering at the secretary.

Mr. Cadwell shrank back. "Even if I wanted to tell you, the mayor hasn't shared her plans. She slipped me a note between meetings. I don't know the contents of the letter." His Adam's apple bobbed as he swallowed hard. "I need to go."

Belle clenched her teeth until her jaw ached. "Thank you for the message and the supplies. Good day."

The secretary stalked away, shooting Beast one last frightened glance before slamming the door shut.

Outside, the screech of tires peeling on the cobblestone road penetrated the cottage's thick walls before fading away.

Silence stretched between Belle and Beast as they stared at the cream-colored sealed envelope and supplies.

"I suppose we should start with the letter," Belle said faintly, stunned by the strange turn of events.

At Beast's grunt of approval, she flipped the envelope over to glance at the interlocking gear pattern embossed in the cerulean blue seal. Carefully, she tore around the seal and removed the letter.

I'll contact you as soon as possible via the radio. Please leave it on. In the meantime, Mr. Cadwell should have picked up a few supplies on his way to deliver this. More later. Lay low and take care.

-M

Deflated by the short missive, Belle's shoulders slumped. "I don't know what I was expecting, but that was a bit of a letdown, wasn't it?"

"Maybe we'll have better luck with the bag?"

Beast untied the burlap sack and removed its contents: two generously filled canteens, dust rags, towels, a book of matches, two tightly rolled blankets, two apples, two bars of chocolate, and jerky.

Nonplussed, Belle scratched the back of her head while she contemplated the supplies. She was thankful, but thoroughly confused. "That was kind. At least we can make this place a little more livable while we wait." She leaned down to study the radio. "Strange, I don't see any wires."

Beast tossed his cloak over the back of one chair at the table and picked up a dust cloth.

"What are you doing?" Belle gestured to the rag.

"I'll start cleaning while you work on the radio." He shrugged. "I'd be useless with all those knobs."

"Thank you. You'd think since I could modify the mechanical unicorn this would be easy, but…" Her voice trailed off as she studied the multitude of knobs, light bulbs, and dials on the unusual radio. Did the one in Maureen's office have all these extra parts? She couldn't remember.

"Good luck." Beast waved with the dust rag and set about his work.

Belle stared at the sight of the bear-like Beast attacking the layer of grime coating the cabinets with such shocking ferocity he kicked up plumes of dust. Shaking her head, she picked up the overly complicated radio, turning it over to search for clues. There were no cables to be found nor a switch on its base. She flipped it back over, testing the knobs one by one, until at last, crackling white noise filled the room. The bulbs on the radio glowed with steady golden light.

Spurred on by her success, Belle adjusted the knobs until

orchestral music sounded from the speakers with crystal clarity. A jaunty tune played.

Beast returned, covered in filth, but grinning widely. "Fantastic!" He studied the radio thoughtfully. "How's Maureen going to contact us?"

Belle shook her head. "No idea. I'll try changing frequencies later."

They stood together, listening to the music shifting into a playful song reminiscent of a festival.

Beast tossed his dust rag aside and held up his arms in a dancer's pose. "Dance with me?"

"What?" Belle blinked. "I don't know how to dance. Just the ridiculous pseudo-waltz from the circus act."

"Good. Neither do I." Beast waited with open arms, his eyes sparkling with mischief and warmth.

"But my clothes…" She pulled feebly at the oil stains ruining her shirt. "I should at least change. There's a spare outfit in my pack."

Beast shook his head. "We still have cleaning to do. Don't bother wasting a new outfit on my account. Besides, mine is just as bad as yours." He pointed to his dusty shirt.

"But why?"

"Because it sounds fun."

Beast's mischievous smile, coupled with the absurdity of the situation, won her over. Laughing, she placed her hands in his waiting paws and he whisked her off her feet into an enthusiastic, off-rhythm dance.

Neither of them knew what they were doing as Beast twirled Belle. Their moves were out of sync with the song, but it didn't matter. The tension in Belle's back melted as she laughed at the ridiculousness of it all. Beast's deep chuckle joined in, and warmth flooded her body.

Soon, the music changed to a slow waltz.

Catching her breath, Belle paused as she looked at Beast. "Should we get back to work?"

"Not yet. May I have this dance, too?"

The raw vulnerability in his voice made Belle's mouth go dry.

Gulping, she nodded, and Beast pulled her closer, slipping his arm lower around her waist. They found their rhythm, made easier by the gentle tempo. Breathless, she looked up at Beast as he twirled her slowly. Catching her stare, he smiled softly as he tucked a strand of Belle's hair behind her ear.

They leaned closer until their foreheads touched as the song drew to a close. Hyper-aware of the points where they touched, Belle's whole body felt electrified. When she trusted her voice to not crack and betray her, she spoke. "Thank you. You were right. That was fun. It helped take my mind off everything."

Beast's voice rumbled deliciously. "Good, I'm glad."

Crackling static drowned out the orchestra on the radio.

"Maybe I need to adjust it?" Belle squinted at the myriad of dials and knobs.

Maureen's voice carried over the radio, obscured by static pops. "Belle? Beast? Are you there?"

"So much for a break," Beast muttered bitterly.

CHAPTER ELEVEN

Two weeks had passed since Maureen's broadcast message, and Belle was still no closer to a decision. Tension spread between Belle's shoulder blades, traveling across her back muscles as she stared at the dormant radio on the table. Clutching a steaming mug of coffee, she contemplated her choices in the quiet kitchen.

The mug's heat was almost unbearable without the thick bandages around her knuckles, but she was grateful that her hands had finally healed. All that remained of her injuries were faded purple bruises. She removed the wrappings for the last time yesterday, and now she wished for gloves. Everything felt overwhelming to the touch.

Snippets of Maureen's words haunted Belle as she carefully took another sip.

"When your hands are healed, I can start the process for ether-poisoning treatment. Send word whenever you're ready."

Belle had never envisioned her future without ether-poisoning. No one in Aetherbourne lived to old age. Either the sickness or the mines claimed everyone in the end. She always assumed she'd perish from the inevitable deterioration from her condition, or the Ringmaster's cruelty would go too far.

Maureen's offer was very tempting, and it was made even more irresistible by her actions over the past several days. She had proven to be a woman of her word, following through with her promise to send much-needed supplies. Belle and Beast didn't want for anything in their cottage as they waited for news. Captain Charity had brought over furniture, groceries, clothes, and books for them. She had even given them a few basic cooking lessons so they could use the stove.

But Belle's mind worried over the future. What if the cure was worse than the disease? Her most obvious symptoms were the visible dark veins on her too-pale skin. The headaches were annoying but not debilitating. What if she lost her strength in the process and couldn't protect Beast? Maureen hadn't mentioned a single word about the town hall meeting that was supposed to have happened. The fear of a mob coming to the cottage doorstep kept Belle awake at night.

Then again, if she could be rid of her discolored veins, she'd no longer look like the image Ringmaster had broadcast to the world. Perhaps she'd be able to venture out and help Beast find answers about his transformation?

Before she could change her mind again, Belle turned the radio knob to the correct frequency and pressed the call button. "Excuse me, Maureen? Are you there?" She cringed, hating how meek her voice sounded.

Only crackling static answered. She reached to turn off the radio when Maureen's voice cut through the white noise.

"Hello? Is everything okay?" The mayor sounded out of breath, as if she'd been running.

Belle's mouth went dry, and she gulped the last dregs of her coffee. Shuddering at the bitter taste, she answered, "I'm here. I was wondering about your offer to treat my ether-poisoning since my hands have finally healed."

Maureen's tone brightened. "Good! I imagine it wasn't fun wearing bandages for so long. Yes, I can give you a screening to see if the cure will work on you. If you'd like, I can be there within the hour to pick you up."

"Within the hour?" Belle's voice squeaked.

"We wouldn't begin treatment today. I only need to take a blood sample, I promise."

"Then yes, please come get me." Belle gulped.

"See you soon!"

With that, the static returned, leaving Belle alone with her thoughts. Pressing her palms to her face, she silenced the panic growing in her as best as she could, taking shuddering, slow breaths. What had she agreed to? She didn't even know how to find her way to the cottage from Duchollow if there was an emergency. She'd only ever seen a fraction of the town from the back of Maureen's truck.

When Belle's nerves settled, she looked at her bedroom door, biting her lip. She'd better tell Beast about her plans, or he'd worry. Shortly after they moved in, he'd resumed sleeping during the day to avoid the bright afternoon sun. She searched for a pen and paper to leave a note, then hesitated. She wasn't entirely certain if he could read. When they read together, she always read aloud to him. He had told her he liked her voice, but she wasn't sure if that was the only reason.

Heart palpitating, Belle pushed the door open softly. Beast was curled up snugly in a nest of pillows and blankets on the floor. Her bed was against the wall, only a couple feet away. He claimed it was easier on him to sleep on the pallet than on the creaky bed, but only after he'd built up a mountain of pillows. Warmth flooded her as she watched him peacefully slumbering. She hated having to wake him.

Belle leaned down and nudged Beast's shoulder. "Beast, I'm sorry to wake you, but it's important."

Slowly, he opened his goldenrod eyes, yawning and stretching like an overgrown house cat.

"What is it?" His words slurred together.

"I radioed Maureen. I'm going to her lab today to see about the ether-poisoning treatment, and I didn't want you to worry."

Beast's eyes widened, and he bolted out of his blankets to stand by Belle. "You did what?" He cleared his throat. "I mean, I want you to have the cure. Are you sure about going alone?"

Belle swallowed hard. "I think it'll be safer with the bounty. I'm not thrilled about leaving you behind, but I'd hate if anything happened to you again because of me."

Beast took her hand into his paws. "Hey, you deserve a cure. You'd be able to go anywhere, be anything. Don't let me hold you back."

"You don't hold me back." Belle squeezed his paw gently.

"If you're cured, I doubt anyone would think you're the circus runaway. You could build a whole new life." Beast's expression was wistful as he squeezed her hand back.

Belle shook her head. "I'm not interested in leaving you behind."

"Maybe you should." Beast bowed his head.

"No." She tucked her free hand under his chin, lifting his gaze back up. "I'd rather stay and help you find answers. You deserve to know what happened and who did this to you."

Beast harrumphed in response.

Outside, the familiar rumble of Maureen's truck approached.

"I need to go. I'll see you later." Belle touched her forehead against his. "Be safe and sleep well. I'll be back soon."

"Be careful." Beast reluctantly released her hand.

"I will. Please get some rest. Maybe I can bring back dinner."

"Thank you." Beast looked uneasy as he mechanically returned her wave.

After donning her cloak, Belle opened the front door and locked it behind her. Maureen's sea-glass green truck emitted steam as it idled, and the mayor nodded at her from the driver's seat when their eyes met.

Belle waved, plastering a smile on her face as she made her way to the back of the truck.

Maureen poked her head out of the rolled-down window.

"Hey, where are you going?"

Belle paused, blinking at the mayor.

"I was going to the back of the truck? As I've done all the other times?"

"Since it's just you today, I think you'll be okay to ride in the front and see more of Duchollow."

Belle hesitated. "What if someone recognizes me from the

bounty?"

"If it'll make you feel better, you can ride in the back again, or you could wear your hood and ride in the cab. The choice is yours." Maureen smiled at her encouragingly.

After carefully tucking her hair into her hood, Belle ambled to the passenger-side door and let herself in.

As she sat down, Belle fidgeted with her cloak and smoothed her linen blouse. "Are you sure this is a good idea?"

Maureen nodded. "Let's go."

"Okay." Belle nodded, swallowing a thousand burning questions as they drove away, resolving to memorize the road home—just in case.

The ride to town was mostly silent as Belle took in the sights. She was surprised to see that the town was only fifteen minutes away. Only a stretch of forest and a smattering of small farms separated the bustling town and their quiet cottage.

As they approached the central plaza, Maureen glanced sidelong at Belle.

"What's wrong?" Belle squirmed in her seat. Without Captain Charity or the radio as a buffer, she felt intimidated being alone with the mayor for the first time.

"Nothing. I just thought you'd be bursting with questions. But you've been so quiet." A small smile graced the mayor's face.

"Oh! Yes, I do have questions." Belle desperately wanted to ask why the mayor was being so generous with her and Beast, but she also didn't want to risk losing access to a cure.

"Ask away," Maureen said breezily as she turned down another street with food vendors lining the walkways. Shops were opening, offering everything from vibrant clothes to fancy clocks to elaborate children's toys.

"Did the meeting go well?" Belle asked quietly. Though she didn't exactly mind being stranded with Beast, she longed to go exploring the picturesque town with him.

Maureen exhaled. "Well, yes, but there's a problem."

Belle looked sharply at the mayor. "Do we need to leave?" Her hand reached for the door handle. "Beast! I need to go back."

"Slow down. It's not that." Maureen looked up, clenching the steering wheel as she hit the brakes, pointing at the sky. "What is that? Ships rarely fly right over town."

Belle followed her gaze. A small airship blotted out the sun as it flew overhead. Pedestrians in the town center took notice too, pointing and chattering loudly. Something came pouring out of the airship, but because of the sun's position, it was impossible to discern what. Moments later, the sky filled with falling papers, eliciting shouts and panicked yelps from the townspeople.

"What the hell?" Maureen's brow creased.

Belle watched in horrified fascination as one paper floated toward them, sticking print-side down on the windshield. In bold letters, the flyer proclaimed, "Warning! Dangerous Beast on the loose. Reward: 2,000 silver pieces, dead or alive." It was accompanied by a grotesque illustration of Beast with a severe overbite, an elongated snout, and exaggerated antlers.

Icy dread settled in the pit of Belle's stomach. "He knows we're here."

"No, he doesn't." The mayor shook her head. "The Ringmaster's stepped up his advertising. His broadcast has been all over Nuzaran."

"Where did he get the money for this?" Belle gestured at the swirling flyers. "The circus makes money, but not on this scale."

"Let's get to the lab. We've got a lot of work to do." Maureen's mouth was set in a grim line.

Reward flyers rained down on Duchollow's town center during the rest of the drive. Maureen slowed her truck to a crawl as the papers flew around, sticking to windshields and hitting pedestrians.

After Belle held her armrest tightly during the stop-and-go traffic, she finally breathed a sigh of relief when they reached the back of Town Hall.

The mayor cut the engine and snatched her keys from the ignition. "What a mess," Maureen grumbled as she got out of the truck, storming to the back entrance to her lab.

Belle scrambled to follow her, pausing briefly as she scanned the horizon for the mystery airship. It was nowhere to be seen.

"Are you coming?" Maureen poked her head out of the door.

Nodding, Belle trudged forward, crunching a flyer beneath her boots. As she bent down to retrieve it, she wondered if the flyers had reached the cottage. She smoothed out the crumpled paper, hoping to discover new information with a closer reading, but no such luck. Wrinkling her nose, she carefully folded the paper and pocketed it. Beast needed to know about this.

Inside, the lab had been radically transformed since Belle's last visit. If it wasn't for the crowded bookshelves lining the walls, she'd have thought they'd wandered into a different room. There were no more hazardous piles of prototypes and parts strewn across the floor. Even the schematics formerly covering the work tables were tucked away, replaced by neat rows of glass vials. An odd chair with visible gears poking out of its high back was pushed up next to the table. A chalkboard had been moved to the front and center of the room, featuring incomprehensible equations written in chaotic handwriting.

"Have a seat in the examination chair. I'll be with you momentarily." Maureen opened a worn cabinet on the far edge of the room and rummaged through it.

Belle warily sat in the strange chair near the chalkboard. An adjustable metal lamp hung directly overhead, but it was currently switched off. After easing into the rigid seat, she soon grew restless. Wondering what else was new in the lab, she looked around, only to blush moments later when her gaze landed on the supply closet she and Beast had hidden in. She pointedly looked elsewhere, refusing to be distracted when her nerves were already in shambles.

Meanwhile, Maureen busied herself getting the lab prepared in a flurry of activity. The mayor stormed around, slamming cabinets and muttering to herself. She placed equipment on the work table near Belle's chair, including more clear vials, paperwork, and empty flasks. Just as Belle thought she was finished, she went into the closet.

"Is there anything I can help with? I feel useless sitting here." Belle shifted in her seat.

Maureen emerged with a syringe, needles, and a small medical kit. "I've got this. It won't be much longer."

"At the risk of you stabbing me with the syringe, may I ask you a question?" Belle unsuccessfully tried to peek at the typeset forms laying on the work table.

"You can ask whatever you wish," the mayor replied as she prepped the needle. "However, there are some things I'm not free to discuss due to their delicate nature. No offense intended."

"Why are you really helping me and Beast? You and Captain Charity have gone out of your way for us. It will be impossible to repay you for your kindness. We appreciate everything, but we don't understand it."

Maureen gave her a sidelong glance. "I believe Darling has already told you some of my past."

So much for getting a direct answer. Belle wanted to hit her head against the table. Instead, she asked, "Is it because Beast is one of Delphine's creatures? We fought the Hounds. I don't think it's too much of a stretch to say they came from the same creator."

Maureen inhaled sharply. "I can't say for certain Beast is one of her creations, but the thought crossed my mind. He looks like the sort of thing she'd create, though the Maker knows why she does such things. Creating and meddling with life is...messy."

"Is that something you're experienced in?" Now that she was finally getting some answers, Belle pressed on. Whatever news she could glean about Beast's origin, she would take it back to him. Now she wished she had let Beast come with her.

"Not in the same way that woman has, no. The closest I ever came to creation was Damek. And that's it. I'd never create another sentient automaton again. The implications are too complicated." The mayor's expression turned stony.

"Beast needs to know if Delphine could be responsible. He suspects her after Captain Charity told us about her, but he doesn't know for sure." Her eyes narrowed. "If you think he's Delphine's work...Is he in danger of being dissected by you in the name of science? Or is he a pawn for you to use against your enemy?"

Maureen blanched. "No, I want to help him, regardless of Delphine's involvement. Something terrible happened to him, whether it was a natural mutation from ether-poisoning or something done deliberately to him. He needs help before he deteriorates."

"What do you mean deteriorate?" Belle frowned. "In the time he's been with me, his speech has improved. He barely spoke a word when we first met. If anything, he seems to be regaining his humanity."

"That could be because he trusts you. If he had no one to talk to, why would he use his voice?" Maureen placed the syringe on a metal tray before picking up a pen and a paper. "As for the deterioration, yes, that's a concern for ether-poisoning, especially if he has some typical form of it. I thought you'd realize that with your condition."

"Realize what, exactly?" Growing dread coiled in her belly, as if her body already knew what the mayor was going to tell her.

Pity filled Maureen's umber eyes. "You get headaches, don't you? Have they increased frequency?"

Belle shrugged. "It's impossible for me to tell if my headaches are from my condition or if it's stress."

"Fair enough." The mayor scribbled a note. "When did the Ringmaster take you again?"

"Ten, nearly eleven years ago. Why?"

"I can't think of any cases like yours. It's almost as if leaving partially stabilized the deterioration, but without proper research, I have no way of knowing for certain."

At the calculating glint in the other woman's eyes, Belle shrank back. "Perhaps I should have asked if I'm in danger of being dissected."

"Sorry, I didn't tell you those things to worry you. I need to make sure I have all the relevant information. I want to heal you, if you'll let me."

"Can you tell me about the cure? Will I lose my strength?"

"Once I have an elixir formulated for you, you'll undergo at least one blood transfusion. Likely, you'll have multiple procedures as the cure runs its course." The mayor swept a rogue braid that had fallen in front of her face back behind her ear. "As for your strength, I don't know if you'll still have that or not. It could be a permanent result of the ether-poisoning, some kind of mutation, or the result of years of hard labor." She jotted down another note. "Your strength is an unknown variable."

Belle leaned forward. "Do you think I should pursue the cure? If you were me, what would you do?"

"I'd get the cure. I wouldn't risk my health, especially with loved ones to protect."

Belle let out a shuddering breath. "Let's get the analysis done, then. I'll think about it. If I'm eligible, I mean."

Maureen readied her pen. "Before I get started, I need to ask you a couple more questions."

Belle tilted her head as she stared at the mayor. What else could she possibly need to know? "Go ahead."

"Is there any chance you're pregnant?"

"What? No!" Belle's face grew far too hot as she gaped at the mayor, aghast. "Beast and I share the same room, but we haven't, I mean…" The words died on her lips as she gestured with her hands.

Maureen choked back a shocked laugh as she wrote a note. "Two things, I didn't say Beast, you did. Second, I'm not here to judge you. I just need to know all the variables for a cure. A baby would complicate things."

"Oh, I see." Belle folded her hands and put them in her lap primly, keeping her gaze down.

"Moving on," the mayor said, flipping the page over. "You were born in a mining town, correct?"

"Yes, Aetherbourne. I haven't been back since I was taken away."

"And you worked the mines as a child?"

A lump settled in her throat. "Yes, I did."

Maureen patted Belle's trembling hand. "That's all I need for today. May I take some blood samples?"

Belle nodded, rolled up her sleeve, and looked away while Maureen drew blood. The slight pinch of the needle was all she felt as she stared at the bookcase, wishing she could read the faint titles from her seat.

"All finished." Belle turned her attention back to Maureen. Two vials filled with her dark shimmering blood sat on the work table behind the mayor. "Let me get you bandaged up."

As Maureen bandaged her forearm, Belle asked, "When will you know if the treatment is viable for me?"

"It should only take a couple of days at most. I have a swatch test of sorts." Maureen paused her ministrations. "I will say this is the first time I've seen ether-poisoned blood that hue. It's interesting, but it doesn't mean the cure won't work. It's just another variable to solve for."

"Thank you."

"Let's get you some food before you head home."

"I'd appreciate that. I want to clean up first, if that's all right."

"There's a small powder room over there." Maureen pointed at another door in the lab, next to the closet.

"Thank you." Belle stood slowly, feeling woozy. As her vision swam, the room appeared to spin.

Maureen caught her by the elbow. "Are you going to make it alone? If you can't manage, I'll bring a washcloth for you."

Belle shook her head. When the room stopped spinning, she responded. "I'll be fine."

Once inside the bathroom, Belle closed the door behind her and turned on the faucet. She needed a moment with her thoughts before the ride home and Beast's inevitable questions. The cool water running over her hands grounded her as she slowly inhaled and exhaled. She splashed her face for good measure.

After drying off, Belle almost felt like her usual self when the loud bang of a door opening was audible through the closed door. It was impossible to tell if it came from the secret door to Maureen's office or the back entrance. Heart racing, she braced against the door as she strained to hear what was going on. Surely, anyone with access to the lab would be safe, but the unknown presence still made her nervous.

Two pairs of footsteps sounded familiar: a pair of boots tapping rapidly on the wooden floor and the other heavy and mechanical.

"Maureen!" Captain Charity's voice boomed.

Belle smiled, feeling foolish for her paranoia, and reached for the door handle. She froze at Maureen's response.

"Not now, Darling." The mayor's low voice sounded like a warning.

"No, it's going to be now." Captain Charity sounded uncharacteristically gruff.

Belle clamped a hand over her mouth, silencing her gasp.

"Do you really think this is wise?" Damek's calm, tinny voice piped up.

"Doesn't matter. We're running out of time. Maureen, either you've got to deal with the Ringmaster, or I will. This has to end," the captain commanded.

Silence fell as Belle tightened her grip on the door handle.

"Maker's moldy knickers, Darling. I'm not alone right now." Maureen's exasperation was audible. "Can't this wait?"

Pulse thrumming, Belle flung open the door. "No, it can't. What do you mean by handling the Ringmaster? What's going on?" She looked between the captain and the mayor. "I need answers. I'm tired of being left in the dark."

"I told you this wasn't wise," Damek muttered, but no one paid attention to the automaton.

Captain Charity and Maureen stared at Belle, both wearing identical guilty expressions.

Belle glowered. "I'm waiting. Tell me why you're running out of time."

"This isn't what it looks like." Captain Charity lifted her hands, palms up. Her sheepish smile didn't reach her troubled eyes.

"Enlighten me. What does this look like?" Despite the confidence in her voice, Belle's stomach churned wildly as she pressed her lips into a firm line to keep them from trembling.

"We haven't betrayed you. We would never." Beads of sweat dotted Maureen's brow.

"You could have fooled me. You're dealing with the Ringmaster? Did he finally name a price you couldn't refuse?" Part of Belle wanted to leave immediately, but she needed answers. She hoped Beast was still safe at home.

Unless it was too late, and someone had already captured Beast.

"Never mind, I'm leaving." Belle clumsily lumbered toward the exit, ignoring the stunned expressions of the others.

"Now you're being unwise." The solenoids in Damek's neck whirred as he shrugged. "Humans."

Belle squared her shoulders. It was a relief to see the automaton back to his functional self, but she was too upset to say as much. "I'm not leaving Beast to be taken."

Captain Charity's eyes bulged. "What are you talking about?"

Belle reached for the back door's handle. "You said you were going to deal with the Ringmaster. It sounded like you were going to take him up on the reward money."

"What? No. If I wanted to be rid of you two, I'd have turned the *Figment* around as soon as I found you in the cargo hold." The captain's curls bounced as she shook her head vigorously. "I'm going to confront the Ringmaster. He needs to be stopped, permanently."

Belle's arm holding the door handle went limp as she dropped her hand in surprise and her jaw went slack. Voice barely above a whisper, she faced the captain. "Why would you do such a thing? He's better connected than you think. If you fail, he'll come straight back here."

Maureen nodded, the copper beads on her braids catching the light and sparkling. "See? I told you it was a terrible plan."

"Do you really think he's going to give up after dropping thousands of flyers? He did that here. We're in the middle of nowhere. What do you think he did in the bigger cities?" Captain Charity threw her hands up as she faced the mayor. "He's left them nowhere to hide."

"I'm sure Belle's come to the same conclusion." Maureen folded her arms. "But running after him isn't going to fix it. It could end badly for everyone."

"Then what's your plan?" The captain retrieved a crumpled flyer displaying the caricature of Beast from her coat pocket and waved it at the mayor. "Because I don't think he's going to stop with these. This was an opening shot."

"I'm formulating one." Maureen frowned deeply as she eyed the flyer.

"What makes you think you'd stop him?" Belle asked. "Before our escape, the Ringmaster always got what he wanted. Last time we spoke, he threatened to kill Beast if he wouldn't perform his act. It wouldn't be the first time he's killed."

Memories of the slain circus tiger and the Ringmaster's

triumphant, bloody sneer came flooding back. Belle shook her head. Now wasn't the time to grieve.

"I can be persuasive." Captain Charity lifted her chin as she struck a power pose, hands on her hips. Seeing Belle's incredulous expression, she amended, "And if that fails, there's always this." She loosely grabbed the hilt of her sheathed electric saber. It was the first time Belle had seen the saber since the *Figment* landed in Duchollow.

"You don't know him the way I do. He's got a small army of henchmen." Belle pointed at the automaton. "And don't let him catch sight of Damek. He'd take him, too, given the chance."

Damek's eyes flashed a warning orange. "I don't want to join the circus." He clutched the captain's arm. "Please don't make me go."

"Damek isn't going on your crusade, Darling." A vein on Maureen's forehead throbbed.

"So you'd have me face him alone? Fine." Captain Charity drew herself up to her full height, which was still several inches shorter than the other woman.

"No, I wouldn't have you go at all." Maureen scowled.

Captain Charity looked at Belle expectantly. "What about you? Do you honestly think the Ringmaster is going to quit?"

"No, but why do you care so much? What's in it for you?" Belle couldn't fathom why the captain was so determined to confront the Ringmaster. It wasn't as if he was going to go door-to-door in the town looking for her and Beast. The Ringmaster still had a show to put on, and his funds weren't infinite. Why risk what peace they'd found?

"I thought we were friends. My mistake." Hurt flashed in the captain's eyes.

Captain Charity's pained expression tugged on Belle's heartstrings. She opened and closed her mouth, but she didn't know what to say. Belle's resolve crumpled as her dull headache flared into sharp pain. She winced, pinching the bridge of her nose.

"Do what you want, but the Ringmaster won't quit. I've known people like him." Captain Charity pivoted with unnatural stiffness. "Come on, Damek. Cinders needs to eat."

"Yes, Captain." The automaton dutifully followed the captain, but to Belle's surprise, they didn't exit through the back door.

Instead, Captain Charity marched to the bookcase in a section several feet away from the mayor's secret passage to her office. She removed an unassuming blue leather book from the third shelf and the bookcase swung open, revealing a new door with a flight of stairs going up. Captain Charity slammed the door behind her.

Belle stared at the perfectly disguised door. Another hidden passage behind the wall of books. How many doors were activated by the books?

"My quarters." Maureen gestured absently to the concealed door.

Belle blinked. "I'm leaving. I need to tell Beast about all this."

"Right. I'll get my keys after I clean this up." Maureen stood and began straightening the paperwork.

"I'm walking home."

"What? You still need to eat." The pen slipped and clattered on the floor, where the mayor ignored it as she stared in shock at Belle.

"I'll be fine." Belle turned away from Maureen and put her shaking hand on the back door handle. "But what about the bounty? What about getting caught?"

"It's not my face on the flyer. I need the space to think. Today has been too much and I don't know what to trust anymore." Belle put her shaking hand on the door handle.

"Wait! Do you even know how to get home?" Maureen wrung her hands. "It's a long walk, even if you were at your best."

"I remember." Belle pulled her hood up and straightened her cloak.

"It's your choice, but if you're protecting Beast, you need to be smart about protecting yourself, too."

Belle looked over her shoulder as she opened the door. "I'm aware."

Maureen sighed. "I'll message you the results when they're in. Please stay safe."

"I'm as safe as I can be." With that, Belle stepped out into Duchollow alone for the first time.

CHAPTER TWELVE

Belle gasped for breath as she stood against the wooden pillar of her covered porch, staring up at the three stone steps that led into the cottage. The trek from Maureen's lab was more arduous than she'd thought. Walking back alone on an empty stomach after having two vials of blood drawn had been a terrible plan. She'd hoped that her alone time would give her clarity about the captain and mayor's intentions, but it ended up being a miserable exercise that made her feel lightheaded and weak.

With a stifled groan, Belle trudged up the stairs. When she reached the second step, the front door flung open with a bang.

Beast lumbered out the door, his bloodshot eyes wild as he looked her over. "What happened?"

Before Belle could answer, her foot caught on the last step, and she careened forward, her cloak tangling around her legs.

Beast caught her, clutching her tightly to his chest, his claws biting into her arms through her shirt. He loosened his grip and looked down at her with a furrowed brow.

"Thank you." Belle's vision swam as she tried to focus on his tired eyes. He looked as exhausted as she felt. "Why didn't you sleep?"

Beast readjusted his hold as he lifted her, pulled her closer, and wrapped her cloak around her like a blanket. As he carried her over the threshold, his warm voice tickled her skin. "I'm glad I didn't," he murmured.

As she rested her head against his soft, russet-colored linen shirt, she felt the tension in her shoulders melt. She closed her eyes, but something in her trouser pocket kept jabbing into her thigh.

The reward flyer.

Bleary-eyed, Belle fished the folded paper out of her pocket. "I have to tell you something."

Beast hummed in agreement as he closed the door behind them. "Let's get you settled, then we'll talk."

Three steps inside, and Belle was fast asleep, clutching the flyer in her fist.

When Belle woke alone in her bed, it was dusk. The gauzy, white curtains billowed in her room, ushering in the chilly spring breeze. She gingerly propped up on her elbows before untangling her legs from the pile of blankets tucked around her. Her cloak was across the room, draped over the mahogany vanity with her boots lined up beneath it.

The flyer was nowhere to be seen.

Her stomach growled at the savory aroma wafting from the kitchen. Spurred on by her hunger and need to tell Beast about the conversations in the lab this morning, Belle padded barefoot through the cottage.

In the kitchen, Belle watched Beast for a moment as he precisely chopped potatoes for the stew bubbling on the stove. His paws mystified her. It was as if someone had taken large human hands and covered them with fur, replaced his fingernails with claws, and added leathery pads to his palms. The old scars Belle had glimpsed beneath his fur made her wonder if that was precisely what had happened.

Paw-hands may have presented some challenges, but he seemed to have no trouble utilizing Captain Charity's cooking advice. All the warm feelings watching Beast cook vanished as Belle tensed thinking about the captain. Their argument about the Ringmaster had her stomach in knots.

Belle gathered herself to inform Beast of all the lab discoveries, but her attention was caught by the crumpled reward notice beside the radio on the kitchen table. The illustrated caricature of Beast leered up at her from the table. At least she wouldn't have to tell him about the flyer.

"Do you want to sit down? I can bring you something to eat while dinner's cooking." Beast threw diced potatoes and a sprig of thyme into the pot.

Belle flushed. She'd forgotten about Beast's keen hearing. "Thank you for taking care of me. This morning...was a lot. I'll tell you about it."

She sat down and, spying the offending image again, crumpled it and threw it in the waste bin.

Beast brought her a fresh slice of honey-wheat bread topped with brie and a cup of water before returning to chop carrots.

Giving in to her hunger, Belle devoured the food and finished her drink, becoming aware of how parched she was. When she was finished, she turned her chair to face Beast.

"The Ringmaster hasn't given up on us." Belle grimaced. "There were hundreds of reward posters raining down on the town this morning, delivered via airship."

Beast nodded as he stirred the pot. "Maureen told me as much. I ended up radioing her after you passed out. I was worried about you."

The muscles on Belle's neck and shoulders tensed. "What'd she tell you?"

Beast turned around, wiping his paws on a tea towel.

"She told me about the flyers, a bit about the cure, and Captain Charity wanting to confront Ringmaster on her own. Maureen was worried that you'd left on your own and that you were upset. I'd like to hear your side."

Full of nervous energy, Belle pushed her empty plate forward and stood up to pace.

"I had my blood drawn to test my eligibility for the cure.

Afterwards, I was cleaning up in another room when Captain Charity came into the lab." Belle wrung her hands. "She told Maureen they were running out of time and that either she needed to deal with the Ringmaster or the captain would."

Beast raised his brows. "As in threaten him? Kill him?"

Belle gaped at Beast. "I thought she meant to turn us in for the bounty."

He tilted his head to the side as he studied her. "I trust your judgment, but have you considered the captain's tendency to stab first, ask questions later?"

Pursing her lips, Belle hesitantly nodded.

"I think if she had wanted to hand us over, she would have done so by now. Why would she bother to teach us to cook—especially me?" Beast pointed to himself.

"To win our trust?" Belle threw her hands up as she shrugged. "Perhaps it was a distraction to keep us occupied until she could negotiate a better price? I know she has helped us, but isn't Captain Charity an airship pirate?"

"Who got us medical help even when we were stowaways?" Beast shook his head.

Belle's frown deepened.

Beast sighed. "I'm not taking her side. I just don't want to sabotage your chance at a cure."

"What if there isn't a cure, and this is a clever ruse?" Her chin quivered.

"On our first day in Duchollow, you pointed out the couple with faded ether-poisoning marks, didn't you? Do you think that was staged?"

Belle halted her pacing, bracing herself against the wall as her shoulders slumped. "I don't know anymore."

Beast closed the gap between them, standing less than a foot away. "I know we don't know Maureen well at all, but do you really think she'd go through the expense of housing and feeding us for weeks for the reward money?"

Closing her eyes as she tried to settle her jumbled thoughts, Belle released a shuddering breath. "I wish I knew. It never would have occurred to me that Captain Charity would want to face the

Ringmaster on our behalf. What if I've ruined everything?" After a pause, she added, "Maureen said she'd still let me know if I'm eligible for the cure, but I'm even less sure about it now."

"Do you have to decide today?"

Opening her eyes, Belle stared at Beast. "Why?"

Beast shrugged. "If no one is beating down our door now, isn't it possible we're still safe?"

"Do you think we're safe?" Belle searched his eyes. "You're more at risk than I am. I don't want to endanger you for a cure that may or may not exist. Even if it is real, it sounds complicated."

"Don't you want to be cured?"

A hysterical chuckle escaped from Belle's lips before she clamped her mouth shut. "Sorry. Yes, I'd love to be rid of my ether-poisoning, but either I can't trust the one with the cure or I've blown my chances with my doubts."

"It doesn't sound like you ruined anything. Maureen's going to tell you the results within the next few days." He tilted his head. "Why are you so worried?"

Belle ran her fingers through her tousled hair. "I don't know what the answer is. Maybe we should just go back to how things were before, hiding out here and focus on finding a way to pay them back for their kindness. If they let us stay, I mean. The people I grew up with—" Her breath caught as she gulped, remembering the agony of her mother's final days. While she was terrified of the same fate, she had a hard time believing that there was a cure that could have saved countless Aetherbourne miners. "My symptoms aren't nearly as bad as those the people I knew back home suffered. Why risk what we safety have? Maybe nothing has to change."

"I don't want everything to stay the same, dammit," Beast growled, pressing his fist against the wall next to Belle, his arm protectively over her. "I want—" His eyes flickered down to her lips, lingering for a beat. He closed his eyes, slowing his breathing. When he opened his eyes again, they shone with a breathtaking warmth. "I want you to be happy and healthy. Don't you want the same?"

Belle's mouth went dry as she met his intense gaze. "Yes," she whispered.

Beast gave her a feral grin. "Good, we agree. It's your decision, but if you want my opinion, I think you should go through with the procedure."

"If the mayor says I'm eligible."

"That's true. And I'll watch over you in recovery."

"But what if something goes wrong or I can't get back to you? Or the Ringmaster comes?" A million other anxious thoughts bubbled to the surface as she fidgeted, picking at a loose thread on her sleeve.

Beast moved his paw to cup the side of her face, tracing her cheekbone with the pad of his thumb. "There's nothing that can keep you from me as long as you want me around. You're strong, but not invincible. I'll tear through this town to find you if anyone tries to separate us."

"Promise?" Belle's voice trembled.

"Promise." Beast's eyes flickered to her mouth again, but when he leaned in, he rested his forehead against hers.

Belle wrapped her arms around his strong waist, pulling him closer. Loud sputtering noises emitted from the stove. Reluctantly, she withdrew her arms as Beast turned to survey the damage.

"I better put that on simmer." He scratched the back of his neck before shuffling to the oven.

After several deep breaths, she straightened her shirt and smoothed her hair. When she finally felt presentable, she sat back down. She was grateful for the respite, even if she had a life-altering choice hanging over her head.

As Beast served her a steaming bowl of stew, he asked, "Why don't we find something fun to take your mind off things?"

"Like what?" Belle blinked. They rarely ventured beyond their property's fence.

"I'll think of something. It'll be a surprise."

Belle stared incredulously. "I think I've had enough surprises for today."

"Well, this will be a good one for tomorrow. Trust me." Beast gave her a winning smile, complete with crooked canines.

Warmth bloomed in Belle's chest as she reached her hand out to hold his paw. "Thank you. I'm looking forward to it."

The midmorning sun streamed through the open window, warming Belle as she read a moody fantasy while reclining in a cozy nest of pillows and blankets on her bed. It promised to be a beautiful day, with milder weather finally making an appearance. He'd promised more food later but needed time to prepare it. He'd sent Belle back to bed with books, coffee, and buttered bread to tide her over while he worked on her surprise. The small plate Beast had brought her earlier sat on the nightstand, with only crumbs remaining from her light breakfast.

Belle was touched by the gesture. He'd actually slept last night instead of keeping his usual nocturnal habits. Though she was anxious to hear from Maureen about her eligibility, Beast's cheerful whimsy made her smile.

The pampering didn't hurt, either. He'd rounded up every extra blanket and pillow he could find in the cottage to provide her with the perfect reading nook. After yesterday's events, it was a luxury to sleep in and read at her leisure.

Taking another sip of coffee, Belle turned the page of the novel. The heroine was brooding again because her lover had revealed he'd been cursed to turn into a wolf every full moon. At least he was fully human most of the time.

Soft knocking broke Belle's concentration. Flushing slightly, she peered over her book at the closed door.

"Come in." Her lips curved into a smile as Beast cracked the door open, his large frame blocking her view of the kitchen.

"Everything's ready." He radiated enthusiasm as he beamed. Bits of flour clung to his evergreen shirt. Looking down at his soiled clothes, he furrowed his brows as he attempted to wipe off the powder. "Well, almost. Wait a moment, please."

Beast closed the door behind him and rummaged through his wardrobe, retrieving a fresh blue shirt. He hastened to take off his shirt, grunting as his antlers became entangled, and replaced it with a fresh shirt while Belle watched curiously from behind her book.

He turned to face her after smoothing his shirt. "Ready now."

Noting her page before closing her novel, Belle climbed down from her reading nest. "Can't wait."

Beast placed a paw on her shoulder. "Hold on, I need something to cover your eyes."

Belle tilted her head and raised her brows. "What kind of surprise is this?"

"A fun one." He looked around the room, his frown deepening.

"What if you cover my eyes with your paws?"

"That should work. May I?" He held up his paws, smiling sheepishly.

Belle softened at his hopeful expression. He hadn't been so playful since their first night in the cottage when he'd asked her to dance during their cleaning break. "Yes."

The heat from Beast's body directly behind Belle sent an electric thrill through her as he covered her eyes with his paws. She fought the urge to whimper when his leather pads brushed against her skin as he pushed her hair back.

"Let's go." Beast's voice rumbled in her ear, his breath tickling her.

She could only nod in response, afraid anything she said would come out as a squeak. Beast carefully guided her out of the room, opening the door after admonishing her to keep her eyes shut.

As they continued down the short hallway, a string quartet played a tranquil sonata with delicate notes over the radio. The scent of florals mingled with savory aromas.

"Open your eyes." Beast withdrew his paws, leaving Belle bereft, until her eyes adjusted to the low lighting.

The dimly lit kitchen was unrecognizable. Candles and rose petals were scattered throughout the room with fully bloomed, bright red roses in an empty glass bottle forming a centerpiece on the table. Plates were filled with pancakes, slices of marmalade bread, ham, and eggs. A bowl full of oranges and apples sat between their plates. The radio, playing soft violin music, had been relocated to the sitting room.

Tears pricked at the corners of Belle's eyes as she faced Beast. She pressed a kiss against the side of his muzzle. "Thank you," she murmured. She leaned back to look at him. "Where did you find roses and fruit this time of year?"

Beast's arms wrapped around her waist. "You're welcome. While I was fixing up the greenhouse, I found some hidden gems. I thought I'd give you a tour later."

"I'd love that."

His eyes sparkled with pride. "Let's eat. We have the whole day to ourselves."

As Beast pulled out Belle's chair, the radio crackled with an all-too-familiar static, extinguishing the music.

"Hello?" Maureen's hesitant voice cut in.

Belle swore under her breath. "It's too soon." Her eyes widened. "I wonder if the test failed."

"Maybe it's good news?" Beast looked forlornly at their plates, the hot food still steaming. He sighed. "I thought we'd have more time."

"Is anyone there?" Maureen grew louder, drowning out the faint white noise.

With growing trepidation, Belle made her way to the radio. Bending down, she pressed the communication button. "We're here. Is everything okay?"

"Yes." Maureen cleared her throat. "The preliminary results of your blood test are in. You're eligible for the cure."

Belle's vision swam as the mayor's words sank in. She braced herself on the edge of the end table as she swayed. With a trembling hand, she pressed the button again. "I thought it took two days for results."

Beast pulled up a chair for Belle. She mouthed her thanks as she sat down, then turned her attention back on the radio.

He crouched behind her, leaning in close as he kept one arm protectively around Belle.

"I didn't want to get your hopes up. The test can be done in a matter of hours. If the results aren't positive before the end of the second day, the procedure is likely to fail. I was worried since your case was unusual that I was going to get mixed results, but the vials passed with flying colors this morning." Maureen's voice hitched. "The results were the same every time I retested."

Belle released a shaky breath. "So, what's next?"

"That all depends on you. I can get started today if you're still interested. You don't have to decide now, but I'm at a critical point in my project for the Festival. If we don't start now, it might be a couple months before I can help you."

"What about Captain Charity and everything we talked about in the lab? Why would you still help me after that?" Belle's knuckles whitened as she clenched her fists.

"My willingness to help you isn't contingent on anything. I truly want to see you happy and healthy." The mayor grew quiet. "As far as Darling is concerned, I can't repair the rift between you two. That's up to both of you."

"One moment, please."

Belle looked at all the effort Beast had put into her surprise. The food sat uneaten on the table, the candles still flickering. They hadn't done anything he'd planned. She was dying to see what he'd done to the rundown greenhouse.

Did she even trust Maureen? After her conversation with Beast yesterday, she didn't know what to think anymore.

"What do you want to do?" He gently squeezed her shoulder, bringing her out of her jumbled thoughts.

"I want to believe the cure will work, but I wasn't ready for this today." Belle gestured to the table. "You planned all this, and I didn't even have time to think about what I'd do if my results came back eligible."

He shook his head. "I can always surprise you another time. Don't let me stand between you and the cure. We'll have all the time in the world afterward."

She gave him a tremulous smile. "Am I crazy for trusting Maureen?"

"She could have turned us in the moment we landed in Duchollow, but she didn't. I think you owe it to yourself to hope for the best." Beast squeezed her shoulder again before releasing her.

Belle pressed the radio button. "Sorry, I needed to think. Are you there?"

"Yes." The tension in Maureen's voice was palpable.

"I'd like to start the cure, but can I eat first?"

"Of course! It'll take me a couple of hours to prepare and have Mr. Cadwell clear my schedule. I'll radio when it's time." The mayor sighed. "Any further questions?"

Belle leaned in to press the button, but Beast covered her hand with his. She looked up at him, her brows furrowed.

"Do you want me to go with you? I can watch over you." Beast's expression was anxious.

"Maybe? But those flyers were distributed across the town yesterday." She rubbed the back of her stiff neck.

"We'll be fine if we take the back way in. What do you want?"

"Is it selfish that I want you there?" Belle wrung her hands. "I don't want you in danger, but it would be good to see your face first when the procedure's done."

"This face?" Beast pointed to his muzzle and antlers, raising his brows. Mirth twinkled in his eyes.

"Yes, that face." She was sorely tempted to stick out her tongue. "I'll ask."

Belle pressed the button. "Is there anything I need to do in advance, and can Beast come with me?"

Only static answered. Seconds ticked by, and Belle wondered if they'd lost the connection.

Finally, Maureen answered. "Pack an overnight bag in case there are complications." The mayor cleared her throat. "Beast can come as well, as long as he knows not to interfere. The procedure is complex and delicate."

Beast rolled his eyes. He snarled, "I know the difference between surgery and torture."

Belle suppressed a smile before pressing the communication button. "He understands. Thank you."

"You're welcome. I'll see you both later." Her words were punctuated by a click, signaling the end of her broadcast.

After a moment of static, the music resumed. The sonata transitioned to the next movement, a frenetic piece with jagged notes.

"So, this is happening, huh?" Butterflies fluttered in Belle's stomach as she gulped.

Beast helped her to her feet. "You should eat, then we can pack. Are you okay?"

Belle met his gaze as she nodded. "I don't know what to believe about Maureen or the captain, but I think they mean well." She bit her lip. "I wish we could have had more time today."

Beast brushed back the loose strands of her hair and tucked them behind her ear. His palm lingered, straying down to cup the side of her face. "I do, too, but I don't regret it. I'm glad you're getting this opportunity."

Belle flushed. "Thank you."

Wordlessly, Beast led her back to the table. The food was divine, though neither felt like talking much. After their meal, Belle did her best to drive away thoughts of medical equipment and everything that could go wrong. She threw her energy into packing extra clothes in her worn knapsack, but it wasn't enough to stop her from trembling.

Beast caught her shaking hands. "Anything I can do to help?" He rubbed her palms, soothing her nerves.

Her eyes glistened. "I'm scared to hope this will work."

Beast squeezed her hands. "Come what may, I'll be there for you." He released her hands and held up the first fairy tale book Belle had read to him at the circus. "Look what I found. I'll read to you while you recover."

Overwhelmed by the thoughtful gesture, Belle could barely whisper, "Thank you."

They embraced, clinging to each other until the radio crackled in the other room.

Maureen's voice echoed in the cottage. "Everything's prepared. I'm on my way."

Belle's fingers tangled in the back of Beast's shirt as she held on tighter.

Beast traced her jawline lightly before leaning in to rest his forehead against hers. "You'll do amazing. It'll be okay."

CHAPTER THIRTEEN

O nly a few minutes into preparations in the lab, Belle was seized by panic. Leather restraints bit into her wrists, escalating her heart rate as she hyperventilated. No one had mentioned when discussing the procedure that she would be bound.

Breathe in, breathe out.

Find something else to focus on.

The metallic contraption in Maureen's lab, which towered over the tilted examination chair, hummed loudly. The machinery housed the flasks of a shimmering elixir that would be fed into her veins at a controlled rate using compressors. Harsh light from the overhead lamp heightened Belle's discomfort as the stiff chair creaked beneath her.

Don't think about the straps.

Memories came unbidden of her early days in the circus. As a child, Belle had rebelled against the Ringmaster, using her strength to throw weights at the horrible man. With the click of the button on his cane, shocks had pulsed through her body, emitting from her copper ankle bracelet until she collapsed. When she'd come to, she was strapped to a rickety old chair with ether-laced chains, left alone in the dark. It didn't take many sessions for her to learn that fighting back led to pain and isolation.

Belle squeezed her eyes shut. Blocking out the view of the restraints helped, but she could still feel the leather and metal buckles against her bare arms. She was dressed in a sleeveless smock for the procedure, affording her some modesty while allowing Maureen access to key veins.

"Is this necessary?" Beast bellowed, his words reverberating in the lab.

Flinching, Belle opened her eyes, careful to avoid looking at her wrists.

"I'll send you home if you don't stop roaring," Maureen warned, her eyebrows forming a deep V behind her clear splash guard. Her words were muffled by a medical face mask and her beautiful braids were twisted into a high up-do.

With hunched shoulders, Beast perched on his stool next to Belle. The glare on his tinted goggles made his expression difficult to read. He reached for Belle's hand, stopping short of touching her. Leaning forward, he spoke in a low, soothing tone as if he were speaking to a frightened animal. "What do you need?"

Belle reached for Beast's paw but was thwarted by the restraints around her wrist. He closed the distance, clasping his paw around her shaking hand.

She focused on the rough texture of Beast's paw, and her breath slowed. Her throat was tight, but she choked out, "The restraints."

Maureen was instantly at Belle's other side, examining the straps.

"Does it pinch?" The mayor's dexterous fingers worked at the buckles, loosening the fit.

Beast released Belle's hand, moving out of Maureen's way as she checked the other wrist.

Belle shook her head. "No. Back in the circus, the Ringmaster, he…" She gulped. "In my early days at the circus, if I misbehaved, he'd bind and abandon me in darkness for hours, sometimes for a day or more. I don't take well to being restrained."

Beast glared at the mayor as he returned to Belle's side. Sitting back down on the stool, he grabbed Belle's hand and rubbed her knuckles. "I'm so sorry this brought back horrible memories."

A harsh chuckle escaped Belle's lips. "I feel foolish getting upset over some straps like I'm a child again."

"You're not foolish. I wish the restraints weren't necessary." Maureen's voice caught. "If you're not held in place, though, you could hurt yourself during the procedure."

"Can you wait to use them until she's asleep?" Beast's voice rumbled.

The machine droned, filling in the silence as Maureen considered the request. "I can, but the timing will be tricky. It'd be best if they're on before the medicine kicks in." She grimaced. "It's going to be intense."

"Take them off," Belle begged. "Please."

The straps slipped off, releasing the tightness in Belle's ribcage. Sensation returned to the rest of her body. She realized her cheeks were damp, but she didn't remember crying. "Thank you," she whispered as she rubbed her arms and drew them tight across her chest.

"You're safe." Maureen brushed back the loose strands of hair that had fallen across Belle's face.

Beast cleared his throat. "May I try something?"

Belle nodded, zeroing in on his face. The hums and whirs of the machinery in the background faded as she focused all her attention on him.

"I'm going to hold your wrists, so when it's time for the restraints, you won't notice the change, hopefully. Okay?"

A lump formed in Belle's throat as she lowered her arms back onto the armrests. "That should work."

Beast moved his stool closer to her chair and gently wrapped his paws around the angry red marks where she'd strained her wrists against the straps. The leathery pads of his paws, coupled with his woodsy scent, were familiar and comforting.

The tension in Belle's body melted. "Much better."

"Don't get any fur in my way. The last thing we need is cross-contamination," Maureen grumbled, but there was no bite to her words. Her eyes crinkled as she looked at them. "I'm inserting the tubes soon after I retrieve the blood for the transfusion."

As Maureen retrieved the pouch of blood and connected it to the machine with a pop, Belle craned her neck to watch.

"Where did you get the blood?" Belle asked, desperate to keep herself distracted.

Maureen's shoulders tensed as she froze for a moment. After checking one of the myriad dials on the machine, she kept her back turned to Belle as she moved onto the next knob, twisting it until it hissed. "Captain Charity volunteered. She has a universal blood type that will work with yours."

Unease and guilt gnawed at Belle. She hadn't spoken to the captain since their fight, but the captain continued to surprise her with her generosity. "Blood types?"

"I'll explain blood types to you another time, but yes, it matters." Maureen readjusted the leather apron over her clothes before picking up a syringe with a long needle. "Ready to begin?"

Belle took a deep breath. "I'm ready." She reclined, wishing she could see Beast instead of the intricate copper ceiling tiles engraved with a botanical design.

As if Beast had read her mind, he leaned down to brush his muzzle against her hand. "You're not alone." His warm breath sent shivers down her back, mercifully distracting her from the sound of Maureen prepping the tubes.

Belle squeezed her eyes shut, unwilling to watch the needles enter her arms.

The medicine burned as it entered her bloodstream. Belle barely registered the restraints locking in place as a scream ripped from her throat.

Beast smoothed back the hair that clung to her damp forehead and whispered in her ear. "I'm here. The sleep medicine will work soon."

Wincing, Belle opened her eyes. "It burns."

Beast rubbed her shoulders. "I know and I'm sorry it hurts. Let the medicine work and sleep."

As Belle nodded, her eyelids grew heavy. She fell into oblivion, too exhausted to worry about the restraints anymore.

Dreams and memories soon filled the void.

Veins of ether crisscrossed through dreary bedrock. The rough terrain poked through young Belle's thin, hole-riddled shoes as she skipped down the mine, swinging her lantern. In the distance, her tools had been abandoned by the section she was supposed to be working. Her parents were too busy extracting the precious element to wonder where their only daughter was.

Her foot caught on a loose stone, and she tumbled forward, crashing into the ground as her lantern went out, plunging her into darkness.

She was all alone.

Belle slipped back into consciousness long enough to see the mayor tinkering with the dials to adjust the machine.

"She's waking up too soon." Maureen grunted, turning a knob as the machine hissed.

Beast's paws caressed Belle's temples as his voice rumbled. "Sleep."

Her eyes fluttered closed.

Memories jumbled together. Mother read to her by the fire, tutting at the fresh ether-poisoning marks crisscrossing Belle's face. Her skin grew paler every day, but it wasn't only Belle's condition worsening.

Mother took to wearing high-collar, long-sleeved shirts and gloves, even when it was humid. Belle spied black spider-web veins across Mother's hands when she removed her gloves before bed.

The veins on Father's forearms were getting darker, too, and extending all the way up his arms and across his neck as if the ether-poison were strangling him.

Belle writhed in the examination chair, thrashing against the restraints, as liquid fire burned through her veins.

"Why isn't it working?" Beast's panicked voice drowned out the noisy machinery.

"It's part of the process!" Maureen replaced an empty blood bag with a fresh one and turned a dial. "Give it time."

Cool relief entered Belle's veins, sending her back to her disjointed dreams.

Memories mixed and morphed into nightmares, turning into a confusing kaleidoscope. Hounds snipped at Belle as she stood in the center ring, lifting three acrobats in a demented waltz while the Ringmaster pointed his cane at her and laughed.

Beast was in chains while Hounds snarled and snapped at his limbs.

The spotlight burned as the mechanical unicorn trotted toward her, chasing the Hounds away before exploding, incinerating everything in its path.

Ragged gasps of breath escaped from Belle as her whole body felt like it was engulfed in flames.

"We're losing her!" Maureen's foggy octagonal glasses were askew underneath her face shield. "This isn't supposed to happen!"

"No." Beast gripped Belle's shoulders.

The machine whined as Maureen pulled a lever, slapping the

side of it before the compressor wheezed, pumping a stronger dose of elixir with each hiss.

Beast's voice was in Belle's ear. "Stay with me. I'm right here. It'll be finished soon."

Belle drifted off.

Happier memories floated to the surface, a disjointed but welcome change.

Dancing with Beast in the kitchen.

Going on a stroll in the garden.

Curled up asleep on the *Figment*. Beast's arm slung protectively over her waist..

Belle woke to Beast's anxious eyes staring at her through his tinted goggles. All the lights in the lab were turned on at full brightness, stinging her eyes.

"Am I awake? Did it work?" Belle's voice cracked. Her sore mouth was parched.

"It worked. You went through hell, but it worked." Beast sighed. "You had us worried for a while."

"I knew you'd be fine." Maureen entered Belle's field of vision and handed her a water glass. Her mask and face shield were gone, leaving behind faint indentations on her smooth, dark skin. "Drink up. You lost a lot of fluids, even with the elixir in your veins."

"Thank you." The cool water soothed her raw throat.

"I'll turn down the lamps so you can see. Be right back." Maureen dimmed the lights and returned with a silver mirror with a floral border engraved in its handle.

Beast furrowed his brows at the ornate mirror but said nothing. Belle made a mental note to ask him about it later.

"Would you like to see the results? It's only the first procedure, but you have a lot to be happy about."

"Yes, please." Belle's hands shook as she accepted the mirror. She gasped when she saw her reflection.

Though remnants of ether-poisoning lingered, her veins were considerably lighter. Hints of color had returned to her translucent skin. Even her charcoal-colored hair had a healthier sheen to it.

"Thank you." Her voice cracked, and her eyes burned with unshed tears. "Could I have some more water, please?"

"On it." Beast left and returned with a full glass.

Belatedly, Belle realized as she sipped her water the straps had snapped. "I'm so sorry." She gestured at the broken restraints.

Maureen smiled. "I'm just grateful it worked. Let me get the equipment out of the way and we'll let you get some proper rest." The mayor busied herself with the machine, releasing the locks on the bottom, and wheeled it to the supply closet across the room.

Belle turned her attention back to Beast, who had disappeared from her field of vision after quickly placing the glass in her hands. "Beast? Where'd you go?"

"Here." His gruff voice was directly behind her.

"Come here. I told you I wanted to see your face first."

"You did already."

"Please?"

"Okay…" Beast's voice trailed off as he shuffled around the examination chair and stopped in front of Belle.

Her lips curved into a smile. "I told you I'd miss your face." Belle tilted her head as she stared, her eyes still adjusting to the light. "Beast?"

"Yes, Belle?"

"Where are your antlers?"

Beast stood before her fidgeting. His antlers had been cut down to his fur. Only two small stumps remained, and they were partially covered by his white fur.

On the work table across the room, his severed, twisted antlers rested underneath a clear glass dome. Nervous energy flowed through Belle as her eyes darted from the antlers on display and back to the stubs on Beast's head. She couldn't believe she hadn't noticed right away that they were missing, but between the lingering effects of the procedure and the bright lights, she had been at a disadvantage.

"Did you pay for my treatment with your antlers?" Belle gasped. "You didn't have to do that. I would have said no."

The gentle humming and occasional clanging of the lab machines filled the silence as Beast removed his tinted goggles and pocketed them. When he looked back at Belle, his expression was pained. "No, it wasn't anything like that. I wanted them gone."

"Oh." Belle leaned back in the stiff examination chair, wincing as the leather stuck to her bare legs. She couldn't wait to change out of the thin smock. "Why didn't you just say so? You were acting so strangely."

Beast scratched the back of his neck as he feigned interest in the visible iron gears of the clock hanging on the wall across the room. "I only glimpsed my reflection in the mirror when Maureen showed you the results of the elixir, but it startled me. I didn't want to shock you while you're recovering."

Belle furrowed her brows. "I suppose, but you still seem off. Are you sure there isn't something else going on?"

Beast looked back at the antlers. "While you were sleeping, Maureen approached me. She asked if the antlers were putting pressure on my skull. I told her they did, and she offered to remove them. She said she'd study them and search for clues about a cure for me. I wouldn't let her put me under while you were unconscious, so her removal options were limited. Eventually, I'll have her remove the stumps, but not until I know you're safe and fully healed."

"How is she going to get a cure from your antlers?" Belle shook her head. "I'm sorry. I didn't realize they were causing you pain."

Beast gave her a rueful smile. "How could you have known if I never told you about it? She's going to confirm if my antlers are organic or if my maker slapped them on me and called it a day."

Belle grimaced. "I see."

"I know it's not exactly a cure, but at least it helps me feel a little less...beastly." He shifted his weight, shoulders slumped.

"I get it. At least you're not hurt, right? And maybe something good will come of this."

Belle struggled to get out of the chair. Standing on wobbly legs, she stumbled over to Beast.

"Be careful. You might not be supposed to be up yet." Beast gulped as she neared him.

"I know, but I'm worried about you." Belle reached to hold Beast's paw, but he shrank back, his eyes downcast.

Appalled, she stepped back. "Did I do something wrong?"

Beast looked up, his posture stiffening. "No. Why?"

Belle cleared her throat as she fidgeted, wringing her wrist. "Forgive me if I've misread things, but did I offend you?"

Beast averted his gaze. "No. You're perfect."

"I am not."

"Look at you. You could have a better life in the town." Beast smiled wistfully as his eyes traveled up Belle's body before finally meeting her eyes. "Even after one treatment, you can barely tell you've had ether-poisoning. Soon, you won't match the description in the Ringmaster's reward. I'm holding you back by playing house with you. You shouldn't be shackled to a beast."

"You're more than a beast. I know your heart."

He snorted, looking away. "For all we know, I have a pig's heart."

Belle closed the gap between them, tracing her fingers along his jawline as she turned his face toward her. "You know that's not what I meant."

"What did you mean?" Beast's voice was gruff, but there was a spark of hope mingled with a yearning in his expression that tugged on her heartstrings.

"Would a beast prepare an elaborate meal and decorate the table with roses to cheer me up?" Belle pressed a kiss to the side of his muzzle, lingering for a moment. Her heart raced while she waited for a response, hoping she wasn't making things worse.

When Beast wrapped his arms around her waist, she tilted her head back to look at him, smirking. "Besides, a pig's heart wouldn't be likely. I don't think it'd keep up with your frame. No, you're human enough."

"I still think you could do better." He wrinkled his muzzle.

Belle sighed. "How many times do I have to prove that I like being with you?"

Beast opened his mouth, looking ready to argue, so she pressed on. "Don't worry. I'll keep proving it over and over again until it finally sinks in. As long as you want to be with me, I'll stay by your side."

"You're impossible." Despite his sullen words, he gave her a lopsided grin.

Pulling him flush against her body, she was sure Beast could feel her heart hammering through her flimsy smock. Heat radiated from him as he gave Belle an inscrutable look.

Beast leaned in, his low voice rumbling pleasantly in her ear and sending shivers down her back that had nothing to do with the breezy outfit she wore. "You know this means I won't let you go."

"You'd better not." Belle kissed the side of his muzzle again, playing with the fur on the back of his neck as Beast traced the small of her back.

"Oh, good. You're back on your feet." Maureen's dry voice cut in, startling Belle and Beast apart.

Even after they disentangled their limbs, Beast kept one arm around Belle's waist as they faced the mayor. She stood on the other side of the lab, poorly disguising her amusement as she coughed.

"Sorry for the interruption, but I wanted to check on my patients. We can cross standing off the list." Maureen gestured to the two armchairs and sofa tucked in the lab's corner. "Are you up for a quick chat?"

Reluctantly, Belle nodded as she crossed the room, smoothing the skirt of her smock on her way to the seating area.

Maureen waved Beast over. "You, too, please."

"Very well." Beast lumbered after them, oblivious to the fresh wrinkles on his linen shirt and his mussed fur.

The clock's ticking, coupled with the low hum of machinery, filled the silence as the mayor picked up the paperwork stacked haphazardly on the coffee table and shuffled through them.

"Has something happened?" Anxious thoughts bubbled to the surface of Belle's mind. She should have known disaster would strike the moment she was on the path to recovering from ether-poisoning. So much for finally catching a break.

Maureen cleared her throat, interrupting Belle's spiraling thoughts. "No, everything is fine. Aside from checking in on your recovery, I have a job offer for you if you're interested."

Belle leaned forward in her seat, her hand intertwined with Beast's. "I'm listening."

Maureen's gaze briefly darted to their joined hands before she shook her head. "Right. Before I tell you, Belle, how are you feeling? No dizziness or fever?"

"Other than some fatigue, I've never felt better." Belle's answer was honest, though she couldn't wait to test her strength again. Perhaps it was vanity, but she didn't want to lose her edge when the Ringmaster still had a bounty out for them.

"Fantastic." A wide grin spread across Maureen's face as she jotted down a note on her paper. "Duchollow hasn't had a public library in years, and I want to change that. There's a building leftover from the town's old days, but it hasn't been touched in decades. I was wondering if you'd like to restore it after you've finished your final treatment."

"Really?" Belle's pulse quickened. "What would it entail?"

"I'll give you the details later, but your first steps would be categorizing the current inventory and coordinating with contractors for repairs and remodeling. I won't lie to you. It needs extensive work and the books are decades out of date. Perhaps a trip to a wholesaler will be in order once it's ready?" Maureen steepled her fingers, leaning back in the overstuffed armchair.

"Wow." Belle's stomach fluttered as she turned to Beast. "What do you think?"

Beast rested his muzzle on his free paw. "I think it'd be the perfect job for you. Just be careful."

"Before I say yes, I'd love to see the library first. I don't want to over-promise what I can do," Belle said, turning back to the mayor. "It sounds like a dream, though."

"Let's plan on it in a few weeks. I should have some time before my project's deadline hits." Maureen adjusted her glasses as she focused her attention on Beast. "It might be a while before I have better answers for you, but I'm going to analyze your antlers soon. A blood sample would be helpful, too."

"Whatever you need." Beast squeezed Belle's hand. "As long as I can come back to Belle."

Maureen folded her hands in her lap as she nodded slowly, pursing her lips. "I'll collect the sample in the morning." She stood and stretched. "I'll set up sleeping quarters for you both so I can check Belle's vitals again in the morning. I know the lab isn't ideal, but I think it'll do for the night. In the meantime, I'll have dinner brought later for you, too, if you're hungry."

"Thank you so much." Belle's stomach rumbled.

"I'll go pick up dinner." Chuckling to herself, Maureen departed the lab.

After a wonderful dinner of mutton chops, sweetbread, and rice pudding, Belle and Beast settled in for the night. A section of the lab was sectioned off to create an impromptu guest room, which included a cot for Belle and a pallet of pillows and blankets for Beast, much like the one he had at home. A partition made of hanging sheets had been erected, blocking out the gas lights on the walls, dimmed in case they needed anything before morning.

Long after they'd said their good-nights, Belle lay awake in her cot, staring at the ceiling. She was afraid to close her eyes, worried her resurfaced memories would return.

Beast shifted on his pallet. "Can't sleep?"

Belle shook her head. "No. I don't want the nightmares to come back."

"They seemed terrible." More gently, Beast added, "At first, I thought it was the pain affecting you, but when you cried out about your parents, I thought it was more than that."

A lump formed in Belle's throat. "I remembered things I haven't thought about in years. I hope this doesn't happen every time."

"I hope so, too. At least it's only two more sessions and you'll be done."

"Thank you." Belle bit her lip as she debated telling Beast about the last part of her dreams. "In the end, it got better. During the end of the session, I thought I heard you calling my name, and the dreams shifted. It was bearable after that."

Nervously, she peeked at Beast. Barely making him out in the dark, Belle wished she had his night vision.

Beast was propped up on his side with his sheets dipped down, gathering around his hips. He was shirtless, having removed his shirt earlier, claiming the blankets were sufficient. Patting the pillows next to him, he asked, "Would you sleep better over here?"

Flushing, Belle nodded. She wasn't wearing the smock anymore, but her soft white nightgown was still on the thin side. Though they shared a room at home, they rarely slept at the same time, so she hadn't thought about her nighttime apparel. Even in the dark, she could feel Beast's eyes on her as she lifted the covers to get out of bed and padded over to his pallet.

Once she lay down next to Beast, he wrapped his arm around her.

"Better?" he asked, pulling her close.

"Much." Sighing, Belle snuggled in.

She was almost asleep, ready to drift into blissful dreams, when a door across the lab creaked open.

Beast startled awake, throwing the blankets off as he bolted upright.

Before he charged toward the source of the noise, Belle scrambled to grab his shoulder and, with her other hand, pressed a finger to his muzzle. She gestured to the sheet barrier, hoping his night vision would allow him to see what she meant.

Beast nodded, Belle's finger still on his mouth.

Wordlessly, they crept out of bed to peek behind the makeshift curtain. By the dimmed gas lights, Damek and Captain Charity exited from the door to Maureen's chambers, followed by Cinders trotting after them. The captain grunted as she pulled something heavy behind her.

"Are you sure this is wise?" Damek's tinny voice echoed in the lab. "It's the middle of the night."

"I'm aware." Captain Charity's voice was terse as she whispered back. "We need to leave now."

"Yes, Captain."

Cinders mewled plaintively as if answering her mistress.

With that, the trio left, exiting the lab's back entrance.

When the lock clicked, Belle turned to Beast. "What was that about?"

Beast shook his head. "Wherever they're going, she has her saber and a huge trunk."

CHAPTER FOURTEEN

Early the next morning, Belle and Beast anxiously waited in the lab's seating area for Maureen to wake up. When the door to the mayor's quarters creaked open, both Belle and Beast jumped to their feet. By the time the mayor descended the stairs, they were by the door.

Lifting her glasses to rub the sleep out of her eyes, Maureen squinted at the clock across the room. "What time is it?" She yawned as she adjusted her frames. "It's not that late. What's wrong?"

"Captain Charity left with Damek in the middle of the night and we were worried something had happened. Neither of us slept much afterward." Belle wrung her hands.

A shadow crossed Maureen's face before she gave them a disarming smile. "She's like that when she's on a job. It wouldn't be the first time she's left at a strange hour when she's heading to a remote destination. Darling is off to procure rare parts for my Festival invention, with a long flight ahead of her."

Belle exchanged an uneasy look with Beast. "But—"

"Everything's fine. Look, why don't I make us some coffee and I can check your vitals before you go home for a proper rest?"

Maureen waved her hand dismissively. "I'm sure Darling will be back soon, and then maybe you two can patch things up."

Three weeks later, Captain Charity and the *Figment* had still not returned. Despite this, the mayor insisted nothing was amiss and the ether-poisoning treatments continued. With each visit, Maureen looked progressively more haggard, with bruise-colored shadows under her eyes. Belle was grateful for Beast's presence during the sessions. Each time, her body was wracked with burning pain as the elixir counteracted the lingering effects from years of poisoning, but it was worth it. After the final follow-up appointment, Maureen informed Belle she'd made a full recovery. There were no more traces of ether in her blood.

Now that her treatments were over, Belle was eager to take the mayor up on her offer to visit the abandoned library and hopefully begin her dream job. Today was the day of the tour, and for the first time in her almost twenty years, she fretted over her clothes. She eyed her outfit anxiously in the full-length mirror in the bedroom. She normally went for function over fashion, though with the outfits Captain Charity had gifted her, even the most casual of clothes had a bit of style to them.

After agonizing over her choices, Belle opted for a creamy blouse with billowy sleeves that tapered at her wrists, a chocolate scarf, a soft brown skirt held up by leather suspenders, and comfortable lace-up boots. Her hair was pinned up, with a few loose strands framing her face. Seeing herself in the mirror was a shock. She looked unrecognizable without translucent skin or black-blue veins. Virtually all traces of the poisoning had vanished, giving her complexion a healthy glow. She could easily blend in with the townspeople of Duchollow.

Taking a deep breath as she smoothed her skirt, Belle made her way to the kitchen where Beast was cooking breakfast and humming along with the radio.

Belle smiled softly at his antics. Between her appointments, he'd made it his personal mission to make their house into a home, starting with the kitchen and cooking all their meals. He altered his sleep pattern to match hers, taking a long nap in the afternoon to avoid the brightest part of the day so they could spend more time together.

"Breakfast is ready." Beast plated her food, his back facing her. "If you get a chance while you're in town, find out where we can get chickens. I think they'd make a nice addition to the garden."

Belle blinked. "Do you think it'd be taking on too much at once?"

He turned around to set their plates on the table. "Maybe. Definitely something worth—" The words died on his lips as his gaze fell on Belle.

"Something wrong?" She anxiously scanned her outfit for runs or stains.

Beast shook his head, wide-eyed. "You look amazing. Are you sure you have to leave so soon?"

A mischievous grin broke across her face as she sat at the table. "Thank you. Do I look like a future librarian?"

Beast shrugged, returning her smile. "I wouldn't know, but I think you're going to do a wonderful job."

He came around behind her seat and wrapped his arms around her shoulders. "Please be careful, though. With the captain still missing, I'm worried about you going into town."

Belle reached up to touch his paws. "I will. You be careful, too. If you sleep this afternoon, lock everything up. I'll have my keys."

"Will do." Beast gave her a reassuring squeeze before sitting next to her. They ate in companionable silence, enjoying their meal and the soft music playing on the radio.

When they were finished, Belle glanced at the clock. "I should have a little more time before Maureen's here. Want help with the dishes?"

Beast looked scandalized as he shook his head. "And mess up your librarian outfit? No."

"You like it that much, huh?" Belle tilted her head.

"Yes." He closed the gap between them and tucked a stray

strand of hair behind her ear. "I like your hair up like that. Especially with that neckline."

Beast leaned in and nuzzled against Belle's neck, partially undoing her scarf and sending heat radiating throughout her body as she squirmed in his arms.

"Careful, your clothes." Beast's breath tickled her neck.

"You don't play fair," Belle whimpered.

"Where would the fun in that be?"

Crisp knocking at the front door interrupted Belle's retort. According to the mantel clock, the mayor was right on time.

"To be continued?" Belle asked as Beast straightened.

He nodded, smirking at her. She leaned in and kissed the side of his muzzle, tracing his jawline. Without warning, Beast wrapped his arms around her waist and pulled her closer.

"So much for my clothes." Belle was breathless as she leaned in to kiss him again.

The knocking grew louder. "Are you ready?" Maureen called out.

"Her timing is uncanny, as always," Beast grumbled as he released Belle and helped her straighten her outfit.

"Coming!" She smoothed her blouse and retied the scarf before dashing off to answer the door.

The mayor stood in the doorway, an amused but exasperated expression on her face. "Finally. May I come in for a minute? I have some good news."

"Yes, come in." Belle ushered in the other woman and closed the door behind her. "Did Captain Charity return?"

For a moment, Maureen's cheerful façade fell, and the smile plastered on her face faltered. The shadows under her red-rimmed eyes were etched deep. The mayor inhaled sharply. "No, but it's okay. She's been gone longer than this before on far more dangerous missions without communication. I won't say I'm not worried, but this is normal." Her grin returned, albeit a little dimmer. "I have some good news for Beast, though."

Beast turned around from the sink where he'd busied himself with the dishes. As he dried off his paws with a towel, he raised his brows. "Really? I didn't think you'd have anything conclusive yet."

"Well, I don't have a cure, but using your blood sample, I can confirm with confidence you are human in origin." Maureen gestured to the stumps still attached to his head. "Whenever you want those removed, I can do so."

"That's fantastic news." Giddiness bubbled up in Belle until her happiness was burst by Beast's troubled expression. "What's wrong?"

"It's wonderful to have my humanity confirmed, but what could have turned me into this?" He gestured to his muzzle and claws.

Maureen nodded. "I have some theories, but I need to do more research. My next step will be investigating mutations related to ether-poisoning. It's not unprecedented for ether to cause all kinds of abnormalities."

"You think this was a mutation?" Beast asked, narrowing his eyes.

Maureen shook her head. "Not exactly. The scarring underneath your fur suggests your transformation was too deliberate for a random mutation. I just need to figure out exactly what was done so I can figure out how to undo it."

Beast snorted. "That simple, huh?"

Belle could see he was hurting, so she tried to lighten his mood. "At least you don't have to worry about having a pig's heart."

Beast scoffed but cracked a lopsided grin. "As far as we know, anyway."

Maureen rubbed the back of her neck as she shot them a bewildered look. "Right. Ready to see the library?" She turned to Belle.

"Yes! I can't wait." She dashed to Beast to hug him tightly. "Be safe while I'm gone."

"I will," Beast murmured, the fine hairs on his muzzle tickling her ear. "You be safe, too."

After reluctantly letting Beast go, Belle followed Maureen out to her truck. She felt oddly exposed going into town for the first time without a cloak or hiding in the back of the vehicle.

As the engine rumbled to life, Maureen said, "Don't worry. You look like anyone else in town. From what I've heard, you're going to love this place."

They were silent on the ride to the library. Belle felt awful for bringing up Captain Charity earlier, but Maureen seemed unfazed, even content as she waved at pedestrians on their way. The mayor parked in front of a two-story stonework building near the town center in a part of Duchollow that Belle had never visited before.

Belle was instantly enchanted by the building, even before seeing the books. It featured arched windows, multiple chimneys, and a tower that jutted above its steeply pitched roof. Ivy climbed up the sides of the building and a few of the windows were broken and boarded up. The short staircase leading up to the entrance had cracks in it, but in her mind, it was as grand as any palace.

"It'll need a massive amount of work and repairs, but it has potential." Maureen cut the truck's engine, a smile playing on her lips. "Ready to see the inside?"

"Yes, please." It took every ounce of Belle's self-control to not run ahead. Her stomach fluttered with each step closer to the door. She knew what a library was in theory, but she'd never stepped foot inside one before.

Maureen grabbed a rolled-up parchment and two lanterns from the back seat before getting out of the vehicle. At Belle's puzzled expression, she held up the paper. "These are the original plans for the library. You can study them yourself later if you'd like."

Belle beamed. "That'll be fun."

Once they reached the double doors, Maureen fished out her massive keyring and opened the lock with an antique ironwork key. The door groaned open into a dark, cavernous room. Faint sunlight streamed in through the few unbroken windows and cracks in the walls.

Maureen held her lantern up to peer inside, casting looming shadows across the ramshackle flooring. "It has gas lighting, but I'm uncertain if it's functional."

"Well, let's go look." Belle took careful steps as she followed Maureen inside the building.

Even in the dim lighting, it was easy to tell this had once been a gorgeous library. Drop cloths covered the furniture, but the room had several reading nooks, some of which were focused on grand fireplaces with detailed floral engravings. Books were stacked haphazardly around the room, some fallen from the floor-to-ceiling shelves. A thick layer of dust coated everything and a musty scent permeated the room. Despite the grime and obvious need for repairs, Belle was in awe. She'd never seen so many books in one place before.

"I think I found the switch!" Belle fumbled her fingers along the wall until the room was bathed in soft golden light.

The walls were dotted with frosted globes, and several chandeliers twinkled, revealing a suspended copper orrery that creaked and groaned as it rotated. The ceiling was painted with a chipped celestial design, a gigantic, faded compass behind the model galaxy. Mesmerized, Belle watched the mechanism rotate, mimicking the planets' orbits. Memories of the orrery in Onyxmark came back to her. She had seen it as a girl when she'd run away from the circus for a day.

"Turn it off before it breaks." Maureen tapped Belle's shoulder and pointed at the ceiling. Some of the model planets had seen better days, and after years of disuse, their orbits threatened to collide with each other.

"On it." Belle blushed as she turned the switch off.

The library descended into darkness again, the orrery slowly creaking to a stop.

"What do you think?"

"It's wonderful." Belle's voice caught.

Maureen grinned. "Just think: this is only the first floor. There's the second floor, and my notes mention the tower holds the Archives."

"The Archives?" Belle raised her brows.

"Yes. It seems there were plans to build a university in Duchollow when ether-mining was booming, but that fell through. Only the library remains today, and it's rumored to house an impressive academic collection called the Archives." Maureen pursed her lips. "I might have to take a peek at them for my research when you're working. If you want the job?"

Belle nodded. "Yes, please. Maybe I'm in over my head, but I think this place will be beautiful when it's done." She pointed at the orrery. "I think I can fix that, too, with the right tools and a good ladder."

"Wonderful. We can talk about details after we finish the tour. I think the staircase is over there." Maureen pointed across the room when a frantic knocking on the open double doors echoed through the vast room.

Both women looked back at the entrance, equally startled by the intrusion. In the entrance, Mr. Cadwell braced against the worn door frame as he took ragged, gulping breaths.

"I've been looking all over for you." He coughed, dabbing the sweat off his brow with an embroidered, monogrammed handkerchief. "There's been word about Captain Charity and the *Figment*. Before departing for Minport, she sent your cargo with the *Curiosity*, which docked earlier this morning. I've asked Captain Lucke to speak with you about it."

Maureen tilted her head. "What's in Minport?"

The color from Belle's face drained, and she nearly dropped her lantern in shock. "The Circus Illume. She's going after the Ringmaster." Cold sweat beaded across her forehead. It felt as if all the oxygen had left the room as her breathing became short and fast. The captain had been telling the truth: she really was going after the Ringmaster. If the pirate failed, it'd spell disaster for their fragile peace.

Beast. She needed to warn Beast.

Belle bolted for the library's open double doors but halted when Maureen's slender hand clamped down on her arm in a vice grip.

"Wait!" The mayor's voice cracked.

Belle turned back to look at her. Behind Maureen's glasses, her brown eyes were dilated as she took gasping breaths. Placing her hand over the mayor's trembling fingers, Belle intended to pry herself loose, until she thought better of it. She squeezed the other woman's hand, hoping it was calming and not painful.

"I need your help. If Darling is going after the Ringmaster, your insight could save her. She's headstrong, and when, not if, her temper gets the best of her, it'll be a disaster. Please." Maureen's lower lip quivered.

"I'd love to help, but I have to warn Beast first. He's most at risk if we're discovered." The tears forming in the corners of Maureen's eyes broke Belle's heart. "After that, I'll give you whatever information about the Ringmaster you need."

"How long have you known Beast? A few weeks? Months?" The mayor withdrew her hand. "Darling has been a constant in my life for years. I can't lose her."

"Do you really think it'll be helpful for me to go with you to meet this other captain?" A knot settled in Belle's stomach as guilt washed over her. Captain Charity wouldn't be involved with the Ringmaster at all if it weren't for her.

"It might." Maureen took a shuddering breath. "This goes beyond Darling being missing, as much as it pains me to say. Damek is in danger, too. The tech I used to create him could be catastrophic in the wrong hands."

"What?" Belle froze in open-mouth horror. She knew the automaton was one-of-a-kind and had gathered his creator was fussy about his condition, but she never suspected he was dangerous. "Isn't it reckless having Damek pilot an airship if he's volatile?"

The other woman looked away. "I've included extreme safety measures in his design, but if they're activated, he'll cease to exist. Please come with me. I'll bring you home immediately afterward."

Belle's shoulders slumped. Every instinct she had screamed at her to run, but she couldn't do it. "I'll go with you, but I need to warn Beast as soon as possible."

Maureen nodded. "I understand. Thank you." She cleared her throat and smoothed the wrinkles on her indigo brocade shirt as she stood straighter. "Let's go. I want to catch the captain before he takes off again."

After a short, tense ride to Town Hall, Belle cringed as she got out of the truck. Her cramped leg muscles ached after sitting in the back seat. She should have taken Mr. Cadwell up on his offer to switch places with her.

Maureen rushed inside ahead of everyone. Belle lumbered after her, wincing with each step. Mr. Cadwell shuffled behind them, dabbing his forehead with his handkerchief.

Inside the foyer, a wiry man in a leather duster slouched half-asleep against the wooden panel wall. Smudged black eyeliner framed his closed eyes. His russet hair cascaded in waves down to his shoulders, adorned with a hat that was excessively embellished with a plethora of black feathers and an intricately engraved pocket watch. Tiny aviator goggles were perched on the brim. His fashion sense could have given Captain Charity a run for her money.

"Captain Lucke, thank you for waiting," Maureen called out as she neared him.

The stranger opened his eyes and stepped forward, removing his hat in a sweeping motion. With his other hand, he shook the mayor's. "I'm glad to be of service, ma'am. I wish it were better circumstances." Captain Lucke's voice had an easy cadence to it. Belle saw him steal a glance at her, and she recognized the look he gave her—one she had seen many times before when people saw her for the first time. His eyes widened as he craned his neck to take in her height.

At least the captain recovered quickly and extended his hand to Belle with a mischievous gleam in his green eyes. "I don't believe we've met, miss. Captain Lucke of the *Curiosity*."

Belle broke eye contact first as she hesitantly shook his hand, the back of her neck prickling. She didn't even want to be here, and now she was stuck making small talk. Her eyes darted to Maureen, pleading for help. "Um, nice to meet you. I'm—"

"My former patient and Darling's friend," Maureen cut in. "Given the urgency of the situation, I'd like to head to my office now."

"Of course." Captain Luke winked at Belle, who blinked in response.

"I'll get drinks." Poor Mr. Cadwell looked ready to faint.

"Thank you, Mr. Cadwell." Maureen unlocked her office and ushered them inside.

Despite recalling the discomfort of the tiny guest chairs during her last visit, Belle sat down in the seat nearest to the wall, not wanting to attract any more attention from the captain. Captain Lucke took the other chair while Maureen sat at her desk.

"Would you mind repeating for me what you know about Captain Charity and the *Figment*? Last I heard, she was on a job to help me prepare for the Festival." Maureen leaned in, her chin cradled in her intertwined fingers as her elbows rested on the cluttered desk, crinkling schematics.

The captain's eyes darted to Belle, no doubt wondering why a former patient of Maureen's would sit in on this meeting, even if she was a friend of Captain Charity's.

Belle fought the urge to fidget in her seat. She wished she would have told the mayor no and gone home. The captain's penetrative stare made her feel exposed.

"Captain Lucke?" Maureen pressed.

"Right." The captain shook his head. "There isn't much to tell, but I'll relay it if it'll put your mind at ease. We were both docked at Voxglen. Captain Charity looked distressed at the canteen. I ordered her a drink, and she told me she had urgent cargo for you, ma'am, but that she had pressing business in Minport. She asked me when the *Curiosity* was heading back to Duchollow, and after I told her when, she asked if I could deliver her cargo in her stead. She paid us her full advance after I agreed to assist."

When Captain Lucke finished, he leaned back, making his chair groan as its legs creaked precariously.

Belle blinked. "That doesn't tell us much, does it?"

Captain Lucke lifted his hands, palms up, as he shrugged. "I wish I had more information, but your secretary was determined that I meet with you, ma'am, even if I have little to tell."

"Well, if Darling was just in Voxglen, heading to Minport, then she's not exactly missing. Minport's about a day and a half's journey via airship in good weather. It's not unlike her to not radio first. Thank you for your time, Captain." Maureen pursed her lips.

"Well, I'd agree, but there's a problem." Captain Lucke held up his index finger, the light catching the stack of rings on it. "I spoke to Captain Charity last week. She should have been in Minport days ago. I told her we had a job in Brassfall first before coming to Duchollow. It seemed like a strange request to have us deliver her cargo when Minport was closer to Voxglen, but she was desperate for us to take it off her hands."

All the color drained from Maureen's face. "What did you say?"

Belle's stomach churned.

"Here are refreshments." Mr. Cadwell carried in a tray with a coffee carafe, mugs, glasses of water, and wafer cookies.

"Thank you, Mr. Cadwell. It sounds like there's more to discuss with Captain Lucke than I had thought." Maureen waved him in.

The secretary placed the tray on the least messy section on her desk before bowing out of the office. After he left, she said, "I need to know exactly when you saw Darling."

"It's been eight days." The captain's brows knitted together as he looked between Belle and the mayor. "What aren't you telling me? Minport is one of the tamest cities she could fly to."

"Never mind that." Maureen glanced at the clocks on the wall behind her desk. For the first time, Belle noticed the city names engraved on the bottom edge of each one, including Minport's, which read an hour behind Duchollow. "Someone will be working at the dock now. Hang on."

Maureen pulled a lever concealed behind a stack of books on her desk. A panel on the wall creaked open, revealing a built-in cupboard housing a telegraph inside. Without another word, she ran over to it and tapped its switch furiously, the machine's keys rattling with each stroke. Just as quickly as she'd begun, Maureen ceased her frantic motions. She folded her arms across her chest as she stared at the telegraph, waiting.

Belle and Captain Lucke exchanged baffled glances.

Moments later, a printed strip of paper came out of the machine. Maureen snatched it and scanned it, swearing under her breath.

"Ma'am?" Captain Lucke rose from his seat. "If there's nothing else, I need to get back to my crew."

"Sit back down, please." The mayor turned to face them both, crinkling the paper in her hands. "This says Captain Charity arrived in Minport six days ago and paid to dock for three days. She never returned. The *Figment* has been impounded by authorities."

Belle blanched. "She wouldn't let anything happen to her ship."

"No, she wouldn't." Captain Lucke sat down. "What do you need?"

The ride back to Belle and Beast's cottage was solemn. When Belle stepped out of the truck, she hesitated as she closed the door. "I'll radio you later with my answer. I need some time to think about it."

Maureen nodded, suppressing a sniffle. "I understand. Take your time, but not too long."

Belle nodded, a lump in her throat. "I will. Take care."

Maureen drove off as Belle entered the house.

Beast looked up from the sitting room. "How was the tour?" His smile faded as he took in Belle's somber demeanor. He crossed the room with long strides before wrapping his arms around her. "What happened?"

Belle took a deep breath. "The library has to wait. There's been word about Captain Charity's last known location. Now, the mayor wants me to help rescue her, but I have to go back to the Circus Illume."

CHAPTER FIFTEEN

The wind whipped around Belle and Beast as they stood at the airship docks. The *Curiosity* loomed over them in all her titanic blue and silver glory, pale sunlight glinting off the delicate swirling embellishments on her bulwark.

"I don't want to be here." Belle's teeth chattered despite her heavy cloak. She'd barely had time to scarf down breakfast and wished she had a coffee to warm her bones. The blustering gusts cut to her core, bypassing the comfortable layers she'd carefully chosen for this chilly spring day.

"I don't like it, either." Beast's brown hood fell low on his face, meeting the top of his tinted goggles. His words were muffled by a plain brown face mask tucked in beneath the goggles. He wrapped his cloak around Belle as he surveyed their surroundings.

Dock workers loaded cargo on the other airships, trading jokes as they stifled yawns. None of the workers spared them a second glance.

Belle leaned in, relishing Beast's warmth. "You don't have to come if you don't want to. It would have been smarter for you to stay home."

Resting his paw protectively on her shoulder, he pulled her closer. "You know I couldn't abandon you."

The dull pain of a tension headache flared across Belle's forehead. She didn't want to rehash the argument they'd had last night. Having Beast along on the rescue mission felt like a terrible idea.

Though she knew helping was the right thing to do, Belle had all kinds of lingering worries after telling Maureen yes. Besides her anxieties regarding the captain's absence, she had even more worries. The mayor had informed Captain Lucke that Belle had fled from the circus, and that was the reason behind Captain Charity's trip to Minport. She'd felt sick when a flash of recognition appeared in the captain's eyes after the revelation.

"So you're the strongwoman turned damsel in distress I've heard about. Fascinating." Captain Lucke smirked as if he'd solved some great puzzle.

After that conversation, Belle had planned to inform Beast she would be returning to Minport to assist with the search, hoping the crew of the *Curiosity* wouldn't turn her over. But her good intentions fell apart soon after she'd told Beast about Maureen's plan. He refused to be left behind, not wanting Belle to face her tormentor or risk capture alone.

Beast finally won the argument when he pointed out that if he stayed behind, the crew could still turn either of them in for the bounty. Belle hoped that being cured of her ether-poisoning would make her worthless to the Ringmaster. But with his vengeful streak, she knew that might not matter. She had begrudgingly agreed. She didn't want to be miles away from Beast during uncertain times. Now the entire crew of the *Curiosity* was in on their secret. It felt like they were courting disaster, but at least they'd be together.

Thinking about letting strangers in on their plight made Belle's stomach churn. "I hope the crew is understanding. I wonder what Maureen told them?"

"The mayor graciously offered to double our fee for our discretion." Captain Lucke appeared behind them, wearing a crushed velvet burgundy vest with matching trousers and artfully smudged eyeliner. His long duster billowed behind him, making him look as if he was about to star in a dramatic performance, not an ill-advised rescue mission. "Coming aboard?" His calculating gaze lingered on Belle longer than necessary.

"Yes." She pulled her cloak tighter around herself.

Beast squeezed her shoulder before nodding at the captain.

"Wonderful. I'll introduce you to the crew. They're eager to meet such an infamous pair." With a flourish, Captain Lucke led the way inside the airship.

Belle and Beast followed, each pulling a steamer trunk loaded with supplies gifted from Maureen. Belle snuck her hand into Beast's paw. He gently stroked her palm as they boarded the airship.

The inside of the *Curiosity* differed vastly from the *Figment*. While the latter had been composed of mismatched materials and looked lived in, this airship gleamed like she was brand new. Ornate gas lamps held by sculpted golden hands lit their path to the bridge, highlighting the polished wooden floors and walnut wainscoting topped by sapphire-blue paint on the corridor walls.

In the bridge, four people sat on stools fastened to the floor around a round wooden table that was similarly bolted. The assembled crew craned their necks to look at Belle. When they saw Beast, their reactions turned visceral. Even camouflaged, he cut an imposing figure.

A diminutive man with a squashed nose was the first to speak up. "Cap, I know you warned us about our special cargo, but is that creature safe to bring aboard?"

"I thought the beast had horns?" A bronze woman wearing a flowing beige shirt stared pointedly at Beast's hood.

Captain Lucke held up his hands, smiling benevolently. "Our job is to rescue Captain Charity and her ship. Maureen has generously footed the bill and is paying us considerably more than the circus master's bounty, so let's treat our guests with respect, shall we?"

"Aye," the uneasy crew members answered unanimously before growing silent.

"This is Belle and Beast, as you surmised." Captain Lucke gestured to them.

Belle's grip on her luggage tightened as she stiffly nodded hello.

Beast huffed as he stared down at each member of the crew, keeping his arm firmly around her.

"Seems her pet is awfully protective," observed a brunette with deeply tanned skin and tattooed constellations dotting her collarbone, revealed by her partially open lace-up shirt.

"He's not my pet." Blushing furiously, Belle wondered if it was too late to find another lift to Minport.

"I don't know," Beast growled in her ear. "That sounds like it might be fun."

"Beast!" Belle gasped, clamping her hand over her mouth. She was simultaneously amused and embarrassed.

Captain Lucke guffawed. "You'll fit in fine here." When the captain recovered, he pointed at the assembled crew one at a time. "Right, introductions. Hazard's the gunner."

The woman in beige inclined her head.

"Hawke is the pilot."

The tattooed woman nodded, eyes still appraising.

"Riggs is our quartermaster."

The shorter man fussed with his crimson ruffled shirt before giving Belle and Beast a tight smile.

"Moody is the cook."

Moody was the only crew member who had not spoken yet. He was a bald man with more jewelry than Belle realized could fit on a person. He nodded, his diamond earrings catching the light and creating miniature rainbow prisms around him.

Hawke whispered something to Riggs, making him chuckle.

Belle felt like she'd made a huge mistake coming aboard the *Curiosity* with Beast.

"Good. Now that everyone's met, let's go over the plan before takeoff." Captain Lucke gestured to the table. "Take whatever seats are available."

The stools were so close together that Belle felt like she was practically sitting on Beast's lap.

"I'm surprised the mayor didn't come with the way she's sweet on Charity." Moody spoke with a light, lilting cadence.

Captain Lucke leaned forward. "She wanted to, but duty called her to stay in Duchollow. It's probably for the best. She's been quite generous with this job." He held up a hefty bag of coins.

Belle's stomach twisted as she was reminded of the meager bag of silver the Ringmaster had paid her father.

"Now, to business." Captain Lucke clapped his hands together. "Belle's going to be our eyes in the circus. She knows the layout best, so she'll be going in disguise for reconnaissance."

"How are you going to do that?" Riggs blurted, then flushed, his round face matching his shirt. "Sorry, it's just, you, uh, stand out." He scratched the back of his neck.

Belle shrugged. "It's a risk, but no one at Circus Illume knows that my ether-poisoning has been cured. I don't think they'd recognize me now, especially without a flashy costume or dark veins, but I packed a wig just to be safe."

Captain Lucke cleared his throat. "After Belle scouts the area, we'll go from there. The other consideration is safely retrieving Damek, the automaton pilot, before his safety measures kick in." At the crew's blank stares, the captain elaborated. "He'll self-destruct."

"Is that all?" Hazard snorted.

"To be honest, I'm surprised we haven't heard reports of a mysterious explosion in Minport." Belle grimaced when she realized everyone's eyes were on her. "It's odd for the Ringmaster to not tinker with a new toy."

"Fair point." The captain rested his chin on his fist.

"I hope Cinders is okay," Beast spoke up, his words muted.

"Who?" Hawke tilted her head.

"Charity's cat. She's a little thing." Beast shifted his weight and dropped his gaze.

The rest of the crew stared at Beast.

Riggs spoke up first. "But what is he doing here?"

"I'm the backup plan." Beast pulled down his mask and bared his sharp teeth, sending Riggs scrambling back.

"I'll take your word for it," the other man stammered.

"If that's everything, let's begin preparations for takeoff. I want to get to Minport as soon as possible." Captain Lucke turned to look at Belle. "I'll give you a tour later. For now, strap in. It's going to be a bumpy ride."

Belle reached for Beast's paw.

After the airship stabilized, Captain Lucke took Belle and Beast on a tour while the rest of the crew attended to their jobs. Belle felt nostalgic for the *Figment* as the captain showed them yet another extravagant observation deck. The *Curiosity* was beautiful, but the *Figment*, despite its mismatched décor and wear, felt more like a home.

"And these are your quarters, Beast." They stopped in front of a room in a narrow corridor. The captain gestured at another door farther ahead. "Belle's room is down the hall. Dinner will be served in two hours."

"Thank you." Beast nodded and his eyes darted to Belle. They exchanged an uneasy look as he entered his quarters.

Belle furrowed her brows. Didn't anyone tell the captain they lived together? The entire point for them both to go to Minport was to avoid being separated.

"Allow me to escort you to your room before I resume my duties." Captain Lucke took her by her elbow.

Wincing at the contact, Belle discreetly extracted herself from his loose hold to pull her luggage between them.

Captain Lucke opened the door to a room with a spacious view. The far wall was entirely made of glass, with a retractable curtain that spanned the length of it. The rest of the room was painted deep blue and decorated with mirrors and miniature floral paintings.

Belle sat her steamer trunk at the end of the bed. "Thank you for the tour, Captain."

He grinned at her, his smile a little too wide for her liking. "My pleasure. Should you need anything at all, ask. There's a call button by the entryway." He nodded to the intercom on the wall, similar to the system on the *Figment*.

"I'll keep that in mind. Thank you." She cleared her throat and fidgeted. "If you'll excuse me, I'm worn out from this morning's excursions. I think I'll have a lie-down."

"Excellent plan. Have pleasant dreams." Captain Lucke winked before leaving.

After the door closed, Belle shuddered. Too much attention for one day.

When the sound of the captain's brisk footsteps faded away, Belle, chewing her lip, looked around her quarters. They were well appointed, given she wasn't part of the crew and this had been a short-notice flight. The comfortable-looking bed was covered in burgundy blankets and pillows. A secretary desk stocked with stationery was tucked in the corner.

Left alone with her thoughts, all Belle could think about was the possibility of coming face-to-face with the Ringmaster soon. The faded scar on her ankle, a souvenir from years of wearing his electrical ankle bracelet, chafed against her trousers as she paced. She halted in front of a round mirror hung on the wall, startled by her haunted reflection and the dark shadows beneath her eyes.

Lumbering back to her steamer trunk, Belle opened it. She packed her delicate white nightgown, toiletries, and a change of clothes in a borrowed carpet bag before leaving her room. Her walk down the hall was brisk as she approached Beast's door, clutching the bag tightly in her right hand. She belatedly wondered if he was asleep after their late night.

Moments later, the door creaked open, and Beast stood in the doorway, his tinted goggles and mask removed, an amused glint in his eyes. "I was wondering if you were going to show up or if I was supposed to go to you." He gave her an appraising look as he folded his arms across his chest. "Or if you prefer the captain's company, I won't stand in your way."

"No, thank you." Belle grimaced. When Beast's frown deepened, she added, "He's not you. May I come in?"

"Yes." He led her through the doorway before locking the door behind them.

Belle raised her brows, a small smile playing on her lips as she followed him inside.

His quarters were as grand as Belle's, though the large bed had been stripped, and the blankets had been added to the pallet made on the floor. On the desk in the corner, a radio played soft orchestral music.

Belle sat her bag on the floor next to Beast's steamer trunk. Suddenly self-conscious, she stuffed her hands in her trouser pockets, shyly glancing over at Beast.

His gaze softened as he sat on the edge of the pallet. "Have a seat."

Belle nodded and sat next to him, snuggling close as she sighed.

Gently, Beast tilted her chin up, the leathery pads of his paw brushing against her skin. "What's the matter?"

"I'm scared about tomorrow. I'm exhausted." Belle released a shaky breath. "Even my old scar was bothering me."

His paw slid to cup the side of her face. "I'm sorry. Do you want to change the plan? There's still time."

Belle shook her head. "I can't think of a better plan, even though this one's risky. I just…" She bit her lip before continuing, "I don't want to be alone right now, and I especially don't like being apart from you."

"I'm not going anywhere." Beast moved to rub her shoulders.

"Good."

Beast paused. "What scar was bothering you?"

"Oh, the one from my old anklet. From the circus."

Beast tilted his head, his expression inscrutable. "May I see it?"

Blushing all the way down to her collarbone, Belle nodded. "Sure." Feeling self-conscious, she repositioned herself to balance her leg across his lap.

Beast gently unlaced her boot before removing it and her wool sock. He pushed her trouser leg up just enough to reveal the faded purple scar around her ankle. With a featherlight touch, he traced delicate circles on her jagged scar, eliciting a gasp from Belle as delicious shivers traveled up her leg.

Beast's eyes burned with intensity she'd never seen before. "Does it hurt?"

"N-no." She ducked her head as her cheeks grew hot.

He continued his ministrations as the soothing song playing in the background drew to a close. "You never finished telling me about the library. Was it everything you hoped for?"

"It was amazing, so much more than I thought it'd be. There were more books than—"

The radio switched to commercials which played much louder than the music.

Beast growled. "Every time, I swear. Hold on." He rose from the pallet but froze as the next ad began.

The announcer's voice echoed in the quarters. "Come see Circus Illume's latest attraction: the She-Beast! Beware her razor-sharp claws. Marvel at her uncanny strength. Wonder at her wicked antlers!"

"You don't think..." Belle couldn't verbalize the horrible thought. What were the odds of finding another creature like Beast when Captain Charity was missing? But the Ringmaster didn't possess the means to create one, so where did he find a new beast?

"I don't know, but maybe." Beast furrowed his brows as he sat back down.

"We need to tell Maureen and inform the crew." Belle's mouth set in a grim line. "This is more complicated than we thought."

In the dying sunlight, the colorful neon sign for Circus Illume twinkled above Belle as she followed the crowd through the gates to the Cacophony Hippodrome. Her long dark-blond wig itched, and her heart hammered as she clutched her bulky carpetbag close, terrified anyone might bump into it and discover the tools and gadgets concealed within.

Somewhere in the crowd, Hazard and Riggs scouted the area. After settling the impound fee for the *Figment* with Maureen's money, they left the airship docks together. Upon reaching the circus, they scattered to cover more ground faster.

The rest of the *Curiosity* crew remained on their airship with Beast, who was not happy about being left behind. He conceded after the broadcast advertisement for the She-Beast that perhaps it was best to err on the side of caution. Even the crew was on edge after hearing about the commercial.

Belle didn't like leaving Beast behind, but if she had her way, he'd be in Duchollow at home. She felt exposed in the crowd despite the wig and the new clothes. Worse, she couldn't shake the feeling she'd be separated from Beast forever if she were discovered.

After Belle had been cured from ether-poisoning, it would be a stretch for anyone to recognize her. Despite her trembling hands, she paid the attendant—an ancient, spindly man who avoided eye contact—and received a red ticket with no issues.

Deep breaths. She could do this.

Tonight's mission was pure reconnaissance. It'd be foolish to attempt anything else with so many people around. The ground was damp from last night's spring rain and mud squished underneath Belle's boots as she canvased the outdoor attractions, trying to avoid splattering the muck on her coveralls.

It was a surreal experience seeing the circus as an outsider. None of the patrons paid her any mind as they seemed engrossed by the various acts on the wooden platforms spread out on the grounds, the warm-up entertainment before the center dome opened for the main event. The familiar scents of roasted chestnuts, cheap ale, and straw mingled together, bringing back memories of challenging strangers to feats of strength before performances and the Ringmaster's punishments afterward if she wasn't lively enough during her act.

Lost in thought, Belle collided with an oncoming patron. She jumped back as if scorched, reaching for her wig to make sure it was secured in place. She hunched her shoulders to minimize her height and kept the carpetbag close to her chest.

"I'm so sorry. I—" The apology on Belle's lips died as the other woman dusted off her dress and wordlessly stalked toward the Cacophony Hippodrome's central building in a billowing flurry of green and gold.

Belle snorted, relieved her panic was unwarranted. While she didn't miss being gawked at, being invisible was new. At least it worked to her advantage as she continued surveying the platform performances. She ignored the clowns mingling throughout the crowd, making grotesque faces as they juggled increasingly ridiculous objects, ranging from pins to wrenches.

On another platform, a bald, scantily clad woman blew violet fire to the delight of the audience. Belle ducked her head down, not wanting to draw the fire-breather's attention. They had not gotten along during her time in the circus, and though Belle had never known why the stuntwoman hated her on sight, she didn't want to find out if the animosity was still there.

Making her way past the platforms, Belle scanned the area for any signs of the She-Beast, but there were only posters with bold letters proclaiming the creature's arrival and a poorly painted silhouette of an extended claw. Soon she found herself precariously close to the trailers. A flimsy rope serving as a barricade and a sign stating "No Trespassing: Circus Folk Only" were before her.

Belle chewed her bottom lip as she looked behind her. Workers were approaching, likely for last-minute preparations for the show. She'd better not risk drawing attention to herself. Maybe after the show started, she could come back to look for Captain Charity. If the Ringmaster had captured Damek, he'd create an act for the automaton, but she hated to think of what he might do to the captain.

She hoped Hazard and Riggs were having better luck than her. Even though they were strangers, part of her wished she could check in with them, but it was impossible to spot them in the crowd.

Clutching her bag, Belle made her way inside the Cacophony Hippodrome's main building, clenching her jaw as she crossed the threshold. She told herself she was looking for signs of Damek in the show, but she couldn't stop thinking about the She-Beast. Maybe the *Curiosity* crew would be amicable to breaking her out if her story was anything like Beast's? Belle mulled over what the crew's price would be for such a blatant theft.

With a pang, Belle thought Captain Charity would help the She-Beast for the pleasure of hitting the Ringmaster in the pocketbook. Shoulders hunched, she shuffled behind the crowd funneling toward the seats and balked when she noticed Cook handing out programs. Belle avoided eye contact, grimacing at the sour taste in her mouth as she drew nearer.

"Enjoy the show, dearie!" The matron waved Belle on, hardly glancing at her as she handed her the program and moved on to the next guest.

Belle wasn't sure if she was relieved or upset about Cook not recognizing her, but it was for the best. It's not like they'd been close friends, or Cook would have helped her escape the Ringmaster's cruel grasp long ago.

In the center ring, the automaton band played a jaunty tune as guests made their way to their seats. Belle chose a seat near the exit, where she could still see the ring and easily slip out undetected. To her relief, there was no sign of Damek on stage.

Belle skimmed the program, but there were no clues to be found about Damek or the She-Beast, only brief text promising a thrilling performance. The arena lights dimmed, the music faded, and a hush fell over the audience. She bit her nails into the stiff wooden armrests as the Ringmaster took center stage wearing his signature bright red coat and top hat.

His voice boomed as he spoke into his glittering megaphone. "Welcome to the Circus Illume! We have a special show for you tonight, with acts ranging from the depths of nightmarish terrors to the heights of dazzling wonders." The colorful stage lights reflected off his toothy grin.

Belle's stomach turned as she sank down in her seat. The show was the same as always, and she nearly got up twenty minutes into it, after seeing the fire-breather do the same tricks she'd done for years, until the Ringmaster took to the center ring again.

"Now for our newest addition: the terrifying She-Beast."

Two stagehands wheeled a massive cage into the central ring, while mechanical platforms rose from the stage floor, transforming the ring into a ballroom, complete with a grand piano being played by an automaton. Inside the cage was a massive creature dressed in a sparkling pink dress that clashed with her amber fur.

Belle froze. The creature was a Hound, with antlers sprouting out of her head.

Fighting back nausea at the revelation, Belle squinted at the automaton playing a waltz on the stage, but it looked nothing like

Damek. This automaton resembled a gilded music box figurine, not the smart-mouthed pilot.

The Hound bayed at the bright lights, drowning out the music. She snarled at the handlers and the Ringmaster as they attempted to extract her from the cage. The audience gasped as the Hound swatted a handler's whip out of his hand, sending it clattering across the stage.

Undaunted, the Ringmaster lifted his megaphone again. "It seems our She-Beast has succumbed to her savage ways tonight, but never fear, our show will go on!"

With a wave of the Ringmaster's hand, the cage was wheeled away as the Hound bellowed and acrobats took to the stage, performing aerial stunts to the automaton's graceful tune.

The Hound's piercing howls halted when the Ringmaster subtly pressed a button on his cane as he tapped it to the music. The average audience member would have missed the gesture, but Belle was all too familiar with the motion: offstage, the Hound probably had been shocked into submission.

Belle had seen enough. Though the horrific memory of the Hound attack on the *Figment* was fresh in her memory, Belle empathized with the pitiful creature in the cage. She needed to search for clues about Captain Charity and Damek before it was too late, but she resolved to help the Hound, too.

As she left, Belle wondered how the Ringmaster acquired a Hound. Back in Duchollow, Maureen and Beast had made it sound as if only his creator and the mayor's rival, Delphine Wyerstone, had Hounds. Beast and Maureen agreed they were probably discussing the same woman, which meant that Delphine must have had dealings with the Ringmaster. Belle's eyes widened. Captain Charity could be in even more dire straits than she'd thought.

When she exited the dome, it took every ounce of willpower Belle had to not run to the trailers. With the show only halfway finished, she'd have some time to search. Though Captain Charity and Damek were her priority, Belle still looked for tracks from the Hound's cage, but it was futile as twilight gave way to night.

Gritting her teeth, Belle stepped past the "No Trespassing" sign into the dimly lit trailer area. There wasn't a soul in sight. A familiar meow sounded by her legs. Her breathing hitched as she looked down. Cinders purred, rubbing against Belle's leg. She looked well-fed but dirty, bits of mud clinging to her soot-colored fur.

"I'm so glad to see you," Belle whispered as she bent down to scratch the diminutive cat. "But where are your mistress and Damek?"

Without warning, Cinders bolted.

Cursing under her breath, Belle followed, minding her footing on the uneven terrain. "Get back here," she hissed, struggling to keep pace with the cat without dropping her cumbersome bag.

Cinders stopped in front of a trailer Belle didn't recognize near the Ringmaster's showy red one. This trailer resembled a prison, with steel beams crisscrossing the windows. The front door had entirely too many locks on it.

Cinders scratched at the door and mewled.

"Good girl." Belle panted as she reached into her carpetbag and retrieved a semi-automated lockpicking device that fit comfortably in her hand. "Keep it down, though."

Inside the trailer, muffled howls grew louder.

Belle hesitated. Would the Captain be in here with the Hound? Though she wanted to save the poor creature, going into the dark with one sounded like an awful plan. What would the abused Hound do when backed into a corner?

Cinders head-butted Belle's leg before resuming scratching at the door.

"I can't believe I'm listening to a cat over reason." Belle's fingers shook as she studied the complex mechanism in the low lighting. She wished Maureen would have left written instructions for it. Taking a deep breath, Belle lined up the lockpicking device, bracing herself for whatever horrors awaited inside.

CHAPTER SIXTEEN

The muffled howling inside the trailer reached a crescendo as Cinders frantically pawed at the door. Sweat dripped down Belle's back as she tried to remember how to work the semi-automated lockpick. It was a deceptively unassuming device, with a tapered metal end that fit snugly into the first lock's keyhole, and a handle with two plain buttons on each side.

Her chest tightened as she realigned the tool, hoping the Hound's handlers weren't waiting inside. With trembling fingers, Belle pressed a button on the tool's handle. At last, the device whirred beneath her hand, rotating and clicking its gears as the tapered end adjusted to the lock's internal mechanisms.

The first lock opened with a satisfying click. Four more locks of varying sizes remained on the door. Belle peered over her shoulder in the poorly lit area, certain someone was going to come to investigate why the She-Beast was howling, but the area was deserted. Not a single trailer had interior lights on.

In the distance, the crowd thundered, and the music swelled. It wouldn't be long before the show ended.

Where were Hazard and Riggs? The Cacophony Hippodrome was large and there was a huge crowd tonight, but it made Belle uneasy that she hadn't seen either member of the *Curiosity* since they left the docks. Where were they searching?

The last lock clicked open. Swallowing hard, she opened the door slowly and gritted her teeth when it creaked. Cinders brushed against Belle's leg before darting inside. Swearing under her breath, she closed the door behind her, immediately regretting it. She'd forgotten to take the lantern out of the carpetbag first.

Inside the trailer, thin, rectangular beams of light entered through the barred skylight, casting the room in eerie shadows. A fetid odor mingled with the smell of sawdust and sweat. Cinders charged ahead, disappearing in the shadows. In the center of the room, the Hound was chained, with her faux antlers laying on a cluttered desk behind her. The orb on her collar glowed crimson. Belle's breathing hitched when the Hound moved, allowing more light to hit the desk. A saber was precariously perched on its surface.

The Hound's baleful eyes glowed icy blue in the darkened room. Without the dress on from her ill-fated performance, she looked feral, but there was underlying intelligence in her expression that gave Belle pause.

"Captain Charity? Is that you?" Her voice cracked.

The Hound ducked her head.

Tears formed in the corners of Belle's eyes as she staggered forward. "I'm so sorry I ever doubted you. I wish I hadn't assumed the worst." She gulped. "You really were trying to help."

The Hound turned away and curled up on the wooden floor like an overgrown dog.

"I know you probably hate me now, but I will get you out of here. I swear it. Maureen's terrified for you. We all were." Belle reached for the Hound's chains but froze as rattling and Cinders' plaintive yowling emitted from a dark corner of the room.

"What was that?"

A thud and a hiss answered her.

Moving to the narrow beams of light, Belle shoved her tool in her pocket and frantically searched through her carpetbag for a lantern. At last, she closed her fingers around one. At last, she closed her fingers around one. Holding the light high, Belle peered into the darkness. In the corner, Captain Charity was bound and gagged, her dirty face streaked with tears. On the wall behind the captain, Damek was spread out in pieces on a flimsy table, like a creature laid out for dissection. Cinders pawed at the chains tethering the captain's ankles to an iron ring drilled into the floor. An all-too-familiar anklet with a crimson orb was shoved on her leg, flush against her shackles.

Belle stepped forward, intending to run to Captain Charity's side. The Hound growled at her, sitting upright with her ears laying back flat.

Lowering the lantern out of the Hound's eyes, Belle spoke in a soothing tone. "Easy, girl. I'm not going to hurt anyone."

The Hound snarled before lying down, keeping her eyes trained on Belle as she inched her way to Captain Charity. When she finally reached the captain, she set her lantern down and untied the cloth gag.

Captain Charity's eyes blazed, reflecting the lantern's light. Her voice was hoarse and cracked. "What are you doing here? He'll kill you!"

Belle gasped as she bent down to examine the captain's handcuffs. Her sleeves were torn away, exposing raw skin around her wrists. "Let's get you free." She promptly unlocked the handcuffs with the mechanized lockpick. They clattered to the floor.

Captain Charity rubbed her wrists before stretching her arms. "That's better already. Thank you."

Belle sat at the captain's feet as she searched for the lock on the shackles around her ankles. "I'm sorry for doubting you."

The captain chuckled. "I heard your apology to the Hound. Did you really think I was transformed?"

"If it happened to Beast, why not you?" Belle pursed her lips. The lock on the shackles evaded her. She could only see smooth metal all around the captain's ankles but no keyhole.

"I suppose that's fair." Captain Charity rubbed the back of her neck. "I'm sorry for disappearing, but I wanted the Ringmaster to leave you in peace. I didn't think it was going to happen after he issued the bounties."

"Yes, but why would you go after him yourself? We were safe in Duchollow. At least, I thought we were." Belle furrowed her brows as she realized the anklet was melded to the shackles. She angled the lockpick against the anklet's crimson orb and experimented by pressing the other button on the device. The orb darkened as it popped out and revealed a keyhole.

Captain Charity sighed, running her fingers through her tangled hair. "It's more complicated than—"

Familiar bellowing outside cut her off.

"Beast!" Belle's eyes widened.

"Why would you bring him back here?" Captain Charity's mouth hung open in horror.

"I didn't! He was aboard the *Curiosity*." Bile rose in Belle's throat. "Get me out of here and we'll help him."

The roaring grew closer.

"I forgot to lock the door behind me!" Belle hissed.

"Maker's moldy knickers." Captain Charity rubbed her temples. "This has to be the worst luck of any rescue."

"Working on it." Belle's eyes darted to the saber on the desk, then the chained Hound. She stalked to the door and locked it before slowly approaching the Hound with the lockpicking device in her hand. The Hound perked her ears up, growling and baring her canines.

"I won't hurt you. I just need the saber. Please."

Belle carefully reached out with her empty hand to the Hound, palm up as one would for a stray dog.

The canine creature sniffed her fingertips and huffed, hackles raised, before allowing Belle to pass.

"What are you doing?" Captain Charity peered at her between her fingers, covering her eyes.

"Getting ready." Belle's expression was grim as she examined the saber. "How do you work this thing?"

"You need the battery pack. It looks like a metal bracelet. The prick tossed it on the desk, too. But—"

Belle located the battery pack behind stacks of She-Beast flyers. It was chunky and too small to fit around her wrist. She held it in her left hand, wrapping the band across her knuckles after loosely tying the scabbard to her belt, and sheathed the saber as she approached the Hound.

"What are you doing?" Captain Charity's voice shook.

"Creating a diversion." Warily, Belle lined up her tool with the orb on the Hound's collar. The Hound barked when the mechanism whirred, and she nearly lost her grip. With her other hand, she patted the Hound's back. "I'm going to free you. No one in here's going to hurt you."

She hoped the Hound understood.

The orb fell out, and Belle readied to remove the collar's lock when muffled voices grew louder outside. The front door's locks clicked open in rapid succession. Belle pressed the button on the mechanism, hoping it'd work fast enough on the collar.

The trailer door swung open to reveal the Ringmaster's lean form in the door frame. The electric lights in the trailer flickered on. A woman stood behind him wearing a dark green cloak over a matching dress with golden embroidery on it.

"I'll retrieve your captain and—" The Ringmaster's eyes widened when he saw Belle. "What are you doing in here? Who are you?"

Behind the Ringmaster and the woman, Beast was in chains, snarling, and wearing a metal collar with a crimson orb. Captain Lucke held Beast's chains, flanked by the rest of the *Curiosity* crew.

Seized with fury, Belle threw her blond wig at the Ringmaster, letting her charcoal hair fall free.

"You!" The Ringmaster's face turned purple as a vein on his forehead throbbed. He held up his cane, readying to strike.

Belle stepped back to the Hound, who glared at the Ringmaster with murderous intent. With a flick of her tool, the Hound's collar fell off. The Hound shook off her chains and snarled at the Ringmaster.

Placing herself in front of Captain Charity, Belle unsheathed the electric saber, pressing the concealed button on its handle. The saber crackled and sparked with blue electricity as she stared down at the Ringmaster. "It's me. My friends and I are leaving."

The Hound stood by her side, growling, with her ears flat back. The creature's gaze locked on the Ringmaster and the blond woman behind him standing in the doorway.

Outside the cramped trailer, Beast roared, rattling his chains.

Captain Lucke held his restraints, barking orders at the rest of the *Curiosity* crew to help. The crimson orb on Beast's collar glowed steadily in the twilight, visible even from a distance.

"Not another step closer, girl, or your precious Beast will be in for the shock of his life. Or perhaps I'll send a jolt to the captain?" The harsh lighting inside the trailer cast strange shadows on the Ringmaster's flushed face, highlighting his jagged scars. His hazel eyes gleamed with malice as he held up his gaudy cane.

Belle's pulse thrummed as she zeroed in on the cane. One press of the button on his cane and the anklet he'd forced her to wear during her years of captivity would emit powerful shocks. A quick push meant a small zap, but when the Ringmaster was feeling cruel, he'd leave her twitching on the floor. He wouldn't be merciful today.

At least he didn't realize that Captain Charity's anklet was missing its crimson orb. Beast was in danger, but to free the captain all Belle had left to do was finish picking the lock on her shackles. Or Captain Charity could do it. Her hands were free. Belle's free hand drifted to her pocket and her fingers curled around the mechanical pick stuck in them.

"What's it going to be, girl?" the Ringmaster sneered.

"I told you we're leaving." Belle clenched the saber handle tighter. If she could get the lockpick to Captain Charity and take the cane away from the Ringmaster, they could make a break for it with Beast.

The Hound's hackles were raised as she crouched in from front of Belle, snarling at the Ringmaster.

"You said everything was under control." The woman behind him fixed Belle with a calculating look as she crossed her arms.

Captain Charity's voice was full of venom. "Delphine. Which pet are you here for?"

It felt like all the air left the room as realization hit Belle.

Delphine.

Creator of the Hounds.

Maureen's rival.

Beast's creator?

Delphine craned her neck to peer around the Ringmaster and flashed a cold smile when her gaze landed on the captain tugging on her tethered chains. "Still bold, even when bound. I can see why Maureen likes you." She scoffed. "I'm here for what's mine: the automaton and the beast."

"No." The memory of the faded scars crisscrossing Beast's body haunted Belle. She longed to wipe the smirk off the cruel woman's face.

"It's too late for 'no.' I already have him." Delphine gestured to the scene outside.

All five members of the *Curiosity* crew held a chain on Beast as he thrashed, to no avail.

"You've lost." The Ringmaster leered. "I'll fetch your anklet."

The Hound lunged and crashed into the Ringmaster, sending his cane clattering to the floor. It rolled into Belle's boot as both creature and man tumbled out of the trailer, knocking over Delphine.

With a high swing of the electric saber, Belle cleaved the cane in half. The air smelled of burned ozone as smoke rose from the singed cane. "Beast! The collar won't do anything now!" she yelled over the chaos, praying he heard her as she glanced outside.

Beast pulled the chains out of Captain Lucke's hands, throwing him into the others as he roared.

"The beast is loose!" The captain's shrill voice cut through the panicked shouts of his crew.

The Hound and the Ringmaster wrestled on the muddy grass, knocking into his trailer, but Delphine was nowhere to be found. Circus folk who had made their way back to the trailers screamed and ran from the rampage.

Confident Beast could handle himself, Belle switched off and sheathed the saber. She crouched by the captain's feet, frantically unlocking her shackles. "Can you stand?" She offered her hand to Captain Charity.

The captain clutched Belle's hand and wobbled as she rose. "We need to grab Damek! Where's Cinders?"

"Hopefully, she's avoiding this mess. I don't mean to be indelicate, but isn't Damek…" Belle chewed her lip, not wanting to further upset Captain Charity after her ordeal. Though Belle hadn't known Damek long, she had a soft spot for the automaton. She couldn't imagine how the captain was feeling about her pilot's fate, but they had to escape while they had a chance. The Hound and Beast couldn't hold the Ringmaster and his cronies forever.

"Isn't he what?" Captain Charity whirled to face Belle, her red-rimmed eyes sparkling with fury as she picked up the automaton's mechanical arms.

Cinders hopped up on the table with the rest of the disassembled parts and meowed, pawing at the dormant automaton's head.

"Oh, dear. This is bad." Damek blinked, his eyes flashing a deep red. "I'm in pieces!"

"Is he going to blow up? Maureen said he had a security feature." Belle backed away from the table.

Captain Charity snorted. "I disabled that 'feature' ages ago. I'm not having a living bomb pilot my ship." She picked up Damek's head and gave him a reassuring pat. "Morning, sunshine. We'll get you put back together after we escape."

Belle wasn't sure Maureen was going to approve of Captain Charity's modifications, but there wasn't time to fret. Spying an open crate shoved under the desk, she asked, "Will he fit in this?"

"Some of him will. Let's go!" Captain Charity shoved Damek's disembodied head between his arms and into the crate.

"Goody." Damek pouted. "There's rubbish in here."

"At least you don't have a nose!" Captain Charity panted. "Belle, give me the saber and take the crate."

Belle obliged, returning the sheathed saber and power bracelet to the captain. Together, they scrambled to pack the rest of Damek's pieces. Captain Charity carried his legs outside while Belle stacked his torso on the crate before following after her.

The brawl was getting worse. The Hound had the Ringmaster pinned against the ground. Beast kept the *Curiosity* crew at bay, backhanding Captain Lucke when he made a grab for his chains.

Delphine appeared from behind the Ringmaster's trailer. She raised her gloved hands. "Enough! I suppose I must do everything myself." She removed her left glove, revealing a golden prosthetic with a bracelet with a single dangling green crystal charm.

"Thankfully, I always have a contingency plan." With a smirk, she tapped the crystal with her index finger.

The Hound stopped her attack, howling in pain as she writhed. Beast bellowed, holding his paws over his ears.

Gritting her teeth, Belle set down Damek's crate before charging. A resounding crack rang out as her fist connected with Delphine's mouth. The other woman doubled over, losing her grip on the bracelet. Belle ripped the jewelry off Delphine's wrist and crunched it beneath her boot.

Both the Hound and Beast ceased crying out. The Hound stared at Belle, then scampered away from the ruckus, racing off toward the woods alone. Beast rubbed his head, looking shaken.

Belle towered over Delphine. "You can stop this madness. Change Beast back!"

Delphine's gaze hardened as she wiped blood tinged with gold off her chin, removing her makeup and revealing her skin's unnaturally pearlescent hue. "Never. He can't be fixed."

Rage boiled inside Belle as she picked Delphine up.

"You can break me, but it won't save your precious Beast," Delphine spat.

Belle scowled and dumped her in the now-empty trailer. Following Belle's lead, Beast rounded up the entire crew of the *Curiosity* and led them into the trailer as well, snarling when they protested.

While Beast stood guard, Belle found the bloodied Ringmaster propped up against his trailer, glaring at her with hate-filled eyes. A fresh wound crisscrossed his old scar from the tiger on his cheek. She grabbed the keys out of the Ringmaster's pocket before carrying him into the trailer with the others.

"This isn't over," the Ringmaster hissed, pressing a cloth to his wound.

"Yes, it is." Belle slammed the trailer door shut, then checked all of its locks before picking up Damek's crate. "Let's get out of here before anyone comes investigating." She trudged forward, hoping they had enough time to get back to the docks before any of the Ringmaster's henchmen grew brave enough to come out of hiding.

Beast followed Belle, carrying the automaton's legs while Cinders perched on his shoulder, her claws digging into his fur.

"How are we getting out of here?" Captain Charity wheezed as she struggled to keep up, wincing with each step.

Before them, the Ringmaster's yellow automobile gleamed under the circus lights, its retractable roof down.

"That!" Belle reached the vehicle first, setting Damek's crate down in the back seat. She held up the Ringmaster's keys before getting into the driver's seat and starting the engine. The automobile rumbled to life. "Get in!"

Beast hopped in the back of the vehicle, not bothering with the door, and sat Cinders on his lap along with Damek's legs.

Captain Charity soon followed, collapsing into the passenger side seat. "Do you know how to drive?" the captain asked, her voice breathless.

"No."

"Right side is go. Left side is brakes. Try not to kill us." Captain Charity closed her eyes, sinking back into her leather seat.

Gulping, Belle pressed her foot on the pedal, revving the engine. The vehicle didn't move.

"Shift gears! Here." Captain Charity opened her eyes and did it for her.

"Thank you." Belle pressed the pedal again, and this time, the automobile took off, mud squelching beneath its tires before peeling out of the Cacophony Hippodrome's grounds.

Captain Charity, Cinders, and Beast braced themselves as Belle drove to the airship dock. She narrowly avoided other vehicles on the road while the captain offered plenty of encouragement and swearing.

When Belle finally parked, she faced the others, beaming. "We made it!"

Beast looked seasick. "Thank goodness."

They all climbed out of the vehicle, awkwardly carrying Damek's parts. Captain Charity saluted the gob-smacked guard on duty with the automaton's foot as they raced past the gates. It didn't take long for them to find the *Figment*. They scrambled aboard and everyone crowded into the cockpit in a breathless mess. Even Cinders was exhausted, curling up in a ball on the floor.

Belle piloted the airship, proud she could remember her crash-course lessons.

When the *Figment* was airborne, Captain Charity said, "I need to take care of something."

"Wait! I'm still taking off." Belle didn't tear her eyes away from the dashboard as she pulled up on the lever.

"You'll be fine. This won't take long. When you reach the right altitude, you'll know. Damek will answer any further questions." The captain's voice grew faint as she departed the cockpit.

"Easy enough to say. Damek's in a box." Belle grunted as she glanced out the window. The dock was slowly shrinking, but the other airships were still visible. The *Curiosity* stood out, moonlight reflecting on its elaborate decorations.

"I'm right here!" Damek protested inside the crate. The rest of his pieces were haphazardly stashed around him, along with refuse.

Belle wrinkled her nose and returned her focus to piloting.

Beast put his paw on her back. "You've got this."

"Right." Belle inhaled and exhaled, trying to slow her breathing as the *Figment* ascended.

A violent shuddering rocked the airship.

Below, the balloon of the *Curiosity* suffered a massive burn hole that caused it to rapidly deflate.

Panic seized Belle. What if someone saw them? Or retaliated?

Another shot fired from the *Figment* and ripped a hole in the other ship's bulwark.

"What happened to the delayed firing?" Belle panted, her hand slipping from the controls. The ship took a hard turn, and she wrestled the controls to correct their course.

"The captain upgraded the ship while it was undergoing repairs," Damek's muffled voice piped up.

The intercom crackled on. Captain Charity's voice boomed in the cockpit. "Everything okay?"

Beast pressed the button for Belle as she clung to the steering with white knuckles. With barely controlled anger, Belle said, "You scared me. What'd you fire at them for?"

Captain Charity's voice was defiant. "I needed to prevent the *Curiosity* from following us. It'll buy time to warn Maureen about their treachery. Did you have anything important on board?"

"Just our trunks and some clothes." Belle swallowed hard. "What about guards? Surely, someone saw that or they'll figure out what happened."

"I'll buy you new stuff. Just keep my ship in the air 'til I get back. Then we can talk. There's a lot we need to catch up on." Captain Charity signed off, the intercom crackling and popping before going silent.

CHAPTER SEVENTEEN

The *Figment* finally achieved cruising altitude with limited guidance from Damek, but Belle still gripped the steering wheel tightly. Though they were flying at a steady clip, she dreaded slipping and causing the airship to oscillate wildly again. Navigation was made marginally easier by the full twin moons, but flying in the dark with no sense of direction was setting her nerves on edge.

"Do you think we should check on Captain Charity?" Belle snuck a glance at Beast. He was crouched on the floor with Cinders, who purred as he cradled her to his chest. "The cannon's recoil might have hurt her."

"I can look for her." He patted Cinders before gently placing her on the floor. The diminutive cat mewled her protests and stretched before curling up next to Damek's foot in the stack of dissembled parts shoved into the cockpit.

"Thank you, but there's no need." Captain Charity stood in the corridor, leaning on the wall for support. She brushed back her frizzy hair before pointing to a meter. "Might want to keep your eyes on the sky and the altimeter. You're losing altitude."

To Belle's chagrin, the captain was right. Gritting her teeth, she adjusted course. When the *Figment* was stable again, she said, "We were worried about you. I thought you might have passed out at the gunner station."

The captain squeezed around Beast and retrieved Damek's head from the crate before sitting down in the copilot's seat, wincing. "I've done worse." She hummed as she studied the myriad of gauges and dials on the control panel before grinning. "You're doing well. If I can't fix Damek, maybe you should be my pilot."

Damek's eyes flashed red, the damaged lights vaguely resembling exclamation points. "Hey, if it wasn't for me, she wouldn't have known how to come out of an ascent."

"I'm teasing. There's no finer pilot than you." Captain Charity patted the automaton's head.

"And Maureen will kill you if you don't fix me." A solenoid inside of the automaton whirred as he grinned lopsidedly.

"There is that." The captain shuddered.

Belle gestured at the sea of wispy clouds and stars before them. "Is there a particular direction we should go? I've been flying in a relatively straight line for a while now, but I don't know where we're heading."

After moving Damek's head to the seat, Captain Charity checked the map on the windshield and the latitude and longitude gauges on the control panel. "We're on course. Do you mind flying longer? I'd like to piece together what I can of Damek before we land."

Belle nodded and resumed piloting. Captain Charity retrieved tools from a patinated brass box under the copilot's seat and started assembling the automaton. Beast stretched his legs out into the corridor and idly played on the floor with Cinders.

The tightness in Belle's chest didn't leave until after an hour had passed without further incident. She kept expecting to see either a patrol ship or one of Delphine's Hound-filled airships in pursuit, but the night sky was blessedly serene. The same could not be said of her thoughts. Why had Captain Charity risked everything to go after the Ringmaster? And why hadn't the Hound in the trailer attacked them?

When the suspense became unbearable, Belle made sure the controls were steady before she turned to look at the captain. Damek's head was now attached to the torso propped up against the wall.

"Better?" The captain grinned as she wiped a grease smudge off her forehead with a stained cloth.

Damek's internal gears whirred. "I can't move my neck. My pneumatics sound weird, and my limbs are twitchy." He held up his mechanical hand, which seemed to move jerkily of its own volition.

"I'll get you fixed up properly in Duchollow, but this isn't too bad, considering the conditions." The captain playfully smacked the automaton's shoulder.

"You mean Maureen's going to fix me?" Damek's pneumatics hissed as he lowered his arm.

"Yes." Captain Charity sighed as she sank back into her seat. "I'll radio her when we're in range after we land in Gattermire for the night. I've got business in town before we head home."

Belle cleared her throat. "Can I talk to you about something?"

"Go ahead." All traces of light-heartedness disappeared from the captain's face as her expression became closed off.

"I am so sorry that I questioned your motives." Belle wrung her hands. "I wish I could take back what I said."

The captain shook her head. "Don't be. Look at what happened with Captain Lucke and the *Curiosity*. It's bad enough that the spineless cowards double-crossed you and Beast, but they also betrayed Maureen. They've known each other for years. She's going to be devastated."

"I know. But I don't think it means you're like that." Belle chewed her lip. She didn't want to break their tenuous peace, but she had to ask. "I still don't understand why you helped us. Why risk yourself?"

The other woman looked away. As she studied the horizon, shadows fell across her face, obscuring her features. "I've told you before that I've known men like the Ringmaster. He'd never let you go. I had to do something."

"But why?"

Captain Charity snorted. "Do you think happy, well-adjusted people become airship pirates? I have a past. We all do. I've had the misfortune of being treated as property until I finally put a stop to it. There may have been explosions involved."

"Oh." She gaped at the captain, but the other woman didn't elaborate further. Belle shifted in her seat, her muscles aching. "If it's too uncomfortable for you to talk about your past, I understand. But can you explain something?"

"What's that?" Captain Charity's tone was considerably cooler as she checked their bearings.

"Do you know why the Hound didn't attack us? For a moment, I thought she would." Belle's gaze lowered. "Instead, she saved us. I hope she made it to the woods safely."

Captain Charity shrugged. "The Ringmaster thought he was being clever keeping her in there with me. Since I didn't abuse the creature, I didn't have to worry about her hurting me. She had plenty of reasons to go after him and Delphine."

"Are the Hounds like Beast? Because if so, I—" A choked sob escaped from Belle as she thought of the Hounds' brutal attack on the *Figment*. It seemed so far away now, but seeing the vulnerable Hound made her question her response.

"Look at me. I know where you're going with this, and you need to stop." Captain Charity squeezed Belle's shoulder with her calloused hand. "The Hounds are not people; they never were. Delphine made her own hyper-intelligent bipedal mutts and took away their free will. You did what you had to in order to save us, and I'm grateful for it."

"How do you know?" Despite her heavy heart, the captain's sure tone piqued her curiosity.

"She's right." Beast had been silent for so long, Belle had thought he'd fallen asleep on the floor, but when she looked back, it appeared he'd been hanging on to every word. "Delphine said she was at the circus for me and Damek. I'm certain that she's my creator. Though I don't remember who I was before I was a beast, I distinctly remember being told I was the first of my kind. The Hounds were kept as guard dogs on my creator's grounds."

Belle's gaze softened. "I see. Still, I wish the attack on the *Figment* could have resolved peacefully." She shook her head. "I'll have to do some soul-searching, but I appreciate the insight."

"If you hadn't done what you did, none of us would be alive today." Captain Charity withdrew her hand and busied herself with checking the control panel.

Belle took a deep breath as she built up the courage to ask her next question. "Do you know how Delphine and the Ringmaster ended up working together? Their partnership was an unpleasant surprise."

"A bit." Captain Charity's jaw clenched. "Delphine heard about the bounty and figured out it was 'her' Beast." The captain winked at Belle. "Sorry, we all know he's your Beast."

"Pardon me?" Belle gaped at the captain's mercurial mood.

Beast chuckled.

"Anyway…" Captain Charity straightened her tattered shirt with a grimace. "Delphine went to the Ringmaster with an offer of one of her Hounds for Beast. That, and money." She snorted. "I didn't hear how much. It was disgusting seeing how easily she manipulated him for her purposes. And he was…awful."

"I'm sorry for what you went through." Belle swallowed hard.

"I was only there a short span compared to you. I can't imagine the torture he put you through." The captain patted her hand.

Belle gave her a half smile. "I think it's safe to say I'm never going back to Minport again. None of us can."

The captain snort-laughed. "That's for sure." She glanced at her longitude and latitude readings again. "Speaking of places to go, we're approaching Gattermire. We'll sleep on the ship tonight and get what we need in the morning. Buckle up. I'm taking the controls."

After a smooth landing at Gattermire's docks, Captain Charity unbuckled her seatbelt and stretched.

"Why don't you two get some rest? I need to radio Maureen and I'd rather not have an audience for the lecture she's going to give me, even if I have it coming." Despite her self-deprecating tone, the captain had a sparkle in her eyes.

Belle nodded, poorly disguising her amusement with a cough. "Understandable. Where would you like us to go? Back to the observation deck?"

Captain Charity lightly smacked her own forehead. "I forgot to tell you. I prepared your room on my way back from the gunner station. When the *Figment* underwent repairs, I thought I'd make it homier in here and converted some of the storage into additional quarters."

"Thank you so much." Belle felt a fresh wave of gratitude for the captain, but she couldn't help but worry about her physical state. "Are you sure you haven't overdone it?"

"I'll be fine with some rest. Your room is down the corridor, third door from the end on the port side. There are extra clothes in the wardrobe. Hope you both sleep well." Captain Charity turned her attention to the radio and nervously fiddled with the dials.

"Good luck with Maureen!" Belle waved goodbye, then followed Beast to their quarters.

When they reached their room, Belle flipped the light switch. Their quarters were far more luxurious than she'd expected, especially for a room that had been previously used for storage. A massive bed dominated the room, big enough to easily fit two of Beast's size on it. Its carved headboard matched the celestial design painted on the wardrobe. The white pillows and cozy blankets looked inviting after their ordeal.

A small bookcase filled with books secured via a leather strap across the center of each shelf was built into the walls. A heavily cushioned sofa faced a window with a fantastic view of the stars peeking over a sleepy town nestled among pine trees in a craggy valley.

Belle was in awe. "She did all this for us?"

Beast closed the door behind them and padded across the room. "Maybe there are still good people in the world." Before she could respond, Beast tapped her on the shoulder. When she turned around to see what he wanted, he pulled her into a tight embrace.

"Beast?" Belle tilted her head, a smile playing at her lips.

"I haven't checked you over since our escape. The Ringmaster didn't hurt you, did he?" He anxiously looked her over from head to toe.

"My knuckles are a little sore, but otherwise, I'm fine."

"Let me see." Beast furrowed his brows as he lifted Belle's bruised fingers and softly stroked them. "Does it hurt?"

His gentle touch made her heart feel full. "No, it's not so bad."

"Good." Beast pressed his muzzle to her knuckles in an almost-kiss.

Belle flushed. "What about you? Were you hurt?"

"No, the cowards used a tranquilizer. They got the dosage wrong, though, because I was awake sooner than they expected."

"I'm sorry that happened to you, but I'm glad you're safe now." Surreptitiously, she checked him for injuries, but to her relief, aside from a bit of mud clinging to his cloak, he appeared unscathed. "The whole time I was back at the circus, I couldn't shake the horrible feeling we'd be separated forever."

Beast moved his paw to cup the side of her face. The heat in his gaze was scorching. "And what did I tell you about that? I'd tear down the whole circus to get you back."

"I know." Belle's stomach fluttered.

Beast tucked her loose strands of hair behind her ear. A pained expression came over his face, and he withdrew his touch, stepping back.

"Is something wrong?" Belle frowned, confused by the sudden shift in his mood.

"It's selfish." He averted his gaze.

"Please?" Belle closed the gap between them, clasping her hand over his paw.

"I don't know if I can be cured, but I can't bear the thought of losing you. I let you down when they put me in chains."

He can't be fixed. Delphine's words haunted Belle.

"You didn't," she said, ignoring her fear. "I thought staying home would be safer for you, but I'm not sure what would have been the right choice with so many people after us." Belle traced Beast's jawline before cupping the side of his face. "I don't think you're selfish." She kissed the side of his muzzle. "I don't want to lose you either."

Beast fidgeted, his eyes downcast.

"Anything else on your mind?"

"It's nothing." He ducked his head, coughing into his fist.

"Are you sure?" She bit her lip.

Beast met her gaze, his eyes filled with yearning. "I've fallen in love with you, but I'm worried I'm going to ruin you. I mean, look at me. What if this is how I am forever?"

Warmth bloomed in Belle's chest and radiated through her body. "I love you, too. We'll figure this out. If Delphine could turn you into this, I'm sure we can find a cure with Maureen's help." Feeling reckless from their escape, she curled her fingers into Beast's shirt, pulling him closer so she could whisper in his ear. "And if not, maybe I could stand a bit of ruining."

Raising his brows, Beast chuckled darkly. "Are you sure that's wise?"

She gave him a mischievous grin. "Maybe not, but I mean it."

"Good."

Beast circled his arms around her waist, enveloping her in his cloak. He sighed as his eyes darted to her lips. "I wish I could kiss you."

Belle flushed. "I'm sure we could figure out something."

A glimmer of mischief appeared in Beast's eyes. "I'm sure we could."

Timidly, Belle brushed her lips against Beast's muzzle, testing the connection. It was as if electricity coursed through her body, lighting up all her nerve endings.

The only thing Belle knew about kisses was what she had read, but she could happily get used to the way Beast trembled at her touch. They leaned into each other's embrace until neither one could suppress their yawns.

"I suppose we'll have to figure it out another day." Belle smiled ruefully.

"Sleep?"

"Please."

Curled up against Beast's side in the most comfortable bed Belle had ever slept in, she wondered if Delphine had told the truth. Could she live with Beast as he was?

There was no question in Belle's mind about how she felt about him. Somewhere between the first time he handed her the apple at her campsite and now she'd fallen in love with him. Though she'd been light-hearted in her response to his worries, she knew there was no guarantee he could be cured. Of course, she could love him as a Beast. But would he let her?

The golden sunlight formed a halo around Beast's silvery fur as Belle traced the outline of his shoulder. Sighing contentedly, she curled back into Beast's arms, intertwining her legs with his.

Her eyes had barely closed before the intercom crackled on. Over the speaker, Captain Charity took a gulping breath before speaking, her words blending together in a rush. "Wake up, lovebirds. We have to leave now. Buckle up!"

Beast groaned, his words muffled as he turned face-down into the pillow. "It's too early for this."

Belle laughed and got out of bed, feeling euphoric after Beast's declaration the night before. She walked to the intercom button and pressed it. "Why are we in a hurry?" The memory of the *Curiosity* going up in flames came to the forefront of her thoughts, instantly sobering her mood. "Is it a patrol ship?"

In the distance, the *Figment*'s engine stirred awake, sending rumbles throughout the airship.

The captain's litany of swearing was muffled by white noise before her answer came through. "No, but one could be on the way. Harnesses are stashed in the couch cushions. Get to it."

Icy dread settled in Belle's stomach. What had happened in Gattermire?

Belle's heart hammered as she made her way to the built-in couch. "Are you awake? We need to move."

Beast threw off the covers and followed her to the seating area, leaving his discarded shirt on the floor. His eyes wandered approvingly to the nightgown clinging to Belle as she fumbled for the harness stashed behind the cushions.

Feeling his gaze on her form, Belle flushed. Even the tips of her ears were red. "Not now."

Beast's voice purred, his hot breath tickling her ear. "Weren't you the one who said you could do with a bit of ruining?"

"Timing, Beast." Belle's mouth went dry at the look in his eyes as he pulled away to sit next to her. He'd never let her live those words down.

Just as they buckled, the *Figment* groaned at the steep takeoff incline. The airship rocked violently as it took a hard turn starboard, throwing Belle in Beast's lap as her belt strained under the stress. A few of the books tumbled off the shelves in their room, slipping over the straps that previously held them in place and clattering to the floor. Everything in the room rattled. Belle clung to Beast, burying her face in his shoulder. She thought she was over her unease about flying, but as the harness dug into her this felt like too much.

"It's going to be okay." Beast stroked her hair and tucked it behind her ears.

"How do you know?" Belle's nails scratched Beast's back as the rattling grew louder.

"Because I didn't find you for it to end this way. I love you." Beast wrapped his arms around her.

"I love you, too." She squeezed her eyes shut as the airship pitched forward. "I hope the captain doesn't get us killed."

Beast hummed his agreement, his claws tracing light, soothing patterns along her back.

At last, the chaos stopped, and the airship stabilized.

Captain Charity's breathless voice echoed in their room. "We're in the clear. When you're presentable, head to the observation deck. I'll fill you in over breakfast. Sorry for the rude awakening."

After untangling her limbs from Beast's and unbuckling, Belle reached the intercom. "We'll be there, but don't you need to keep us airborne?"

Damek's tinny voice echoed in the room. "I'm sufficiently repaired to maintain our current altitude and speed."

Belle blinked. When did Captain Charity have time to sleep?

Beast stood by the open wardrobe, tugging on a caramel-colored shirt and black trousers. He grinned when he caught Belle staring. "Shall we?"

When Belle and Beast arrived at the observation deck, Captain Charity was already setting up breakfast on the long table. The only visible evidence of her recent captivity were the haunted shadows under her eyes. Belle suspected the loose, long-sleeved white blouse and tan trousers concealed the worst of her injuries.

The captain smiled when they entered the room. "Have a seat."

Belle was thankful for the stocked wardrobe so that she and Beast could have fresh clothes as well. The trousers and blouse belted around her waist fit perfectly.

"Sorry about earlier." Captain Charity rubbed the back of her neck. "I was so out of it last night that I didn't explain what I needed to do in Gattermire. I didn't mean to catch you two unawares."

Belle fought the urge to bounce her foot. Her whole body felt like it had jitters. "Are we safe now? What happened?"

Captain Charity handed them each a plate of warm bread, cheese, and sliced ham as they poured their own coffees. "I was busier in Gattermire than I intended to be." The captain yawned as she leaned back in her seat.

"You never said what we were stopping for." Belle took a sip of coffee. It was a new flavor, richer. Heavenly.

"Right. Maureen needed more materials for her project, and I picked up a few spare parts for Damek." Captain Charity gulped her coffee. "While I was in town, I accidentally discovered the manufacturer of the Ringmaster's orbs and sabotaged it on my way back. The detonator went off while I was only a few buildings away. I thought I'd been spotted, so I wanted to leave immediately. Sorry about the abrupt takeoff."

"Good." Beast snorted and took a long drink of his coffee.

Belle covered her open mouth with her hand. "What about the workers? Weren't you worried about getting caught?"

"I sounded the fire alarm first. There shouldn't have been anyone inside." Captain Charity shrugged. "As for getting caught, I took a gamble. There's no word on the radio about what happened in Minport. No new bounties. No word about the Hound on the loose, either. The silence is eerie."

Fear coiled in Belle's stomach. "Do you think the news will stay quiet about this, too?"

The captain rested her elbows on the table. "I can't imagine either Delphine or the Ringmaster are going to lie low forever. I wanted to deal a blow while I had a chance." She ran her fingers through her copper hair. "I hope the Hound got away. I was growing fond of her."

"Me, too." Hesitantly, Belle asked, "What's stopping Delphine or the Ringmaster from going to Duchollow?"

"I can't speak for the Ringmaster, but I know Delphine wouldn't dare step foot there. Not after last time." Captain Charity's expression hardened as she retrieved something from under her seat. She held up a collar similar to the ones the Hound and Beast had worn. "Before I smashed up the plant, I grabbed a few for Maureen to run tests on. Maybe we can find out how these are controlled and bypass them the next time we come across Hounds."

"Good. As long as I don't have to wear one," Beast cut in, his gaze locked on the dormant orb. "I don't want to be a test subject."

"The only testing you'll be going through is for your cure." The captain gave him a confident smile.

"Delphine said I can't be fixed." A shadow fell across Beast's face.

Belle snuck her hand into his lap and gave his knee a reassuring squeeze. "She's probably lying."

Captain Charity nodded. "She'll say anything to keep you under her thumb. Trust me."

With that, the three finished an oddly silent breakfast before preparing for landing.

The sun was setting by the time they arrived in Duchollow. A strange feeling bubbled over Belle as she stole a look at Beast as they unbuckled from the couch in their room. It wasn't exactly a revelation that they loved each other, but it had been unspoken until last night. The idea of going home together seemed to carry heavier weight after his confession, compounded by Beast's fear he couldn't be cured.

Beast caught her look and inclined his head to the bed. "Do you think Captain Charity would miss the bed if we took it home?"

The mischievous glint in his eyes made Belle flush. "I'm sure she would." Then, before she could cower away, she added, "Maybe we could get one of our own."

The grin Beast gave her was positively feral.

Whatever response he'd been about to give was cut off by Captain Charity's voice over the intercom. "I'll open the hatch. Not sure if we'll have a welcoming party or not. I couldn't reach Maureen."

For the first time, the unflappable captain sounded nervous.

The pneumatic system of the recently installed hatch door hissed as it opened. Beast held Belle's hand, gripping it a little too tightly. His cloak was in tatters and his goggles missing along with his face mask. This was going to be the most exposed he'd ever been in Duchollow. Belle had debated waiting on the ship until dark, but both the captain and Beast wanted to return home as soon as possible.

Captain Charity tapped her boots impatiently and tucked her copper hair behind her ears as the last of the door's reinforcements unlocked. Damek was strapped to a flatbed, unable to walk without malfunctioning after the captain's rushed repair job. Cinders kept the automaton company, curled up on his torso as she purred.

The door opened, and the captain winced.

"Are you going to be okay?" Belle gave Captain Charity a sympathetic look.

"How mad do you think Maureen's going to be?" The captain bit her lip.

"I think she's going to be thrilled to see you, but you should ask her yourself." Belle pointed to the dock.

Maureen waited at the end of the loading dock. As soon as she spied the captain, she bolted up the bridge.

Beast pulled Belle out of the way as the mayor dashed inside the *Figment* and enveloped Captain Charity into a tight embrace.

"Darling, never scare me like that again." Maureen brushed the captain's hair back.

"You know I can't make that promise." Before the mayor could object, Captain Charity caught her lips in a delicate kiss.

Cinders emitted a squeaky meow, breaking the spell.

Her octagon-shaped glasses knocked askew, Maureen straightened, her brows furrowed as she took in the sight of Damek strapped to the flatbed.

"Hello, Mother." Damek's face contorted into a deranged half smile, a wire on his mechanical cheekbones shorting and sparking as his grin transformed into a grimace.

"Darling, what happened to Damek?" Maureen's mouth pressed into a thin line.

"We should go, right?" Belle whispered to Beast.

He nodded and took her hand, but before they exited, Maureen called out to them.

"Wait, I'll take you two home. The truck is parked over there." The mayor gestured to the vehicle hastily parked near the dock before pointing at the captain. "We'll talk more about what happened to Damek after I check you over for injuries."

"Yes, ma'am." Captain Charity's contrite façade slipped as her eyes sparkled.

As the daylight dimmed, Belle couldn't help but glance at the sky for rogue airships. As they got into the truck, she wondered whether whatever means Maureen had for keeping Delphine out of Duchollow would be enough.

CHAPTER EIGHTEEN

Three days after the *Figment* returned to Duchollow from Minport, there was still no information about the *Curiosity* crew, the Ringmaster, or Delphine. After days of not knowing if retaliation was coming, Belle took out all of her pent-up nervousness and anger on the antiquated irrigation system connected to the well in Beast's garden. Sweat dripped down her back despite the unseasonably chilly weather and the heavy rain clouds threatening to burst overhead. She wanted to surprise Beast by restoring the well while he took his midday rest, but with her agonizingly slow progress, she feared that he'd wake before she was finished.

Ever since Beast had surprised her with the elaborate breakfast, she'd wanted to reciprocate his gesture with something as meaningful. Their recent misadventure had solidified her resolve, but Beast was difficult to surprise. He insisted on doing all the cooking—which might have been for the best. Belle hadn't taken as well to the captain's cooking lessons. His only other hobby was the expansive garden, but she knew nothing of growing things. However, she could tinker. Although he never complained, she could imagine how difficult it was for him to manually draw water from the well.

After retying her hair back with a ribbon, Belle glared at the broken irrigation system. Between rusted parts and misaligned gears, the machine certainly had seen better days. Every time she thought she'd fixed a problem, another one crept up—even after she'd replaced the compressor. She finally spotted the culprit: a small gear hopelessly entangled with thick, viny weeds.

After retrieving a knife from the toolkit gifted by Maureen, she cut the vines and grunted as she pulled the jammed gear free. She quickly located a replacement in her kit and swapped in the new gear, wincing as she scratched her grime-covered hand. Gloves would have been useful, but all thoughts about her ruined hands disappeared when she turned the main knob. The mechanism groaned to life as its gears rotated, pumping well water through the complex system. In the garden, water dripped out of copper pipes and sprayed over each row of vegetation like gently falling rain.

With a wide grin, she shut off the valve. Beast would tell her if any adjustments needed to be made to the pressure, but at least she could return his grand gesture. Humming as she worked, Belle cleaned up her tools. There was a spring in her step as she headed back inside. Beast would wake up soon, and she couldn't wait to show him her surprise.

After cleaning up, Belle quietly opened the door to their bedroom, a small smile on her lips as she tiptoed to his pallet. She leaned down with the intention of gently tapping his shoulder to wake him up but froze. The bed was empty.

Frowning, she checked the other rooms, but he was nowhere to be found. Had she missed him going outside? She returned to the garden, her heart rate picking up. Feeling foolish, she called out, "Where are you? I want to show you something that I hope you'll like." She squinted. The garden was empty, save a lone rabbit scurrying off for the trees.

"Beast? You okay?" Stomach churning, she crept farther into the yard. The field behind the cottage appeared to be deserted.

Threatening rain at any moment, the clouds hung heavy in the air. Her pulse thrummed in her ears as she continued searching. Behind Belle, the door to the greenhouse opened with a loud creak. She startled, jumping back with a yelp.

"What's wrong?" Bits of dirt clung to Beast's clothes and fur. The overcast sky had darkened enough that he pushed his goggles over his furrowed brow.

Resting her hands on her knees, Belle took several shuddering breaths as her heart rate slowly returned to normal. "You scared me. I thought something happened to you."

Beast lumbered closer and pulled her into a tight embrace. "I'm not going anywhere."

As she leaned into his steady arms, Belle suppressed the urge to cry. She hated feeling that if they weren't constantly vigilant, everything would be ruined. Even the coziness of their home wasn't enough to ease the fear that they were being watched. Beast had suggested starting work on the library's restoration, but she'd refused multiple times yesterday, saying that she didn't want to bother Maureen while she was preoccupied with Captain Charity's recovery and Damek's repairs. While both were valid excuses, the truth was she couldn't bear to leave him after seeing him in chains again.

"I was worried. What if—" She couldn't bring herself to finish the sentence as she kneaded her fingers in his filthy shirt.

"I know." He rested his muzzle on her forehead, his claws tracing soothing, featherlight circles on her back.

"Thank you."

Beast leaned back, meeting her gaze. "You mentioned a surprise?"

"Yes! I fixed up the well. The automation works and now it should take less time to water your garden. I hope it helps. I'll need you to give me the specifics later so I know how long you need the system to run."

Beaming, Beast replied, "Thank you so much! Do you have any idea how much time you've saved me? I—" He abruptly stopped and tilted his head to the side as he looked past her.

"What's wrong?" Belle frowned as she heard the familiar rumble of Maureen's truck coming up the road. "Did we have plans today?"

"No, we didn't."

Captain Charity's voice called out from the front of the cottage. "Are you two home?"

"Coming! We're outside. Meet you at the table." Belle took Beast by the paw as they trudged to the front of the house.

They found the mayor and the captain already seated at the table outside, both snickering, when they rounded the corner.

"Did we interrupt something?" Captain Charity raised her brows as she pointed to their muddy clothes.

Beast laughed and Belle shook her head as they sat down. She was relieved to see the captain's humor and health had returned, though shadows persisted under the fiery woman's eyes. Belle hoped she was getting the rest and care she needed.

"No, we were working on garden projects." Belle brushed off a speck of dirt, accidentally smearing mud across her already ruined shirt. Defeated, she folded her hands in her lap with a sigh.

Maureen concealed her smirk with a cough. "I see."

Eager to change the subject, Belle asked, "How are Damek's repairs going?" She wanted to ask about the captain, too, but the pirate tended to dodge personal questions.

The mayor shot Captain Charity a murderous glare. "After hours of adjustments, he's finally stopped short-circuiting."

The captain shrugged. "Well, his gait has never been smoother."

Maureen rolled her eyes.

Belle hesitantly asked, "Has there been any news?"

The mayor shook her head. "Not a word, and fortunately, no oddities at the dock or strange airship sightings."

"That's some good news." Belle picked at a loose thread on her sleeve.

"What's wrong?" Beast nudged her.

"I'm torn between staying hidden and feeling like it's useless. The Ringmaster, Delphine, and the *Curiosity* crew all know we're here." Belle sighed before gesturing to the mayor and the captain. "I mean, I don't want to put Duchollow at risk. What you both have done for us is incredible. I'm so sorry."

"No, you're right." Maureen adjusted her glasses as she leaned in. "It's terrible that the *Curiosity* crew turned out to be traitors and that extreme measures were taken to keep their ship grounded." She gave the captain an exasperated look. "There's nothing we can do about it now."

"Except for paying off the dock workers to keep quiet about our escape. Thank you, by the way." Captain Charity clasped the other woman's shoulder and winked.

"It'd be cheaper on me if you'd straighten up," Maureen muttered, shaking her head. "I've had your clemency documents drafted for years."

The unrepentant pirate stuck out her tongue. "And I've been telling you for years that you're better off with me continuing my pirate ways. How else are you going to get your supplies or sabotage Delphine's plans?" She folded her arms behind her as she leaned back in her seat.

Belle looked between them, bemused. She felt like she was on the cusp of figuring out something important, but it eluded her.

Maureen cleared her throat. "Anyway, I think it's time to strike against the Ringmaster. I doubt anything will happen to him legally, but I have friends at Duchollow's radio station. How would you feel recording about your time at Circus Illume and exposing the Ringmaster for the monster he is?"

"You want me to do what?" Belle immediately tensed. Beast put his arm around her shoulders, a comforting weight that kept her grounded as she stared at the mayor.

"I thought if more people heard about your experience, it might hurt him in the pocketbook. Delphine has too much influence with politicians for us to do anything about her now, but the Ringmaster doesn't have that luxury." Maureen took a breath. "I know it's a big ask."

"What about Delphine? Won't she protect him?" Belle bit her lip.

Captain Charity scoffed. "Doubtful. He's failed her, so she'll drop him."

"It's your choice, but I think you should do it." Beast's voice rumbled. "You could finally start the library restoration project without worrying about him coming after you. He'll be too busy dealing with the bad publicity."

Belle considered his words. Maybe going along with the broadcast would be the first step in truly being free of the circus. She wanted to be brave, but she couldn't help gulping before answering, "Okay, I'll do it. When do we start?"

"Wonderful." Maureen stood up and pushed her chair in. "How about after you both clean up? I'll take you into town."

"What?" Belle's pulse quickened as she anxiously looked to Beast.

He nodded. "Let's get it done."

After they changed clothes, Belle felt light-headed as she followed Beast to the truck. Despite her excitement about taking action against the Ringmaster, she couldn't help but worry that he must be even more determined to get them back.

Hours after Maureen dropped Belle and Beast off at their cottage, Belle curled up on the sofa intending to read, but she couldn't focus on her book. She stared into the middle distance, replaying the day's events in her mind.

Her emotions were raw and conflicted. Before today, she'd never talked about her past at length to anyone. Even Beast had known only snippets of what she'd been through. She had always been afraid if she opened up, all her old wounds would fester.

After Belle told her story in the radio station studio, instead of being buried under the weight of her past, she felt an unexpected lightness. After the recording session, Maureen mentioned a town hall meeting about the broadcast she'd host soon. If it went well, Beast could start coming into town. Belle was dangerously close to letting the hope into her heart that she and Beast could build a life together. Maybe she could even take him back to the plaza, as she'd wanted to do the first time they saw the town from the back of the truck.

Still, she was terrified that the broadcast would be a beacon for any of their enemies to come find them. Delphine and the *Curiosity* crew already had full knowledge of who had harbored them. It wouldn't be too much of a stretch to suppose that since the Ringmaster had captured Captain Charity, he also knew.

The back-and-forth between anticipation and anxiety was more than enough to drive her to distraction. So much so that she didn't hear Beast cross the room to kneel by the sofa, worry etched into his features. She realized too late that her book had fallen from the armrest onto the wooden floor.

"Are you okay?" His eyes were anxious as he looked her over. "I called your name a few times."

Belle startled. "Sorry. I have a lot on my mind. What do you need?"

"I'm worried about you."

Belle sat up, cringing at the stiffness in her neck. She'd contorted her tall frame to fit on the sofa, and now she was paying for it. "About me? What about drawing extra attention to ourselves with the broadcast?"

Beast moved to sit next to her. "It worries me a little, but I don't think it could do more harm. Everyone who wants to hurt us already knows we're here. I hope the broadcast bankrupts the Ringmaster."

"I do, too." She gave him a sidelong glance. "How are you feeling about what Maureen said about you possibly meeting more townspeople?"

Beast scratched the back of his neck. "I'm not much for crowds, and I love our home. But if this works, I'd be happy to visit you at the library or pick up supplies for the garden without having to ask you to do it for me."

"See? I knew you'd come around." Belle bit her lip.

He tapped her shoulder with the pad of his paw. "You never answered my question. What was on your mind? It must have been a lot for you to abandon reading."

Belle fidgeted. "I had a ridiculous thought despite everything."

Beast tilted his head as he reached for her hands to still them. "Please, tell me."

A faint blush spread across her face. "Do you remember the plaza clock tower on our first day in town?"

He nodded, his brows drawn together in confusion. "A bit. Mostly, I remember trying to stay hidden in the back of the truck. Why?"

All of Belle's words came out in a rush. "I thought it'd be a fun place to have a picnic with you."

"What?" Beast blinked.

"I told you it was silly." Her cheeks burned.

"No, it's not. Just not what I was expecting." He pointed at her, lifting his brows. "You were thinking of spending time with me even back then?"

Belle gulped at the feral expression on his face. "Yes, why?"

There was a feral gleam in Beast's eyes. "You've had it bad, haven't you?"

She looked down. "Maybe."

Beast cupped her face. "You don't have to be embarrassed. I fell for you the moment I met you. I wouldn't have gone along with your terrible escape plans if I didn't have feelings for you."

She snorted. "Thank you, I think."

His gaze softened. "There's my girl."

The silence was comfortable as Beast held Belle's hands until he stood up abruptly.

"Let's do it." He headed to the kitchen, leaving Belle puzzled in the sitting room.

"Do what?" She craned her neck as he rummaged through their cabinets.

"Go on the picnic tonight. I can't imagine the town is full of night owls. Let's go see the clock tower."

Belle stared. "You want to go out tonight with everything going on?"

Beast beamed as he retrieved a worn picnic basket from a cupboard. "Yes. We should take your mind off things. Besides, you barely ate dinner and I'd love to repay you for fixing the well."

"Don't you think it'll be too risky?"

Beast crossed the room to stand in front of her and put his paws on her shoulders. "We'll go under the cover of darkness wearing cloaks. If anything feels off, we'll leave. But I think it'd do us both good to go out. Please?"

Belle smiled ruefully as she nodded. "Okay, you win."

Happiness radiated from Beast as he helped her up from the sofa. "It'll be fun, trust me. Come help me pack."

There was a chill in the night air as they trekked to the heart of Duchollow, picnic basket and blanket in tow. They both wore cloaks with their hoods up, and Belle carried a lantern, though Beast's night vision afforded him enough visibility to guide their path to town.

Going into town on foot in the dark took significantly longer than riding in Maureen's truck, but once Belle stopped jumping at every rustle of a tree branch, she smiled as she held Beast's free paw. For the first time she could recall, they felt like a normal couple out on a date.

Beast caught her staring as they neared town. In the low light, Belle couldn't read his expression, but she was sure there was a mischievous glint in his eyes. Instead of the teasing she expected, he squeezed her hand gently.

Upon arriving at the deserted plaza, Belle was captivated by the enchanting town center. The clock tower was illuminated in shades of blue and purple, drawing attention to its celestial features. The stars on the clock's face shimmered, making the plaza look even more magical than it did in the daytime.

"Worth it?" Beast's voice rumbled pleasantly as he leaned in to whisper in Belle's ear.

"Yes," Belle breathed, throwing her arms around him. "Thank you for this."

He moved the picnic basket to return her embrace. "You're welcome. I'd do anything to get you smiling again."

Beast removed his mask and then set up the picnic. Hot cider warmed their bellies as they ate leftover bread, cheese, and chocolate by gaslight.

When the clock struck midnight, the lights danced, reflecting off its star pattern as it chimed a soft lullaby.

As Belle turned to him, her eyes sparkled. "This was definitely worth it."

Beast set his mug down to wrap his paws around her hands. "I hope I can always be the reason you find happiness."

Belle leaned in to kiss his muzzle. "And I hope I can do the same for you." When they parted, she shivered.

Beast wrapped his cloak around her. "Ready to go home?"

Her teeth chattered as the breeze picked up. "Please."

"Let's get you warm."

The next morning, Belle was content in Beast's arms, sleeping well past her normal time. Their nocturnal adventure had led to a late night, and she had no plans of moving until she absolutely needed to do so.

Insistent knocking on the door dashed all hopes of a tranquil morning in.

Belle cracked her eyes open, frowning. They weren't expecting company. She extracted herself from Beast's hold to tap his shoulder. "Beast," she whispered. "There's someone at the door."

"Tell them to go away," Beast grumbled.

Belle nearly hit him with a pillow before he bolted up, throwing off the blankets.

"Wait, are we in trouble?" Despite his disheveled fur, Beast was fully alert as his gaze darted wildly around the room.

"I don't know." Belle hunted around the room for a robe to cover her flimsy nightgown.

"Want me to make them go away?" Beast flexed his claws.

"I'll go with you." She found her black robe embroidered with crimson roses, and her fingers fumbled to tie the sash.

Maureen's muffled voice called, "Are you up?"

Belle's shoulders sagged, the tension lessening in her back. "Oh, well, it's just—"

The mayor's words cut her off. "I need to talk to you both. Broadcast day came sooner than I thought. Can you both come with me?"

CHAPTER NINETEEN

The hardback wooden chair in the crowded auditorium storage room was too small for Belle. Her hunched muscles ached as she fidgeted. Beast paced, nervous energy radiating from him as his cloak, billowing behind him, swished with each step. He narrowly avoided tripping over somber black ballet costumes haphazardly stacked against the dark paneled wall and colliding with a colossal timpani drum.

The door opened with a whining creak and Captain Charity poked her head in the room. Under the poor lighting, her skin paled, highlighting the dusting of freckles across her nose and shadows under her eyes. When Belle caught her gaze, the captain winked, some of her swagger returning.

"How'd it go?" The wobbly chair groaned beneath Belle as she shifted her weight.

"Better than we thought it would." Captain Charity gave them a thumbs up. "Maureen's ready for you two."

Belle gulped as Beast stopped pacing to help her out of her seat. His steadying touch grounded her trembling hands.

"Show time," Beast rumbled, his low voice only for her ears. He donned his plain black face mask, concealing his muzzle.

Belle cracked a smile, but her stomach clenched as they followed the captain to the stage. When Maureen had arrived on their doorstep this morning, she never would have guessed the mayor was going to ask them to come to the town hall meeting. She'd spent the day in panic over the decision and now felt torn between relief that the meeting was nearly over and terror that they'd made a huge mistake.

"Do you think everyone will have pitchforks and torches?" Beast whispered, snapping her out of her spiraling thoughts.

"I hope not." She shuddered at the thought of a furious mob. "Still think this was a good idea?"

He squeezed her hand as he nodded. "I'm tired of hiding. If the meeting goes well, maybe you can show me the library."

The tension in her shoulders lessened as she squeezed his paw back. "You have a deal."

The austere theater was brightly lit, prompting Beast to don his tinted goggles. Even Belle had to shield her eyes after glimpsing the packed house as Captain Charity guided them on stage. She understood why the meeting had been moved to a theater. She imagined most sessions weren't so crowded and lively.

Maureen stood at a podium speaking into a microphone, while Secretary Cadwell typed minutes on a clunky typewriter at a long table onstage. "I've invited Belle and Beast here this evening so you can put a face to your new neighbors after today's broadcast. I won't ask them to recount the events again, but they've agreed to answer a few questions."

The captain sat down next to the secretary, leaving the two seats free. The theatrical lighting cast the crowd in shadows, making the audience appear faceless and featureless. There already was a long line behind the microphone set up between the aisles. It took all of Belle's self-control to not stare at the line as she sat next to the captain.

Beast sat on the end, wisely choosing to keep his hood up and paws folded in his lap. There was no disguising his bearlike build, but his outfit helped him almost pass as a giant man—except for the tufts of white fur poking out around his goggles. Belle slipped her hand beneath the table to rest it between his paws.

Stomach souring, Belle's eyes briefly darted to the exit before turning her attention to the first speaker.

"I thought you said he was a beast? Looks like a man to me. Maybe we could use him at the docks." A stout man with an impressive steel-gray beard spoke into the microphone. His eyes darted to the stage as he nodded at Beast.

He nodded back at the stranger. Belle would bet anything his mask covered up a grin.

"Thank you, Gilbert." Maureen's lips twitched, the ghost of a smile on her lips. "Did you have an actual question?"

Gilbert swept his dusty cap off his head before answering. "I'm all in favor of the town taking in these two, but is this going to jeopardize the safety of Duchollow?"

"No, it won't." The mayor steepled her fingers, leaning over the podium. "The Ringmaster has no claim on Belle and Beast. There's nothing he can do to compel them to come back. He illegally purchased Belle as a child and wrongly imprisoned Beast. We're not harboring anyone, only protecting victims from their abuser."

Captain Charity waved from her seat, her eyes sparkling with mischief. "No one has come here looking for me. I think we're safe."

Gilbert's eyes crinkled as he looked at the captain. "At least you keep us in business, Captain. Thank you, Mayor."

The tension in Belle's shoulders lessened as she sighed. If the rest of the questions and comments were this easy, maybe tonight wouldn't be so bad.

A woman wearing a stiff mauve dress and pearls took the microphone next. "How do we know their account is true? The Circus Illume has been in operation for years. I remember taking my children to it when they were only knee-high, and now that they're grown, they've taken their children. I find this story hard to believe. It must be a scheme."

Several other suspicion-filled voices chimed in with similar comments. Belle slumped in her seat as Maureen tried in vain to gain control of the crowd, but their swelling voices drowned her out.

Beneath the table, Beast balled his paws into fists, muscles tensed as if he was ready to pounce.

"I've got this," Belle whispered to him, resting her hand on his thigh and hoping she sounded more confident than she felt.

Maureen stopped talking and Mr. Cadwell stared as Belle made her way to the podium. "May I?" She pointed to the microphone.

"You don't have to do this." The mayor placed her hand over the microphone, muffling it. "This isn't how I thought it'd be at all."

"I know." She held out her hand, waiting.

The mayor handed her the microphone. "Good luck."

Clutching the microphone like a talisman against her fear, Belle faced the crowd. The lighting was less harsh now, and she could make out the faces in the audience. Their expressions ranged from sympathetic to skeptical to angry and scared.

Taking a shuddering breath, she willed her voice not to shake. "Good evening. I'm Belle." She swallowed. "I understand there are questions about the validity of our story. Would you like to see my scars? Some of them I can't reveal without breaking decorum, but here's one."

Belle sat the microphone on the table before unlacing her boot, then pulling it and her sock off. She rolled up her trouser leg, revealing the faded, angry purple scar around her ankle, before she picked up the microphone again. Wearing only one shoe, she padded awkwardly to the edge of the stage. "Here are the marks left by the Ringmaster's treatment. He forced me to wear an electroshock anklet for nearly ten years after he purchased me from my father. When I outgrew one, he'd wait until my ankle was rubbed so raw that I couldn't perform before he replaced it. If I dared do anything to displease him, with the press of a button on his cane, a shock would shoot out of the anklet."

The townspeople muttered, giving each other uncomfortable looks.

"This isn't even the worst of my scars. Sometimes, the Ringmaster wanted a more personal touch. He'd strike my rib cage with shock sticks." She paused, her eyes meeting the accusing woman. "I was a child the first time he shocked me. There's nothing family-friendly about the Circus Illume."

The speaker pushed her way to the front of the crowd to get a look at Belle's ankle. "How could it go on so long? Aren't you a strongwoman?"

Belle shook her head. "It's hard to use that strength when the electricity's coursing through my body, setting every nerve ending on fire."

"I—" The woman opened and closed her mouth.

"Beast's treatment was just as horrific after he stumbled across my campsite and was captured by the circus. The Ringmaster hurt my only friend, the first real friend I'd ever had." Each word crackled with Belle's raw emotions. "We gain nothing from telling our stories from the Circus Illume, except for the hope the Ringmaster can't hurt us again. We just want a home."

Maureen's voice rang out in the auditorium. Even without her microphone, her voice was strong. "You heard her, folks. Can you find it in your hearts to welcome Belle and Beast into Duchollow?"

Murmurs of assent rose in the audience, filling the hall. Even the woman who'd been accusing moments ago nodded.

"Outstanding. Meeting adjourned." The mayor banged a gavel as the captain slumped forward in her seat and the secretary packed away his typewriter.

As the crowd shuffled out of the auditorium, Maureen rushed over to Belle and Beast. "Well done. I knew you two could do it." The mayor wiped the sweat off her brow. "I apologize for putting you two on the spot this morning, but it had to be done. You'll both be free to go into town."

Belle felt giddy with anticipation as she looked at Beast. "Are you sure it's going to be this simple?"

Maureen nodded. "I've lived here for years. You'll never meet a more loyal, protective community."

"Is this the same community Lucke is from?" Beast cocked his head to the side.

The captain's expression soured. "No. He's not from around here. He and his crew made port here a few times over the years."

Maureen stepped forward, her eyes cutting to Captain Charity. "There's bound to be bumps, but I think you're going to be pleasantly surprised."

Nodding, Belle followed them off the stage, closely followed by Beast. Though she appreciated the mayor's confidence, doubts plagued her. Visions of an angry, torch-bearing mob descending on the cottage dominated her thoughts.

"Hey, still up for taking me to the library tomorrow?" Beast nudged her, pulling her out of her spiraling thoughts.

Brows furrowed, Belle whispered back, "Are you sure?"

"I think it'd do us both a world of good to get out of the cottage. And you miss it, right?"

With a tight smile, she nodded. "I'll ask Maureen for the keys when we're on the way home. We'll leave early tomorrow."

The next day, Belle and Beast entered Duchollow just after dawn when most of the town was sleeping. Rosy lights bathed the colorful shops near the plaza in soft hues. The vendors at the food stalls were busy lighting their tiny stoves and brewing rich coffee. Birds sang their good morning songs as they hovered near the stalls, waiting for scraps left over from food preparations. No one interrupted their morning stroll to the library.

The tension Belle had been carrying since last night's meeting melted as she opened the building's creaky double doors and led Beast inside. When she carefully turned the lights on low, his eyes went wide.

"I'm surprised you don't spend all your time here. This place feels very...you." He stood in the center of the room, his gaze fixed on the faded celestial pattern painted on the ceiling as he placed his knapsack on the floor next to a towering stack of weathered books. The low gas lamp chandeliers and wall sconces reflected off the suspended, dormant orrery. Specks of dust floated and glittered in the beams of sunlight peeking through the broken windows. "I love it."

Belle beamed as she set her pack down and rummaged through it. "I'm glad you like it." She retrieved a cleaning cloth and held it up. "Are you sure this is what you want to be doing on your first official day in Duchollow? You can go exploring anywhere you want in town or pick up supplies for your garden."

"There's nowhere I'd rather be." Beast's eyes crinkled. "I get to spend the day with you. Everything else can wait."

Despite the flutters in her stomach, she couldn't resist a smirk as she tossed him a rag. "Even if it means scrubbing this filthy place from top to bottom?"

He caught the cleaning cloth with a flourish and a wink. "I don't mind getting dirty. Lunch in town?"

Arching her brows, she playfully flicked his shoulder with her cloth. "First one to finish their half chooses where?"

"You're on." He waved his rag in salute before He waved his rag in salute before scampering to the nearest bookcase and furiously scrubbing at the built-up grime on its shelves.

"Wait! We're starting on the Archives. Top to bottom!" Her protests turned into cackling as Beast raced up the winding staircase on all fours.

Laughter and howling shrieks filled the library as they cleaned. Belle pressed a dusty handprint on Beast's back. He retaliated by strategically covering her cobalt blouse from hem to collar in paw prints.

In retaliation, she grabbed both of their rags and chased him between the bookshelves, leaping over stacks of books strewn about the room. She narrowly avoided a collision with the cart-like machinery used to transport books on miniature tracks from the Archives down to the main desk on the first floor. Beast recklessly sprinted ahead, soon cornering himself in a narrow corridor lined with shelves precariously full of rare volumes.

With a mischievous glint in her eyes, Belle tossed the cloths at him. They exploded with plumes of dust as they hit his ruined shirt.

"It's like that, huh?" Beast grabbed her by the waist.

Belle broke free of his grip and pinned him against the bookcase by his wrists. He strained against her hold, to no avail. Leaning in close, she brushed her lips against his ear as she replied, "It's like that."

"If you say so." He gave her a feral grin before lowering his mouth, eliciting a whimper from her as his muzzle caressed her neck.

"Oh, that's not playing fair." She panted as he nipped at a sensitive spot near the base of her throat.

Beast stopped his ministrations to growl in her ear. "Who said I was playing?"

Undone, Belle shakily released his wrists before wrapping her arms around him to pull him closer. Her eyes fluttered closed as she whispered, "More."

With a low growl, he switched places with her, pinning her against the bookcase. As he leaned in to lavish attention on her neck, Belle stumbled backward, knocking a book off the crowded shelf with a resounding thud.

The spell was broken as he looked mortified at the fallen volume. "I'm so sorry. I know how you feel about your books."

Laughter bubbled out of Belle as she shook her head. "It was worth it. Let me check the damage."

After wiping her hands on her trousers, she picked up the book and frowned at the grime sticking to the cover. She retrieved a spare cloth from her pocket and did her best to clean the filth. When she finished, she gasped as she opened it, turning the pages rapidly.

"What's wrong?" He peeked over her shoulder.

Belle held up the stained and cracked leather-bound book. In faded gilded lettering, it read, *Incidents of Outlandish Transmutations,* surrounded by indecipherable runes etched into the cover.

"It's a book documenting early experiments in alchemy and ether. As old as it is, I bet it predates knowledge about the risks of ether-poisoning. Look, there are even diagrams of transformed rats." She grimaced as she flipped through the pages of rats with too many eyes and appendages, then looked up to meet Beast's mortified gaze. "Sorry, it's gruesome."

"You think this will help Maureen's research?" Doubt seeped into his voice as he tapped an illustration of a rat whose teeth had elongated to the point of curling into tusks.

"Maybe? It couldn't hurt to ask." She tapped the cover absently. "What's a book like this doing in the Archives?"

"Are you guys in here?" Captain Charity's voice floated from downstairs.

Belle jumped, then burst into laughter at the put-upon expression on Beast's face. Neither of them had expected company.

"It's always something," he muttered as he helped her straighten her crooked blouse.

"Is there anything on me?" She tilted her head as he made a show of carefully inspecting her outfit.

"You're fine." He brushed a loose strand of her hair back before briefly resting his forehead against hers.

Pocketing the book, Belle took his arm as they descended the stairs together.

Captain Charity waited for them in the center of the room, fingers looped into her belt as she surveyed them with a calculating stare. "Everything okay? I called your names a few times."

"We've been cleaning the Archives upstairs." Belle held up her cloth, willing herself to not blush.

The captain's gaze lowered to the dusty paw prints covering most of Belle's shirt. She snorted. "Cleaning, huh?"

"Yes. Have to get the library in shape so Miss Bookworm can get to the fun part of organizing the collection." Beast slung his arm around Belle and grinned.

Captain Charity bit her lip as she shook her head. "I see. I thought since it was Beast's first official day in town, I'd treat you both to lunch and show you where some of the best spots are. Maureen said she'd join us, too." She smiled slyly. "If we're not intruding."

"We can always finish cleaning later. Let's go." Beast nudged Belle. "And we can show Maureen the book you found."

"True." She smiled warmly at him before turning her attention back to the captain. "We'd love the company and a tour. Thank you."

"Do you want to get cleaned up first?" Captain Charity gestured to their grimy outfits.

Covering her face with her fingers spread wide, Belle replied, "Good idea. This probably isn't the best look for our first outing in town."

After Belle and Beast changed into their spare clothes, Captain Charity took them to a lovely café that featured potted plants and antique vases decorating the room. Maureen waited at a spacious table in the corner with a steaming mug of coffee the size of a bowl. The other patrons didn't stare at Beast, more interested in their lunches, so Belle took that as a win. Though the town hall meeting last night had ended well, she was relieved the patrons in the restaurant gave them space.

After exchanging pleasantries and ordering food, Belle fished the transmutations book out of her knapsack and slid it toward the mayor. "I found something in the Archives today that might interest you."

"What's that?" Maureen paused mid-sip, her eyes fixed on the book. Steam fogged her glasses, obscuring her expression.

Belle folded her hands in her lap, resisting the urge to talk with her hands and risking knocking over their drinks. "It fell off a bookshelf while we were cleaning. I took it because I thought it might help with your research for his cure."

Captain Charity snorted at the word "cleaning" as Maureen reached for the ancient text. The mayor's expression turned dreamy as she flipped the pages and muttered to herself.

It took all of Belle's self-control to not fidget as she waited for the other woman to finish examining the book. She was rewarded for her patience when Maureen's eyes shone with a manic gleam. "This could be it! Maybe there's a link to ether-poisoning and Beast's condition, after all." She thumbed through the book, skimming until she got to a passage with shape-shifting rats on it. "I'll need to read more and finish up testing for my invention, but we might be close to a cure before the Festival."

"You mean there actually might be something useful in that?" Beast stared at the mayor.

"If this book is accurate. Yes." Maureen's eyes glowed as she retrieved a notebook from her pocket and scribbled in it.

"But what was a book like this doing in the Archives?" Belle asked.

Maureen looked up from her notes, her lips pursed. "Good question. I'd love to know."

Any further speculation was cut off by the arrival of their food. Despite Belle's happiness that her instincts about the book had been correct, she couldn't help wondering what Maureen had known about the Archives before asking her to work at the library. She couldn't shake the feeling there was more to this story than altruism.

CHAPTER TWENTY

"I could hop on the *Figment* right now and be on a beach tomorrow collecting shells," Captain Charity grumbled as she reassembled a bookshelf while Belle and Beast rearranged the furniture on the library's first floor.

"I wouldn't have guessed you were a beachcomber." Belle grunted as the bookcase she carried with Beast wobbled. "A little more to the left, please."

"On it." He adjusted his grip as Belle guided him.

Together, they righted another fallen bookcase. After a week of deep cleaning, the library was considerably less filthy but still in dire need of repairs, fresh paint, and straightening. Belle was curious about what had happened to the library during the years between its closure and now, as much of the furniture had been knocked over or broken.

She was thankful for the library project as a distraction. Both Belle and Beast had been preoccupied with thoughts of the book on transmutations they had given to Maureen. Unfortunately, testing the hypothesis was taking longer than the mayor expected, leaving everyone involved on edge as she threw herself into her research. With the Festival fast approaching and the deadline looming for the mayor's secretive invention, Belle wasn't confident when the cure would arrive, so she dealt with her anxieties by sprucing up the library. The physical work helped clear her mind and allowed her to sleep soundly, as she was too tired to lie awake worrying.

Beast accompanied Belle every day to work on the library's restoration, but this morning, the captain surprised them both by coming along. Captain Charity followed them inside after driving them in Maureen's stead. The airship pilot proved herself adept with tools as she reassembled bookcases.

"I feel like I'm going out of my mind listening to Maureen. When she's not working on the cure, she's perfecting her Festival invention. She's so close, and I know she can do it, but there's no living with her when she's obsessing. The lab is in chaos and Maker help you if you accidentally move anything important." The captain gritted her teeth as she adjusted a too-tight screw. "Hope I didn't strip this. There we go."

Belle wiped her brow before sitting on a lumpy armchair nearby and took a long drink of water from her canteen.

Beast flopped down on the other armchair and drank from his canteen before replying, "I'm sorry working on my cure has made her like this."

"She's always like this when she's deep in a project. I swear, it's part of her process." She shrugged before grinning brightly. "It's also why I'm sure she's going to succeed with the cure. It's part of her pattern."

"Do you really want to go to the beach, though?" Belle asked.

Captain Charity flushed and scratched the back of her neck. "No, I don't want to make Maureen anxious, and I need to make sure she stays safe, too. Maybe I can convince her to go with me after the Festival if she's not busy."

The front door of the library creaking open made all three of them jump.

Maureen poked her head inside, her bloodshot eyes framed by dark circles and crooked octagonal glasses. "Sorry to interrupt, but Beast, I need you to go to the lab for a fresh blood sample. I'm getting close to a tangible solution, but it needs testing."

Beast dropped his canteen, sputtering and spilling water as he stared at the mayor. Belle recovered first and used a spare rag to dry the soaked rug.

"Thank you." His voice shook as he helped her clean up.

"Don't worry about it. I've got this." Belle touched his paw. "You should go with Maureen."

He drew a shaky breath as he stood and nodded at the mayor. "Let me finish up here and we can go."

Maureen blinked, turning her attention to Belle and Captain Charity as if noticing their presence for the first time. Almost as soon as she looked at the captain, she looked away. Turning to leave, she called over her shoulder, "You two can come as well, so you know what to expect when it's time. The equipment is nearly ready."

Belle buzzed with anticipation. She hadn't allowed herself to daydream much about life after a cure for Beast, but now she was dying to know what he'd looked like before his transformation. Although she was eager for him to be healed, her curiosity got the best of her. Her imagination came up with a blank when trying to conjure an image of Beast as a man.

Not even Captain Charity's sarcastic grumbling as she shuffled behind the group could dampen Belle's enthusiasm. "Oh, goody, the lab again. It's not like I was avoiding there to escape someone's mood swings or anything."

The lab was so much worse than Captain Charity had hinted at. While Belle had seen the mayor's workspace in a state of disarray before, this was pure mayhem. Maureen's secret work-in-progress was at the epicenter of the chaotic maelstrom. Whatever it was, the machine was massive, dominating the room along with the schematics and spare parts strewn everywhere.

On the other side of the lab, an ornate silver metal mask and matching bracers rested on a Beast-sized examination chair. The mask resembled a metallic wolf's head with crimson eyes. Clear tubing snaked around the arm of the chair and out of one bracer.

Damek swept the chaos, collecting fallen parts into multiple piles in the room's corner. "Have you three come to talk her down? She hasn't slept in twenty-eight hours." The automaton greeted them, adding another hunk of scrap metal to the organized mess.

Belle's jaw dropped. As much as she wanted a cure, she didn't want Beast endangered because of sleep deprivation. "Why don't you get some sleep? Can't we test this out tomorrow?"

"I'll sleep after this." Maureen waved her hand dismissively, suppressing a yawn as she gestured to the complex chair. "Beast, have a seat."

He eyed the mask warily as he sat down. "It's a little snug, but I can fit."

"Let me adjust the settings. We won't test the tubes today. I just need to see if everything fits." She fidgeted with the base of the chair, and the armrests expanded, making more room for his frame.

When the mayor placed the mask on Beast, the gears that made up its intricate design whirred, adjusting the size of the mask until it completely covered his face but leaving an opening for his mouth and a strap around the back of his head. The bracers accommodated his strong forearms similarly, clicking into place.

"You look like you're off to a costume ball." Belle furrowed her brows at the odd machinery.

Beast cracked a smile, his canines poking through the open mouth of the mask.

"It looks like everything fits. Let's draw your blood so I can test my theory." Maureen removed the strange mask and bracers.

Beast shuddered as the mayor stored the equipment. "Are you sure those are necessary?"

"Yes, I'm sorry." Maureen prepped the vials and syringe.

Belle wiggled past the work table to stand by Beast and squeeze his paw.

He sighed, holding her hand a little tighter. "I'll live with it, then."

After Maureen drew two vials worth of Beast's blood, she smiled triumphantly. "We might start testing as soon as tomorrow."

Belle and Beast stared at the mayor.

Belle's heart hammered. She hoped his cure wasn't as violent as hers.

As if reading her mind, he whispered in her ear, "I'll be fine."

"I should be comforting you. I'm sorry." She rested her head against his shoulder.

"If my calculations are correct, and they usually are, the procedure should go smoothly. But first, let's get you home to rest." The mayor took two steps forward before swaying on the spot.

"I'm driving," Captain Charity said firmly, catching her in her arms.

"Thanks, Darling." Maureen yawned, leaning into her.

"Finally, she agrees to something sensible." Damek shook his head, solenoids buzzing as he tidied stacks of schematics.

Black thunderclouds gathered overhead as Captain Charity drove them home. The air smelled of petrichor, and the birds gave warning caws as they took shelter. Maureen had insisted she tag along, saying that she could tell them more about the cure on the way, but by the time they'd driven around the block she was hunched over in the passenger seat sound asleep.

When they reached the cottage, Belle exited the vehicle with Beast, waving goodbye to Captain Charity.

"What is it?" Belle didn't miss his hackles rising as they approached the porch.

"I'm not sure. Something feels off." He snarled as he stepped in front of her, reaching for the door handle.

The truck idled as Captain Charity leaned out of the open driver's side window. "Is something wrong?"

Beast bared his teeth as he opened the door. "Something doesn't smell right."

Belle followed Beast inside. The lights came on, but neither had turned on the switch. The Ringmaster leaned against the wall, holding a cane in one hand and a chain leash in the other, two growling Hounds tethered to him. He wore a crumpled flamboyant red suit and smeared eyeliner ran down his cheekbones. Jagged rips crisscrossed his pants and coat.

There was a manic gleam in his eyes as he stepped closer, sharply tugging on the chain. The bipedal canines trailed behind him. "Charming place you have here." The Ringmaster's conversational tone clashed with his unhinged appearance as he looked around the room. "Shame you have to leave it."

"Get back!" Beast stood in front of her.

"No, you get help!" Belle stepped around Beast and planted her feet firmly in front of him. She hoped he had the sense to listen to her pleas, but his breath was hot on the back of her neck as he growled at the trio of intruders before them.

The storm rattled their cottage, a flash of lightning illuminating the Ringmaster's teeth as he grinned and released the leashes. His pets leapt, aiming straight for Belle. Their chains dragged behind them, clanging against the wood floor.

She braced herself for impact, but Beast pulled her out of the way, his claws digging into her side. She tumbled into his chest, and they collided against the wall with a thud.

Far too close for comfort, the Hounds crashed into the front door. Their limbs became entangled, and they growled as they snipped at each other. Their chains whipped, striking the walls and leaving gashes in the woodgrain.

"Enough." The Ringmaster's voice rang out. The snarling stopped with a click of his cane as shocks coursed through the whimpering creatures. They twitched before coming to a seated position, whining as they ducked their heads.

"Did you really think you'd escape me?" Thunder cracked outside and rain pelted against the roof as the Ringmaster stalked closer, a shock stick emitting blue sparks in one hand and his black cane in the other. The air clinging to his tattered suit smelled of ozone and cheap beer.

As Belle helped Beast up, she whispered, "Go get Captain Charity. I've got this."

Her heart hammered as he stared at her.

"I can't leave you with him," Beast snarled.

"You can and you will."

"Oh, that's just precious," the Ringmaster spat.

"I'll be fine." She set her jaw.

Beast growled as he charged toward the open door.

"Get him." The Ringmaster held up his cane, his finger hovering above the shock button.

The canines snapped to attention, their fear evaporating as they scrambled after Beast.

"Looks like it's just us again." The Ringmaster's lip curled as he leered.

Over the whistling gales of wind and pouring rain, Beast bellowed, "The Ringmaster's inside with two Hounds!"

Belle thought she could hear the truck rumbling. Hope surged in her chest, only to be dashed as both creatures dragged Beast back inside, ripping his soaked shirt. Beast staggered from the door, flinging his attackers toward the Ringmaster. The scowling man retreated against the wall across the room, his hate-filled gaze never leaving Belle.

Wind howled through the open door. Rain pooled around the entrance. Another flash of lightning revealed the all too familiar crimson orb collars on the canines as they shook off fat droplets of water.

Belle's gaze fell to the tatters on the Ringmaster's filthy red suit, where it appeared claws had reduced a trouser leg to ribbons. "Keep his dogs busy," she whispered to Beast as he neared.

He grunted in response, lunging toward the larger gray one.

Belle stretched her stiff neck and cracked her knuckles as she approached the Ringmaster.

"Don't come any closer, girl." He waved his shock stick.

Dodging his attack, she swiftly grabbed the cane out of his hand. She smirked as she snapped the device in half. "No more pets for you."

The Ringmaster threw back his head as he guffawed. "Do you really think I'd be foolish enough to let you defeat me the same way again?" The light of the gas lamps glinted off a charm on his good sleeve. It glowed crimson, similar to the charm Delphine had used to control the Hound at the circus trailer.

"What?" Belle sputtered until the russet-colored animal leapt at her. The Hound landed painfully against her side, and they tumbled to the floor. The writhing canine's rank breath was far too close, making her retch.

Finally, Belle freed herself with a swift backhand to the foul muzzle. Wincing, she stood. Saliva dripped from his mouth as he snarled and crouched low, hackles raised. This time when he charged, she was ready. By leveraging his momentum, she flung him backward, narrowly missing Captain Charity and Maureen as they dashed inside.

Belle was disappointed that the captain didn't have her saber. Instead, Captain Charity wielded a wrench while the mayor clutched her mechanical screwdriver.

The captain's boot pressed down on the leash while the creature was prone. She caught Belle's eye as she struggled to keep her footing. "I can't hold it long."

Maureen hovered behind the cornered animal, her eyes trained on the collar's orb.

As the Hound rose, shaking the chain, Belle rushed over to catch him and pinned his arms behind his back. He strained against her hold. It took all her restraint to prevent her grip from causing permanent damage to his ribcage.

"Hurry," Belle grunted.

"On it!" Maureen deftly popped out the crimson orb with her tool, deactivating the Ringmaster's control. With another swift movement, she unlocked the collar, which clattered to the floor. Instantly, the canine became still and stopped snarling as Belle released him.

Despite his suddenly mild manner, she remained vigilant. Instead of lashing out, he shook his head as though he were disoriented. With a feeble whine, he retreated into a corner, his tail drooping.

Across the room, Beast and the other Hound fell through the coffee table, breaking it in half. They rolled off the debris, neither appearing ready to surrender. The creature slashed at Beast, narrowly missing his eyes. Beast countered with a forceful headbutt, causing his opponent to yelp.

"Hang on, I'll remove this one's collar, too." Maureen raced forward, Captain Charity at her side.

"You'll do no such thing!" the Ringmaster's cruel voice rang out.

Belle swore. She'd lost track of him while worrying about Beast. Where was he?

Unfortunately, she didn't have to wait long for an answer. Behind Beast, electricity sparked as the Ringmaster held his shock stick poised to strike. Time seemed to move in slow motion for Belle as she sprinted across the room, vaulting over fallen furniture. She launched herself at the Ringmaster. The force of the collision knocked the vile man over, sending the shock stick flying.

Maureen knelt by the dazed Hound, dexterously removing the collar while Captain Charity helped Beast stand. The captain anxiously peered at the mayor as she worked.

Belle caught the Ringmaster by the throat. Beneath her fingertips, she could feel his pulse thrum. "This ends now."

"You don't have the nerve." He curled his lip in disdain even as he choked.

For a terrible moment, all the pain from years as the Ringmaster's captive came flooding back to Belle.

The Ringmaster, wielding his shock sticks, loomed over nine-year-old Belle after she'd botched her stunt.

Locked in a dark trailer, ten-year-old Belle's stolen books provided the Ringmaster kindling for the night. The air still stank of smoke the next day.

The Ringmaster's sneer as he stepped over the body of the short-lived circus tiger.

Fifteen-year-old Belle, left alone in the dark yet again, wondering if the Ringmaster was going to starve her for real this time.

Beast's final plea for help before the Ringmaster shocked him into unconsciousness.

Leaning in close, Belle gritted her teeth. "I'm not like you."

With that, she let him go. The Ringmaster fell to his knees, gasping and glaring at her.

Belle ripped the cuff-link charm off the Ringmaster's sleeve before trudging toward the fallen shock stick. Electricity fizzled as she crunched his favorite toys beneath her boots.

"I said it was over." Her breathing was ragged as she stumbled. Beast ran over to hold her up.

"You need bandages and pain medicine." Beast furrowed his brow as he brushed her hair back. Drenched and covered in scratches, his clothes were utterly destroyed.

"So do you. What are we going to do with him?" Belle pointed to the fuming Ringmaster. "And them?" She jabbed her thumb at the Hounds as they licked their wounds.

Outside, the thunder quieted into a gentle rumble as the wind died down.

"I have a few ideas." Maureen's gaze hardened.

CHAPTER TWENTY-ONE

Two days after the break-in, the early morning light streaming through the open windows brought the damage inside of the cottage into stark reality as Belle and Beast redoubled their cleaning efforts. The shattered coffee table and bits of cushioning from the sofa littered the sitting room. Deep scratches crisscrossed the wooden floor and marred the walls from the entryway through their sitting room. Worst of all, the scent of wet fur still lingered, prompting Belle to open all the windows. The gentle breeze did little to eliminate the pungent scent.

Beast was somber as he swept up pieces of smashed radio. The shallow scratches and bite marks on his arms were healing, barely visible through his pale fur. "This was a new low, even for that vile man." He wrinkled his nose as he held up one of the broken dials. "We could have at least had some music while we fixed this mess."

"We don't have to do this today." Belle wrung her hands, eyeing the note on their kitchen table written in Maureen's small, scrawling handwriting.

Yesterday, while they'd slept off the adrenaline rush after the confrontation, Maureen had stopped by the cottage to install a new lock. She'd left a note about a breakthrough in Beast's cure. She would be ready for them as early as today. After that, both Belle and

Beast had wavered between hope and fear as they counted down the hours until the mayor's arrival. Cleaning was the distraction they both needed, or so Belle had thought, but now she had doubts.

"It's the first chance we've had to clean since the break-in." He gestured to the debris piled haphazardly against the hallway. "I'm tired of looking at all this, aren't you?"

She bit her lip. "Yes, but it's your cure day."

"Potential cure." Beast raised a single claw. "It'll be one less thing to worry about while I'm hopefully on the mend."

Belle fidgeted. "I know, but I wish that I could have had time to take your mind off of things."

Beast placed the remains of the radio on the kitchen table and strode back across the room. He tucked his paw under her chin and tilted her face toward him so she wouldn't miss the searing look in his eyes. The leathery pad of his thumb lightly rubbed against her bottom lip. "You being here with me is enough. Besides, there's not enough time for us to do what I'd like to…and with your injuries, you're in no state for it, anyway. It can wait until I'm cured."

Oh.

A teasing smile tugged at Belle's lips. "My injuries aren't that—"

Familiar knocking on the door cut off the rest of her reply.

"We're here!" Captain Charity's cheery voice was muffled by the newly reinforced door.

"Right on time," Beast muttered under his breath in a rumbling growl.

Slipping out of his arms, Belle gave him a quick kiss on the side of his muzzle before answering the door to the captain and Maureen. The mayor looked better rested than she had in several days.

"Sorry we're running late. I was checking in on the Hounds." A shadow passed over Maureen's face before she brightened. "At least they seem to cooperate."

Belle's pulse quickened. The mayor had been vague about the details of the Hounds and the Ringmaster's location. With everything going on, she hadn't wanted to push, but she couldn't help asking as she let in the captain and mayor. "What about the Ringmaster?"

Maureen's mouth set in a grim line. "He won't talk. I'm sure Lucke helped him, but I don't have proof yet. Give it time."

"Maker's moldy knickers," the captain muttered under her breath as she nearly tripped over the debris stacked in the entryway.

Maureen looked pointedly at the faint scratches on Beast's arms. "Are you feeling up to the procedure? It's going to take a lot out of you."

"I'm ready. Our bags are packed." The shaking in his clenched paws betrayed his confident tone.

Belle's stomach felt like it was in knots. She desperately wanted Beast cured, but she was terrified. How much more complex was his experimental process going to be than her own procedure? "Are you sure you're well enough? Those bite wounds are still healing."

Beast brushed back a strand of her hair. "I'll be fine. This is the first step in starting our lives together."

She traced his jawline tenderly before leaning in to rest her forehead against his. "Okay. I'll be right there with you."

When they broke apart, their friends pretended to examine the shattered radio, but the captain's red-rimmed eyes glistened with unshed tears.

Maureen's eyes were suspiciously bright as she cleared her throat. "Let's go. I'll get you a new radio to celebrate your recovery."

When they arrived at the lab, Maureen ushered Beast to the custom-built examination chair, where the disturbing metal mask and gauntlets balanced on the armrests. A strange astringent smell mingled with the familiar scents of old books and strong coffee. Ominously intricate machinery nearly as tall as Belle surrounded the chair, including several stands housing IVs filled with shimmering blue liquid.

Captain Charity brought Belle a stool before assisting the mayor with the vast array of knobs and dials on the equipment. The machinery hummed to life, occasionally emitting hisses and groans as internal gears turned. Belle barely had time to give Beast a quick kiss and hold his paws as the mask clicked into place, adjusting to fit his head. Maureen tightened the gauntlets around his forearms, checking them over before inserting the tubing.

"Flip the last switch, Darling." The mayor kept her eyes trained on Beast as the mask's eyes lit up a deep crimson.

When Captain Charity flipped the switch, the machines looked like they were breathing the way they moved in sync, pneumatics wheezing as the machine pumped elixirs into Beast.

A lump formed in Belle's throat as his grip tightened around her hands. She laced her fingers with his as he thrashed, straining against the creaking restraints. His bellows drowned out the noise of the machines. With another swift movement, she unlocked the collar, which clattered to the floor.

"Do something!" Belle's heart hammered as he slumped in his seat, unnaturally still.

Beast blinked woozily as Maureen and Captain Charity removed the equipment and dimmed the lights low enough for his comfort. His appearance was unchanged. "What happened?" he rasped.

"The elixir didn't take." Maureen spat the words, slamming her fist down on a table and scattering a pile of notes. Grumbling under her breath as she gathered the papers, she muttered, "Why didn't it work?"

Beast closed his eyes, clenching the armrests. "I shouldn't have dared to hope."

"Can we have a moment?" Belle shot the others a look.

Captain Charity took her mumbling partner by the elbow. "We'll be in the next room." They departed through the hidden entrance in the bookcase leading to the mayor's office.

When the door closed, Belle leaned over Beast and carefully tapped his paw. "Beast?"

He opened his goldenrod eyes slowly. Defeat was etched into his features as his shoulders hunched.

"I should have known it wouldn't work." His hoarse voice was barely above a whisper.

"It was only the first try. Maureen hasn't had the transfiguration book long. I'm sure she'll come up with a new plan." Her heart ached at his broken expression.

"What if it never works?" His gaze lowered. "I can't keep you shackled to me."

"Please look at me."

Reluctantly, he looked up.

"I'm not shackled to you. Besides, you were wrong about something." She touched her forehead to his. "This wasn't the first step to starting our lives. We're already together, so we should make the most out of what we have. Cure or no cure, I'll be with you so long as you'll have me."

Beast wrapped his arms around her, pulling her down to straddle his lap. With a trembling paw, he cupped the side of her face. "I don't know what I did to deserve you, but I'm grateful. I love you."

"You didn't need to do anything. I love you for who you are. Simple as that." Belle ran her fingers through the fur on the back of his neck.

"I've got it!" Maureen burst through the bookcase entrance a moment after it squeaked open, waving her notes. "I'll cure the Hounds, then we'll try again." Her expression soured. "But first, we need to get through the Festival. We only have a few days left to prepare."

Belle's eyebrows rose. "What do you mean, 'we'? What festival?"

"You didn't tell them?" Captain Charity poked her head in the lab through the open door, then stepped through the entrance. "No wonder they look so confused."

Maureen pushed one of her beaded braids out of her face, and she pursed her lips. "I meant to tell them sooner, but between working on a cure for Beast, the break-in, dealing with the Hounds, and, oh yes, actually finishing my invention, it slipped my mind."

Belle gave Beast a quick kiss on the side of his muzzle before wriggling free of his paws. Straightening her blouse as she gathered her thoughts, she gave the mayor a pointed look. "Now's as good of a time as any to tell us what's going on."

"Right." Maureen placed her stack of papers on the closest work table and pushed her glasses up. "With the Ringmaster refusing to reveal how he entered Duchollow with two Hounds and Delphine's movements unknown, I think it'd be best if you and Beast came with me to Onyxmark."

Despite her tumultuous feelings, Belle smiled softly as she remembered her first escape from the Circus Illume, spending the day at the orrery in Onyxmark. Though her freedom had been cut short, not even the Ringmaster's cruelty could eradicate her memories of the dazzling bejeweled solar system model.

"Won't we be at more risk in a new city? From what little I know of Onyxmark, it's huge." Beast leaned forward, resting his muzzle on his paw.

Maureen shook her head. "There's a risk either way, but the Ringmaster breaking into your home worries me. He must have had some inside information to know where you lived. I never told Lucke or the *Curiosity* crew about your location."

"Unless he used the Hounds somehow to track us?" Belle tucked her chin in her hand, mirroring Beast as she thought. "Would something like that even be possible?"

Captain Charity's eyes widened. "That never occurred to me. What about you?"

Pinching the bridge of her nose, the mayor groaned. "No, but it is now. Wonderful. Another variable."

"Speaking of the Hounds, is it safe to keep them in Duchollow?" Belle bit her lip. She felt terrible for the Hounds, but she couldn't help wondering if the abuse they'd suffered made them impossible to rehabilitate.

The mayor put her hands in her pockets and shrugged. "The Hounds are being well-cared for and protected. They'll pose no risk to the community while I'm away. Luckily, they've been docile since the Ringmaster's control over them ended."

Belle narrowed her eyes. She hated ambiguity, but there was another matter, far more pressing than the mayor's caginess. "What about Beast? He's still recovering, and he stands out in a crowd."

Sighing, Maureen rubbed her temples. "I was hoping he would be cured before I came up with this idea. What would you do? Our options aren't great. Either Beast stays in Duchollow, potentially a vulnerable target, or comes with us. I don't think Delphine would expect him to attend the Festival."

"Would Belle be safer in Onyxmark?" Beast shifted in his seat as he looked at the mayor.

"Yes, undoubtedly, but it'd be worse to split you two up. I know it looks like I have unlimited resources, but they're finite."

"Then we'll go to Onyxmark, if Belle wants to go." He reached for her hand and squeezed it. "What do you want to do?"

Belle ran her free hand through her hair. "I don't know. I'd rather not move you, but the idea of sitting at home wondering if more Hounds will show up feels like a terrible plan."

"I'll be fine."

"Are you sure? We don't even know what the Festival is or what Maureen's bringing to it." Frowning, she turned her attention back to the mayor. "Won't you be too busy with your invention to help us?"

Maureen blinked before her mouth broke into a wide grin. "Not at all! The Festival celebrates Nuzaran's technological advances and rewards ingenuity. My machine is going to alter the landscape for the better for everyone. Do you want to see it? I think my work will particularly interest you, Belle."

"Shouldn't we get Beast home so he can rest?" She gave him an anxious look, but his attention was completely on the mayor.

"Let's see what she's done. I'm curious. Aren't you?" His tone was light and teasing.

Belle was intrigued, but she'd rather wait to find out what the mayor was up to. They had more pressing matters to attend to if they were going to go through with this plan. Unfortunately, she made the mistake of looking back at Beast, who was giving her puppy dog eyes.

Defeated, she sighed. "Fine, I'd love to see it."

"I thought you said it wasn't ready for a demonstration?" Captain Charity blanched as Maureen dashed toward the bookcase to the right of the secret entrance.

"Nonsense. It'll be fine." The mayor removed a plain blue book on the shelf, revealing a panel with an array of buttons and switches. In a flurry of movements, she pushed a combination of buttons before throwing a switch.

In the center of the lab, the floor groaned and creaked as a hidden trapdoor revealed itself, creating a massive square hole between the work tables. Pneumatics hissed and gears turned as a platform raised up from the newly created opening until at last, a complex machine comprising a copper frame housing an array of glass vials with wide bases, gears, and tubing weaved between everything. In the center of it all, a metal rod with a spherical end protruded from the top of it.

Belle couldn't take her eyes off the machine. "What does it do?"

Maureen twisted a knob on the machine. "It creates an artificial replacement for ether. Best of all, there are no ether-poisoning side effects. I've run the numbers."

"That's incredible!" Belle took a sharp intake of breath. She knew the mayor had previously created machines to keep the ether-miners out of danger, but knowing that no one else would have to suffer the way she or countless others had was staggering. "What do you call it?"

Captain Charity covered her face with her hand and shook her head. "Don't ask her that. Maureen's terrible with names. You should have heard what she called Damek before I rescued him."

Scowling, Maureen cut her eyes at the captain. "Thanks, Darling. The name is a work in progress, but I'll come up with something. Now, for the demonstration!"

Reluctantly, Captain Charity was at the mayor's side, pouring ingredients retrieved from cabinets into several of the machine's vials, leaving one of the giant vials empty.

"Goggles on!" Maureen pointed, and Captain Charity soon produced tinted goggles for everyone.

Belle barely had time to adjust her eyes to the tinted lenses before the mayor turned a knob and toggled a switch on. A blue flame lit underneath the filled glass vials, and crackling electricity arced from the central rod.

Both Beast and Belle covered their ears when the machine emitted a loud boom, shaking the lab.

"Everything's fine! Don't panic!" Maureen's voice was shrill as she flipped more switches and adjusted the dial. The machine sparked and groaned in protest.

"See? Not ready!" Captain Charity gritted her teeth as she covered her ears.

"Not helping! Flip that." Maureen nodded at a switch, her own hands full as she turned two knobs.

The captain did so, and the noise instantly quieted down. Steam billowed around the machine, but it seemed otherwise intact. All the vials were empty, save the last one, which was now filled with shimmering, blue-silver liquid.

"Ta da!" With a flourish, Maureen pointed to the liquid. "My invention needs some fine-tuning, but it'll be ready on time."

"That's incredible." Beast turned to Belle. "Are you glad we stayed?"

"I suppose..." Her ears were still ringing, and exhaustion hit her in a wave. "Can we go home now?"

"Let me clean up here, and we'll get you two home." Maureen stretched, wincing as her back popped. "The Festival is only a few days away. If you two are going, and I think you should, I'll need to know soon."

Beast rose from his chair and nodded.

Belle rubbed her temples to ease her headache. "I think going to Onyxmark with you two would be for the best. I'm not completely sure about the idea, but at least it's a plan."

"Excellent! Leave the arrangements to Darling and me." Maureen beamed, just as the machine mutinied with a spark. "Oh, stop that." The inventor swatted at the machine playfully as she flipped a switch.

"Everything will work out." Beast's voice rumbled in Belle's ear as he put his arm around her.

The sputtering machine coughing out more smoke did not inspire her with confidence.

In what felt like the longest week of her life, Belle counted down the days until the Festival by throwing herself into the library restoration project. By the time there were only two days left until their departure, she felt ready to explode from a combination of nerves and anticipation. To her disappointment, Beast had turned down her invitation to join her at the library, saying his garden needed attention.

She wasn't worried that he had his own work, but the sadness permeating his smiles broke her heart. When Beast thought she wasn't paying attention, the brave front he put on flickered and despair settled in. The bleak look in his eyes broke her heart.

Unfortunately, Belle had forgotten today was the day the contractors would begin the arduous task of repairing the cracks in the library's walls, undoing the damage left from years of neglect. The clanking of mechanical ladders unfolding, coupled with the workers' chatter and raucous laughter, set her teeth on edge as she tried to focus on the task at hand.

Across from the racket, she stood in front of a bookcase with a deep frown on her face, book in hand. Behind her, a trolley filled with more books waited to be shelved. "How did I miss this one?" Swearing under her breath, she realized that in order to fit in the missing volume, she'd have to slide over a book from each shelf. Her stiff muscles burned as she stretched, eyeing the stack of books with disdain.

A loud buzz sounded directly behind her, the droning boring into her skull. Belle narrowed her eyes as the contractors lined up a series of steam-powered cat-sized machines against the wall. The machines had treads that had no trouble sticking to the wall as they climbed vertically, stopping to coat the cracks with a plaster-like substance, gears cranking as their mechanical arms pivoted.

Meanwhile, the crew climbed the ladders to cover the untarnished sections of wall with a fresh coat of paint. A few workers stayed at the base of the ladders, manually adjusting their position with the turn of a groaning crank.

"I can't do this right now." Shoulders slumped, she waved goodbye to the contractors and lumbered to the library's exit.

Outside, she sat down on the stone steps, resting her back

against the door frame. The day promised to be a humid one, a reminder that summer was around the corner. Heat prickled on the back of her neck as she buried her face in her hands. So much for a distraction.

After a few moments of self-pity, Belle lifted her head to watch the busy street. The midday sun beat down on the citizens of Duchollow as they went about their business, stopping to chat between errands. The rumble of automobiles blended with the street vendors calling out their lunch specials.

Belle smiled to see people going about their normal lives, but a twinge of sadness wormed its way into her thoughts. Even though they technically had the freedom to go into town together, Beast hadn't seemed interested in mingling with the townspeople. He never said it aloud, but he seemed convinced he couldn't have a normal life so long as he resembled a creature. Before the attempt at a cure, he had seemed tentatively interested in the town, but now it was as if he'd given up on the idea.

Burying her face in her hands, Belle wished she could ease Beast's burden.

"What are you doing on the ground?" Captain Charity's teasing voice pulled her out of her melancholic thoughts.

Belle looked up, startled to see Beast standing behind the captain wearing his tinted goggles and wincing in the bright sunlight.

"Taking a break from the contractors." She grimaced. "I can't get anything done while they're working." She peered around the captain at Beast. "What are you two doing in town? I thought you were working in the garden today?"

"I was." He shifted his weight as he fidgeted. "But Charity says she has something important for us."

Belle's heart leapt to her throat as a myriad of potential disasters swirled through her mind. Had the Hounds escaped? Or had Maureen's sleep deprivation caused a disaster in the lab? Mentally chiding herself for jumping to conclusions, she shakily stood. "Is there a problem?"

Captain Charity clasped her shoulder, giving her a reassuring squeeze with a slender calloused hand. "Everything's fine. I promise it'll be fun, but you both need to come with me."

The tension in Belle's back lessened, but her nerves were frayed. She bit her lip, hoping the captain would elaborate. When she didn't, Belle sighed. "It's not like I was getting much work done, anyway."

"We shouldn't be gone long. Maybe the small break will help you get your focus back." The captain gestured down the street. "And we're within walking distance. Let's go."

Captain Charity led them to a charming tailor shop three blocks away. In the storefront window, mannequins wore everything from intricately detailed dresses to formal suits. The ornate sign above the storefront read, "Madam Dawkins, Clothier."

"Dawkins?" The surname sounded familiar. Belle furrowed her brows.

"Maureen?" Beast's voice rumbled.

"Her aunt." The captain straightened her blouse before opening the door.

A tiny woman with a wide grin and pins sticking out of her braided bun greeted them at the door. Her eyes had the same sharp gleam as the mayor's. "Come in, come in. Maureen's placed a rush order for you two."

Inside the shop, Beast warily eyed the pins sticking out of the enthusiastic tailor as he placed himself between the stranger and Belle.

"Don't be shy. I'll start with you first." For such a frail-looking person, Madam Dawkins had no trouble extracting him from Belle and shooing him into a dressing room. He shot her a pleading look before the curtain closed.

"What's all this about?" Belle whispered.

Captain Charity held her stomach, silently shaking with laughter at Beast's predicament. When she regained her composure, she replied, "We remembered there are a lot of costumes at the Festival and Maureen got the brilliant idea to get you both outfitted. If you'd like, you can attend instead of staying aboard the *Figment*."

A thrill went up in Belle at the idea of actually experiencing the festivities, but her pragmatic side won out. "Aren't we painting targets on ourselves by using your ship?"

Captain Charity grinned. "I took care of it. We won't be recognized, trust me."

Madam Dawkins came bursting out of the fitting room. "It's your turn!" She pointed her measuring device at Belle.

Beast looked harried as he shuffled over to the captain.

"In you go, dear." The tailor escorted Belle by the elbow into the dressing room. "I just need to take down some numbers so I can finish the pieces."

The dressing room was devoid of clothing, only indecipherable sketches and lists of measurements pinned to the deep blue wall. Belle was disappointed there was nothing to try on. "We don't get to see the costumes?"

"It'll be a surprise!" Madam Dawkins waggled her finger as her automated measurement device whirred and expanded to the former strongwoman's full height. The tailor scribbled rapidly in her notebook, humming off-key as she wrote. "There! All done." With a snap, the rapid measuring ceased.

"And we don't need to try on anything?" She raised her brows as they left the dressing room.

"It'll be fine. I've tailored your clothes before, young lady." The seamstress sniffed.

Beast perked up at that tidbit of information. When Belle reached his side, he leaned over to whisper, "If it's anything like your librarian outfit, it'll be fantastic."

The tailor gave him a toothy grin. "I like him. He appreciates art."

Belle gave her a polite nod. "Thank you for everything."

"My pleasure." Madam Dawkins squinted, staring at Captain Charity's ring finger. "My niece still hasn't made you an honest woman?"

Laughing, the captain shook her head. "Not yet."

The older woman tutted. "Hang in there. I'm sure she'll come around." She pointed at the captain. "In the meantime, try to stay a little more grounded. It'll help."

Captain Charity flushed crimson. "I'm trying."

Madam Dawkins' expression softened. "I know you are. Give it time and tell Maureen to bring you over for dinner sometime soon. I miss you both."

The captain clasped her hand. "I will."

As they left and walked down the street, the captain elbowed Belle. "See? That wasn't such a bad surprise, was it?"

"Haven't we had enough surprises lately?" she replied, shaking her head. "I'm grateful for the disguises, but it still feels risky."

"Trust me, there's a plan in place." Captain Charity lowered her voice and stood on her tiptoes to whisper in her ear. "Isn't it worth it to see him happy?"

Belle snuck a look at Beast, who seemed happier than he had in the last couple of days. The corners of his mouth were upturned as he waved to a passerby. Sighing, she admitted, "I suppose you're right. You know it's useless to whisper in front of him, right? He can hear everything."

"It's true." The corners of Beast's eyes crinkled as he smirked.

Captain Charity guffawed. "I should have known better. So what do you think the tailor's making for Belle?"

As Beast lit up discussing outlandish costume ideas with the captain, Belle wished she could join in their light-hearted teasing. Her worries dampened her mood, and she couldn't help wondering if they were courting disaster, even if they had clever disguises being made.

Two days later, Belle and Beast stood at the airship docks, each donning a knapsack and lugging wheeled steamer trunks behind them. They stared at the unfamiliar airship towering over them.

Sunlight glinted off the jet-black balloon of the *Starlight Specter*, highlighting the rigging keeping it in place. A shining celestial design that featured shades of blue, green, purple, and silver accents adorned the ship's body. A copper and steel sun flanked by twin moons jutted out from the bow.

"What happened to the *Figment*?" Belle asked. The captain had previously said that they were taking her ship to Onyxmark. Were they at the wrong dock?

"You're not the only one going incognito. It's the same airship." Maureen wiped the sweat off her brow as she approached the loading deck. Stacks of massive trunks were behind her, each on a mechanized wagon coupled together like a small train.

Belle squinted at the airship. It was the same size as the *Figment*, but completely unrecognizable with the new balloon and fresh paint job.

"She's beautiful, but she doesn't look like my ship." Captain Charity pouted as she pulled her trunk alongside her to stand next to them.

The hatch door, speckled with green and copper patina, let out a hiss of steam. Internal mechanisms clicked as its bolts unlocked, taking far longer than Belle recalled.

When the door finally opened, Damek peered at them. His fully repaired metal body gleamed, and Cinders wrapped her tail around his mechanical legs. The lights of his eyes changed from serene blue to flashing warning orange.

"Why are you still standing there? My internal clock says we should have started preflight preparations five minutes ago," Damek's tinny voice whined.

"We're coming. I was having a moment," Captain Charity grumbled as she tugged on her case with a little too much force, knocking her off-balance.

Maureen was by her side in an instant and caught the captain in her arms.

"Still on about the *Figment*'s disguise?" Damek shook his head. "It was this or get a new ship. It's temporary."

Belle could have sworn the automaton rolled his eyes, but that would have been impossible.

Captain Charity gritted her teeth. "I know."

"Thank you for helping us." Belle grabbed the captain's luggage in addition to her own. "I know this has to be hard on you."

The captain flushed crimson before ducking her head. "You're welcome. I know it seems silly, but the *Figment* is home."

"As soon as it's safe, we'll change her back again." Maureen smoothed Captain Charity's copper hair back before kissing her forehead.

"We won't be doing anything if we don't get a move on." Damek tapped his foot, resulting in heavy, repetitive clanging.

"Wonderful. They're both in moods today," Beast muttered in Belle's ear as they entered the cargo hold.

Belle hoped the rest of the flight went better than boarding.

The interior of the *Figment* was unchanged, and Captain Charity's stiff posture relaxed upon entering the ship. "That's my girl," she said, patting the familiar worn wall of the cargo hold.

Unfortunately, Maureen tensed as she loaded her yet-to-be-named invention in the hold, then immediately began fretting over the placement of the crates. The drone of the engine echoed through the ship, drowning out her worries.

Belle and Beast exchanged amused glances as they helped reposition the cargo, moving faster when Damek impatiently reminded everyone over the intercom they needed to leave soon. Onyxmark was a six-hour flight from Duchollow in ideal conditions.

Once loading and take-off were complete, she and Beast took up residence on the enclosed observation deck with Cinders, away from the tension in the cockpit. The three were content to spend the flight curled up on the sofa facing the glass dome window. Beast dozed, leaning against her while she read, with Cinders fast asleep on his lap. Between page flips, she stole glances at him as he slept, absently running her fingers through his fur.

The intercom crackled on, and Captain Charity's chipper voice echoed throughout the room.

"Good afternoon! It's nearing three o'clock and we're about to land. Make sure you're buckled in."

Beast blinked awake and stretched, disturbing Cinders from her slumber. The diminutive gray cat scampered away as Belle suppressed a chuckle.

"Oops." He scratched the back of his head. "Is it time already?"

Belle nodded as she pointed to the dome window. "Look."

Outside, the dense forest gave way to jewel-tone buildings and spiraling towers of steel and glass that jutted skyward. Orderly airships dotted the cloudless sky. Though she was still nervous about bringing Beast to the city, Belle felt lighter as they approached Onyxmark.

"What's on your mind?" Beast tapped her shoulder.

"I was thinking about the orrery. Remember when I told you about my unsuccessful escape attempt?"

His gaze softened. "I do. That was here, wasn't it?"

"If it's still here, I'd love a chance to take you to see it. It's incredible." Her eyes shone.

"I'd like that." Beast finished adjusting his harness as the *Figment* descended, ending all conversation.

After a smooth landing, everyone helped Maureen load her wagons for the Festival exposition. After the final crate was loaded, the mayor gestured toward the corridor. "Thank you for your help. Why don't you three change while I set up? The opening ceremony is this evening."

"Are you sure you want to go alone?" Captain Charity gestured to the precious cargo. "Even with the wagons, it's still a lot of gear."

"I'll be fine, thank you. If you could grab me a change of clothes, I'd appreciate it. I'd rather not wear this to the ceremony." Maureen gave her a tired smile as she pointed at her smudged coveralls.

"I can do that. Good luck!" Captain Charity leaned forward and kissed Maureen. When they parted, the captain shooed Belle and Beast. "You two might want to get out of sight before we open the hatch."

Butterflies fluttered in Belle's stomach. "O-okay. We'll see you soon!"

As they departed for their quarters, Beast asked, "Have you seen the costumes yet?"

"No, I didn't have a chance. Why?"

A mischievous gleam appeared in his eyes. "No reason. I think you'll like them."

In their room, Belle held up her dress, removed from its garment bag, and gasped. She wished she knew more about fabrics because the material was incredibly soft, and she'd have given anything to have more clothes made with it. The fitted bodice of the ballgown was black, gradually lightening to deep blue, then indigo, and finally violet at the bottom edge of the full skirt. Star-shaped crystals and round planet-shaped crystals covered the entire gown. Accompanying the dress was a silver crescent moon mask and delicate black boots.

She lifted and turned the dress, admiring how its iridescent sheen shimmered in the light. "Wow, Madam Dawkins did this as a rush order?"

Beast hummed in agreement as he finished putting on his jacket. "No complaints from me. How do I look?"

Belle tore her eyes away from the dress. Her heart thundered in her chest as she took in Beast's profile. "Stunning."

His suit matched her dress, transitioning from black to blue to violet from the top down. Under his jacket, he wore a high-collar onyx shirt with a celestial cravat. A billowing cape lined with indigo material obscured his silhouette further. In his gloved paws, he held a golden sun-shaped mask, large enough to complete his disguise.

Giving a little twirl, Beast grinned. "The boots feel a little strange, but at least they fit and there won't be an inch of fur showing. We should be okay."

A lump formed in Belle's throat. Maybe they would get to enjoy themselves after all. Clearing her throat, she finally responded. "That's wonderful."

Beast pointed at the dress. "Are you going to get dressed?"

Flushing crimson, she nodded. "Give me a few minutes."

Beast leaned against the wall as he waited, looking entirely too dashing for her to focus.

After some difficulty figuring out how to put on the dress without wrinkling it, Belle was nearly finished getting ready, save the stays at the back of the bodice. "Beast? Can you help me with this?" She peered over her shoulder only to find he was already on his way.

"It'd be my pleasure." Beast's voice rumbled deliciously in her ear as he leaned in close enough for the heat radiating from his body to warm her. "You look amazing."

"Thank you. You were right, I do like the costumes."

Beast chuckled, then grumbled under his breath. "I don't know if I can tie this. Between my paws and the gloves, it's tricky. I don't want to ruin your gown."

Belle reached behind her to grab his paws and placed them on her waist. "Maybe I don't have to get dressed just yet. They didn't say how long it'd take to set up."

His breath caught as she lowered his paws to her hips. "Belle, what—"

Rapid, familiar knocking on the door sounded.

"Again?" He seethed as she smothered her laughter in her hand.

"Coming!" Belle answered the door, holding the bodice in place.

Captain Charity stood in the doorway, donning a white half-mask with a gold finish. The rest of her outfit made her look like a storybook pirate, complete with a feathered hat, buckled leather corset over a breezy shirt, and a patchwork lace skirt.

"Are you ready yet?" The captain snorted at Belle's attempts to keep the bodice up. "Let me help you with the stays. Opening ceremonies start soon, and I need to get Maureen her change of clothes."

As Captain Charity finished tying the stays, Belle snuck another look at Beast, who held his mask in one paw.

He caught her gaze and gave her a feral grin. "Glad we came?"

Belle closed the distance between them, looping her arm around Beast's free arm. "Yes, let's go."

"Don't forget your masks!" The captain called after them, her laughter echoing in the corridor.

CHAPTER TWENTY-TWO

Captain Charity carried Maureen's bag as she led Belle and Beast through the packed streets. Messengers and mechanical delivery carts weaved between the sea of people wearing everything from elaborate masquerade costumes to casual outfits. With the Festival underway, Onyxmark was even more fantastic than Belle remembered. Lanterns and green and gold banners lined the road to the Exhibition Hall. Garlands of white flowers swayed in the warm evening breeze, giving off a heady, sweet scent.

Street food vendors called out their wares, their voices mingling with the chatter of the crowd and the soft orchestral music playing over concealed speakers. Belle was thankful they'd eaten on the ship since no one wanted to risk Beast removing his mask in public, but she dearly wanted to bring back a few savory dishes to the *Figment* to sample.

At last, they reached the massive glass and steel Exhibition Hall dome. Two golden banners spanned the height of the spherical building, framing the grand double-door entrance. In swirling script against a background of deep green flowers intertwined with gears, it read "Welcome to the 103rd Grand Festival."

The spacious interior of the hall resembled a botanical garden, with seating areas nestled between food stalls and stately palm trees. To the delight of the attendees, a troupe performed small stunts, from balancing on motorized unicycles to juggling to elaborate dances.

Belle couldn't help but wonder if any former Circus Illume performers were amongst their number. The performers made her wish her crescent moon mask covered her entire face, not just three-quarters of it. Though she had no reason to think she knew any of the performers, their presence made her uneasy.

"What's wrong? Your nails are digging into my suit." Beast tapped the hand that held his arm too tightly.

"I'm sorry. Just nerves, I suppose," she whispered back. She took a deep breath and loosened her grip as she reminded herself that none of the performers had any reason to be looking for her. The Ringmaster was safely locked away in Duchollow.

Determined to enjoy herself, Belle turned her attention back to the inventions on display as they made their way along the winding path and past the performers toward the showcase. There were a vast array of technological marvels, including heavily modified hot air balloons, hovering carriages, chemist booths, and all kinds of devices with incomprehensible functions. Belle wished she could view them closer, but even if she had time, the inventors weren't ready for curious guests. Many inventions were cordoned off, and automatons even guarded a handful. At last, they finally reached Maureen's booth nestled in a secluded corner.

"There you are!" Streaks of sweat and grease covered Maureen. Behind her, the transmutation machine glistened. "I wish someone would have mentioned all the greenery in here. This humidity isn't good for my machine."

Over an intercom, an enthusiastic announcer's voice reverberated throughout the hall. "Everyone, please make your way to the central stage. Chancellor Elmstone will give her opening remarks in ten minutes."

Maureen swore as Captain Charity handed her the bag of clothes. The mayor gave a clunky remote to the captain. "I need more time, but I guess I'll figure out the humidity issue later."

"I'll lock up. Good luck." With the press of a button, a gilded cage materialized and unfolded around the transmutation machine. The bars were spaced enough so that onlookers could still view the intricate device, but the control panels and vials were inaccessible.

"Has it always been able to do that?" Belle's eyes widened.

The captain nodded. "Maureen's worried about sabotage. If you look around, she's not the only one."

"Seems excessive," Beast deadpanned.

The captain's expression darkened. "You'd think, but the lengths some competitors will go to win might surprise you."

Before Belle could ask more about what she meant, Maureen was back at their side, donning her own costume which coordinated with Charity's outfit. Her costume was in hues of indigo and silver, and she wore trousers tucked into thigh-high boots.

"You're having me attend the opening ceremony in a pirate costume?" Beneath Maureen's scowl, there was a glimmer of amusement sparkling in her eyes.

"Lead the way. You look stunning." Captain Charity fanned herself.

"You're a tease, Darling."

"Never."

Beast offered his arm to Belle, and they all made their way toward the central stage.

By the time Belle, Beast, Maureen, and Captain Charity arrived, all the metal benches surrounding the central stage were full. They had to stand at the very back, though even from a great distance, the stage was impressive. Towering copper statues of inventors from eras gone by, overgrown with flowering vines, decorated the platform.

"Please welcome Chancellor Elmstone and the Festival council to the stage!" The announcer called over the speakers amongst crackles and static pops barely audible over the excited crowd.

The lights dimmed and the audience fell into a hush as Chancellor Elmstone walked across the stage in a shimmering white gown under a bright spotlight that highlighted her teal-dyed hair. Assembled behind her were eight people in costumes, each wearing a solid color in jewel-tone hues. The wizened chancellor looked tiny on the huge stage, even standing behind a raised podium. "Thank you all for coming to the 103rd Grand Festival. I've been attending these for a long, long time, but I can say with confidence there has never been a finer selection of entrants for the invention exhibition. Competition this year will be fierce."

The audience politely chuckled, though several participants eyed each other warily.

Belle's attention drifted from the chancellor's words. She peered at the line of masked people sitting behind her on the stage, curious about their costumes. Though the mono-color costumes were equally stunning, the woman on the end wearing gold caught Belle's eye as she shifted in her seat to adjust her ballgown. Her featureless gold mask seemed to look straight at Belle. She couldn't shake the prickling feeling of being watched. Her eyes darted to the sides of the hall, calculating her exit options. Should they leave?

When Belle looked back at the stage, the golden woman faced the chancellor, hands folded in her lap. Belle slumped in her seat. All the remarks about the cutthroat competition must have gotten to her. There was no reason for anyone to pay attention to her or Beast. Their costumes allowed them to blend in with the others.

"And now, let the Festival begin!" The chancellor swept her arm toward the stage behind her.

An orchestra rose from a concealed platform in the center of the stage, and ethereal music sounded, beginning a dreamy waltz. The audience moved out of the way as workers moved fast to clear the benches and make way for a dance floor next to the stage.

Beast turned to Belle with a sweeping bow, his golden sun mask sparkling. "Shall we dance?"

Beneath her own silver moon mask, Belle grinned. "I'd love to."

Belle couldn't help thinking of the first time Beast asked her to dance in the kitchen the day of her ether-poisoning cure as he took her into his arms. It was surreal placing her hands on his gloved paws in the crowd of people. She never would have dreamed something as simple as dancing in public would be possible for them, but there was something beautifully anonymous about losing themselves in the music. With their masks on, she could pretend they were just an ordinary couple enjoying a night out. Across the dance floor, Captain Charity twirled Maureen. Both women beamed when the captain caught the mayor in a low dip.

Belle sighed as she leaned into Beast's arms, thankful for the respite.

As the sun set, fairy lights strung above the dance floor twinkled on. Electric lamps surrounding the walkway flickered on as well. Outside, the sky darkened as night fell. A loud boom from outside the hall thundered. Beast and Belle clung to each other tighter, but then loosened their hold when the other dancers cheered. Over the lake next to the Exhibition Hall, fireworks sparkled and exploded in dazzling hues.

Belle leaned against Beast's chest as she took in the view. The fireworks were gorgeous—doubly so as they reflected in the lake.

"There you two are. Sorry we lost sight of you." Captain Charity appeared at their side with Maureen on her arm. Both looked considerably disheveled, their outfits wrinkled. "Ready to head back?"

Beast gave a long-suffering sigh. "If we must."

Maureen smirked. "We should. Tomorrow's the exposition." Her eyes widened behind her mask. "Oh, no, it's tomorrow. What if it goes wrong?"

Captain Charity kissed her cheek. "You will do wonderfully. Let's get some sleep. You'll feel better in the morning."

Back in their quarters, Beast quickly removed his cloak, gloves, suit jacket, and shirt. At Belle's raised brows, he shrugged. "It was getting warm under those layers."

"I see." She reached for the stays on the back of her bodice.

Beast's paws closed gently around her hands. "May I?"

"Yes, please."

As he slowly loosened the stays, he cleared his throat. "About earlier…" His voice trailed off.

"What about earlier?" Her heart fluttered. Had she offended him while they were getting ready? They weren't shy about physical touch anymore, but it never went beyond kisses. Either something interrupted them or one of them would shy away.

He coughed. "Nevermind. It's untied now."

"Thank you." She held up the front of her gown as she faced him.

His gaze was downcast, shoulders hunched. The gas lighting gave his silver fur a faint halo.

"Beast?" With her free hand, she rested her hand on his chest. "Did I upset you?"

He met her gaze as he shook his head. "No, I just—" He inhaled, then the rest of his words came out in a rush. "I'm worried about hurting you or pushing too far."

"Have I pushed you? I'm sorry if I took things too far today." She withdrew her hand, only for him to clasp it with both of his paws.

"You could never."

"I feel the same way about you. What do you need?"

"You." Beast closed the distance between them, nuzzling against her neck as he breathed her in. "Maker, you're beautiful. Always thought so."

"Is that why you brought me the rose so soon after we met?" She wrapped her arms around Beast, enjoying his warmth.

"Maybe. Or maybe I wanted to make you mine." Beast lightly nipped at the base of her neck, eliciting a gasp from her. He pulled back as his gaze burned with need. "Are you sure this is what you want? Because I'd give anything to have you make that sound again."

Heat enveloped her as she nodded.

"Good." His canines grazed the side of her neck.

They both froze as a buzzing alarm sounded in the corridor.

"What now?" Belle groaned.

"Is that the new security system?"

"Probably." Extracting herself from Beast's embrace, she peered out their door's peephole. Captain Charity thundered through the corridor, her black nightgown billowing as she wielded her electric saber.

"Looks like trouble's found us." Belle set her jaw. "Help me get dressed?"

Beast's eyes lingered on her slipping gown before sighing. "I suppose we should."

The shrieking alarm grew louder with each passing second as he struggled to retie the stays on the back of her wrinkled ballgown.

"Any luck?" She peered out their door's peephole again. Belle couldn't see the captain, but her distinctive swearing echoed in the corridor.

"I'm sorry, it's not working." He huffed as his paws fumbled, dropping the stays.

Outside their quarters, Maureen dashed barefoot, wearing one of the captain's breezy dresses. There was a tool clenched in her hand, but she was gone before Belle could clearly see what it was.

Belle swore under her breath. "We're running out of time." She stalked across their room to her steamer trunk, removed her gown, and pulled on a simple linen dress, still wearing her delicate boots from the opening ceremony.

Beast's goldenrod eyes went completely round as he took a sharp intake of breath.

A faint blush crept across her cheeks as she reached for the door handle. "I'll be right back."

Shaking his head, he furrowed his brows. "I'm going with you."

"It's not worth risking your anonymity."

He took her hands in his paws, tracing a light pattern on her thumbs. "I couldn't live with myself if something happened to you."

She gave him a crooked smile. "Seems we're at an impasse because I feel the same about you."

Shouting echoed in the corridor.

"Let's go." Belle flung open the door, Beast following closely behind her as they raced toward the yelling.

As they neared the cargo hold, she put her arm across his chest, stopping him in his tracks. "Stay back in case the hatch opens. Don't want any dockworkers to spot you."

Beast grumbled his assent. Balling her fists, Belle crept into the cargo hold.

Maureen leaned out of the open hatch, the light from a streetlamp streaming inside.

"Anything?" the mayor called. The alarm chirped, echoing in the close quarters.

Captain Charity's voice was muffled when she answered. "Only minor damage to the hatch, scratches around the keyhole."

Maureen's posture stiffened. "Great. That narrows nothing down."

"I'll go ask security if they've seen anything before I check on your invention."

"Thank you, Darling. I'll reset everything." Maureen hunched over a control panel and pressed a button, silencing the shrill alarm.

"Anything we can do to help?" Belle tapped the mayor on the shoulder.

Maureen jumped, letting out a high-pitched yelp.

Gasping, the mayor's finger shook as she pointed. "I didn't hear you come in."

"Sorry, I didn't mean to scare you. The alarm worried us." Belle nodded at the security system. "What set it off?"

Maureen gritted her teeth. "There's no trace. They took off as soon as the alarm sounded."

"At least the alarm worked as a deterrent."

The mayor grunted in response as she checked the system's panel again.

Beast stepped closer, wrinkling his nose. "Whoever did it, their scent is impossible to discern. It smells like chemicals by the hatch. Highly acidic and astringent."

The mayor rubbed her temples. "I'll get a contamination kit and have Captain Charity wash down when she's back. Maybe run some tests." The mayor sighed. "You two should try to get some sleep."

"Don't forget to sleep, too." Belle cast one last worried look at Maureen before they departed for their quarters. In only a few short hours, they'd need to wake for the first full day of the Festival.

CHAPTER TWENTY-THREE

After a restless night, Belle woke before Beast. He'd slept with one arm curled protectively around her waist, his expression troubled even in his sleep. Carefully, she slipped out of his hold and made herself presentable. After slipping on her shoes, she made her way to the dining hall.

Maureen and Captain Charity were already seated at the table. Both had dark circles under their eyes as they clutched mugs of steaming coffee. A platter of assorted pastries sat next to the carafe of coffee, but their breakfast remained untouched.

"Looks like you two slept about as well as we did." Belle helped herself to a raspberry pastry and coffee as she joined them. "Anything new?"

Maureen pinched the bridge of her nose. "No, I'm afraid not. At least whatever chemicals were used didn't hurt us."

"And your invention was unharmed." Captain Charity took a sip of her coffee. "I wish we had better answers, though."

"I do, too. In the meantime, I still have to name my machine," Maureen grumbled.

"There's time. Judging won't begin until this afternoon." The captain gave her a tired thumbs up.

Belle perked up. "What's the plan for this morning?"

Maureen glumly took a bite of her pastry. "Before last night, I would have told you and Beast to relax on the ship until this afternoon to stay safe, but now, I'm not sure. I suppose you two could come with us, but it might draw attention if there are guests at my booth during contest preparations."

Belle sat her mug down. "Well, I actually had an idea. Do either of you have a map of Onyxmark?"

The other women both stared at Belle, their heads tilted to the side.

Finally, Captain Charity answered, running her fingers through her bedhead. "Yes, but why?"

"Are you sure this is a good idea?" An obsidian lion mask muffled Beast's voice. His suit was deep burgundy, coordinating with Belle's matching gown.

"Yes. Please let me surprise you for once. Besides, Maureen gave me her prototype communicator." Belle patted her embroidered clutch. Inside, it contained money and a clunky device that operated like a smaller version of their radio back home. While she was concerned about the break-in attempt, she didn't want to sit around the airship worrying.

The boots covering Beast's clawed feet made his movements clumsy, and he held onto her as she guided him down the airship's ramp. Following Captain Charity's map, she led him through the packed streets. The city was arranged in a basic grid pattern, which was helpful given the way her mask, a pearlescent tigress with inlaid onyx stripes, restricted her vision. She was thankful that today's mask covered her entire face as they made their way through the crowd.

"There!" Belle pointed across the busy street.

"Is that what I think it is?" Beast stopped in the middle of the sidewalk, staring up at the magnificent dome-shaped marble building in front of them. The first floor featured celestial stained-glass windows. On the roof, a copper sun rotated, reflecting beams of sunlight.

"It's the orrery." Underneath her mask, Belle's eyes misted. It felt like it had been a lifetime ago since she'd come here as a runaway. "Would you like to go in?"

"I'd love to." Beast linked his arm with hers. "I can see why this is where you made your escape. It's stunning."

"Wait until you see the inside."

Belle was relieved to see most of the orrery patrons also wore costumes, some even more elaborate than theirs. She had worried they'd stick out until she saw an entire group wearing coordinating peacock costumes, complete with sparkling trains trailing behind them. Brightening, she tugged on Beast's gloved paw as he studied the paintings of constellations on the wall.

"Come on, the best part is ahead!"

The lift to the second floor was a massive gilded cage. As it ascended, they had a perfect view of the mural of the solar system that spanned both floors. As impressive as the painting was, Belle couldn't resist peeking at Beast. She wished they didn't need their disguises so she could see his expression.

At last, they reached the elaborate model solar system made of copper and jewel-tone orbs for the planets. Huge gears rotated, spinning the ten planets around the lit sun in the center of the room.

Mechanical copper and crystal models of the stars above Nuzaran in different seasons decorated the walls. The vaulted midnight blue ceiling had star-patterned stained-glass windows near the peak, letting in a dazzling light show that changed with each spin of the copper sun on the roof outside.

Beast wrapped his arm around her as they watched the planets make their orbits together.

"Thank you for sharing this with me. I've seen nothing like this before."

Belle rested her head against his shoulder. "I'm glad you like it. It's surreal being back here after everything that's happened."

When the room became too crowded as more visitors filed in, Belle and Beast made their way toward the exit.

"Should we grab lunch and eat on the ship? There were stalls on the way to the dock," she said as Beast opened the door for her.

He rumbled his assent.

They'd only taken a few steps outside when static crackled from within Belle's clutch. Belle and Beast ducked into a nearby alley, wrinkling their noses at the trash piled up against the building.

Fishing out Maureen's device from her bag, Belle stared at it, dumbfounded as Captain Charity's stressed voice came over it. "Where are you two? I've been radioing for the last thirty minutes!"

Heart racing, Belle pressed the button to answer. "We just left the orrery. I think all the copper might have interfered with the signal."

"Whatever the case is, I'm glad I finally reached you two. Come quickly to the booth. Someone sabotaged her machine. Judging starts in a couple hours."

"We're on our way." With trembling hands, Belle clicked off the portable radio and stashed it in her clutch.

"Why not send us to the airship?" Beast adjusted his mask. "I thought you said Maureen didn't want us at her booth."

"Your guess is as good as mine." Dread settled in the pit of Belle's stomach as they made their way to the Exhibition Hall.

Belle and Beast weaved through the crowded streets, their progress slowed by their impractical costumes. The breeze picked up, worsening visibility as petals rained down from the floral garlands strung between streetlamps. Thoughts of returning to the disguised *Figment* tempted Belle as they drew nearer to the Exhibition Hall. With every brush against the other pedestrians, her nerves went on high alert. She was less concerned about what would happen if her mask slipped. She could only imagine the onlookers' horrified screams if Beast's lion mask slipped.

However, there was probably a good reason Captain Charity asked for them to come to Maureen's booth and not the airship. What if the *Figment* was being watched?

The crowd pressed in on all sides, knocking Belle's hand out of Beast's gloved paw.

"Belle!" From several feet ahead, he twisted around, towering over the Festival-goers.

Cursing her distracted thoughts, she shoved past the other pedestrians, ignoring their disgruntled looks. "I'm coming!"

She didn't dare say "Beast" surrounded by strangers.

A passerby stepped on her dress and ripped its hem, making Belle wince as she fought to reach Beast. At last, she caught up with him, reaching between annoyed strangers to grab his attention. She sighed as his paw closed around her hand. Holding onto each other tightly, they entered the Exhibition Hall.

A guard in a crisp forest-green uniform with fussy brass pauldrons stopped in front of them, barring the entrance to the invention showcase. Behind her, a rope that hadn't been there yesterday blocked their path. The guard's rust-colored hair was pulled into a tight plait, revealing a no-nonsense face as she fixed them with a stern look. "Only authorized personnel past this point. All the contestants are preparing for judging. You may return in two hours."

Belle gulped, her thoughts racing as she contemplated her next move. It would be simpler to go straight back to the airship, but her doubts still lingered about its safety. She hoped Damek was okay.

"Ma'am?" The guard's thin eyebrows furrowed.

Thinking fast, Belle reached into her clutch and fished out an ornate pamphlet. "My program says it's open to the public for the duration of the Festival."

The guard's cheek muscle twitched as she gritted her teeth. "I'm afraid that's changed. There's been an incident. You need to leave."

"They're with Maureen Dawkins! Booth 967." Captain Charity jogged up behind the guard wearing an oil-stained apron over coveralls. Grease and sweat marred her face.

"This is highly irregular." The guard looked the disheveled captain up and down, her lips tightly closed.

"Have you met the inventors here? They're all odd." Captain Charity winked as she slid the barricade over. "Let's go. Maureen's waiting on you two for those critical adjustments."

The guard lifted a finger, opening her mouth to speak.

"Thank you for all your hard work!" Belle waved at the sputtering guard as Captain Charity tugged her and Beast toward the showcase.

As they passed other contestants fussing over their entries, the captain muttered, "Remind me to teach you how to talk to guards. Step one, you don't."

Belle scratched the back of her neck. "Sorry, she caught me by surprise."

"You did fine. You just need a little more finesse next time." The captain chortled. "I can't believe you thanked her for her work."

Beast snorted, shaking his head.

All humor disappeared as they arrived at the booth. The remains of the cage sat in a sad pile of bent copper pieces in front of the machine. Several of the bars had melted in spots. Behind the invention, the mechanized wagon was loaded with crates.

Beast coughed, his mouth muffled by his mask. "That chemical smell is back. Much stronger here."

"Thank you for confirming my theory." Maureen appeared from behind her invention. Her apron was splattered with oil stains. Goggles with filthy lenses in dire need of cleaning replaced her octagonal glasses.

"How did this happen?" Belle gestured to the extensive damage.

Maureen pulled the goggles down and removed a fresh handkerchief from her coverall pocket to scrub them as she nodded toward her machine. "Unfortunately, the cage isn't even the worst of the damage. Look at this."

Nearly all the giant glass vials were riddled with holes and cracks. Gears had popped out of alignment, and cloudy fluid pooled around the base of the machine.

"How did no one notice this happening?" Belle's stomach churned at the mechanical carnage.

"I have a few ideas, but it's not safe to say more here." The mayor clasped her hands together in front of her heart. "I'm not one to beg, but I need your help to get this functional again. Can you two please help?"

Humidity prickled against Belle's skin, giving her dress a wilted appearance. The hall was much too warm to accommodate the tropical plants artfully placed between displays. She cleared her throat. "Of course, we'll help, but is it salvageable? It looks…bad."

Maureen set her jaw. "Everything is salvageable. It's rare for things to be so bad that they are beyond repair."

"Can we fix it in time, though?" Captain Charity pointed to the clock in the park-like walkway between booths. It was a quarter past the hour. "We've got just under two hours before the judging starts."

"We can try. I have enough spare parts."

"Tell us what you need." Beast rolled his shoulders.

Maureen pointed to the crates sitting on her mechanized wagon. "Can you help unpack? Damek helped load, but I couldn't possibly bring him here."

As Belle resigned herself to further ruining her costume, she wondered why Damek was still a closely guarded secret. She wanted to ask the mayor or the captain about him, but for now, they had bigger concerns. Instead, she lifted the first of many crates. "On it. Where do you want this?"

An hour later, Belle wished she had removed her tigress mask before getting her hands dirty. Sweat clung to her face. She desperately wanted to towel off, but her dress was completely covered in muck. There was nothing left to clean with. She felt more sorry for Beast, who couldn't dare lift his helmet-like mask. Between his fur and the costume, he must have been miserable.

The work kept her hands too busy to linger on such thoughts as she replaced the shockingly heavy vials in the invention with care. She couldn't afford to break any of them. There were no more replacements left.

"How's it coming?" Maureen called from the control panel.

"Last vial." Praying to whomever was listening, Belle placed the vial in the final slot. "How did you do this before? That angle is difficult to maneuver!"

"Damek and judicious use of pulleys in the lab," Maureen grunted as she turned a wrench. "Is it in yet?"

The vial squeaked in protest as Belle screwed it in. She held her breath until it clicked into place. All the tension rushed out of her. "Done!"

"Excellent." Maureen craned her neck to look at Captain Charity as she waited by the booth's built-in faucet. "Water time!"

The captain gave her a mock salute before connecting the hose to the machine and turning its knob. As the interior tanks filled, Beast and Belle loaded the crates of broken parts back onto the mechanical wagon.

Humming to herself, the mayor placed the alchemical ingredients in the fresh vials, their liquids swirling inside and reflecting colorful hues.

"What about the cage?" Belle pointed to the twisted copper remains.

"Just move them out of sight for now. I'll fix it after judging." Maureen squared her shoulders. "Let's do a test run."

Captain Charity turned off the faucet and removed the hose.

"Everyone, get back. It's go time!"

Once the others retreated to the walkway, Maureen flipped the lever. Nothing happened. Swearing violently, the mayor rubbed her temples. "What now?"

As soon as she asked, the machine sputtered to life. The weak pops and groans grew into hisses and whirring as it powered on to its full potential. Gears cranked as they turned, and soon steam billowed around the invention, obscuring its creator as she turned more knobs and pulled levers.

Belle was grateful the machine no longer flashed violently, as it had during the test run. She'd forgotten to ask if they'd need goggles, though as the noise continued, she considered suggesting earmuffs for future tests.

Finally, the racket stopped, and the clouds of steam dissipated as shimmering blue liquid filled the largest of the vials. Captain Charity and Beast whooped, and even as exhausted as she was, Belle cheered, too.

"Outstanding work, everyone." Maureen beamed, wiping the sweat off her brow. "I'll make a few more adjustments so it's not such a slow start, but otherwise—"

"Attention, contestants! Judging begins in fifteen minutes." The cheerful announcer's voice reverberated in the Exhibition Hall.

Belle's mouth went dry. "We need more time!"

Maureen shook her head, pointing at their stained costumes. "It'll hold. You two get out of here and go change clothes before the judges arrive."

Belle gulped as her gaze darted to the now dormant machine. It looked as if anyone so much as breathed on it, the whole thing would collapse. "Good luck."

Beast offered his arm to Belle. "Think the guard is still around?"

"I hope not." She grimaced. "We have enough problems."

As they rounded the corner, judges and onlookers alike surged toward the showcase, waiting for the disgruntled guard from earlier to move the barricade.

Belle swore under her breath. "Fantastic. What—"

Beast's paw over her mouth silenced her as he pulled her behind a cluster of palm trees off the main path that was barely wide enough to conceal them.

Beast pulled her flush against his body and leaned in to whisper in her ear. "I can think of worse places to hide."

Heat prickled at the back of her neck, a combination of the humidity of the botanical garden and proximity to Beast. She could only nod, slipping her hands underneath his suit to grab the back of his shirt as the chatter of the approaching crowd grew closer. She buried her face in Beast's shoulder and hoped they wouldn't get caught, but she still agreed. Their hiding place could have been worse.

"Demonstrations begin in ten minutes, starting with Booth 1! Good luck to all the competitors." The chipper announcer's voice echoed over the intercom, sending the excited chatter of the eager attendees to a fevered pitch.

Belle tugged on the back of Beast's shirt as she whispered, "How are we going to get out of here? They keep coming."

"Let's give it a few more minutes, then we'll go. If only a couple of people spot us, we'll be fine."

She looked down at their grease-stained, rumpled costumes. "We're going to attract attention with the state our outfits are in."

"Doesn't matter anymore. The showcase is open to everyone now, but we'll walk fast if it makes you feel better."

She hummed her appreciation as she leaned into his embrace, longingly thinking about their washroom aboard the *Figment* and a change of clothes.

At last, the murmur of the crowd sounded farther away.

"Want me to check if it's clear?" Belle whispered.

"Yes. It's entirely too warm here."

Belle disentangled herself from Beast's embrace, then peered around the trees. There were a few stragglers walking along the cobblestone path, but behind them, no one was coming. As soon as the passersby disappeared from view, she crooked her finger. "Now's our chance."

They were nearly out of the hall when the guard caught up with them.

"Wait! Shouldn't you be at the demonstration?"

"Don't worry about it," Beast huffed.

Arm in arm, they briskly left the Exhibition Hall, leaving the befuddled guard and her questions behind.

After a quick rinse and change of clothes, Belle and Beast returned to the hall wearing their celestial costumes from the first day of the Festival after determining yesterday's outfits were clean enough. They only had three costumes for the duration of their stay in Onyxmark.

"Up next is Booth 967!"

"That's Maureen." Belle pulled Beast's paw as they picked up the pace.

The crowd pressed in around them as they ventured farther into the showcase area. Enthusiastic Festival-goers marveled at all the inventions on display while the inventors spent half their time preening for the audience while giving each other suspicious looks. Above the rows of booths, the modified hot-air balloon floated. Its inventor even let a few brave souls climb aboard as a part of a demonstration. Its noisy, jerky flight made Belle grateful that Maureen's machine was earthbound.

An excited murmur grew louder from the direction of Booth 967. Captain Charity stood on an improvised platform using an empty crate, wearing a pristine indigo blouse over crisp pants, reminiscent of Maureen's favorite outfit. There were no signs of grime on the copper-haired woman as she addressed the chattering audience.

Behind her, the machine gleamed as if the sabotage had never happened. The only sign of the hasty repairs was Maureen's wagon parked neatly behind it. The quick outfit change, Captain Charity's showmanship, and the invention's sudden tidiness reminded Belle uncannily of the circus.

Shaking her head at her distracted thoughts, Belle joined Beast at the back of the crowd. She found herself thankful for her height so that she could see over the enthralled audience, though she frowned when she didn't spot the mayor. Where was Maureen?

"Does it really replace ether?" A reporter called out, holding a clunky recording device at the front of the crowd. Her bowler hat was askew, revealing short, wild black curls.

"Yes, it does. Using a few common elements, the machine transmutes in a fraction of the time and resources it takes to mine and distill ether." Captain Charity lowered her voice dramatically, making the audience come closer. "Best of all? It doesn't have dangerous side effects of ether-mining."

"What's it called?" Another reporter's pen hovered above his notepad as he craned his short neck up to look at the captain.

Belle leaned forward. Last she'd heard, Maureen still hadn't named her invention.

Captain Charity squinted at the reporter. To her credit, the captain didn't hesitate as she proudly announced, "The Transmutation Engine."

"Can we see a demonstration?" the first reporter asked, waving her photographer over with her free hand.

The slim photographer struggled under the weight of his camera stand, but after wrestling with the equipment, he set it up on the outer edge of the audience.

Captain Charity's confident smile faltered, but only for a moment. "We're waiting until the judges arrive, which should be soon—"

The intercom crackled on.

"And now it's time for Booth 967's demonstration!"

The captain's brows rose. "Or we'll do it now."

Soon, Chancellor Elmstone and her entourage of colorfully masked council members parted the chattering audience and arrived at the booth.

"You're not Mayor Dawkins." The chancellor pursed her lips as she frowned at Captain Charity. "Where is she?"

From behind The Transmutation Engine, Maureen stepped out, wearing an indigo outfit that coordinated with her captain. Her goggles had been polished, gleaming under the bright lights of the hall.

The mayor nodded at the judges and the chancellor as Captain Charity stepped off the platform to stand beside the mayor. "Please allow me to show you the wonders of The Transmutation Engine." Maureen gave the captain a look before her professional smile returned. "Thank you so much for coming, everyone."

Without further ado, the mayor went to the control panel and flipped the lever with a flourish. To the amazement of those watching, the machine started up smoothly. It whirred to life, the gears smoothly rotating as they cranked.

Belle clutched Beast's gloved paw as the familiar steam rose from the machine, shrouding Maureen and Captain Charity in the thick smoke. A soft boom emitted, making a few onlookers yelp, but their panic quickly abated as the steam cleared. In the last vial, the silver-blue ether swirled hypnotically. Captain Charity offered the mayor a small vial. The mayor stepped close to The Transmutation Engine, turned on a spigot, and filled it with ether.

"Here it is for the judges to test: some of the purest, most stable ether to exist." Maureen handed the vial to the chancellor.

Chancellor Elmstone pursed her lips as she regarded the vial. "Thank you for the astonishing demonstration. We will certainly give this a closer look."

One of the masked judges, a woman in gold, spoke in a lilting voice. "If this is legitimate, this will change the landscape of Nuzaran for the better. Well done."

Maureen's eyes widened, all the color draining from her face. Captain Charity tapped her shoulder, and the mayor recovered with a fake cough. "Thank you for coming."

Belle smiled at the mayor's reaction to the compliment until she couldn't shake the feeling of being watched. The hair on the back of her neck bristled as she turned to look over her shoulder. Behind her, the guard from earlier marched briskly away from the booth. How long had she been standing there? Had she been watching the demonstration? Or keeping tabs on her and Beast?

The judges and the crowd jostled past as they left the booth, bumping into Belle and pulling her out of her worried thoughts. The journalists rushed Maureen to ask a few more questions before following the others to the next booth, leaving Belle and Beast behind with the mayor and the captain.

When the excitement died down, Maureen closed her eyes and leaned against her machine, holding her hands over her heart. Captain Charity stood next to her, an unsettled expression on her face.

The mayor sighed. "That was entirely too close for comfort."

"But you did it! Congratulations." Belle beamed as she and Beast approached the mayor.

Maureen opened her eyes. With the goggles lifted above her head, the lenses left prominent rings on her face, highlighting the dark circles under her red-rimmed eyes. "Thank you, everyone, for helping with the repairs." She inclined her head toward Captain Charity. "And thank you for the name. It's brilliant."

The captain straightened up and smiled tenderly as she brushed one of the mayor's braids back. "I'm happy to help. I'm sorry if I overstepped, but I know how hard you've worked on this and what it means to you."

"I'm grateful for it, truly." The mayor sucked in a shuddering breath. "Unfortunately, we have a problem. I think Delphine's among the judges."

"What?" Belle's stomach churned as she stared at Maureen.

Beast's breath hitched.

Maureen opened her mouth to speak but was cut off by the announcer's voice booming over the intercom.

"The judges will deliberate soon. Please come back tomorrow for the award ceremony and reception to follow at the central stage. Congratulations to all the competitors for a wonderful display for the 103rd Grand Festival."

"Let's secure the machine and get back to the ship. It's safer to talk there." Captain Charity's expression looked haunted as she glanced over her shoulder.

It didn't bring Belle any comfort that she wasn't the only one who felt like they were being watched.

CHAPTER TWENTY-FOUR

T he atmosphere aboard the *Figment* was glum as Belle, Beast, Captain Charity, and Maureen sat in the dining hall in silence. Belle picked at the fried prawns in her takeaway box, but she had no appetite. Next to her, Beast snuck pieces of the prawns to Cinders under the table. Between bites, the diminutive cat tapped his leg for more.

Belle smiled wistfully at Cinders' antics, despite her troubled thoughts. Unable to stand the quiet anymore, she pushed her takeaway box forward. "Are you sure the judge is Delphine?" She winced as she felt the dull throb of the beginnings of a tension headache. Cradling her head between her hands, she asked, "What would she gain from being here?"

Maureen rubbed her temples. "I'd know her voice anywhere, but it's hard to say if my anxiety is clouding my judgment. Without seeing her face, I can't tell for sure."

Captain Charity's eyes narrowed. "It wouldn't surprise me if it was her. Who knows what she'd get out of being a judge? But she does love to play games."

After unsuccessfully nudging Beast for more food, Cinders hopped up on his lap and head-butted his arm until he gave her scratches. She curled up and purred contentedly.

Beast hummed in agreement, petting Cinders. "If it was her, I couldn't detect her scent. Every time I've been around her, she has an odd, cloying smell, like roses and chemicals." He sighed. "Of course, as crowded as the hall was, it would be difficult for me to know for sure."

"I hate that the judges all wear costumes. This would be so much simpler without them." Maureen slumped in her chair.

"Why are they masked?" Belle took a sip of water.

Maureen sighed. "The costumes have been a tradition since the invention portion of the Festival rose to prominence, around the 20th year of it. It came about after a scandal involving bribing judges. The whole contest was thrown into question, so they came up with the scheme of keeping the nominated council's identity secret. The costume became so popular that attendees started wearing their own designs."

"How are the identities a secret if they're nominated?" Beast leaned forward, annoying Cinders. The cat leaped onto the table, flicking her tail in distaste.

"The previous council nominates them," Captain Charity answered. "Though it's still not a perfect system. People still gossip."

"But why would Delphine be nominated?" Belle tilted her head.

The mayor threw her hands up. "Unfortunately, she has powerful friends. Even with the rumors about the unsavory work she's done, she's rich enough from her inventions. It's plausible."

"You'd think she'd rather be in the competition than be a judge if she's known for her designs." Belle rubbed her chin.

"You're right, it makes no sense." Maureen balled her fists in her lap.

"Any ideas on what we should do? Do Beast and I stay aboard?" Belle held up her hands.

"I'm stumped. You could stay aboard and risk another break-in, or come with us and risk discovery. Or, maybe I'm mistaken, and there's nothing to worry about the judge." Maureen scratched the back of her neck.

"What if we still attend the Festival but keep our distance within range with your communication device?" Belle bit her lip. "It's not a perfect plan, but if we're not seen as a group, it might help."

"That could work. Then we leave as soon as the award ceremony is done." Captain Charity put her arm around the mayor. "What do you think?"

Maureen removed her glasses to rub her eyes. "Part of me thinks we should just grab my invention and take off now. It's not worth these doubts and fears, is it?" Her shoulders sagged. "My technology could change the face of Nuzaran for the better. I can't let fear stand in the way of progress, can I?"

Cinders, bored with the proceedings, knocked an empty cup on the floor, then hopped off the table and left with her tail in the air.

Everyone stared after the feline.

"Right. I think that's enough of a plan." Captain Charity stood up and stretched. "I'll clean up."

"Thank you, Darling. I'll help, then I'll go to bed early." Maureen stifled a yawn.

Belle stood, helping Beast out of his seat. "We will, too. Good night."

Back in their quarters, as Beast reached to turn off the beaded crescent moon lamp on his nightstand, Belle rolled over to face him, rustling their crisp sheets.

"Do you think we're doing the right thing going to the Festival tomorrow?" Her gaze lingered on the ballgown laid out across her steamer trunk. It was an all-white corseted gown embroidered with realistic roses.

"With the limited choices we have, I think so." Beast tilted his head as he looked down at her. "Do you?"

A lump formed in Belle's throat as a few tears streamed down her face. "Sometimes, I wonder if we should have made our own way after escaping the Ringmaster. I'd hate for anyone to be endangered because of us." She drew a hiccupping breath. "But then I think about all Maureen and Captain Charity have done for us. Without them, we wouldn't have our home, my cure, or any hope of curing you. It feels selfish, but I'm also so glad we found them."

With a light touch, Beast wiped away her tears. "There's nothing wrong with wanting to have a chance at a better life. Delphine and Maureen's feud goes back well before us, and it's a badly concealed secret that Captain Charity is an airship pirate. How she gets away with being in public is a mystery to me. I don't think our presence will endanger them more."

After turning off the lamp, he pulled her into his arms and ran his paws through her hair.

Belle snuggled into his chest and sighed. "You're right. I just wish I knew the right answer."

Beast pressed his muzzle against her forehead. "Me, too. Let's sleep on it."

The next day, the humidity was worse inside the Exhibition Hall, which seemed to amplify the aroma of the blooming plants mingling with the metallic scent from the ether emissions of the machines on display. Belle was thankful for her domino mask and her breezy white ballgown, but she felt sorry for Beast in his layers. His mask coordinated with hers, made to look like an ancient marble statue overgrown with roses. Even his suit looked statuesque, with faux moss and roses covering his cape.

"We can go back to the ship if the heat's getting to you. How are you holding up?" Belle tapped his shoulder.

The announcer cut in over the intercom. "Make your way to the central stage. The award ceremony begins in five minutes."

Beast huffed as they picked up their pace. "I'll be fine. At least it's the last day we'll have to hear the announcements."

By the time they finally reached the center of the hall, the benches were nearly filled. Luckily, they found two seats at the end of a row. Beast sat on the outside edge while Belle sat next to an attendee who kept her starry-eyed gaze on the vine-covered copper statues on stage. She didn't seem to mind that Belle's elbow was precariously close to her ribcage.

"They're up front." Beast pointed a gloved paw to the first row. Captain Charity whispered into Maureen's ear, soliciting suppressed laughter from the mayor.

Triumphant music swelled over the intercom and multicolored lights shone up from below the massive statues of past inventors on stage. A hush fell over the crowd as Chancellor Elmstone stepped up to the podium. Amethyst hairpins adorned her teal-dyed hair and matched her violet suit.

Behind the chancellor, the colorfully costumed Festival council sat in throne-like chairs in a semicircle. Their outfits were also more elaborate today, with jewels embedded in their featureless, face-covering masks.

"Thank you all for coming to the 103rd Grand Festival Invention Showcase. This year's entries were nothing short of spectacular." The chancellor cleared her throat. "Before I announce our winner, we have two honorable mentions. Cornelia Parson for her Revised Broadcast Network."

She paused, allowing time for Cornelia to stand and wave, a smile plastered to the inventor's face.

Chancellor Elmstone shuffled her papers. "And our other runner-up is Horatio Ward for his Automated Hot-Air Balloon."

Horatio beamed and waved from his seat, a fresh bandage covering his left cheek.

All eyes were back on the chancellor as she spoke. "For the first time in years, the judges were unanimous in their decision. Congratulations to our grand prize winner, Maureen Dawkins and her Transmutation Engine. Her invention will truly revolutionize ether production."

The lights focused on Maureen as she swayed a little on the spot. Captain Charity caught her, supporting her by the elbow. Applause broke out in the audience, though some of the other inventors glared at her.

"Please come to the stage and say a few words." The chancellor nodded at Maureen.

On stage, the woman in gold stood, carrying an ornate trophy made of golden gears and sculpted emerald-encrusted flowers. Maureen and Captain Charity froze on the stairs leading up to the platform. Their eyes locked onto the golden judge. A knot formed in Belle's stomach. This was a nightmare.

"This can't be good," Beast whispered. "What do we do?"

"I don't know. Is it her?" Belle's heart hammered. She looked behind them, scanning for exits.

The suspicious guard from yesterday stood at attention at the back of the crowd.

Adrenaline thrummed through Belle as she looked for a way out of this disaster. They were truly stuck. The communication device concealed in Beast's trouser pocket was useless with so many people around. The other communicator was with Captain Charity.

The roses from Beast's mask brushed against Belle as he leaned to whisper, "Should we leave?"

Sweat beaded beneath her domino mask. "I don't know. That guard is back."

On stage, Chancellor Elmstone beckoned Maureen forward. "Don't be shy. Come on up!"

Captain Charity whispered in Maureen's ear, jerking her head toward the judge. Belle wondered what the captain could have said to make the mayor resume climbing up the steps. The captain stayed by her side, never taking her eyes off of the judge holding the trophy.

Belle tensed, wondering if she should simply push her way past the woman seated on the other side of her. Beast looked as if he were having similar thoughts, ready to spring into action at a moment's notice.

When Maureen reached the stage, Chancellor Elmstone shook her hand. "Well done."

The masked judge approached Maureen and handed her the trophy made of gold gears and emerald flowers before returning to her seat among the judges. The mayor smiled tightly as she handed her trophy to the captain before speaking into the microphone resting on the podium.

"I'm deeply honored to be here." Maureen's voice was steady as her captain stood guard behind her.

Despite the tense circumstances, the mayor's demeanor calmed Belle's nerves. She unclenched her fist and held on to Beast's arm instead. He was not so easily soothed, the tension in his muscles palpable.

Maureen cleared her throat. "The Transmutation Engine is more than a marvelous piece of technology. It represents hope for a better tomorrow. Imagine a future where our poorest communities won't have to live in fear of the mutations that come from living near ether-mines. Though progress has been made over the last decade to automate the process, there have been spills and environmental disasters as companies cut corners with their machines."

The mayor took a shaky breath, and Belle's heart went out as she remembered what Captain Charity had said. Maureen's production cycle had been too slow for greedy companies, and so they'd all gone with Delphine's questionable machines.

"All the components of The Transmutation Engine are sustainable, and certified testing confirms it creates ether without the mutating element. I'm excited to see how this technology will change Nuzaran for the better. Thank you again."

The audience erupted into a thunderous standing ovation. As Belle clapped, all she could think about was if such an invention had existed earlier, her family and community could have had completely different lives. At least now, no one would suffer the same fate.

"Should we get out of here?" Beast asked, his voice barely audible under the roar of the crowd.

Maureen looked like she was having similar thoughts as she grabbed Captain Charity's free hand, both retreating to the stairs.

Belle was more than ready to get away from the crowd. "Yes, let's—"

An explosion of glittering silver confetti fell from concealed devices on the glass and steel ceiling. Outside, the sky provided a stunning backdrop as the last bits of rosy sunlight faded into twilight. Festive music swelled over the speakers, and the audience scrambled to get out of the way as the mechanized process turned the stage area into a dance hall.

"Not this again." Belle groaned, shaking her head.

"Belle!" The crowd surged as the seats were cleared away, separating Beast from Belle.

"Dammit." Belle pushed through the crowd to reach Beast, wincing as someone stepped on the train of her dress. At last, his gloved paw closed around her hand.

Beast swept her into his arms into a tight embrace. "We've got to stop letting that happen."

Breathless, Belle could only nod.

"And for our first dance of the night, our winner, Maureen Dawkins, will open the ball with her partner." The announcer's voice cut in over the music.

"I thought his part was done," Beast huffed.

Maureen and Captain Charity blinked at the bright spotlight as they stood on the edge of the dance floor. Captain Charity shrugged before curtsying to Maureen. Maureen bowed, and the two began an elegant waltz to the delight of the audience.

Belle peeked over her shoulder. The guard was still at her station, her expression inscrutable as she observed the crowd. A new song began, and attendees, judges, and even the chancellors entered the dance floor, surrounding Maureen and the captain.

Beast nudged Belle. "Maybe we should stay and make sure they're okay?"

She could practically hear the grin in his voice as he added, "I wouldn't say no to dancing with you again."

Belle suppressed her grin with a mock stern expression. His enthusiasm was contagious. "One dance, then we're out of here."

"Deal." With that, Beast led her to the dance floor, positioning themselves close enough to see their friends, but far enough away to avoid drawing attention.

As she rested her head against Beast's shoulder while they swayed to the slow song, Belle wished she could enjoy herself more. She tensed as she saw how close the judges were to Maureen. The golden judge stopped mid-dance with her partner, right behind the mayor.

Belle nudged Beast. "Look."

He drew her closer as they watched the judge in gold take off her mask, wipe off her freckled forehead, and brush back her black, curly hair as she laughed with her dance partner.

"That's not Delphine," Beast deadpanned.

"No, she's not." The tightness in Belle's chest loosened. "Maybe everything will be fine."

"Dancing, then?"

"Yes."

Belle felt lighter as Beast twirled her on the dance floor, laughing as he put her into an exaggerated dip at the end of the song.

As she caught her breath, Beast offered his arm to her. "One dance, as promised. Back to the ship?"

They turned to leave, only to bump straight into the guard, who ignored them and kept going forward, straight to Maureen and Captain Charity as they tried to extract themselves from the dance floor.

"What now?" Belle pulled Beast along as they followed the guard, blending in with the curious onlookers.

"Stop right there, Captain Charity! I have a warrant for your arrest. You're wanted for airship piracy." The guard waved a wrinkled flier at the captain.

Belle's heart dropped.

Maureen stepped in front of her partner. "And I have the captain's pardon, signed and dated here. I think you'll find your information out-of-date." From her breast pocket, she retrieved an official-looking document, complete with a signature and an embossed indigo seal and held it up for everyone to see.

"What's this?" The guard peered at the paper, scowling. "Everything appears to be in order, but something seems off."

"Are you trying to imply something?" Maureen looked down at the guard over her octagonal glasses. "As mayor of Duchollow, it's my right to grant pardons. Captain Charity has done nothing but act with honor. I can't say the same about you embarrassing her here."

Behind the mayor, the captain turned crimson as she stared at the document, wide-eyed.

The guard blinked, as if realizing for the first time who she was addressing. "M-my apologies, ma'am." She bowed stiffly and practically sprinted to the nearest exit while onlookers murmured.

Maureen cradled her arm around the shell-shocked captain. "We'll be taking our leave now. Thank you again for the honor, but my partner deserves better."

The couple parted through the stunned crowd, Maureen guiding Captain Charity by the small of her back.

"Let's see if they need help loading up the booth." Belle tapped Beast's shoulder.

They took a meandering path through the lamp-lit invention showcase. Once they were sure no one was watching, Belle and Beast headed toward the booth. As they rounded the corner, they came to halt near Maureen and Captain Charity engaged in an animated discussion.

"Why are we stopping?" Beast whispered.

Belle frowned and pressed a finger to her lips before pulling him behind a cluster of trees off the path.

"How could you pardon me like that? I never quit piracy!" Captain Charity's voice cracked, laced with emotion as she helped load the machine onto the mechanized wagon.

"Say it any louder, and the guard will hear you." Maureen grunted as she loaded her toolbox. "We both knew you couldn't stay a pirate forever."

"But you decided for me!" The captain placed a box a little too heavily on the cart.

"And I'm very sorry about that, but I had a pardon on hand for emergencies. I couldn't let her arrest you."

"I could have escaped."

"And then what? I'd never be able to step foot here again."

"Onyxmark isn't that great."

"Not the point. My invention—"

"See? I knew you were picking the machine over me."

"No, I wasn't. I will always choose you." Maureen closed the distance between them and got down on one knee. "Marry me?"

Belle covered her mouth, hoping her gasp wasn't audible.

Captain Charity snorted. "This is how you want to ask me, after all this time?"

"Well, no..." Maureen sighed. "I don't want to lose you."

Captain Charity helped her up. "We can talk about it more at home. I'm still cross with you."

"I will make this up to you."

"You better."

Behind the trees, Belle wrung her hands. "Booth, or back to the ship?"

Beast shook his head and held his paws up. "I'm not getting involved in that. Ship, please."

As they turned, a familiar voice came from behind them.

"Leaving so soon?"

Beast tensed. "It's her."

Icy dread crept up her back as Belle peeked over her shoulder. At the edge of Maureen's booth, Delphine stood wearing a blue dress holding a matching, featureless mask in her gloved hand. She was flanked by the chancellor and a masked judge in green who carried Maureen's trophy.

"Congrats on the win, Maureen." Delphine's voice dripped with saccharine sweetness. "We have so much to catch up on."

CHAPTER TWENTY-FIVE

Fear rooting her in place, Belle stared in horror at the scene unfolding at Maureen's booth. Without the camouflage of the palm trees, she and Beast were exposed, standing on the well-lit path in the Inventor's Showcase.

There was a muffled hitch in Beast's breath as he turned around to look, too.

"Should we run?" he whispered. The artificial roses on his marble-patterned mask had a wilted appearance as they were partially crushed, likely from when Belle had pulled him behind the tree earlier.

"What if that draws more attention? I didn't see where the annoying guard went." Belle's voice was strained. She couldn't tear her gaze away from Delphine who was flanked by Chancellor Elmstone and a masked judge in a green dress. At least the trio didn't seem aware of her or Beast, but the thought didn't bring Belle any comfort, as both Maureen and Captain Charity were the center of attention.

"You left so fast, you forgot your precious award," Delphine simpered, holding out the gold and emerald trophy. The lantern light on her piled-up golden hair gave her a soft halo and made her blue embroidered dress sparkle.

Maureen's posture was rigid as she paused and nearly dropped the crate she was carrying to her mechanized wagon.

Captain Charity was the first to recover. She wiped her palms on her fancy dress before holding a hand out. "Here, let me take that. I'll load it up for Maureen."

Delphine hesitated, holding the award closer to her beaded blue gown. "I don't know if I should hand it over to a known pirate."

The captain's lip twitched. "Ex-pirate. I've got a clean record now, didn't you hear?"

"Is that so?" The other woman tossed back her golden hair.

"That's enough, Delphine." Chancellor Elmstone held her hand out, exasperation etched into her features as she gave the ex-pirate a sidelong glance. "If Maureen has pardoned the… captain, that's good enough for me. It certainly should be for you, but if not, I'll give her the trophy."

Delphine lowered her gaze as she handed the trophy to Captain Charity. "My apologizes, Chancellor."

The captain smirked as she took the award and carefully placed it in one of the wagon's crates. "Don't even think of it."

A sigh escaped Belle. Maybe they'd get out of this unscathed as long as the chancellor was around to mediate. She tugged on Beast's arm and nodded toward the exit. Her skirt rustled as they turned.

"Were you expecting company?" The masked judge pointed at Belle and Beast.

Belle considered fleeing, but then immediately dismissed the idea. It'd be more suspicious to run. Reminding herself that she and Beast were masked, she took a deep breath before she took Beast's arm. Beast's steps were slow, but aside from the trembling in his paw, he put up a brave front as they approached the booth arm-in-arm.

"We're the muscle," Belle said brightly when they reached the others.

"Perfect timing. Can you rearrange these crates? We need to make room for The Transmutation Engine." Maureen gestured to the boxes of spare parts that had been loaded up haphazardly on the wagon during the demonstration.

Delphine's arched brows rose as she studied Belle and Beast. "If they're your muscle, why are they still costumed?"

The green judge shrugged. "I'm sure they have their reasons. I hate to think of what the humidity has done to my face under my mask, but it's staying on until I retire for the night." She stretched and yawned. "Speaking of which, I'm going to go back to the festivities before I change my mind."

Belle and Beast busied themselves with the crates under Captain Charity's direction, though Belle couldn't resist stealing glances back. The chancellor and Delphine remained while the other judge departed. Leaning down to pick up crates in her white gown had not been one of Belle's best ideas, but at least she had given a plausible excuse for lingering in the booth.

As Maureen carefully unscrewed the invention's delicate vials and placed them on the ground, Chancellor Elmstone cleared her throat.

"Are you sure I can't persuade you to stay in Onyxmark longer, Maureen? There are several of us who would love to discuss The Transmutation Engine with you further." The chancellor nodded at Delphine. "I know you two have had your differences but imagine the possibilities if you collaborated."

Maureen sniffed as she continued her work. "No, thank you. I won't be making that mistake again. I want to ensure the safety standards of The Transmutation Engine remain high. I'm also done with listening to people slander my partner. I won't stay in Onyxmark a minute longer."

The chancellor sighed as she fussed with one of her amethyst hair pins, teal-dyed hair escaping in a wild curl. "I suppose it was too much for me to hope I could convince you otherwise. We'll leave you to your packing, but please reach out to me anytime. My office is always open to you."

Looking up from the vials, Maureen nodded. "I appreciate the sentiment."

"Come along. There are plenty of people waiting to speak to you, Delphine." The chancellor crooked her finger at the other woman.

Belle struggled to suppress an indignant snort. She knew Delphine had powerful friends after making the barons richer from her mining machines. Though the idea made her feel ill, she imagined the golden woman's influential connections extended to high-ranking politicians, too. Delphine clenched her fists at her side. As she stared down Maureen, she sneered. "What happened to the scrap metal? A failed transmutation?" She inclined her head toward the pile of twisted copper laying exposed on the wagon's trailers.

Maureen's expression hardened. "An ill-fated attempt at sabotage. Someone tried to ruin my machine, but they didn't succeed. They broke some parts, but I came prepared."

"Lucky for you." Delphine leaned forward conspiratorially. "You know, I recently experienced sabotage, too. One of my suppliers was recently blown to bits. How long has your captain's record been clean?"

"Delphine, what are you implying?" Chancellor Elmstone's brows furrowed.

"I don't think my record is any of your business." Captain Charity's tone was quiet and deadly as she set her jaw. "Since meeting Maureen, I've tried to do good. She makes me want to be a better person. For her, I'd do anything, even become respectable."

Maureen stepped between them. "Didn't the factory that blew up sell the orbs used for prisoners? What sort of business would you have with that?"

Delphine sneered. "Keeping my guard dogs safe."

Belle was amazed that her hands didn't shake as she helped Beast rearrange the last of the crates. This conversation was headed toward dangerous territory. As she subtly searched for a distraction, a dark stain along the back side of the invention caught Belle's attention. A quick glance confirmed a hose was still attached to the faucet from the demonstration.

"Hey, Maureen, I'm going to clean off the engine before loading it. Wouldn't want any of this residue to do anything strange while in transit," Belle called, hoping her fake nonchalance was enough. Perhaps the threat of getting her fancy dress dirty would be enough to send Delphine away.

At Maureen's nod, Belle turned the knob of the faucet. Cold water shot out of the hose as she made a show of rinsing off The Transmutation Engine while Beast scratched the back of his collar, head tilted to the side.

Chancellor Elmstone retreated away from the booth, eyeing the scattering water droplets with disdain. "Come on, Delphine. Clearly, they're busy loading up."

Delphine ignored the chancellor and stepped around her. "Hold on, you never answered my question. A pardon wouldn't let you off the hook for any damages to the factory."

Belle feigned slipping on the slick floor of the booth, letting the hose fly out of her hand. The spray hit Delphine, drenching her from head to toe in a matter of seconds. As the other woman screeched, Belle scrambled to pick up the hose and shut off the faucet.

"Oops, my hand slipped. Must be from the—" The sentence died on her lips.

Delphine's rouge washed off, along with whatever makeup she was wearing. Her sun-kissed skin was now considerably paler, with gold and dark green veins visible across her pearlescent skin.

"What happened to you?" Chancellor Elmstone covered her mouth with her hand.

"What did you do to yourself?" Maureen peered over her octagonal glasses. "This isn't run-of-the-mill ether-poisoning."

"You are the last person who should judge me for pushing the limits of science and alchemy." Delphine jabbed her pointer finger in the mayor's direction before fixing her hate-filled gaze on Belle and Beast. "And don't think your friends' weak disguises have fooled me. You should know by now I'll always recognize my creation when I see it."

Without waiting for a response, Delphine abruptly left, leaving behind a trail of water as she retreated in a huff.

Beast muttered to Belle, "Maybe that's why she didn't let me see her when I was created."

"I feel like I've missed something important." Chancellor Elmstone's gaze fell on Belle and Beast before flicking back to Maureen. "Good luck with your journey home. Remember, you don't have to be a stranger."

"Thank you, Chancellor. Right now, we just want to leave." Maureen put her arm around Captain Charity as the chancellor departed.

Belle nodded, though her thoughts had taken a darker turn. What had Delphine meant about Maureen? What would she do now that she knew Beast was here?

The morning after the Grand Festival, Belle slept off her aches from frantically loading up Maureen's equipment. Grateful for the luxurious bedding in her and Beast's quarters aboard the *Figment*, she rolled over to curl into Beast, but her head landed on a cool pillow. When she reached for him, her hand came up empty, finding only more blankets. She cracked one eye open.

Beast's side of the bed was *empty*.

Grumbling as she rubbed her eyes, she finally spotted him looking out the dome window, shielding his eyes with one paw as hazy sunlight formed a halo around his silver fur.

"Beast?"

He turned to face her, an amused glint in his eyes as he smirked. "Your bed head is spectacular this morning."

As Belle brushed back her hair, she snorted. "And I wonder whose fault that could be?"

Holding his paw over his heart, Beast was the picture of innocence. "Me?"

"Yes, you. Why are you awake already? I thought you'd be exhausted after carrying the spare parts all the way to the ship last night. We should have some time before we land in Duchollow." Belle sat up in bed, the covers dipping down over her thin nightgown.

"The encounter with Delphine brought back memories I'd rather forget. I gave up trying to sleep." He furrowed his brows. "I don't think we're headed to Duchollow."

Belle threw off her blankets and shuddered as her bare feet met the cold floor. She padded across the room to Beast's side and squinted at the view of dense pine trees and craggy mountains in the distance. There weren't any mountains between Duchollow and

Onyxmark. The ones near Duchollow's valley weren't nearly so rocky and certainly didn't have snow-capped peaks.

"Where are we?" Belle shivered, leaning into Beast's chest for warmth.

The intercom crackled on. Damek's modulated voice echoed in their room. "Good morning! Captain Charity requests if you're awake and somewhat decent to please meet her and the mayor in the dining hall." He paused, as if weighing his words. "I'm not sure why she's questioning your character. From what I understand about organic life forms, you two are upstanding."

Beast chuckled as he rose to press the intercom button.

"Thank you, Damek." Beast's eyes traveled down Belle's form, lingering on the dip in her hips highlighted by her nightgown. "We'll be there shortly."

After scrambling to get dressed, Belle and Beast made their way to the dining hall, where Captain Charity slumped in her seat and guzzled black coffee. Across from her, Maureen looked more alert, though there were dark circles under her eyes as she sipped coffee while making notes in her leather-bound journal.

The scent of sweet tarts and fresh coffee made Belle's stomach grumble.

Maureen gave them an apologetic smile as she gestured to their places at the table. Their breakfast was already plated and a carafe of coffee sat next to two empty mugs. "Sorry it's early, but I've got news that couldn't wait. Please help yourself."

Beast poured their drinks and Belle almost returned the mayor's smile, but the haunted look in the other woman's eyes unnerved her.

"Thank you. Is everything okay?" Belle's pulse quickened. "Delphine isn't after us, is she?"

Captain Charity shook her head. "No, the skies have been clear. I stayed up with Damek to check." She yawned and stretched before grinning. "I still can't believe you drenched her. Nice work."

Belle blushed. "I couldn't think of anything else to make her go away. Maybe your influence is rubbing off on me." Her breath caught as she remembered the hate-filled look in Delphine's eyes when her makeup had washed away. Part of Belle felt a twinge of guilt for inadvertently exposing the unnatural gold veins, but she would have done anything to get Beast away from his tormentor. "Does she have ether-poisoning? What was that?"

Maureen cleared her throat and closed her notebook. "That's actually part of what I'd like to discuss. I believe Delphine has done transmutation work with ether, but instead of trying to create a more stable version, she changed it to be more reactive. That's what she's used for mutation experiments. I think she tested it on herself, along with her Hounds, and even Beast. That's why my cure didn't work."

Belle and Beast gaped at the mayor.

"What?" He dropped his apple tart, his attention focused on the mayor.

"When we were at university together, she was obsessed with alchemy and transmutation. She thought it held the key to cure illnesses and perhaps even spark life in machines." Maureen's shoulders sagged. "As did I. Together, we created Damek, though she wanted more, pushing for research into ether-poisoning. She helped me in the early days of researching its cure, long before I could find a solution. Our work together stopped when I realized she wasn't trying to find a cure. She was trying to unlock the combinations for radical changes."

"What does that have to do with Beast?" Belle slipped her hand over his free paw.

"I think Delphine experimented on animals before herself, and that's how she ended up with Hounds. As for Beast, perhaps he was a failed attempt at alterations, or she was using him to find a cure for her condition." Maureen rubbed her chin. "I'm not sure yet how it's exactly connected, but there's no denying a link."

"I think she'd already done something to herself before my creation." Beast's voice was full of disdain. "I remember only fragments from my time in captivity, but I recall she never let me look at her."

"But why would she willingly give herself some kind of ether-poisoning? It's ruined so many people's lives." Belle winced, thinking of her sickly mother's final days.

Maureen shook her head. "When we were close, she was obsessed with pushing the limits of science and alchemy. I would not put it past her to experiment on herself while chasing perfection."

Captain Charity cut her tired eyes at her partner and scowled. "I wouldn't say you were close if she was using you for her designs."

Maureen bowed her head. "I wonder about that. What if I'm no better than her?"

"You are. You wouldn't make the same choices she has. You actually have principles. But enough talk of the past. Want to share your plan?" Captain Charity laced her fingers with the mayor's.

"Right." Maureen lifted her head, though her gaze was still downcast. "I need to collect more volatile samples of ether for a solution similar to my ether-poisoning cure. I'm going to test it on the Hounds first to see if my theory is correct. Curing them is key to Beast's cure. I can feel it. We're taking a detour on the way home."

The tightness in Belle's chest eased as she squeezed Beast's paw. "That's great news. Where are we heading?"

"Aetherbourne. The town is abandoned, but according to my research, some of the most extreme cases of ether-poisoning transformations have occurred near there, on both people and the local wildlife. We'll need to pick up protective gear on the way, but Darling has a lead on that."

A pit formed in Belle's stomach.

Beast held her hand tighter. "Is that where…"

A lump formed in Belle's throat. "Aetherbourne is where I'm from. Are you asking me to go back?" Her eyes widened. "And what do you mean abandoned?"

CHAPTER TWENTY-SIX

The clouds over Aetherbourne were no longer soot-filled as Belle remembered, but the ramshackle town was still miserable. She hardly recognized the landscape overgrown with prickly weeds and dotted with squat, drab shacks ruined by rotted, broken boards. At the edge of the town, the dormant mine slumbered. Rusted ether-mining equipment littered its entrance.

Inside the *Figment*, Belle took a shuddering breath, pressing her palms against the cool glass of the observation deck window in an effort to steady her nerves. The landing had been rough, with poor lighting in the hilly town and no dock workers for Damek or Captain Charity to radio.

When Maureen had proposed her plan to go to Aetherbourne, Belle wished she would have asked more questions. She was anxious to know if the former miners had escaped to start new lives elsewhere or if everyone had succumbed to ether-poisoning, as her mother did all those years ago. She couldn't help but wonder if her father had left town with his 2,000 silver coins or if the ether-poisoning took him, too. Had his daughter's freedom bought him a new life?

"You don't have to go back there." Beast wrapped his arm around Belle's waist, his warm breath tickling her ear. "I'll help collect the samples, then we can turn our backs on this place for good."

Belle shook her head and leaned into his embrace. "If this leads to a cure for you, I'm going to do whatever it takes. Besides, none of the new protective gear will fit you, remember?" She sighed. "I wish it was anywhere but here."

"You shouldn't have to hurt yourself for my cure to happen. It's not worth it." Beast's voice was a low growl as he held her closer.

Despite her conflicting emotions, Belle couldn't resist turning toward Beast to tap his muzzle playfully. "I'll be fine. And don't be ridiculous. You're worth it. Don't tell me you wouldn't do the same for me."

Damek's chipper voice came over the intercom. "Captain's done inspecting the landing gear! Only superficial scratches on the ship. She said to meet her and Maureen in the cargo hold."

When Belle and Beast entered the cargo hold, they had to watch their steps or risk walking into crates haphazardly stacked near the door. The room was more cramped than ever. New supplies were packed between parts of The Transmutation Engine, crates were stacked in precarious rows, and the mayor's mechanized wagon was shoved against the hatch door.

Amidst the chaos, Maureen set up a makeshift storage space for the canisters of samples to be collected while the captain inspected the new ether-resistant suits. From what Belle could see, they resembled diving suits she'd seen illustrated in a book once, though they looked made of lighter material. The bubble glass helmets would be less cumbersome and offer more visibility than their underwater counterparts made of copper.

"When do we suit up?" Belle forced herself to ask cheerfully, startling the engrossed mayor and captain.

Maureen adjusted her octagonal glasses as she regarded Belle and Beast. "It'll be a few hours before I'm ready, but if you want to stretch your legs, you're welcome to go exploring. Keep your distance from the mine." She furrowed her brows. "If this place is too painful for you, Belle, I can always see if Damek could help with the sample extraction. He wouldn't even have to wear gear."

"Negative on Damek," piped up Captain Charity as she checked the suits for holes and tears. She peered up at them over her work. "If Belle can't help, we'll be fine, but Damek is much too delicate for lifting heavy equipment or navigating the tunnels. I'm not losing my pilot in the mine. No offense."

"I could always reinforce his joints. You know I wouldn't intentionally put Damek in harm's way," Maureen wheedled.

Before the conversation could devolve into an argument, Belle held up her hands. "I appreciate everyone's concern, but I'm okay. Let's just focus on getting what we need. In the meantime, I'd love to get some fresh air." Considering her phrasing, she admitted, "Well, as fresh as the air is around here, anyway."

Beast slipped his paw into Belle's hand and gave her a reassuring squeeze. "We can always come back to the ship if it's too much."

Maureen nodded before rummaging through the gadgets on her makeshift workbench made of repurposed parts. "Before you go, take these so we can tell you when we're ready."

The mayor handed Belle a radio, along with a rectangular green-gray machine with two copper wires protruding from the top of it in a V-shape. A radial dial on its surface calibrated measurements in units of 10, though what those units represented was unclear. Currently, the needle rested at 0.

"What's this?" Belle held up the strange new device.

"It's an ether-radiation detector. The higher the number is, the more the risk of ether-poisoning is present. Being cured of ether-poisoning doesn't make you immune." Maureen cut her eyes at Beast. "And I'd rather not find out how ether-radiation might further alter Beast."

Beast snorted, pointing to his prominent canines and bear-like visage. "What else could it do to me?"

"I don't know, but I'd rather not risk all hope of a cure because of a lack of safety precautions." Maureen pointed at the detector, her expression grave. "If that dial reaches above 50, get back to the ship immediately."

Beast gulped. "Will do."

"Thank you." Belle called over her shoulder before unlocking the hatch. She tapped Beast's shoulder. "Ready?"

"I suppose…" Beast fidgeted. He donned his tinted goggles but went barefoot and without a disguise for the first time in days.

"We can stay aboard if you're worried. Maureen's not exaggerating when she says the ether-poisoning was rampant here. Most people I knew growing up either had it or someone in their family did." Belle nudged his arm gently.

Beast looked down where their arms met, frowning. "I'll carry one of the devices. Let's go see your hometown."

As Belle handed him the detector, she gave him a wistful smile. "I'll give you a tour, but I'm warning you, there's probably not much to see."

"Lead the way."

Outside, Aetherbourne was both as Belle remembered in her fragmented memories and completely alien without the filthy smoke in the air from the old processing equipment or chatter of miners coming and going from their grueling shifts. She and Beast walked arm in arm along the outskirts of the town, both in quiet, contemplative moods. The only sounds were their footsteps and the faint crackles from the ether-radiation detector as it hovered between 10 and 20.

"Where do you want to go first?" Beast asked, breaking the silence.

"Is it strange that I want to visit Mother's grave?" Belle pointed to the graveyard, startlingly large for a small mining community, on the hill overlooking the town. "Father didn't even let me go to her burial. I had to work with the rest of our crew. He only went on his lunch break and came straight back to the mines. He never spoke of her again."

"I'm so sorry." Beast hugged Belle tightly. "I know you said your childhood was awful, but I didn't realize—"

Belle shook her head, a lump forming in her throat. "There are plenty of reasons I don't talk about my family."

Together, they made the trek up the hill to Aetherbourne's unfenced graveyard. Crude stone graves with only names and dates etched into their surfaces littered the hill. Unlike other cities, where more ornate statues of the Maker in all her glory were commonplace, it looked less like a cemetery and more like semi-organized rubble.

Cringing at the state of the graveyard, Belle stooped to clear the weeds and grass overtaking the stones, reading the names to herself. Most of the names, those of miners long gone from her memory, meant nothing to her. And that was if she'd ever known their names. There wasn't much time for socializing in the mine.

Beast knelt to help clear stones, reading the names aloud to her in case they found the site of her mother's marker.

In the middle of the fourth row, Belle cleared away the weeds and choked back a gasp.

Beast was at her side in an instant. "What's wrong?"

"I found her. And Father, too." Belle's breath caught as she reread the marker. The stone was slightly larger than the others, likely paid for with Father's silver. "Hannah Beaumont died 24 years of age. Jeremiah Beaumont died 32 years of age. Parents of Ava Beaumont."

Beast tilted his head. "Who's Ava? Did you have a sister?"

Belle shook her head. "No. That's my birth name, but it means nothing to me."

Beast put his arm around her. "I'm so sorry."

"Me, too." Tears burned Belle's eyes as she read the date. "Father didn't get to enjoy his silver long. He died the same year he sold me."

"Do you think he knew?" Beast asked quietly.

The radio crackled in Belle's pocket. Captain Charity's muffled voice spoke. "We're ready to suit up. Ready to head out?"

Belle retrieved the radio and clicked the call button, her eyes fixed on her parents' graves. "We're on our way. See you soon."

Beast studied her, his tinted goggles obscuring his expression.

"Are you sure? We could look at your old house after we're done. Maybe find answers there?"

As they headed back, Belle shook her head. "I don't need to see the shack. Let the past die. I'd rather focus on the future with you."

At Beast's stunned silence, she smiled softly. "Let's go get those samples and get you cured."

The ether-mine's opening seemed to swallow up the sunlight streaming into its entrance. Belle held up her lantern, revealing the rusty sage green elevator and an empty minecart sitting on filthy rails that led to the lower level. She wrinkled her nose at the all-to-familiar earthy, damp scent. Despite the filter in her breathing apparatus, it was overpowering.

How many times as a girl had she descended into the mine's depths on the squeaking, unsteady elevator, carrying too much gear, without a filter to protect herself from the putrid smells?

Aside from the towering amber drill to the left of the elevator, everything was nearly as Belle remembered from her childhood, though it was unnervingly quiet without the noise of the miners at work, punctuated by the hisses of the siphons collecting ether.

After the short trek from the *Figment* to the mine, Belle was sweltering in her ether-resistant suit. The oxygen tank strapped to her back and the crate of canisters that would store the ether samples that she carried in her free hand compounded her discomfort.

The radio strapped onto her right arm crackled on. Beast's disembodied voice came through the crackling static. "Is everything okay?"

Belle smiled at the concern in his voice as she set down the canister crate. She pressed the radio's call button, holding her arm up to the speaker covering her mouth on the glass helmet. "I'm still adjusting to the suit, but otherwise, everything's fine. You would hate wearing one of these."

"If it gets too dangerous, please get out of there."

Before Belle could reply, Maureen cut in. The delay between her speaking live and over the radio waves gave her a strange, out-of-sync echo. "We won't stay long. Even with the suits, I'm not willing to risk contamination. No one is going into the depths as soon as I power on the drill. She's in good hands, Beast."

"She'd better be," Beast growled. "I'm grateful for the chance at a cure, but not at the risk of endangering Belle."

At Maureen's pointed look at the ether-radiation detector, Belle spoke quickly. "I'll be safe, but we need to get to work. Give Cinders extra scratches for me. I love you."

"I love you, too. Come back safe," Beast answered as Cinders mewed in the background.

"The sooner we finish, the sooner we can get these miserable suits off." Underneath Captain Charity's glass helmet, sweat beaded on her forehead and her hair hung in short, frizzy copper curls.

Belle nodded, eager to leave the mine behind.

Maureen pointed to the menacing drill looming over them. "The detector should buzz if we're in danger, but I'd rather finish up before that happens."

"Agreed." Belle swallowed hard as the three walked side-by-side to the drill. "Wyerstone" was painted on the side of the machine in peeling green letters.

"One of Delphine's," Maureen said, her voice dripping with contempt.

Belle's stomach churned. Being back in Aetherbourne was hard enough without finding out there was a connection to the cruel woman, especially so close to their encounter at the Festival.

"If there's still ether, why did they stop mining here?" Captain Charity asked, bringing Belle out of her musings.

Maureen answered as she held up the detector, its needle wavering between 60-70 units. "Even with the automated drilling, no one could stay in Aetherbourne long term without contracting ether-poisoning. In the end, everyone left or succumbed to the disease. A few were fortunate to get away to get treatment, but most didn't make it."

Belle's eyes burned with unshed tears. She couldn't risk removing her helmet to wipe them away. Blinking furiously under her helmet, she spoke when she could trust her voice not to shake. "Should we get started then?"

Maureen nodded and set about inspecting the drill, removing several panels to expose its mechanical interior before removing her pack of spare parts. She rummaged through it, occasionally setting equipment to the side as she worked. "I should be able to rig this to mine again."

After several minutes of Maureen swearing and tinkering with the machine, Belle hesitantly asked, "Is there anything we can help with?"

Behind the mayor, Captain Charity shook her head and dramatically made an X with her arms.

Still deep in the machine's guts, Maureen didn't look up as she gritted her teeth. "No, it's these damn gloves. They're too thick for me to deal with these wires, but I don't dare take off my gloves. My plan didn't account for the loss in dexterity. I just need to think it through."

"I see." Belle's gaze dropped, landing on the detector laying on the ground. It read 70 units.

"It doesn't help that it's one of Delphine's shoddy machines," Maureen grumbled.

Filled with nervous energy, Belle paced the perimeter of the room, made more difficult by her cumbersome suit. There had to be another solution.

When her boot connected with an abandoned pickaxe, the answer was so obvious she felt ridiculous for not thinking of it sooner. She stepped on one end of the tool to prop it up, not wanting to risk bending over with the oxygen tank strapped to her back.

Upon closer inspection, the pickaxe looked fine, probably in better condition than the ones Belle had used as a child. She took a couple of test swings, and when nothing fell off the tool, she smiled.

"What are you doing?" Captain Charity called, holding up her lantern.

Belle held up the pickaxe. "Thinking about getting ether the old-fashioned way."

Maureen looked up from her work and frowned. "What do you mean?" Her eyes widened. "You can't be serious."

"Why not? I remember what to do. Let's get this done before the detector reads any higher." Belle pointed at the device with her tool.

"How are you going to get to the ether? I'm going to have the same problem powering the elevator. There's no way it'll work after all this time." Maureen furrowed her brows. "You're not taking the rails, are you?"

Belle shook her head as she moved past the drill to the edge of the cavern. "There should be stairs right along…here." Her sentence trailed off as she found the old opening, her light shining all the way down the steep, narrow steps to the mine's lower level. "It looks stable enough. I used it before when the elevator was more faulty than usual."

When Belle turned around, Captain Charity anxiously peered down the stairs.

"Are you sure you're up for this? Who knows if the structure is still solid?"

Belle nodded. "I can't say with certainty that it's ever been safe here, but we've got to do something."

Maureen inhaled sharply as she read the dial on the device. "We need enough to fill the bottles in the bag. Are you sure you can do it fast enough? This is already reading 70 units. I'd hate to be here much longer. We can always regroup and try a different plan."

"I've got this, but can you show me how to open the canisters? These are different than the ones I remember." Belle asked.

"Of course!" Maureen retrieved a canister from the crate. "There's a lever here on the top, see?" She demonstrated as the container opened with a pop. When she pressed down on the lever, it sealed shut, and she put it back in the crate.

Belle gave her a thumbs-up before attaching her lantern to the belt on her suit, freeing her hands up for the canister crate and pickaxe. "Sounds easy enough. I'll be back soon."

"Wait, take the detector with you." Maureen slid the device between the cannisters. "Are you sure you can carry everything?"

"Yes. There's no need for all of us to go down."

With a final wave at the mayor and captain, Belle descended the narrow stairs, minding her footing on the ancient steps and ducking under the low support beams.

Finally, Belle reached the lower level of the mine and was greeted by pitch-black darkness. By her lantern's light, she journeyed through the strange, familiar tunnels until the path opened up into a wide cavern.

Veins of silver ether glittered on the stone walls all the way from the ground to the ceiling. Drills and pickaxes left at their posts were propped against the cavern's edges, as if their operators had left for a break and never returned. She peeked inside mine carts left on the dilapidated tracks, hoping to find raw ether, but only a thick layer of dust remained.

After setting down the crate of canisters and the detector, Belle found a section of ether veins to mine.

Progress was slow going at first, between Belle's limited movement in the suit and worrying about the possibility of falling debris cracking her glass helmet, but eventually, she found a comfortable enough rhythm.

Her work was interrupted occasionally by Maureen radioing to ask for readings, but it didn't take Belle long to fill all six canisters with powdery silver ether. By the time she sealed the last canister, the detector read 80 units and she was drenched with sweat. Her body ached from the repetitive motions and restrictive suit.

As Belle gathered up her tools, the radio crackled on.

"Belle? Is everything okay?" Cinders' plaintive mews punctuated Beast's words.

"I'm fine. The plan hit a snag, so I mined the ether myself."

"You did what? That was incredibly dangerous. We don't even know if the ether will cure anything!" Beast roared, making her wince.

Hurt by Beast's response, Belle was sullen as she answered. "I volunteered. I'll explain back on the ship. If you feel that badly about it, give me a massage later. I'm all kinds of sore. The important thing is we have the samples now."

"You could have told her thank you," Captain Charity's voice chimed in over the radio.

"I will. Back on the ship." His tone softened as he continued. "I am grateful, Belle, but I'll breathe easier once you're out of the mine."

"Me, too. Give me some time to pack up and we'll be on our way."

After Belle gathered her supplies, she began the long climb to the surface. For the first time as she left the mine behind her, she felt a spark of hope. She prayed the ether would lead to a cure for Beast. But first, Maureen had to test her theory on the Hounds waiting for them in Duchollow. Maybe they'd be all cured, and Delphine's terrible work could be undone for good.

Returning to the *Figment* took much longer than Belle had expected. To prevent ether-radiation from coming aboard with them, Maureen had prepared a portable decontamination station halfway between the airship and the abandoned mine. Their bulky suits were removed, sanitized, and stored in sealed metal trunks. Afterward, all three took turns showering under lukewarm water with sterile-smelling soap and changing into fresh clothes. When the process was over, the sunset bathed Aetherbourne in golden light.

Once all the clean equipment was loaded onto Maureen's mechanized wagon, they trekked back to the airship. While Belle appreciated mitigating the risk of ether-contamination, she was exhausted by the time she reached her quarters. She stumbled across the threshold as soon as she pushed the door open.

Beast rose from the sofa, leaving behind the radio, and strode across their room to catch her in a tight embrace.

"Are you okay?" He brushed back Belle's damp hair, tucking it behind her ear as he anxiously looked her over from head to toe.

"I'm fine." Belle yawned, her eyelids growing heavy as she leaned against his chest. "Tired and sore, but happy we got the samples. Captain Charity said we'd take off in the morning so we can all catch up on rest."

"I think that's the best idea she's had yet." Beast's warm breath tickled her ear as, to Belle's amusement, he picked her up in a bridal hold and carried her to bed.

When Beast laid her delicately on the soft white covers, the laughter died on her lips and her voice caught at the intense expression in his eyes. "What is it?"

Beast cupped the side of her face, tracing along her jawline. "I thought I was going to lose you to the mine after everything we've been through. I wouldn't have been able to live with myself if something had happened to you."

Belle's fatigued muscles burned as she pushed herself up to a seated position and placed her hand over his paw.

"Hey, I told you it was worth it to me." Belle kissed the edge of Beast's muzzle. "You need to stop fretting. I'm here now, and we can leave this lifeless place behind."

Beast's shoulders slumped. "But what if it was all for nothing? We don't even know if this ether is going to lead to a cure."

"We won't know until Maureen's had time to work out a formula and test it. Now, will you stop worrying and come to bed?" Belle tapped him on the nose lightly, earning a grin from Beast.

"I'll try. I owe you a back rub. Turn over."

Belle happily obliged and sighed as Beast got to work on her back, being careful not to catch his claws on her tender muscles as he kneaded them.

As Belle grew drowsier, she mumbled, "Look on the bright side. We have a home to go back to, there's a possibility of a cure for you, and the Ringmaster's behind bars." She yawned before adding, "I think I even turned twenty in the middle of everything. When I was growing up, I didn't think that would happen."

To Belle's disappointment, Beast's movements paused. "When was your birthday?"

Struggling to keep her eyes open, Belle replied, "I have no idea. Sometime in the spring, but I never really got to celebrate it. I'm just happy to begin my first year completely free of ether-poisoning."

Beast huffed as he got back to work on her back.

Belle wanted to ask him what bothered him, but soon, sleep overtook her, and she drifted off to dreams of their cottage.

CHAPTER TWENTY-SEVEN

After two days back at their cottage, Beast happily went back to tending to his garden, leaving Belle with too much time to think. She wished she could take her own advice and look on the positive side. She couldn't shake the feeling that something was wrong, though on the surface, everything seemed fine.

Their flight back to Duchollow had been uneventful, and no one had suffered ill effects from the ether-mine, thanks to the detector and protective gear. Maureen promised to send updates as soon as she was ready. There'd been no word of Delphine and the Ringmaster was secure in his cell. So why did something seem off?

The sound of the front door opening interrupted Belle's spiraling thoughts, nearly causing her to fall off the kitchen chair.

"Belle? What's wrong?" Beast stood in the kitchen, his fur and shirt caked in dirt and sweat. Though it was still morning, the day promised to be a warm one, with summer-like humidity.

Belle took a sip of her now-cold coffee and grimaced.

"I'll be fine. I guess it's my turn to worry needlessly." She gave him a weak smile.

"I'm sorry. I'd hug you, but…" Beast lifted his filthy paws.

Belle snort-laughed.

"That's better." He tilted his head. "Why don't you go check on the library? Maybe more of the renovations are done."

Belle perked up. She hadn't been back to the library in days, and now that Beast had brought it up, she missed it terribly. "That's a wonderful idea. Do you want to come with me after you clean up?"

Beast shook his head. "Not this time. I'll head into town to pick up groceries and a few things we need for the house. We're low on everything. See you at dinner?"

Belle blinked. She'd thought he'd want to go with her, but he had a good point. His thoughtfulness touched her. "If you're sure you want to run errands by yourself, okay. I'll see you at dinner."

As she left, Beast called, "I'll cook tonight, so don't worry about anything."

The walk into town helped clear Belle's head, as she was anxious to see how the library renovations were progressing. Work hadn't stopped while they were away at the Festival. Today was the crew's day off, and she looked forward to having the library to herself.

When she arrived, she gasped at the transformation. The cracks in the walls had been repaired, and the newly wired light fixtures bathed the room in comforting golden light. There were still signs of the work to be done—like the unfinished sections of wood flooring —but it was feeling homey.

Belle made her way to the central desk where her catalog system waited for her return. She had grand plans of organizing the library's impressive collection for the checkout system, and soon she was happily sorting through cards, checking on volumes to make sure they were in stock, and creating new cards for the shipment of books due to arrive any day.

Soon it was nearing lunchtime, and Belle's stomach rumbled. She'd forgotten to pack a lunch in her haste to go back to the library. She wished Beast were with her to go out to eat until inspiration struck. After tidying up the cards scattered on the desk,

Belle made her way to Town Hall, hoping that Maureen and Captain Charity were around.

When she arrived, Mr. Cadwell was at his desk, deeply engrossed in a slim book of poetry while he sipped tea.

"Hello, Mr. Cadwell," she said softly, hoping to not startle the secretary. They'd never really gotten off on the right foot—something she hoped to change.

Unfortunately, the poor man jumped, dropping his book and bumping his tea. When he recovered, he faced Belle with a polite smile. "Ah, Belle. What can I do for you?"

"I was wondering if Maureen or Captain Charity were free for lunch. Did they already take off?"

A strange expression crossed the secretary's face as he shook his head. His professional smile didn't quite reach his eyes. "No, I'm afraid they're otherwise indisposed with a project. The mayor gave explicit instructions that they're not to be disturbed."

Feeling deflated, Belle gave the secretary a polite nod. "Well, I'll try again another time. Have a good day!"

After a productive but lonely day, Belle was ready to be home. As she drew nearer, she noticed Maureen's truck parked out front. For a moment, her heart skipped a beat. Was there a breakthrough in the cure already?

Belle's steps slowed as she tilted her head in confusion. Lights were strung up along the side patio of the cottage, and the radio played soft music in the background. The scent of something delicious wafted on the warm evening breeze, beckoning her home.

By the time Belle reached the porch, Beast had come around the corner of the cottage smiling at her.

"Welcome home! You said you didn't know when your birthday was, so we threw you a party. Come on, everyone's here. I've got a surprise for you."

As Belle took his paw, she took a deep breath. She was a little disappointed that there wasn't news of a cure. Now wasn't the time to ask Maureen about it after everyone had gone through all this trouble for her. No one had ever thrown her a birthday party before. For tonight, she could just be happy.

Belle barely felt Beast's loose hold on her arm as he guided her around the corner of their cottage, too preoccupied with the transformation of their gazebo. Garlands of white roses decorated its pillars and lanterns hung along the roof, bathing everything in warm light. Maureen, Captain Charity, and Damek sat at the ironwork table, which was set with mismatched jewel-tone wine glasses filled with sparkling wine and covered dishes.

In the center of the table was a round cake, its top decorated with a crescent moon made of white frosting shaped like roses. The rest of the cake had a swirling celestial pattern of blue, purple, and pink dotted with white stars.

Behind Damek, the radio—relocated from their living room to a small end table—played soft piano melodies.

Belle turned to thank Beast, but the words caught in her throat. Finally, she squeaked out, "Thank you."

With a gentle squeeze on her arm, Beast murmured, "You're welcome. Let's sit. Everyone's waiting for you."

As Beast guided her to the bench beneath the gazebo, Belle nodded, not fully trusting her voice yet as she blinked back tears.

On her right, Damek riveted to face her. His tinny voice brimmed with enthusiasm as his eyes lit up. "Happy birthday!"

"Happy birthday!" Maureen and Captain Charity got up to engulf Belle in tight hugs from behind, crowding out Beast and Damek.

"Thank you so much. Everything's beautiful." Gratitude hit Belle in another wave. Her eyes misted as she smiled at her friends' generosity.

"Let's get you something to eat. Then, presents!" Beast peeked over Captain Charity's shoulder to grin at Belle.

Removing covers from the dishes revealed some of Belle's favorite take-out food, including barbecued chicken on sticks, rice balls, and stir-fried vegetables. Between bites, Damek kept everyone entertained asking questions about human birthday rituals, perplexed by the concept of cake and gifts but happy to be present.

Belle assured the automaton that the cake was divine, especially since the pink batter had been made with strawberries from Beast's greenhouse.

After everyone's plates and goblets were empty, Beast asked, "Ready for presents?"

Belle's eyes sparkled. "You all didn't need to get me anything. It was enough that you organized the surprise."

Captain Charity smirked as she stood on slightly wobbly legs and winked. "We know, but presents are fun, so enjoy."

With that, the captain began clearing dishes. When Captain Charity reached for Belle's plate, the light caught on her left ring finger, reflecting on a band of silver and gold inlaid with opal in speckled hues of green, purple, and indigo.

It took Belle a moment for her thoughts to connect the meaning of the ring and its placement. When it clicked, Belle beamed. "I see congratulations are in order."

"Thank you. Maureen finally made me an honest woman. It took her long enough." Captain Charity laughed as she placed the stack of dishes next to the radio.

"It's not like you made it easy, Darling," Maureen grumbled, scowling until the captain blew her a kiss.

"You wouldn't want me any other way." Captain Charity sat back down at the table. "We still haven't decided if we're going to have a big party or elope, but…" Her brow creased as her gaze darted between Beast and Maureen. "We'll decide when things have settled down."

"I'm getting closer. Just give me a little more time." Maureen clasped her hand over her mouth when Belle and Beast both looked at her sharply.

"You're getting closer to a cure?" Belle's heart hammered wildly.

"I think so, but I don't want to get anyone's hopes up tonight. Let's get back to presents and forget what I said for now." Maureen's eyes were wide and panicked as she wrung her hands.

Beast nodded, his expression still stunned. "Agreed. Can you hand me the presents behind you, Maureen?"

Soon a pile of presents wrapped in recycled newspaper and

decorated with fresh flowers secured with ribbons crowded together on the table in front of Belle.

"I almost don't want to open them. They're gorgeous!"

"Oh, yes, you do. Start with mine." Captain Charity handed her a small package stacked on top of the larger presents.

Careful not to tear the envelope, Belle opened a set of fancy pens, a leather-bound journal, and a voucher to the bookstore for more money than she'd ever thought she'd have for books.

"This is—" Belle choked with emotion, unable to finish her sentence.

"You're welcome." Captain Charity grinned.

With shaking hands, Belle opened the next gift. Maureen gave her a phonograph with several cylinders' worth of music.

"Now you don't have to wait for the radio station to play your favorites," the mayor explained as she demonstrated how it worked.

"It's incredible. Thank you." Belle nodded to Beast, who was giving the phonograph a starry-eyed look. "I think Beast loves it, too."

To Belle's surprise, Damek gave her new fingerless gloves made of flexible leather, custom-tailored to her hands. She immediately put them on.

"Thank you, Damek." Her heart warmed at the automaton's gesture.

"You're welcome. I understand humans have vulnerable skin. I didn't want you to hurt your hands again like when you helped me." Damek's eyes glowed in the fading sunlight.

"I'll treasure these."

"There's one more." Beast shyly handed Belle a small rectangular velvet box.

"But you've already done so much!" Belle protested as she opened the box, then gasped at the detailed necklace inside. A dozen crystal red roses hung from the dark green chain that resembled stems and leaves. The central rose dangled lower than the rest and was framed in a delicate clockwork heart. "Thank you. Are you sure it's not too—"

Beast shook his head as he pressed his paw against her lips. "You're welcome."

Captain Charity faked a yawn and shot a meaningful glance at Maureen. "I think it's about time we head home, don't you?"

"Already?" Damek's internal gears whirred as he spoke. "But I was learning so much about human customs."

"There will be plenty of time for that in the future." Maureen stood, and Captain Charity followed suit. "I hope you had a wonderful birthday, Belle."

"It was the best I'd ever had," she replied honestly. "Thank you for an amazing night, everyone."

After they had exchanged goodbyes, Damek reluctantly followed Maureen and Captain Charity to the front of the house, while Belle and Beast lingered by the gazebo.

Beast scratched the back of his neck as he fidgeted. When he caught Belle looking at him, he smiled ruefully.

"Did you really enjoy yourself?"

Belle threw her arms around Beast. "Of course I did. You're a sweetheart." She planted a wine-soaked kiss on his muzzle.

Beast's eyes crinkled. "I'm glad. I've got one more surprise for you. Follow—"

Maureen called out, "Mr. Cadwell? What brings you here?"

Wordlessly, Belle and Beast made their way to the front of the house to see the secretary gripping his knees with his hands to catch his breath.

Mr. Cadwell straightened before speaking. "Chancellor Elmstone just arrived in Duchollow and wants to see you about something urgent."

Maureen's brows rose. "What does she want that she couldn't have radioed about?"

The secretary gritted his teeth. "It seems Delphine has been determined to smear your name since the Festival's completion. While the chancellor is wary of Delphine, she's made it clear she's looking into the accusations. Worse, she's brought guards who are supposed to transfer the Ringmaster to the capital for his trial."

Maureen rubbed her temples. "Okay, that's a lot. Can you send a message to the chancellor that I'll meet with her first thing tomorrow?"

"I would, but there's a problem." Mr. Cadwell gulped. "Her motorcar is already parked at Town Hall waiting for you."

Maureen's shoulders slumped. "I see. Can you inform her I'm on my way?"

Mr. Cadwell gave her a curt nod. "I'll leave right away."

After the secretary departed, Belle asked, "What was that about?"

Captain Charity ran her fingers through her hair. "If the chancellor's involved, it can't be good."

Maureen pinched the bridge of her nose. "No, it can't be." She gave Damek a pointed look before facing Captain Charity again. "Can you go the back way and take him home? Chancellor Elmstone doesn't need to be around him."

Damek shuddered, his mechanical limbs clanking against his torso. "Agreed."

"Will do." Captain Charity nodded, setting her jaw.

Beast looked between the three of them. "What does Damek have to do with the chancellor?"

"Absolutely nothing, if I can help it." At their confused looks, Maureen sighed. "I'll explain another time. We'd better get this over with. Sorry to leave on a sour note. I hope you have a wonderful night anyway."

After Maureen, Captain Charity, and Damek left, Beast wrapped his arms around Belle's waist. "Let's save your other surprise for a different night. I'd rather not have it spoiled by this."

Sniffling, Belle nodded. Just once, she wished they could have a celebration without a dark cloud hovering over them.

Far too early the next day, Belle woke to a familiar knock at their front door. Next to her, Beast groaned as he released his hold on her chest and cracked one eye open.

"I suppose we should have expected this?" Beast's voice was sleepy as he stretched.

Nodding glumly, Belle grabbed a robe and attempted to smooth her bed head before leaving their room to investigate.

Belle opened the door to a distraught Captain Charity and gave her a quizzical look. "What's going on?"

The captain fidgeted. "Chancellor Elmstone wants to speak to both of you. She's insisting."

They stared at the captain.

Beast spoke first. "Why?"

"I don't know. I told Maureen I could take the two of you into hiding, but she said that was a bad plan." Captain Charity shrugged as she smiled ruefully. "I'm sorry."

Belle exchanged a look with Beast, then shook her head. "Maureen's right. Let's get this over with and see what the chancellor wants." She glanced down at her robe. "After we get dressed."

CHAPTER TWENTY-EIGHT

As Captain Charity cut the truck's engine, she turned to Belle and Beast. "Are you ready for this?"

Belle nodded as she reached for the door handle. There was a time not so long ago that an unplanned visitor and summons to Town Hall would have sent her into a panic, but now she was merely annoyed at having her morning disrupted. "Yes, let's get this over with."

A pearlescent motorcar with pristine chrome details was parked out front. Teal velvet curtains obscured the unfamiliar vehicle's back windows as Belle tried to peek inside. All she could see was the disinterested driver reading a newspaper.

Beast climbed out of the truck behind Belle. "The chancellor doesn't seem to mind standing out, does she?"

"It would seem that way." As Belle finished speaking, the front door of the Town Hall burst open.

Mr. Cadwell poked his head outside, dabbing his forehead with an embroidered handkerchief as he gave them a stern look. "Finally! Everyone's waiting inside the lab."

"Why the lab?" Belle whispered to the captain, blinking as the secretary darted back inside.

Captain Charity tensed before opening the door. Without

turning around, she replied, "Maureen's office is too small. Plus, it'll be easier to prove a point to the chancellor in the lab."

Frowning, Belle linked arms with Beast as they followed the captain inside.

Two sofas and four stuffed armchairs had been moved into the lab's cramped seating area. Maureen scribbled notes from one sofa, while Chancellor Elmstone and a petite woman balancing a portable typewriter precariously across her lap occupied two of the armchairs.

Belle turned to ask Beast where he wanted to sit, but he was frozen, staring at something across the room. Not wanting to attract the chancellor's attention, she surreptitiously tilted her head to see what the problem was.

Her stomach dropped as her eyes locked with a russet-colored Hound pacing on the other side of the lab. The creature stopped and sat protectively in front of a second one with gray fur. Two handlers kept them docile by feeding them chopped beef and murmuring soothing words.

Belle recognized these as the two Hounds that Maureen had taken in after the Ringmaster's break-in. Though this pair acted like anxious dogs, it was difficult for Belle to shake her memories of the attacks on the *Figment* and her home.

Slowing her breathing to mask her unease, Belle nodded at Maureen.

"Good, everyone's here now." The mayor's tight smile did not quite reach her eyes. "This is Chancellor Elmstone and her secretary, Ms. Palmer. Chancellor, you met Belle and Beast at the Festival, though you probably won't recognize them without their masks."

Both the chancellor and her secretary turned around, audibly gasping when they craned their necks to stare at Beast.

Chancellor Elmstone coughed into her fist. "I beg your pardon. Maureen told us of your condition, Beast, but she did not do you justice." She inclined her head toward the creatures. "We're also still recovering from our introduction to the, ah, Hounds."

Beast cracked a wry smile. "Don't worry about it."

Ms. Palmer swayed in her spot, looking ready to faint.

Maureen cleared her throat. "Why don't you all take a seat?"

Captain Charity sat down next to Maureen while Belle and Beast took the sofa across from the chancellor and secretary. Belle felt a prickle of unease having the canines at her back, but firmly reminded herself that they weren't the same as they had been under the Ringmaster's control. It wouldn't help whatever Maureen was trying to prove if she let her nerves show.

Hoping to distract herself, Belle snuck a sidelong glance at Beast. His stiff posture was reminiscent of a cat with his hackles raised. She slipped her hand into his paw.

Both the chancellor and the assistant gaped at their intertwined fingers.

Maureen closed her notebook with a snap. "Chancellor Elmstone, you asked to speak to Belle and Beast?" There was an undercurrent of annoyance in her voice, barely disguised by her polite smile.

"Yes," Chancellor Elmstone replied, her fingers forming a steeple. "I've heard troubling accounts of your background, both in your radio broadcast and from Maureen." Her eyes flickered to the mayor and the captain. "However, I've also had conflicting reports from Delphine Wyerstone. Despite her odd actions at the Festival, she's a respected member of several influential circles. I'd like to hear your version of events."

Captain Charity looked ready to argue, but a nudge from Maureen quieted her. She crossed her arms and shook her head.

Belle and Beast exchanged weary glances. How many times were they going to relive their trauma?

Squeezing Beast's paw for reassurance, Belle gathered her courage. With more bravado than she felt, she asked, "Chancellor, did you say that you listened to our broadcast?"

Chancellor Elmstone blinked owlishly. "Why, yes, nearly everyone did. The radio rebroadcast it because it was so popular.

What a sensational tale! To think that one of Nuzaran's biggest attractions was conducting itself in such a way."

Resisting the urge to roll her eyes, Belle breathed deeply before speaking. "Respectfully, you already know our story. Reliving the events that led to our escape is harrowing. The broadcast was enough to warrant an investigation into the circus and led to the Ringmaster's arrest. Our testimony has been typed so that we don't have to face our tormentor again during his trial. What are you hoping to learn?"

Ms. Palmer halted her typing as she sputtered, "That's the chancellor you're speaking to!"

Belle flushed, hoping she had said nothing that would lead to further trouble, but she'd reached her limit.

"I agree." Beast's low voice was almost a growl as he leaned forward. "What do you hope to gain today?"

Chancellor Elmstone's thin eyebrows rose. "There's no question of the Ringmaster's guilt and Delphine Wyerstone's involvement with these Hounds. But frankly, you, Beast, are disturbing. She denies all wrongdoing and claims that Maureen is the one responsible."

Chaos erupted at the chancellor's pronouncement. Captain Charity, Beast, and Belle were all on their feet talking at once. The canines howled, distressed by the noise, while their handlers attempted to soothe them.

"Enough." Though Maureen didn't raise her voice, her commanding tone silenced everyone. She fixed the chancellor with a hard look. "Chancellor, Delphine's accusations are categorically false. She is the one who sold experimental creatures to the Ringmaster. You can ask him yourself. If you do some digging, you'll find she had huge shipments of the same orbs used in his restraints. Her patented technology was used for the Hounds' collars and Belle's anklet."

"You mean orbs from the same factory that mysteriously blew up with no one inside?" The chancellor gave Captain Charity a shrewd look.

To her credit, the captain didn't blink as she set her jaw. "The same."

"I see." Chancellor Elmstone sighed. "I'm sorry for bringing up old wounds. Before I bring charges against Delphine, I need to be sure."

Maureen pulled a face but recovered before the chancellor looked back at her.

"I assure you, Maureen is not my creator. Delphine is." Beast rolled up his shirt sleeve, revealing his silvery fur. "Would you like to see the scars where she stitched me together?"

Shaken, the chancellor shook her head as she shrank back in her seat. "No, that won't be necessary."

"Weeks ago, the Ringmaster, the *Curiosity* crew, and Delphine kidnapped both Captain Charity and Beast. They had a Hound that Delphine controlled with an orb. After we'd escaped the circus again, the Ringmaster showed up at our home with two more creatures. What further proof do you need?" Belle's voice rose as she glared at Chancellor Elmstone.

"Now, there's no need to raise your voice," the chancellor placated.

Belle clenched her free hand. "Isn't there? What is it you need from us?"

To Belle's surprise, the chancellor chuckled. "I believe you. I just needed to be sure. Now, can someone explain to me why these... Hounds are in the lab?" The way she said "Hounds" made it sound like she'd swallowed something distasteful.

"I'm going to cure them of the experiment that Delphine performed on them. I can't imagine the agony she put them through to make them bipedal." Maureen folded her hands in her lap. "But first, I wanted to show you Delphine's creations so that you understand exactly what kind of immoral experiments she's performed."

"That's very noble of you. Wouldn't it be less cruel to put them out of their misery?" The chancellor's gaze flickered to Beast.

Belle's stomach churned. Would the chancellor order Beast to be put down? Could she do that? "Isn't it better to give them a chance at recovery?"

Before the chancellor could reply, Maureen answered, "There's no need for them to be punished for Delphine's actions. I have a cure nearly ready for them. I'm going to prove they can be restored. By doing so, I hope to perfect a cure for Beast as well."

"I look forward to it. When are you performing the procedure?" Chancellor Elmstone looked skeptical, as did her secretary.

Maureen looked at Captain Charity before responding. After the captain gave her a curt nod, the mayor responded, "Tomorrow. I need today to prepare."

"Tomorrow?" Belle asked, dazed.

"Yes." Maureen stood and pointed to the lab's exit. "Now, Chancellor Elmstone, Ms. Palmer, if you'll excuse us, I have a lot of work to do. I'll call you back when it's done."

After the chancellor and secretary left, Belle sagged against Beast. Still in shock, she whispered, "Tomorrow?"

Belle fidgeted in the too small, stiff chair as she regretted not bringing a book or two with her to Town Hall, but she was grateful she'd had the foresight to wear her hair up. The oppressive humidity made the leather of her seat stick unpleasantly.

It could have been worse, though. Squeezed in the chair next to her, Beast frowned as he tugged on his white linen shirt. Belle couldn't imagine wearing a shirt over fur in the afternoon heat.

Two days had passed since Maureen's pronouncement about the Hounds' cure. Earlier this morning, Mr. Cadwell had radioed to let them know the procedure was nearly finished. Hours later, Belle and Beast were still waiting in the cramped lobby chairs. Chancellor Elmstone's presence made matters worse, along with Ms. Palmer's incessant typing on her portable typewriter.

"How much longer?" The chancellor tapped her fingers against the armrests as she shot Mr. Cadwell a mutinous glare. "We've already stayed in Duchollow far longer than I intended. I have business to attend to in Onyxmark. Not all of us have the luxury of conducting personal experiments on a whim."

Belle didn't care for the chancellor's tone, but part of her also wondered about the long wait. If it weren't for her friendship with

Maureen, she'd still be working in the library with Beast. Though some sections of the library weren't finished, it would be a matter of weeks before the building could be ready for the public. Soon, she'd be able to hire and train librarians.

From his desk, Mr. Cadwell peered over a stack of correspondence at the chancellor. "Soon. I was informed the poor creatures needed more time to come out of their anesthesia and have their vitals checked. I'm sure Mayor Dawkins will apologize for the unavoidable delay."

Beast huffed as he leaned back in his chair. Grimacing, he leaned in to whisper in Belle's ear, "I don't mind waiting, but these seats are awful."

Belle hummed in agreement. "Want to go stretch our legs?"

As soon as the words left Belle's mouth, the door to the mayor's office opened. Maureen emerged, looking exhausted but victorious. Her octagonal glasses were askew and dark circles shadowed her bloodshot eyes, but she gave them a radiant smile and a thumbs-up.

When Maureen spoke, her voice was so hoarse that her words were unintelligible. After clearing her throat, she tried again. "The Hounds are awake! Follow me, but please, don't make loud noises. They're going to be sore for a while, even with a strong dose of elixir."

"Finally! Let's see what the fuss is about," grumbled Chancellor Elmstone.

Ms. Palmer packed up the typewriter in a plain black case, snapping it shut with a click as she nodded. "I wonder if they're still bipedal?"

Belle didn't dare respond as she shakily stood. She hadn't allowed herself to imagine what the Hounds might look like post-treatment, lest she get her hopes up again for Beast's cure.

As Ms. Palmer and Chancellor Elmstone followed Maureen through the office door, Belle looked back at Beast. He hadn't budged, staring slack-jawed at where the mayor had stood.

"Ready?" Belle offered her hand to Beast.

Dazed, he blinked before focusing his gaze on her. "No, but I'll have to be. I can't believe she did it. I'm almost afraid to look. What if her cure only works for the Hounds?"

Belle offered her hand to Beast as he struggled to rise from his seat. "Then Maureen will keep trying until she gets it right."

"Fair enough." He cracked a grin before his smile faltered. "I'm nervous, but you've given me hope."

"That's more like it. Let's go before the chancellor has a fit."

"Might be worth it," Beast rumbled as Belle kissed the side of his muzzle.

Inside the lab, it smelled overly sterile, as if it had been scrubbed with all the cleaning elixirs Maureen had on hand. A partition made of extruded aluminum and heavy blue curtains blocked the view of the surgical station. Behind the curtain, the sound of paws tapping on metal mingled with low voices murmuring reassurances.

Maureen stood next to the partition, leaning against Captain Charity. Next to them, the chancellor and her secretary were attempting to peer past the curtain.

"There you two are!" The chancellor fixed her cool gaze on Belle and Beast. "We thought you were right behind us."

Belle narrowed her eyes. The sooner the chancellor left, the happier she'd be.

"Sorry, I needed a moment." Beast stretched to his full height, towering over everyone save Belle. "It's difficult getting out of those chairs."

Ms. Palmer's eyes widened as she gulped, craning her neck to look up at him.

Chancellor Elmstone pursed her lips, looking as if she were ready to complain again.

"It's fine." Maureen's stern gaze lingered on the chancellor. "I'll be happy to answer your questions, but please remember to keep your voices down, as you would with any shy animal. They've been through quite the ordeal."

"Yes, fine," Chancellor Elmstone snapped. "Can we get it on with? I still have to coordinate transport of the criminal and get back to the capital. I hate to think of the paperwork piling up at my office."

At the mention of transporting the Ringmaster, Belle's chest tightened. She'd sleep better knowing he was miles away.

Captain Charity gritted her teeth as she pulled back the curtain. Two large dogs with wolf-like features sat side by side on a metal table as their handlers fed them treats. Thick bandages were wrapped around both dogs. The dog on the left had tufts of russet fur sticking out between strips of freshly changed gauze, while the one on the right had wisps of gray fur on her exposed ears. Despite the dogs' haggard appearance, their eyes were bright and friendly as they wagged their tails.

A lump formed in Belle's throat as she looked from the cured Hounds to Beast. He couldn't take his eyes off the playful dogs.

"Incredible," breathed Chancellor Elmstone.

Maureen placed a finger to her lips before letting the dogs sniff her hand, which made them wag their tails more enthusiastically. When it seemed like the dogs were ready to jump off the table, the handlers coaxed them back to sitting with more treats.

"I think that's enough excitement for my furry patients. Let's give them some space." Maureen smiled as the gray dog gave her a nudge.

The chancellor meekly nodded as she, Ms. Palmer, Captain Charity, Belle, and Beast followed Maureen to the seating area across the lab.

Tears prickled in the corners of Belle's eyes as she took a seat on the sofa next to Beast. When she could trust her voice to not crack, she asked, "Were there any complications with the procedure?"

"It was a delicate process, especially when it became clear I'd have to do some surgery for parts that had been…manually added in during their creation." Maureen exhaled slowly as she rotated her wrists, grimacing. "We nearly lost them due to blood loss. If it weren't for a generous veterinarian, they wouldn't have made it."

Belle covered her mouth.

"They're going to be fine, as long as they leave their bandages alone." Maureen shook her head. "I'll need to get cones."

Beast leaned forward. "What do you mean by added parts?"

Captain Charity's shoulders slumped. "Maureen found extra bones. At first, we thought it was mutations from ether-radiation, but it became clear there was something more."

"Dog bones?" Belle removed her hand as she watched Maureen's expression darken.

"Human bones." Maureen shuddered while Captain Charity rubbed her back. "It was horrible."

"How did you cure the creatures?" Chancellor Elmstone rested her chin on her hand.

"Fortunately, my theory that unstable ether was a factor in the Hounds' transformation was correct. I synthesized an antidote via The Transmutation Engine. The rest was a careful balancing act of manual surgery and utilizing elixirs." Maureen steepled her hands. "I also found something else. These dogs are native to farmers outside of Glimmerdrift, far away from any ether-mines."

"What does that mean?" Ms. Palmer asked, the keys of her typewriter clacking as she rapidly typed.

"The Wyerstones used to have an estate near Glimmerdrift. I'm not sure if they still do." Maureen paused as she leaned forward. "I've told you everything I know now. Will you please look into Delphine Wyerstone's part in manufacturing these creatures? It is troubling enough that she's conducted unethical experiments on animals, but to add human remains into the mix, too..." Her eyes blazed with fury as she gave the chancellor a pointed look. "Something needs to be done."

"Well, you have not proven Delphine was involved." At the scowl on the captain's face, Chancellor Elmstone raised her hand. "However, I think I have enough for an inquiry."

Beast and Belle stared at the chancellor. Would Delphine finally face consequences?

"Thank you, Chancellor. I appreciate you taking this matter seriously." Maureen folded her hands in her lap. "If there's anything else you need for the investigation, please let me know. I'll be happy to help serve justice."

Chancellor Elmstone's thin lips curved into a smirk. "I'm sure you would be." As she rose, Ms. Palmer packed away her typewriter and hastily stood at attention. "I'll be heading back to Onyxmark now. Thank you for bringing this to my attention." Then she inclined her head toward Beast. "Is there hope for him? Can you make him a man again?"

Belle clenched her fists, hating how the chancellor talked about Beast as if he wasn't in the room.

Maureen answered, "Yes. I've only a few tests to do, and I should have a cure for Beast. That is if he wishes to undergo what will be a complex procedure."

Chancellor Elmstone looked properly chastised when she turned to Beast. "I'm sorry for what has happened to you." Her eyes flickered to Belle. "To both of you. I hope your cure goes smoothly, Beast. Take care."

"You, too," Belle replied, stunned.

"Thank you," Beast rumbled.

After the chancellor and her secretary left, Belle and Beast exchanged wide-eyed looks as they waited for Maureen to close the door.

When the mayor returned, she sighed. "I'm sorry the chancellor was, well, how she always is. It was the only way I knew how to get her to pay attention to what I've been telling her about Delphine for years. I think we got through to her."

"What about Beast's cure?" Belle thought she'd burst if she didn't have an answer soon.

"I'll have to run a few more tests, but if it works, I'll need to have a supply of blood on hand." Maureen grew pensive.

"I see." Belle slipped her hand into Beast's paw as he hung onto the mayor's every word.

"A universal blood type would be best." Maureen hesitated before adding, "Belle, you'd be a perfect candidate. You've already had an ether-poisoning cure, and that might be useful for the transfusion as Beast's undergoing treatment. Would you be willing to donate?"

"Yes, obviously. Anything to help." Belle squeezed Beast's paw.

He wrapped his arms around her. "You're too good to me."

Snuggling into Beast's arms, she replied, "You'd do the same for me."

Captain Charity nudged Maureen. "I told you it wouldn't be a problem."

"I'm glad. Beast, let's get started on those tests. We should have results by the end of the week." The mayor gestured to the back of the lab where vials were already waiting on the counter next to clean syringes.

Belle's stomach fluttered as she watched Beast walk with Maureen, deep in conversation. With the Ringmaster in custody, and now Delphine being investigated, maybe they'd have a shot at starting their lives together.

CHAPTER TWENTY-NINE

ays later, Belle absently swirled her lavender lemonade, watching as the ice cubes spun in a mini vortex, as she wished she would have dressed cooler today. Summer was in the air, from the bright blooms in the outdoor cafe's planters to chipper birds hopping between tables for scraps. The other patrons' light-hearted chatter grated on her nerves. Beast was late to their daily lunch date.

Though Maureen had said she'd know the results of Beast's blood tests by the end of the week, by now Belle knew not to grow impatient waiting—even as seven days turned into ten with no news. Both she and Beast filled their time with projects. They understood through unspoken agreement that if they were busy, they wouldn't have time to worry. So Beast tended to his garden while Belle oversaw the final stages of the library's renovations.

Despite their differing schedules, Belle and Beast met for lunch every day, both as an excuse to connect and as an opportunity to help him grow accustomed to the townspeople of Duchollow. It had been Beast's idea, which made it even more surprising that he was late.

Familiar anxiety coiled in Belle's stomach as she picked at her cooling lunch. With the Ringmaster transported to Onyxmark and no gossip about the inquiry into Delphine, there wasn't anything but their routine to focus on. Beast was usually the first to arrive, hoping to claim a table with extra legroom. Where was he?

"Belle! I'm sorry to keep you waiting." Beast sounded out of breath as he approached the table. "I have a good reason, though."

Belle looked up from her drink, ready to tease him for making her worry, when she noticed Maureen standing behind Beast, her eyes shining brightly despite the dark circles under them.

"Are the results in?" Belle dropped her fork as she looked between them.

"Yes." The mayor radiated joy as she beamed. "It's going to work. Let me grab a chair and we'll talk about it."

Belle stared after Maureen's retreating form as Beast took his place across the table.

"Maureen ran into me on my way and told me the results first. I didn't realize how late I was. I'm sorry." Beast scratched the back of his neck.

Abandoning her lunch altogether, Belle stood and wrapped her arms around him. "It doesn't matter. I'm so happy for you!"

"Me, too." His paws dug into her arms as he held her tighter. "Fair warning. The process is going to be more complicated than we thought."

Belle's smile dimmed. "What do you mean?"

"Have a seat, and I'll give you my best educated guess." Maureen returned, balancing a chair in one hand and two drinks in the other. She placed the glasses on the table and pushed one toward Beast before sitting down.

After everyone had a seat, Maureen leaned forward, clasping her hands together. "I'm sure you both have a lot of questions, even though I briefed Beast a bit. I'll try to answer everything but realize that much of this is still theoretical. However, I can say with confidence that Beast can be cured with one big caveat: it's probably going to take at least two procedures."

"That doesn't sound terrible. What's recovery going to look like?" Belle frowned at the uneasy look between Beast and the mayor.

Maureen sighed and took a deep gulp of her water. "That's one variable I'm uncertain about. The Hounds are well on their way to recovery. Another week, and they may be bandage-free. But Beast..." She gestured toward him. "His physiology is more complicated. Before I begin the procedure tomorrow, I'm going to take a radiograph of his skeletal structure."

Blinking as a thousand questions bubbled up in Belle's mind, she landed on the two most pressing. "What's a radiograph? And tomorrow?"

"I need to take a picture of Beast's bones with a special camera that utilizes ether-radiation. It sounds fancier than what it actually is." Maureen's lips quirked into a self-deprecating smile. "And yes, unless the radiograph reveals anything especially unusual, the procedure will take place tomorrow. Beast wanted to start as soon as possible."

"Is that okay?" Beast's brows furrowed. His tinted goggles obscured his eyes, but his concern was palpable. "I didn't mean to spring it on you like this. I might have been too enthusiastic when I said yes."

Belle's mouth went dry as she shook her head. After taking a sip, she answered, "No, it's your decision, and I agree with you. The sooner we can do this, the easier I'll breathe. However, I am worried about your safety." To Maureen, she asked, "Do you truly have everything you need?"

"Amazingly, yes." Maureen ticked off each item on slender, calloused fingers. "The elixir, pain medication, your blood donation, and the lab are all prepped, along with my guest quarters. If you'd like, Belle, you can stay with Darling and me while Beast is recovering. It's right above the lab."

Belle's eyes glistened with unshed tears as she rose to engulf the other woman in a tight hug. "Yes, please! Thank you so much!"

Maureen reached up and patted her back. "I'm glad I can help. I need to go clear my schedule and tell Darling that the procedure is on. Beast can fill you in on the rest."

Belle returned to her seat, wiping tears from her eyes as the other woman stood.

"Thank you, Maureen. We both appreciate everything." Beast's low voice was choked with emotion.

The mayor's gaze softened. "I know you do. Hopefully, I can undo the damage Delphine has done to you. Beast, if you could come to the lab after you're finished here, I'll take the radiograph. Belle, I'll see you tomorrow."

After Maureen left, Belle slipped her hand in Beast's. "Are you sure you're ready? This is happening so fast."

Beast touched his forehead to Belle's. "I've been ready to be a man again from the moment I first met you. Let's do this." After a beat, he leaned back. "But first, I have a surprise for you. Meet me in the garden tonight?"

Belle frowned. "Tonight? I thought I'd head home and start packing."

"Aren't you training the new librarians after the crew goes home? I thought you said that was today?"

All thoughts of the library had gone out of her head. "I can reschedule."

Beast shook his head. "You're already going to lose out on at least a few days while I'm recovering. Let me take care of the packing, please." He wrapped his paw around her hand. "Besides, I still haven't given you your second birthday surprise. It'll give me the time I need to get it ready. Please?"

Melting under his earnest expression, Belle relented. "Okay, you win. But as soon as training is done, I'm heading home to help."

"Deal."

After a tortuously slow afternoon of coordinating the renovations that would need to be completed during Beast's planned recovery period and training future librarians, it took all of Belle's willpower to not run out of the library's doors when she was done for the day.

By the time she reached their cottage, the sun was dipping low in the sky, turning it a hazy purple-pink. Swearing under her breath about the lateness of the hour as she fished for her keys, Belle was surprised when Beast opened their front door.

"I'm sorry it's so late." Belle's shoulders slumped. "I left as soon as I could."

Beast pulled her into a loose hug, rubbing her back. "I knew you'd be busy today. Everything's taken care of. Whenever you're ready, we'll go to the garden."

Belle leaned into his embrace, sighing happily as he worked the tension out of her stiff muscles. "Give me five minutes."

As the last rays of sunshine faded, Beast led Belle to the greenhouse behind their cottage. Belle gasped at the dramatic transformation. No wonder he'd been so busy.

There was a new addition built onto the west side of the greenhouse, along with a high latticework fence covered in vines. They walked under the wide arched trellis leading inside to an enclosed garden. Lanterns, their flickering flames warm and inviting, dotted the winding gravel path between rose bushes in full bloom.

The path ended at an ironwork bench, covered by a second arched trellis, overgrown with vines.

"This is beautiful, Beast!" Belle's eyes shone. "Thank you."

Beast beamed. "I'm glad you like it, but this isn't even the best part. Sit with me for a moment."

Intrigued, Belle sat down next to him, content to snuggle into his welcoming embrace.

"Watch this." His breath tickled her ear as he pointed to the vines on the trellis and the fence.

As the sky fell into twilight, small buds opened, unfurling into delicate silky-white blooms, their sweet scent wafting through the air. The whole process was over in minutes, but Belle was spellbound by their beauty.

"That was amazing. You did all this for me?" She turned to Beast, mouth agape.

"I wanted to create something you could enjoy year-round, no matter what time of day it is. These are moonflowers, and they only bloom at night." Beast smiled ruefully as he continued, "Inside the new addition, I made you a reading nook surrounded by roses. I thought about taking you in there first, but I didn't think I'd be able to tear you away from the new books."

Belle cupped the size of his face, tracing along his jawline. "There's nowhere I'd rather be than with you."

She pressed a kiss on the side of Beast's muzzle, and he took a shuddering breath as he closed his eyes.

"What's wrong?"

Beast opened his eyes and reverently tucked Belle's hair behind her ear. "You know what the hardest part is? When you look at me like that, I wish more than anything to be fully human again."

Abruptly, he rose from the bench, offering his paw to her.

Belle tilted her head as she accepted his paw and stood with him. "Really? Why's that?"

"So I can do this." Beast wrapped one arm around Belle's waist and pulled her flush against him while his other paw traced her curves. His teeth nipped at her neck, eliciting a moan from her. "And so I can keep going." His voice rumbled against the delicate skin of her collarbone. "You don't know what you do to me."

Heat pooled in Belle's stomach as she gasped. "I'm getting an idea." With shaking hands, she pulled Beast closer to whisper in his ear. "Let's get you cured so I can show you what you do to me."

"I'd love nothing more than that."

The feral look Beast gave her was enough to make her knees shake, but it didn't stop her from letting her fingers trace the muscles of his shoulders down to the small of his back.

Chuckling darkly, Beast shook his head as he pulled her back down to the bench. "Let's get through tomorrow first. Maybe I need to have Maureen make me a fortifying elixir if I'm to survive you."

At the mention of the procedure, Belle's mood cooled. Tomorrow was approaching faster than she was ready for. Fear mingled with hope as she thought of her own procedure to cure her ether-poisoning. How much worse was Beast's ordeal going to be?

Refusing to give into melancholy, she lifted her gaze to Beast's, raising her brows.

"So how many books are we talking about inside the greenhouse?"

"I knew you couldn't resist. There's a small bookcase full." Beast's golden eyes gleamed with mischief. "And there's a daybed built for two inside."

Belle grinned. "Lead the way."

In retrospect, falling asleep in a glass greenhouse with no curtains was not one of their better plans. Belle woke up with her hair damp from the humidity and mussed from curling against Beast's bare chest.

She opened her eyes, dazed by the unfamiliar surroundings, the sunlight streaming over the daybed painfully bright. Shielding her eyes and wincing, Belle tried to warn Beast as he stirred beneath her.

"Wait! Don't open your eyes—"

Beast yawned, rubbing the sleep away as he sleepily smirked, sitting up. "Why? Are you indecent? Because—" As he opened his golden eyes, the rest of his sentence turned into a mix of swearing and roaring as he groaned and clamped a paw over his eyes.

"It's too bright." Belle weakly patted his shoulder. "Are you going to be okay?"

"I need a few minutes." Beast rubbed his temples, growling a string of obscenities. "I hope Maureen can at least do something about my eyes. I'm so tired of this."

Belle scooted closer to Beast and played with the scruff of fur at the back of his neck. "Ready for today?"

Slowly cracking one eye open, a paw shielding his gaze, Beast nodded. "As ready as I'll ever be. Let's get this over with."

Hours later in the lab, Belle wished she had Beast's confidence as she watched Maureen set up a remodeled version of the complex device she'd used on him before. She summoned all of her courage to keep her hands steady as she held Beast's paw while Maureen adjusted the equipment.

Beast tilted his head and gave her a concerned look. "Are you going to be okay?"

Smiling weakly, Belle shook her head. "I should ask you that."

"I'm fine. Ready for this to be done." His eyes sparkled with mirth. "I hope you still think I'm handsome after the procedure. What if I'm better looking as a beast?"

Belle choked back a laugh. "I'll let you know as soon as you're awake."

Beast's expression sobered as he wrapped both of his paws around Belle's hand. He smiled as his gaze dropped to the rose necklace on her neck before meeting her eyes again. "I'm lucky to have you by my side. Whether this works or not, the only thing I want is to see you when I open my eyes again."

"I'll be here when you wake, right where I belong."

From across the room, Maureen coughed. "I'm sorry to interrupt, but it's time to begin. Are you ready?"

"Yes." Beast lifted Belle's hand to his muzzle before releasing her. He brushed her hair back, his eyes sweeping over her as if he was memorizing her features. "I'll see you soon."

"Soon," Belle repeated softly, kissing his muzzle.

The last thing she saw before turning to leave was Maureen fitting the metal wolf mask over Beast's head. When she powered on the machine, its eyes glowed red as the machines connected to it hissed.

It took all of Belle's strength to go up the stairs to Maureen's and Captain Charity's quarters above the lab.

Belle wasn't sure what she expected the quarters of a somewhat reformed airship pirate and mayor to look like, but it felt instantly homey as she ascended the stairs. The space smelled like vintage books mingled with the lingering scent of freshly baked bread. The sitting room had an inviting leather sofa and twin damask-patterned armchairs, with built-in bookcases lining the walls.

Nerves still frayed, Belle distracted herself by looking at the ornately framed photographs cluttering the mantel. The oldest of the group showed Maureen graduating from university, her diploma clutched tightly in her hand. Captain Charity was a constant in the later portraits. In one notable photograph, Maureen held the captain in a dramatically low dip, their faces covered by a spectacular feathered hat.

Belle smiled and hoped she could have a collection of photos of her and Beast someday.

She yelped when Damek's monotone voice called out as he entered the sitting room from a door she hadn't noticed.

"Hello, there! Captain Charity wants you to know she put your bags in the guest room and said to make yourself at home. If you need to know where anything is, please ask."

When Belle caught her breath, she smiled at the automaton. "Thank you, Damek."

"My pleasure."

Feeling self-conscious, Belle fidgeted as Damek continued to stare at her, his lit eyes unblinking. Cinders strolled into the room, purring happily as she wrapped her tail around Belle's leg.

"Hi, Cinders." She leaned down to give the cat scratches. "I suppose there's nothing left to do but wait, huh?"

Damek pointed to the books. "Maybe you could read to pass the time?"

"Good idea." The automaton's thoughtfulness warmed her fragile heart, and she happily perused the extensive collection before settling down on the couch with a stack of books. Cinders hopped on her lap, and Damek sat in an armchair, eager to listen to her read aloud.

Long after the sky turned dark, Belle had trouble focusing on the words on the page. She rubbed her eyes as she lost her place.

"Do you need to sleep?" Damek asked, his gears clicking as he looked up at her.

Belle shook her head. "What if something happens during Beast's procedure? Or if they finish early? I don't want to miss anything."

"I do not require sleep, only charging. I'll keep watch and let you know the moment anything changes with Beast." The automaton rested his mechanical hand over the place where his heart would be if he were flesh and blood.

Careful of the pinch points in the automaton's joints, Belle hugged him. "Thank you. I'll get some rest."

Damek's internal motors whirred, and a curious chipper noise emitted from his voice box. "I don't understand the human need for contact with their appendages, but you're welcome. Pleasant dreams."

With that, the automaton stood guard outside the guest bedroom, stoically watching the entrance into the quarters.

Emotionally spent, Belle stretched out on the guest bed, luxuriating in the softness of the hand-stitched quilt cocooning her. Cinders hopped up on her chest, purring contentedly before falling sound asleep. Belle soon followed, giving into exhaustion.

Hours later, Damek's tinny voice startled Cinders into digging her claws into Belle's exposed arm. She jolted awake and cursed as she rubbed her sore arm. The diminutive gray cat hopped off the bed, her tail high in the air as she flounced away.

Belle's muttering stopped when she heard what the automaton was shouting.

"Maureen says Beast will wake up any minute now. Come quickly!"

Belle threw the quilt off and quickly smoothed the wrinkles on the shirt she'd slept in. She eyed her bag at the end of the bed, but decided she'd rather keep her promise to Beast than worry about her clothes.

As she bolted out of the bedroom, slowing only to shove her boots on, Belle asked, "Any word about how he's doing? Did it work?"

The joints in Damek's neck creaked as he watched her hop on one foot while hastily lacing her boots. "She didn't say."

Belle tensed. "I'd better go then. Thank you!"

After racing down the narrow stairs, Belle arrived in the lab breathless. Maureen was waiting for her, barely suppressing a yawn as she waved.

"Is Beast okay? Did it work?" Belle thought her hammering heart would burst if she didn't get answers soon.

"It's too early to say how successful the first procedure was, but his vital signs are stable." Maureen hesitated, her eyes flickering over to the curtained off portion of the lab. "It was a complicated operation, and I'm still not sure if I'll be able to undo everything Delphine has done. But you should be able to ask Beast yourself. Just… Remember, he's been through a lot, okay?"

A lump formed in Belle's throat. Fighting back tears, she nodded and followed Maureen to the partition.

Captain Charity exited the curtained off area smiling softly as she met them. "He's stirring. Breathing is steady."

"Can I go in?" Belle wrung her wrists.

Maureen nodded. "Of course! I'll check his fluids while you sit with him."

"I'll make some coffee." Captain Charity rubbed the sleep out of her eyes.

"Thanks, Darling." Maureen beckoned Belle forward. "Let's go."

Belle was almost afraid to step over the threshold toward where Beast rested on a custom-sized hospital bed. Gathering her nerve, she nervously peeked over Maureen's shoulder as she followed the mayor inside.

Beast was surrounded by more machines than Belle had noticed when she'd departed. The sight of him hooked up to the IV and electrodes strapped between the thick bandages encasing his body made her tear up again. She hoped the pain was worth it.

Maureen immediately went to work, checking over the machines as they emitted incomprehensible beeps and the occasional puff of steam.

Wiping the tears from her eyes, Belle furrowed her brows as she studied Beast's slumbering form. His shoulders weren't as rounded. They were still broad, but considerably smaller than she remembered. The layers of bandages made it impossible to make out the familiar contours of his face. How much had changed?

She was sorely tempted to run her fingers along his jawline, but she didn't want to cause him further pain. His paws were wrapped up so tightly she couldn't hold them.

"Belle?" His familiar gruff voice startled her out of her observations.

"Beast! Your eyes…" She stared at his eyes, no longer owlish and goldenrod. Instead, they were honey brown, with decidedly human pupils.

"Don't tell me you don't like them." He coughed before closing his eyes, huffing as he drifted off.

"Beast?" Belle anxiously peered down at him, watching the steady rise and fall of his bandaged chest.

"He's going to need more time." Maureen put her hand on her shoulder. "Let him go back to sleep. I'm sorry. I thought he was ready too soon."

Belle nodded as she sat down on the low stool next to Beast's bed. "I'll wait as long as he needs."

Belle woke to the sound of strange humming and beeps, yelping when the light filtering through high, narrow windows hit her eyes.

After her eyes adjusted, she tried to get a better look at her surroundings. She didn't recognize the copper-tiled ceiling at first. It took her a moment to realize she was in Maureen's lab, although no longer on the stool next to Beast's hospital bed.

When Belle said she'd wait as long as Beast needed, she didn't expect to fall asleep sitting up. She could still taste the coffee on her breath from drinking countless cups last night, determined to be awake when he woke again. But after spending hours sitting vigil at his side while Maureen came in periodically to read the machines regulating the elixirs that kept him stable, she shouldn't have been surprised.

As she rubbed her stiff neck, Belle wondered if it had taken both Maureen and Captain Charity to move her to the cot across the room.

"Bad dream?" Beast's low voice was thick with sleep. Next to him, the intricate machinery whirred as it pumped swirling blue fluids into his IV. A small orange light flashed above one dial accompanied by a beeping sound.

Belle shook her head. "No, I just forgot where I was. Didn't mean to fall asleep. How are you feeling?" She squinted at Beast, though the layers of bandages covering most of his body made it impossible to determine his silhouette.

"Terrible, but better now that I know I can see you in daylight without needing tinted goggles. A few hours ago, Maureen turned on the lights to check my eyes. She and the captain had just put you to bed and didn't want to wake you." Beast pointed to his honey-brown eyes. "At least this part of me is fully human again. Don't know about the rest of me."

"That's wonderful news!" Her brows furrowed as she considered his words. "But why did you say terrible? Are you hurting? Maybe the pain reliever needs to be increased?"

"I feel…strange." Beast shrugged, rustling the white blanket loosely covering his lap and wincing as he sat up. "I never was fully comfortable in my transformed body. I always felt like my limbs were too large, but now everything feels weird. And I think I might have pulled the stitches on my face."

Belle threw off her blankets and padded across the room on her bare feet, briefly wondering where her boots were. Leaning over Beast, she noted a dark spot on his right cheek.

"It looks like you did. Should I go find Maureen?"

As if in answer, a machine beeped again.

"Why does that keep making noises? Is it supposed to do that?" Belle's frown deepened.

Beast shook his head. "No, it's fine. Maureen should be back any minute. The beeps mean it's nearly time to switch out the elixir."

Smiling wryly, Belle sat down on the stool next to his bed. "How long was I out? It seems like you have her whole routine memorized."

"Only a few hours. She's changed out the elixir once." Beast feebly moved his wrapped paw to pat her hand softly.

Belle supposed the appendage could be a hand now, not a paw. Which also made her think of something else that'd been on her mind lately. She tucked her chin into hand, lost in thought.

"What's wrong?" Beast nudged her hand, prodding her to look back down at him.

"Well, assuming this procedure works, I can't keep calling you Beast." Belle crossed her legs on the stool as she struggled to find a comfortable position. Her muscles still ached from her poor posture last night.

Something feral sparked in Beast's eyes. Though the bandages obscured his mouth, she could tell he was grinning underneath his dressing. "Why not? I can think of other reasons you could call me Beast…"

The lights in the lab brightened and shortly after, Maureen entered the curtained off room, clutching her journal as she doubled over in laughter. "Next time, I'll announce my presence."

"Hi, Maureen." Belle blushed deep crimson as she scratched the back of her neck. Despite her embarrassment, she wasn't done with Beast yet. Turning her attention back to him, she asked, "But really, what do you want to be called?"

Beast huffed. "Honestly? I haven't given it much thought. Until I see what I look like underneath all of this, it doesn't matter to me." His gaze dropped. "Part of me was hoping my memories would come back, but perhaps it's best they haven't. I'm not sure I want to remember the transformation process."

Maureen pursed her lips as she nodded. "Unfortunately, the elixir is only able to revert your body back to the way it was, not uncover your memories. But you're right; that might be a blessing. Even with the elixirs, I've had to do a few surgeries to course-correct where it looks like there were…" She paused as she considered her words. "…Manual interventions in your transformation."

"Sounds like a polite way of saying vivisection." Belle clamped her hand over her mouth, shooting Beast an apologetic look. "Sorry."

"It's okay. At least now I'm on the way back to normal, right?" Beast inclined his head toward the mayor.

Sighing, Maureen jotted another note in her journal before meeting his hopeful gaze. "I'm not sure yet. You've certainly made progress in a short amount of time, but until I've taken more radiographs and I can look underneath the bandages, it's difficult to say what normal will look like for you."

"Human again? I'd even settle for mostly human." Though Beast's tone was light, the hint of unease in his voice made Belle's heart ache.

"I think we'll get you there." Maureen moved to Belle's side. "Can I take your seat for a few minutes? Looks like I need to change some of the dressings."

"Of course!" Eager to see what lay beneath Beast's bandages, Belle had to restrain herself from hopping off the stool while the other woman retrieved a tin of medical supplies. She watched over Maureen's shoulder as she cut away all the bandages between his right eye and his mouth.

Unfortunately, when Maureen peeled back the layers, all that was revealed was dried blood and stitches. "I'll need to clean this up. Hang on."

As Maureen rummaged through the tin of supplies, Beast caught Belle's stare. "Am I hideous?" he asked playfully.

"I doubt it, but you probably should hold off talking until I clean this up." Maureen clicked her tongue. "If you're curious to see the progress, there should be a hand mirror in the washroom cabinet. Maybe Belle can get it for you?"

Belle nodded. "Do you want to see?"

Beast shut his eyes as Maureen dabbed his stitches with flannel. When she withdrew the cloth, he said, "I am curious, so if it's not too much trouble—" He hissed as she moved to another section of stitches.

"On it." Belle hated to leave him in pain, but she hoped the mirror would boost his morale after his ordeal.

By the time she'd returned with the ornate mirror, Maureen was done cleaning and checking over Beast's stitches.

"Ready to look?" Belle beamed, holding up the mirror.

Beast's gaze grew pensive as he looked at the chrysanthemum-embossed mirror. "Yes."

Maureen moved back, allowing Belle to squeeze next to Beast. As he studied his reflection in the mirror, her breath caught. Dark stitches crisscrossed faded scars on his much smoother cheek, his face no longer covered by thick fur. Rather, he had a fine dusting of silver-white scruff peppered with black covering pale skin, as if he were a man who had skipped shaving for a few days.

Her gaze landed on his mouth. It took her a moment to realize the obvious: his muzzle was gone. He had full lips that were curled into a teasing smirk, revealing his elongated canines.

"Like what you see?" Beast asked, wincing as his stitches pulled.

"I could ask you the same thing." Belle's stomach fluttered. Despite his teeth, he looked human. She wondered if the rest of him was as radically transformed. She was enamored with the glimpse of humanity she could see, including his scruff and scars.

"I don't remember what I looked like, but I'll take this over being a bear-creature." Beast flinched as Maureen applied pressure to his stitches with the flannel.

"Careful, it's started bleeding again. When it stops, I'll reapply the gauze." Maureen's expression softened as she added, "I am happy for you. It looks like the elixir is taking effect."

"What's next?" Belle asked.

"After I get him dressed, I need to take another radiograph to compare to his skeletal structure before the procedure." Maureen eyed the nearly empty bag of elixir. "Speaking of which, do you think you could wheel Beast to the machine?"

"I'm happy to help."

"That's my girl," Beast muttered, earning another blush from Belle.

Maureen made a choking sound that dissolved into laughter as she looked back at Belle. "You might want your boots back on before we go. They're under your cot."

Belle glanced down at her bare feet. "Right. Thank you."

As she retrieved her boots, Belle couldn't help but think she was going to be in the best kind of trouble when Beast was fully healed. She couldn't wait.

CHAPTER THIRTY

"Stop pacing. You're making me want to pace, too, and I can't." Beast's teasing tone cut through the silence that had stretched since Maureen departed. The fresh vial of elixir hooked up to his IV seemed to have energized him. He sat propped up in his bed, watching Belle stride back and forth in his room.

As the hours ticked by, the lab's walls felt like they were closing in. The constant low humming from the machines in Beast's curtained off room wasn't helping, either.

"Sorry." Belle rubbed the back of her neck. "All this waiting is making me anxious. I'd like to know how close you are to recovery. I feel selfish being so impatient, but I just don't want you hurting anymore."

Beast inclined his heavily bandaged head toward the stool next to his bed. "I appreciate that. Why don't you come sit with me instead?"

Belle hesitated, worried she wouldn't be able to stop fidgeting and that she'd annoy him by tapping her boots against the metal stool. Deciding that being near Beast was still a better alternative than pacing around the cramped room, she nodded.

"I wish I could hold your hand," Belle admitted as she sat down. "I hate feeling helpless."

Beast nodded. "Maureen reminded me again, no touching with the bandages so fresh." He gave her a feral grin. "I have no idea what has her so concerned that I won't be good."

"No idea, really?" Belle laughed.

"And I have even more reasons to celebrate. The radiograph painted a positive picture," Maureen's cheerful voice called out as she entered the curtained room. She beamed as she approached them. "It looks like a few more days of the elixir and you should be restored. No more surgeries should be necessary."

"How long will the healing take?" Belle gestured to Beast's bandages.

Maureen pursed her lips. "I don't know. The elixir could speed up the healing process, especially since we're talking about at least two to three more days of treatment, but we're heading into uncharted territory here."

"When can I get out of bed?" Beast asked.

"Not until the infusion of elixirs is done. Your muscles and bones are still shifting." Maureen peered over her octagonal glasses at him as she lifted her pointer finger. "You're in a delicate state right now. Absolutely no unnecessary movements."

"Yes, ma'am." Beast groaned as he readjusted his reclining position. "I can barely sit up in bed. You won't find me walking around."

Belle carefully patted his arm, mindful of his wrappings.

Maureen's expression softened. "When the procedure is done, you might need to reteach your body how to move, but who knows? After a period of adjustment, you might surprise us and get around with ease."

"I hope so." Beast turned to face Belle, his gaze warm. "It'll give me something to look forward to."

"In the meantime, Belle, do you want to sleep in a real bed tonight?" Maureen asked, eyeing the low cot. "You're welcome to use my guest room again. I can't imagine you're getting the best rest in here."

"I'd rather keep an eye on Beast. I appreciate your offer, though." The other woman's thoughtfulness touched Belle.

"Are you sure? I'm not really doing anything that interesting."

Beast shrugged, hissing when the slight movement proved to be too much effort. "I really don't mind if you take Maureen up on her offer. I don't want you to lose sleep over me."

Belle shook her head. "I'm fine, really."

Maureen shook her head. "Darling is out picking up dinner. We'll bring it to you later. Just don't forget to take care of yourself, too, Belle. Beast is going to need you more over the next few days, maybe weeks, while he's vulnerable."

"You hear that? I need you." Beast nudged Belle's knee with his arm.

Blushing lightly, Belle nodded. "I will."

As Maureen turned to leave, she gave Beast a mock stern glare. "Now, be good so the elixir can do its work. I'll be back soon."

Long after the sun went down, Belle stretched out on the cot. She was comfortably full, though she felt a little bad about eating around Beast while he couldn't have solid food. He ribbed her about it until she snort-laughed.

"Are you sure you want to stay with me?" Beast asked, shifting in his bed. The light from his machine shone blue, casting him in a peculiar light.

"Of course I do." Belle pulled her crisp blankets tighter. More quietly, she added, "It feels strange sleeping without you next to me. I don't like it."

"Me neither."

The silence stretched between them until Beast chuckled.

"What's so funny?" Belle propped up on her elbows, squinting to see him in the dim light.

"At least when I'm able to sleep next to you again, your hair won't get so wild from laying on my fur."

Thankful for the cover of darkness, Belle muttered, "I'm not sure the state of my bed head will improve much when you're fully healed."

Beast guffawed. "You've got a point. Love you."

"I love you, too. Sweet dreams."

"I'm sure they will be."

Beast's teasing setting her mind at ease, Belle drifted off with a contented smile.

Shrill beeping from the elixir machine and frenetic scuffling startled Belle out of a deep sleep. The lab was pitch black, but the light on Beast's machine was crimson red, bathing the room in an eerie red glow.

"Shit! She's waking up. We should have tied her up first," a vaguely familiar voice hissed.

Adrenaline rushed through Belle as she threw her blanket off, stepping onto the cold floor in her bare feet. Though she couldn't place the intruder's voice, she could make out the silhouettes of four people surrounding Beast as he groaned.

Grabbing the closest intruder, Belle threw them across the lab, crashing them into her cot. When another rushed at her, she effortlessly picked them up and tossed them onto their moaning, fallen conspirator.

"Get away from him," she seethed, balling her fists.

The remaining two intruders shrunk back.

"I'll handle this." A confident masculine voice spoke behind Belle.

Was there a fifth intruder?

Whirling around to deal with the new threat, a stabbing sensation in her arm halted Belle. She looked down to see a syringe emptying its contents into her bloodstream as her vision grew woozy. She staggered toward her assailant, but it was too late. Her legs buckled beneath her, and she fell to the ground with a thud.

The last thing Belle saw before the world went black was Captain Lucke's leering face as he leaned over her. "That's for the *Curiosity*."

Belle woke with a throbbing headache, dimly aware she was in the lab lying on her cot. All the muscles in her body ached and there was a dull pain in her left hand where someone had inserted an IV.

The memories of the attack came rushing back to her as she bolted up, the IV tugging painfully as she looked toward Beast's bed.

A strangled yell ripped from Belle's throat.

His bed was gone. Only the machine remained, without the vial of elixir. There were dark, ominous fluid stains on the floor. It was eerily silent, with its light off.

Captain Charity and Maureen rushed to her side. Both had dark circles under their eyes.

"Belle?" The captain knelt by the cot, pressing her cool hand to Belle's forehead. "I'm relieved you're awake. Whatever the intruders knocked you out with, it was powerful." She gulped. "Maureen wasn't sure if you'd wake up."

"I'll be fine. Where's Beast?" Belle searched their faces as the couple exchanged uneasy looks.

Maureen spoke first. "We tried to come down as soon as we heard the fighting, but the intruders barricaded our door. By the time we broke it down, they were gone, along with Beast, and you were passed out with a syringe buried in your arm."

With shaking fingers, Belle reached for her IV.

"What are you doing?" Captain Charity closed her calloused hand around Belle's. "It's not safe to take that out yet."

Shaking with fury, Belle shook her head. "I don't care. Beast is gone. I couldn't protect him. He could be miles away. Before they knocked me out, I saw Captain Lucke and at least four others, probably his crew."

"How?" Captain Charity looked back at Maureen. "I have heard nothing about the *Curiosity* in ages, have you?"

Maureen's mouth set in a grim line. "No, but I intend to find out." She knelt beside Captain Charity. "Belle, I know you're worried and angry, and you have every right to be. But we will find

Beast. We're already working on a plan. So, please, keep the IV in and listen."

Belle lifted her chin. "I make no promises, but tell me your plan. No one is going to stop me from going after Beast."

"We found something." Captain Charity's voice was barely audible as she gestured to Maureen.

The uncomfortable cot beneath Belle squeaked as she leaned forward, staring at the strange object in the mayor's hands. "You found that in the lab?"

Maureen held up the broken machine in both hands. Its remains, a smashed speaker, knobs, and ruined electronic parts, resembled a cross between a radio and the communication system aboard the *Figment*. "It appears to be a broadcasting device. From what I could discern, it transmitted any noises it picked up live, like a radio broadcast."

Belle's face grew hot as she thought of the late-night conversations she'd had with Beast in the lab, and long before that, the time they'd hid in the supply closet. "And it's been on this whole time? Since when?"

"We don't think the device has been here for longer than a few weeks. Maureen found it in the cabinets in this curtained off section of the lab." Captain Charity suppressed a yawn and stretched. "After she found it, we combed the entire lab while you were unconscious. This appears to be the only one."

"Most likely, the device was planted around the time of the Hounds' cure." Maureen's brows furrowed. "Unfortunately, the most likely culprits make the situation much more complicated. Whoever they were, they made embarrassingly short work of my security systems. I'll need to rework all of my processes."

"The chancellor and her secretary?" Belle rested her chin on her right hand. Her eyes widened. "But the Ringmaster went on the same airship back to Onyxmark as them and the chancellor promised to look into Delphine."

Grimacing, Maureen nodded. "Like I said, it makes things more complicated. What's worse is we don't know if they acted together or separately. Between the two, Ms. Palmer would have had more opportunity, as I was in several meetings with Chancellor Elmstone during their time in Duchollow. But why would the secretary plant the device?"

"Does anyone else have access to the lab?" Belle rolled her shoulders as her tension intensified. She couldn't help letting her gaze wander to the bare space where Beast's bed should have been with him in it.

Maureen shook her head. "Only us, you, Beast, and Mr. Cadwell. I rarely have people here. Even when I have parts brought in that can't fit through the door, the delivery drivers bring them to the back entrance that's locked the rest of the time."

"Mr. Cadwell wouldn't have a motive to do this, would he?" Belle hated to think the polite gentleman would have a sinister side to him. Despite their rocky introduction, she had grown fond of him.

"No," Captain Charity and Maureen said in unison.

"Mr. Cadwell's been a dear friend for years. It's also his fault that I'm still mayor, despite trying to step down every election." Maureen sighed. "I've told him countless times I'd rather spend my time in the lab, but Mr. Cadwell reminds me I have a gift for helping others. When a project has consumed my time, or an emergency like this comes up, he's the first one to cover for me."

"Remember how scared he was when he first met you and Beast?" Captain Charity asked, a slight smile gracing her worn face. "Mr. Cadwell is lovely, but he's not the bravest. I don't think he'd last as a double agent for Delphine or anyone else."

"Fair enough. So what's the plan?" All of this talking made Belle want to rip out the IV attached to her hand and go after the *Curiosity* crew herself.

"I'm going to talk to Mr. Cadwell to see if he remembers anything from Chancellor Elmstone and Ms. Palmer's visit. His memory is impeccable. If either did anything odd, he'd be the first to know." Maureen wrung her wrist. "Then the next parts get murkier. I plan on sending a message to the chancellor to see what she knows. I'll have to choose my words carefully."

"Meanwhile, I'll be getting into touch with some old friends to see if anyone knows about Captain Lucke and the *Curiosity* crew.

Someone is bound to have seen something." Captain Charity narrowed her eyes. "We'll find Beast."

"I hope so. He's still so unstable from the procedure." Belle's lip trembled. "What can I do to help? The longer we sit here, the more useless I feel."

Maureen laid her hand on Belle's shoulder. With her other hand, she brushed back Belle's hair as a mother would. "I can't even imagine the pain and worry you're going through, but right now, the most important thing you can do is let the IV finish the job. Please let yourself heal. You're going to need your strength."

"But what if it's too late for Beast? He doesn't have the elixir with him. What if—" Belle clamped her hand over her mouth, unable to voice her fear.

Maureen squeezed her shoulder gently. "Beast is vulnerable right now. That's true. I don't think he's in immediate danger from not having the elixir, but he needs it in order to finish the process. I'm confident Captain Lucke is delivering him to Delphine, and while I'm the last one to say anything positive about that woman, I doubt she's going to let Beast die."

Captain Charity's mouth set in a grim line. "She's more likely to change Beast back."

Horrified, Belle fought the urge to scream. "That's not much better."

"I know." Maureen stood, looking weary. "We don't know what sort of state we'll find Beast in, so it's important to rest now."

"Try to get some sleep," added Captain Charity. "The moment we learn anything at all, we'll tell you."

"I'll try, but this feels wrong." Unease settled in the pit of Belle's stomach as she carefully lay down, flinching as her IV tugged.

"I'm sorry. Hopefully, when we wake you, there will be better news." Maureen smoothed the covers over Belle before leaving with Captain Charity.

Belle thought she'd be staring at the ceiling for hours, but exhaustion won, and sleep overtook her.

It felt like mere moments had passed before Belle drowsily woke to someone calling her name.

With enormous effort, Belle cracked her eyes open to squint at the source of the noise. Her eyes widened when she resisted the anxious expression on Maureen's face as she called Belle's name again, leaning over the cot.

Belle threw the covers off and sat up to face the mayor. "Did you find Beast?"

"Not yet, but I just spoke to Mr. Cadwell. He said that during one of my meetings with the chancellor, Ms. Palmer had excused herself, claiming that she had a personal errand to run, and left the lobby after telling Chancellor Elmstone she'd head back to her hotel room. Though she couldn't have gone through my office, it wouldn't have been impossible for her to break into the lab's back entrance."

"Are there signs of forced entry?" Belle asked, her heart racing.

"None that I could see. But listen, there's something more pressing: I radioed Chancellor Elmstone. She was frantic. Ms. Palmer is missing." Maureen drew a deep breath before holding Belle's hands. "And the Ringmaster has escaped from prison."

Belle's mouth fell open. "He's what?"

"I know. Something horrible is happening. I'm certain Delphine's at the center of it all." Maureen clenched her free hand. "We'll put a stop to it, no matter what."

"Anyone ready for a bit of piracy?" Captain Charity entered the curtained-off room with a triumphant gleam in her eye. "I have a lead on the *Curiosity*."

Heart racing, Belle thrust the hand with the IV toward Maureen. "Get this thing out of me and let's go."

CHAPTER THIRTY-ONE

Much to Belle's dismay, they did not immediately board the *Figment* and chase down the *Curiosity* after Captain Charity announced she had a lead. But Maureen made a convincing argument about checking for further sabotage before immediately chasing after Beast's kidnappers. Though the mayor's reasoning was flawless, it felt like with each minute Beast slipped farther away.

Maureen and Captain Charity's animated discussion about the *Figment* brought her out of her worried thoughts.

The mayor pursed her lips. "If it truly is a trap, it wouldn't do for all three of us to get caught in it. You should stay behind, especially in your condition."

Visions of the airship detonating upon boarding came to Belle's mind unbidden. Clamping her hand over her mouth, her eyes widened.

Captain Charity cut her eyes at Maureen. "No one knows the *Figment* better than I do. You should stay behind, too. If she blows up in my face, that's expected. I'm the captain. You don't need to risk yourself."

Maureen crossed the room and took both of Charity's hands in hers. "Darling, we're already in danger. I'll go with you. I know what to look for, and I have tools to help." Her eyes softened as she leaned in to kiss the captain's forehead. "Anyway, I wouldn't want to live without you. Now, stop arguing."

Captain Charity gave her a dazed smile. "Yes, dear."

Belle looked away, wishing she could give them some privacy. Her heart warmed at their tenderness, but she felt a twinge of guilt as she thought of Beast in captivity, unable to move thanks to his incomplete procedure and thick bandages. She should help with his rescue mission, not sit idly by on her cot.

"Is there something around the lab I could do to help? Or anywhere else?" Belle did her best not to sound desperate, but it was hard to keep it out of her voice.

"Actually, yes." Maureen grimaced. "We need to check your home for sabotage, too." The mayor sighed as she ran her fingers through her hair. "This is becoming a much bigger task than I thought it'd be. Maybe we need to let the townspeople know what's going on and get some volunteers to do a sweep around town."

Belle tensed at the mention of her and Beast's cottage. "I'll go straight home to look."

"But what if you going home is a trap, too?" Maureen wrung her hands.

"If you think Delphine's behind this, don't you think she'd guess you'd leave me behind? What if that's the trap?" Belle crossed her arms.

Maureen looked ready to argue, but Captain Charity put a finger to the mayor's lips. "That sounds like a reasonable plan. Why don't you take Damek with you for an extra pair of eyes?"

"Wouldn't that be playing into Delphine's hands? She might make a move for him too after all these years." Maureen pinched the bridge of her nose. "Too many variables and not enough data."

"Delphine could just as easily be waiting for the lab to be unguarded to take Damek, too. I don't want to spend all day trying to out-think her. Not when Beast needs me." Belle stretched her hand and rubbed the tender skin where the needle had been.

Throwing up her hands, Maureen conceded, "That's fair. Wasting time second-guessing ourselves is exactly what Delphine wants us to do."

"Want us to give you and Damek a ride home before we head to the dock?" asked Captain Charity.

"Yes, please. Thank you." Belle shakily stood up from her cot, threw her arms around both Maureen and the captain, and enveloped them in a tight hug. "I appreciate everything you both have done for me and Beast. I'll keep Damek safe, I promise."

Maureen spoke first. "I'm sorry we couldn't protect Beast better, but I promise you we're going to do everything we can to get him back and finish the cure."

"We won't let that bitch win," Captain Charity added, earning watery chuckles from Maureen and Belle, who were both teary-eyed.

"No, we're not." Belle felt a bubble of hope and held on to it. She wouldn't give up now.

After gathering Damek, changing into studier clothes, and hauling her trunk from the guest room, Belle waited in Town Hall lobby for Maureen and Captain Charity with the automaton.

Damek hadn't stopped whirring since Belle told him everything that had happened since they last saw each other.

"Maureen and Captain Charity didn't tell me anything!" The automaton complained. "I asked about Beast, and all anyone told me was that the procedure was going well."

"I'm sorry, Damek."

The automaton shrugged, making his shoulder joints creak. "At least I'll be of use to you. My sensors will detect any strange devices via their frequencies." His shoulders drooped. "Except for the listening device, apparently. I feel like my sensors have failed me."

Belle hugged him. "You didn't fail us. I appreciate your offer to help."

Damek lowered his arms and returned the gesture with a mechanical impression of a hug. "You're welcome. I'm honored to help, though I wish the circumstances were different. I miss Beast."

Blinking back tears, Belle looked away, pretending to look for the others. "I do, too. I don't know what I'll do if he—"

"We'll find him." Damek's calculated certainty warmed Belle's heart.

"Ready to go?" Maureen and Captain Charity entered the lobby. They'd both changed into thick denim mechanic's uniforms that covered their arms and legs despite the hot summer day.

"Yes, thank you." Belle furrowed her brows as her gaze landed on the goggles atop Maureen's head.

Maureen pointed to her new goggles. "These have sensors in them, similar to Damek's. They'll pick up any frequencies from devices that shouldn't be on the airship. I haven't had many opportunities to test them, but they should work."

"If you'd teach me how to use them, you wouldn't have to endanger yourself," grumbled Captain Charity.

"We're done talking about it. Come on, Belle's ready to go." Maureen tugged on the captain's arm.

Outside, they all piled into Maureen's truck. As the mayor turned the key, Belle tensed for a moment, wondering if someone had sabotaged it as well, but the engine purred loudly as usual.

"Let's go!" Captain Charity cheered.

As Maureen backed up the truck, there was a great popping noise as the tires crunched over something. A sad hiss emitted from all four tires as they went flat.

"Those bastards!" Maureen hit her steering wheel when the chaos was over.

Belle nodded, feeling rattled. It could have been so much worse than flat tires.

"Let's see if Mr. Cadwell can drive Belle and Damek home. We can walk," Captain Charity suggested, brushing her copper curls out of her face.

Maureen nodded glumly. "We need to be prepared for anything."

After an awkward, quiet ride with Damek and Mr. Cadwell, Belle was relieved when they arrived at the cottage.

As she unpacked her trunk and helped Damek out of the posh black vehicle, Mr. Cadwell leaned out of the driver's side window.

"I am truly sorry about Beast. Though he and I were never close, I can tell he's got a good heart. I hope you are safe, and that you find him in time."

"Thank you, Mr. Cadwell." Belle's lips trembled as she smiled.

With that, Mr. Cadwell drove off, leaving Damek, Belle, and her trunk behind.

Belle gulped as she approached the front door. It felt surreal entering the cottage without Beast waiting inside.

Before she could insert the key, Damek stepped in front of her with heavy steps. "Allow me to go first. I can sense anything that emits signals, remember? It'll be safer."

A lump formed in Belle's throat. Not trusting her voice, she nodded as she stepped out of the way. The automaton finished unlocking the door and entered the foyer. She left her trunk on the porch as she followed the automaton inside the darkened house.

"Do you want me to turn on the lights?" she asked as Damek made his way through the kitchen. Though she didn't blame him at all for missing the listening device in the lab, she was less certain about letting him go first now.

"My sensors function in all light conditions, but if it helps you, that would be fine. Let me inspect the switch to check for interference." Damek stared unblinking as his eyes turned blue. "It is fine. You may proceed."

Warm light filled the room as Belle turned the lights on, but it didn't make her feel any more at ease. Their home looked much the same since they had left only days ago to begin the process for Beast's cure, but it felt as if they'd been gone for weeks. Without Beast's presence, it felt foreign.

"I've found something." Damek stopped in front of her and Beast's bedroom. His eyes glowed a warning orange.

Icy dread went up Belle's back as the automaton opened the door. Lying on the bed was a strange, small machine. It resembled what the listening device in the lab might have looked like before it was destroyed.

"Wait, Belle—" Damek's eyes flashed red as she scooped up the device.

"Delphine, Ringmaster, Chancellor, or whoever you are, let Beast go while you can. I'm coming for him and there's nothing you can do to stop me."

The device crackled. "I'd like to see you try," Delphine's disembodied voice echoed in the bedroom.

Belle dropped the radio on her bed, stunned. So much for it only being a listening device.

"Belle, run!" Damek threw his clunky automaton body over the device as it emitted ominous beeps.

She dove into the hallway as the device exploded. "Damek!"

Hazy smoke billowed from the open door. Eyes watering, Belle coughed as she stumbled back into her bedroom.

"Damek!" The automaton's name ripped through her throat as she searched for him in the burning bedroom, flames devouring the bed.

Her boot connected with solid metal. Damek's left arm and leg had been blown off. Bits of his missing limbs were strewn across the room, looking like little more than scrap.

"Damek?"

No response. His eyes were dark.

Blinking back tears, Belle scooped Damek into her arms and carried him out of the room, cradling his head against her shoulder. As she left, she grabbed the radio in the sitting room, hoping someone would answer her call for help before the fire spread.

Belle held Damek's limp body on her lap as she sat on the grass several feet away from the burning cottage. The radio sat next to her, playing soft music as she waited for the fire brigade. Fortunately, Mr. Cadwell had answered Maureen's Town Hall radio, promising to send help immediately.

Dried tears and sweat streaked her face, but she couldn't bring herself to care enough to wipe away the grime. She had promised to protect the one-of-a-kind automaton, and instead, he sacrificed himself for her. Maureen and Captain Charity would be devastated.

Rage mingled with grief as Belle looked back at the house. The fire was spreading. Plumes of black smoke billowed from the back of the cottage. The cottage groaned as a section of the roof was consumed by the hungry inferno.

How long until the whole house was reduced to ash?

A clanging of a bell sounded in the distance. Down the road, steam emitted from a fire truck's engine as it barreled toward the cottage. Behind the speeding red truck, Mr. Cadwell's sleek black vehicle kicked up dirt as it raced to catch up.

As soon as the truck came to a stop, the fire brigade scrambled out, armored from head to toe in their brown and orange gear as they charged into the burning cottage. A squat crimson machine rolled out of the back of the fire truck on treads, its body composed of two huge tanks of water with a long nozzle jutting out from the top. Gears groaned while the firefighter driving the machine adjusted the angle of the spout toward the back of the cottage.

One firefighter made a beeline for Belle, his helmet tucked under his arm.

"Are you hurt? We were told there was a woman home when the fire started." He crouched in the grass next to Belle, confusion etched into his features as he looked from her to Damek's lifeless body.

Belle shook her head. "I'm fine, thanks to Damek. He saved me." At the firefighter's blank look, she added, "The automaton."

"Are you sure you're unhurt? How long were you in there? The call said there was an explosion. Did you breathe in smoke?"

"It took me a few moments to find Damek. He warned me to get out of the room before the device exploded, but I wouldn't leave without him." Belle took a tentative deep breath and coughed. "I'm fine."

"Why did you go back? It's a machine." He squinted at Belle, his thin brows raised.

Clutching Damek's body tighter, Belle glowered. "Damek saved my life. I couldn't let him burn."

"Why isn't Belle being examined for injuries? At the very least, get her a blanket and water. The poor woman is probably in shock." Mr. Cadwell's timid nature vanished as he loomed over them.

Behind Mr. Cadwell, Captain Charity and Maureen glared at the firefighter.

Without another word, the firefighter retrieved a blanket and canteen of water from the firetruck, all but throwing the items at Belle before donning his helmet and joining the rest of the brigade.

Mr. Cadwell wrapped the blanket around Belle's shoulders. "I'm sorry for yet another tragedy. I'll go wait for the fire brigade's report." Before Belle could thank him for his kindness, the secretary departed.

Captain Charity took the firefighter's place and sat next to Belle. "How are you?" Her gaze landed on the unresponsive automaton. "Oh, Damek. What have you done now?"

Maureen shut the radio off and sat down on the other side of Belle, silent as she leaned over to shakily touch Damek's scorch-marked cheek.

"I'm so sorry. Damek dove in front of me. He saved my life." Belle sniffed. Taking a shaky breath, she added, "The device we found worked both ways. I told whoever was listening that I was coming for them. Delphine answered me right before it exploded."

Captain Charity muttered a litany of swear words.

Maureen paled. "She spoke over it?"

Belle nodded glumly. "She didn't seem surprised to hear from me."

"She's always been unhinged, but she's gone too far." Maureen scowled, balling her fist.

"Was the *Figment* safe?" Belle asked, almost afraid to hear the answer.

"Yes," Captain Charity replied slowly. "I have a few more diagnostic tests to run on the controls, specifically the landing gear, but otherwise, I think it's safe to say that she didn't sabotage the airship."

"I'm still going to check a few more things." Maureen held her arms out toward Belle. "May I see Damek? I need to catalog his damage."

Reluctantly, Belle handed the automaton over to his creator.

Maureen's lip trembled as she traced where his eyes should have been lit before turning his body to examine where his mechanical arm and leg were missing.

"I'm so sorry." Belle hung her head.

"You've done nothing wrong. If Damek sacrificed himself for you, that was his choice. What's the point of the world's first and only self-aware automaton if he doesn't make his own choices?" Maureen gave her a watery smile.

"He was incredibly brave." Belle hiccupped as she choked back a sob.

"What's all this 'was' business?" Captain Charity asked as she leaned closer. "I don't think the damage is irreversible. Look: his head is intact. He needs extensive body work and a reboot."

"Really?" Belle's eyes widened.

"I think he's fixable," Maureen said slowly, pursing her lips. "There's damage, but I think I can do it."

"I hope so." A tiny spark of hope ignited in Belle's chest.

Captain Charity put her arm around Belle. "You don't have to stay here while the fire brigade works. Do you want to leave? We could get you a fresh change of clothes."

Belle shook her head. "No, I need to see it for myself."

"We'll stay with you, then." Captain Charity gave Belle a reassuring squeeze.

Together, they watched the fire brigade work. The smell of smoke lingered in the air, even after the flames went out.

Eventually, Mr. Cadwell returned, lugging Belle's trunk from the porch. "The chief reported that damage was limited, but the bedroom is gone and the roof is weak. Your trunk is unharmed."

"Thank you for your thoughtfulness." Belle gave him a warm smile.

"I'm happy to do so. I'll load the car. Whenever you're ready to leave, just say the word." Mr. Cadwell returned her smile before leaving.

"What now?" Belle ran her fingers through her hair. "I need to go after Beast, but what about Damek?"

"Why don't we regroup and then go?" Maureen gestured to the cottage. "I can work on Damek aboard the *Figment*. It's impossible to do anything else for the house today. I'll have Mr. Cadwell make arrangements for repairs while we're gone."

Turning to Belle, Captain Charity asked, "Do you think you'd be up to being my copilot until Damek wakes up? We've got a long flight ahead of us."

"Yes, I'd be happy to help," Belle softly replied. "Are you sure I'm the right person for the job?"

"I can think of no one more determined to get to our destination." Captain Charity tilted her head. "Unless you're not up for leaving yet? If you need time, I understand."

Belle drew a shuddering breath. "It's just a building. We can rebuild when Beast's back. Let's go get him."

Aboard the *Figment*, Belle sat in Damek's seat, carefully avoiding smashing her knees into the console.

"Where are we headed?" Belle asked as she watched Captain Charity adjust the dials and knobs.

"Leverport, home to the most dangerous smuggling rings." The captain grimaced. "I don't think it's a coincidence it's a stone's throw from Glimmerdrift. Delphine's family has owned the property for generations. If she's there, the chancellor is full of it because she said that Delphine was hard to find. We told her to look there first."

"Unless Delphine recently returned there." Belle said slowly. "Or it's a trap?"

"It probably is," agreed Captain Charity as she settled into her seat. "Ready for takeoff?"

Belle traced the delicate roses on the necklace Beast had gifted her for luck. She was grateful it had been safe in her trunk, especially as she had debated packing it when Beast was preparing for his procedure.

"I'm ready." Belle buckled in, her eyes on the horizon.

CHAPTER THIRTY-TWO

Far below the *Figment*, a few stray clouds obscured the golden sunlight streaming down on the wooden buildings reinforced with oxidized copper beams. From this height, Leverport didn't look like the hub of dangerous secrets and illicit trading that Captain Charity had warned Belle about. Instead, it looked like a peaceful seaside town, the kind that tourists would flock to for their health.

Keeping her hands steady on the steering, Belle glanced at the sleeping captain, curled up in her seat with a light blanket thrown over her. She hated to wake Captain Charity, but with Damek out of commission, the two of them had taken turns piloting the *Figment* through the night. The captain had completed the bulk of the overnight flying, trusting Belle to handle most of the day, but she's insisted that she wanted to manage the landing.

The tension in Belle's neck and back were painful reminders that she was too tall for Damek's chair, let alone sitting in tight quarters for hours on end, but at least she'd had a break sleeping in her quarters last night. The captain didn't get such a respite during Belle's turn piloting.

Sighing, Belle reached forward with the intention of gently

waking the captain. The intercom crackled on as Belle's hand touched Captain Charity's shoulder.

Damek's tinny voice echoed in the cockpit. "Good afternoon! I'm about 35% functional. Maureen told me I could give you both a status update."

Captain Charity's eyes shot open as she bolted upright.

"Did I just hear Damek?" Half of the captain's copper curls were flattened from laying against her seat while the rest stuck up at comical angles.

"You did! It sounds like Maureen's made good progress." Belle couldn't help the wide smile plastered on her face. After all the terrible events of the last several hours, the good news was a balm for her weary soul.

Captain Charity hit the call button so hard Belle thought it was going to break. "You mental bucket of walking bolts! I can't believe you got yourself blown up."

Belle frowned. She hated to think of what would have happened if Damek hadn't pushed her out of the way of the explosive device.

Before Belle could voice her displeasure, Captain Charity continued, "I am so proud of you, but please never scare me like that again. How are you doing?"

"My cognitive and speaking functions are back, but everything else is in critical condition. One of my sensors is out and I need new limbs, but Maureen says the outlook is positive." Damek's motors whirred. "How is Belle? Was she hurt in the explosion?"

Belle leaned forward over the receiver. "I'm fine, Damek. Thank you so much for saving me. You're the bravest automaton I know."

"You're very welcome. I'm glad I could be of help." Damek's voice sounded almost cheerful. "Maureen wants to talk to you, too."

"Good afternoon," Maureen's tired voice came over the intercom. "As you heard, Damek still has a lot of work to be done, but I can finish it here. He should be able to help with the next leg of the flight. Stop by the lab before you disembark. I have something important for the mission."

"Sounds like a good plan. Leave the airship pirate business to us." Captain Charity winked at Belle. "Belle will be an expert in no time."

"That's alarming," Maureen answered dryly.

"So much for my pardon, huh? It's almost like having a pirate for a fiancée is useful." Captain Charity smirked, holding a finger to her lips.

Belle covered her hand with her mouth, unable to completely smother her laughter.

Static pops punctuated Maureen's terse reply. "It was never about the piracy. You know better than that."

"I'm teasing, love. Good luck with Damek, and thank you." Captain Charity's expression softened.

The intercom shut off with a crackling sound as the bustling three-story airship dock came into view. Like the rest of town, the architecture looked almost cheerful, with no sign of disrepair or neglect.

"This is the place you warned me about?" Belle's brows rose.

Captain Charity nodded, her expression grim. "Don't be fooled by the appearance. You'll never find a more dangerous port. Keeping the peace is key to keeping business running. If you screw up here, everyone will come after you."

Belle gulped. "I see."

After a smooth landing, Captain Charity and Belle stopped by the airship's makeshift lab for their new equipment.

While Maureen explained the tracking devices in the plain copper rings, Belle tried to listen, but all she could think of was Beast. She appreciated the captain was taking so many opportunities to make her feel like she was contributing to his rescue and giving her much-needed levity, but her patience was wearing thin. All she wanted was to search for Beast.

Damek, partially restored, was strapped to a work table. He already looked so much better than Belle expected, but it still hurt her heart to see scorch marks and scuffs on his metal face.

The automaton's lit blue eyes met Belle's as she put on her ring. "I'd do it again."

"Thank you, but I hope it doesn't come to that." Belle placed her hand on the worst of his damaged jaw.

Captain Charity slid the copper ring on her right hand. "I hope you're ready to take over piloting again, Damek. Belle's good, but we all miss you."

"I can't wait to be back to flying," Damek replied. "It's been too long."

Maureen wrapped Belle and Captain Charity into a tight hug. "Both of you, be careful. Keep those trackers on hand. If we get separated, it could make all the difference."

Belle twisted the unassuming ring, her lips turned down. She never wanted to wear a tracker. It reminded her too much of her time at the circus, but she understood Maureen's reasoning.

"We will. Thank you for everything." Belle straightened. It wouldn't do Beast any good if she wasted more time moping.

Belle left for the hangar to check over her outfit again while Captain Charity lingered in the lab to finish her goodbyes. The captain had taken a lot of pride in dressing her like an airship pirate, complete with a comfortably cinched blouse, fingerless gloves, fitted trousers with concealed pockets carrying custom brass knuckles, and reinforced leather boots.

The hangar doors opened with a pneumatic hiss. The captain looked troubled but smiled brightly when she saw Belle. "Let me do most of the talking. You look like an enforcer, but a few words out of you and everyone will realize what a good girl you are."

Belle laughed, despite her worries. "Are you sure about that? With Beast missing, I feel capable of anything."

Captain Charity's humor vanished. "We can't show our hand, okay? Just trust me. If the *Curiosity* crew is here, I know exactly where we're going."

"The dock?" guessed Belle as they exited the *Figment*.

Captain Charity shook her head. "No, we don't know what they're flying these days. I doubt their name is on their airship, anyway. We're going to Haven."

Belle didn't have time to ask what Haven was as Captain Charity briskly led her along the boardwalk to a pub with a freshly painted sign that read "The Copper Triangle." Inside, the packed bar was filled with all manner of folk from preening, elegantly dressed patrons to shifty customers wearing low hoods and dark goggles despite it only being two o'clock in the afternoon. No one seemed to pay either the captain or Belle more than a cursory glance before returning to their drinks and business.

Captain Charity confidently led the way, nodding at the barkeep on their way to what appeared to be a plain supply closet with a lock on it. The captain fished an iron key from her pocket and unlocked the door.

"This is where the real business happens. Lock the door behind you, okay?" Captain Charity's stern expression looked foreign on the usually carefree woman. "It's critical that we follow the rules here."

Belle nodded, her eyes wide as the captain opened the door to reveal a staircase.

The stairwell was lit with electric lamps that flickered ominously. Graphic murals of airships and their crews performing all manners of piracy covered the walls. One portrait was of a young, smirking Captain Charity wielding her electric sword in one hand with a heavily locked trunk in the other.

Belle's eyebrows rose. If they made it out of this alive, she'd have to ask about the painting. All thoughts of the portrait vanished when they reached the bottom of the stairs as they came face-to-face with a studded metal door. The antique plaque affixed to it read "Haven."

"Are you ready?" Captain Charity mouthed, preparing to unlock the door with another key.

Belle nodded, and the captain opened the heavy door to a wild pub alive with patrons gambling and talking over each other. In the center of the room, a band played a raucous song with increasingly suggestive lyrics while beautiful bartenders served drinks.

Sitting at the bar with his back to the pub entrance, Captain Lucke boasted to a small crowd gathered around him. "This is the job to end all jobs, I'm telling you. Easiest money I've made. And I've already gotten away with it."

None of Haven's patrons gave Belle and Captain Charity a second glance as they made their way across the room. Still, Belle couldn't help looking over her shoulder. At the bar, all eyes were on Captain Lucke as he retold the story of Beast's capture. His bold red coat hanging off the edge of his stool was reminiscent of the Ringmaster's.

Belle's fingernails bit into her palms as she clenched her fists.

"Remember what we came here to do," Captain Charity whispered, placing a comforting hand on Belle's back as she guided her to a corner booth with a clear view of the *Curiosity* crew.

Wincing, Belle nodded as she squeezed into the booth. If it weren't for the captain's constant reminders that it would be a disaster to start trouble in Haven, she'd have picked Lucke up by his collar and demanded to know where Beast was.

Leaning over the small table, Belle asked, "Does the plan still apply if he sees us? Should we have come in disguises?"

Captain Charity shook her head. "We wouldn't have been let inside Haven if no one recognized me. Lucke won't start anything here, either. If he doesn't see us, maybe he'll slip up. If we can find out what they're flying in, we might be able to get to Beast while the crew is still drinking."

At the bar, a man stood on swaying legs as he pointed a crooked finger at Captain Lucke. His rough voice cut through the din of the talking patrons and bawdy music. "I don't believe you. So what, you retrieved someone's trained pet?"

"No, a creature unlike anything you've ever seen." Captain Lucke took a deep drink from his huge mug. "Part man, part bear, all monster. Security was tight when we retrieved the brute, but my crew and I were better." He saluted his crew as they cheered.

A squat crew mate with a ruffled shirt raised his mug. It took Belle a moment to remember his name was Riggs, the crew's quartermaster. "To Captain Lucke! Without him, we wouldn't have made all that sweet coin."

Belle's temples throbbed as the beginnings of a headache formed. "How much more of this do we have to listen to?"

Captain Charity grimaced. "Hopefully, not much. Eventually, they'll run out of steam and stop drinking. We need to keep our wits about us, especially if we're going to follow them back to the airship in the dark."

A barmaid with glossy curls and a friendly smile placed two full mugs on their table. "Sorry for the wait. Here's your ale. On the house, as always, Captain." The barmaid blushed faintly.

"Thank you, Anna. As always, I appreciate it." Captain Charity reached for her mug with her left hand, the light catching the stones of her iridescent engagement ring.

Anna's eyes narrowed as her gaze lingered on the ring. Without another word, she left in a huff.

"What's with her?" Captain Charity took a sip of her drink, making a bleak face. "This used to taste better."

Belle took a sip of the bitter ale and immediately gagged. At least she wouldn't have to worry about getting drunk off this swill. She hoped they wouldn't have to stay long.

After hours of listening to Captain Lucke's boasting, Belle was ready to scream. Before she could ask Captain Charity if they couldn't just grab the other captain, Lucke stood and blew a kiss at Anna, the barmaid, who giggled as she pocketed her tip.

"I'd better go check on my prize. Thank you for your hospitality."

The *Curiosity* crew followed their captain, though some of them had trouble keeping a straight line as they walked. The captain, despite his heavy drinking, appeared to have no such trouble.

As soon as the crew left, Captain Charity stood and stretched. "Ready?"

Belle's temples throbbed, her legs cramped, and her back ached, but despite everything, she smiled as she nodded. They were finally getting somewhere.

Belle and Captain Charity followed the *Curiosity* crew down the poorly lit streets of Leverport. The seaside town looked decidedly less charming than it did during daylight hours. With scant gas lamps dotting the boardwalks, their path felt perilous. There were no barriers between the ocean and the rickety, creaking boards.

Captain Lucke and his crew sang a bawdy song off-key, making it easier to follow them to the packed docks from a distance. Under the dim lights, the airships ranged in size from tiny two-person vessels to enormous airships armed with prominent cannons. Many of the airships were notably nameless, though they passed by a few had memorable names like *Maiden's First Kiss* and *Hot John's Getaway*.

At last, the crew led them to a nameless generic cargo ship. Belle was relieved there were no huge cannons visible on the side of the mid-size airship, but from her time on the *Figment*, she knew not to be fooled by appearances.

Belle's stomach churned as she waited for Captain Charity's next move. They hadn't discussed how to handle confronting the crew. Their time was running out as a bald man with too much jewelry adorning his face unlocked the hatch.

"What's taking so long, Moody? Can't hold your drink?" a woman's voice called while the rest of the crew guffawed.

"Better than you, Hawke." Moody found the correct key, and the hatch opened with a click. Most of the crew filed inside, save Captain Lucke. He lingered on the boarding platform as he whistled, drinking from a flask.

"Lucke! I'm surprised to see Delphine hired you back after the bad business with the Ringmaster. That woman hates incompetence." Captain Charity strode forward into the light, one hand on her sheathed electric sword.

"Charity?" Captain Lucke squinted. His grin widened when he focused on her. "She said you'd come. Too easy."

Belle's unease grew as she stood guard at Captain Charity's side. She dug into her pockets, fingers curled around her new brass knuckles, their unfamiliar weight a welcome distraction.

"Something feels off," Belle whispered in the captain's ear, never taking her eyes off Lucke.

Captain Charity nodded almost imperceptibly.

"Whatever she's paying you, I can double it." Captain Charity stepped closer, her free hand open.

Captain Lucke tossed his long hair back. "I doubt that, unless the stories I heard about you are true. Rumor has it you're pardoned. That mayor girlfriend of yours took care of it."

Captain Charity lifted her chin. "Fiancée. And yes, I've been pardoned. But this is a personal matter. I know we've had our history, good and bad, but you know I'm a woman of my word. Let's make a deal. I'd rather get Beast to safety. You don't want to deal with Delphine. Look at the ship she's given you."

Belle tensed as Captain Lucke guffawed.

"You really think this is about money?" He pointed at them with a shaking finger. "You blew up the *Curiosity*."

"Lucke, be reasonable. If given the chance, you would have done the same to the *Figment* if I'd double-crossed you." Captain Charity shrugged. "Why help that insane rich woman out, anyway? Take the money and run. There are better marks."

Captain Lucke shook his head. "There are, but they wouldn't bring me near as much joy as this will." Throwing back his head, he yelled, "They're here!"

The rest of the crew came running out of the airship, all wielding weapons.

Belle's pulse raced as she slipped on her brass knuckles.

"I'm disappointed, but not surprised, Lucke." Captain Charity drew her electric saber. It crackled to life in her hands, bathing her in an eerie blue glow.

It was five against two, but Belle wasn't worried about fighting an inebriated crew. Her biggest fear was that she'd hit too hard to question the crew about Beast's whereabouts. With that thought, she slipped the brass knuckles off, leaving them in her pockets.

"What are you waiting for? Get them!" Captain Lucke ordered.

The *Curiosity* crew swarmed toward them, clumsily brandishing their weapons. Moody the quartermaster fell over as he waved his daggers, while the rest of the crew struggled to remain upright.

If it hadn't been Beast's safety on the line, Belle would have laughed at the absurdity of it all. Instead, she effortlessly disarmed the crew, throwing their weapons into the sea as Captain Charity kept Lucke at bay with her electric saber.

When the crew was fully disarmed, Belle used a spare rope from a nearby mooring to tie the crew to a gas lamp.

Captain Charity pointed her sword at Lucke's throat. "Where's Beast?"

"You'll have to try harder than that if you think you can scare me," Captain Lucke spat.

Belle cracked her knuckles as she strode over to him. She picked him up by the shoulders and held him over the choppy water.

"Give me one good reason I shouldn't drop you." She loosened her grip just a bit, and he slipped lower, his boots touching the water.

"W-wait! I'll tell you where he is! He's on board. Our client hasn't made the exchange yet. Don't drop me. I can't swim," Captain Lucke blubbered, his stinking breath making Belle's nose wrinkle in disgust.

Belle looked back at Captain Charity, brows raised. "Think he's telling the truth?"

Captain Charity nodded. "I've played cards with him enough times." She pointed the saber at Lucke again. "Do you have any more crew aboard?"

Lucke shook his head, gulping. "N-no."

"Get over there." Captain Charity pointed to the rest of the bound crew.

Captain Lucke scrambled over.

"I'll go check on Beast if you've got this?" Belle called as she headed to the ship.

"What? Wait!"

Belle sprinted into the airship's cargo hold. A roughly bandaged figure was buckled into a cot strapped to the wall in the corner of the room.

"Belle?" Beast's hoarse voice was barely audible.

"I'm getting you out of here." She charged forward, heart pounding.

"No, run!" Beast coughed as he strained against the restraints.

The hatch snapped shut.

"Good to have you aboard, Belle." From the other side of the cargo hold, the Ringmaster stepped into the room, the light catching his predatory grin. "You're just in time for takeoff."

The chilling touch of the ether-laced handcuffs chafing against Belle's wrists was all too familiar. She glowered at the Ringmaster as he snapped a crimson orb anklet on her leg, irritating her old scar. Chains shackled her to a bench against the wall next to Beast's cot, just out of range to touch him.

Belle couldn't believe she'd run straight into a trap. The worst part was that she knew she could easily overpower the Ringmaster, but she'd seen a crimson orb poking out of the bandages covering Beast's weakened body. All the Ringmaster had to do was press the button on his cufflinks and jolts of electricity would course through an already weakened Beast. Her surrender was immediate.

The Ringmaster smoothed his blond mustache and smirked. "You're entirely too predictable. One little threat to your precious Beast and you crumple. I suppose Delphine's enhancements to the collar were persuasive. Who knows what the extra current would do?" His gaze traveled pointedly to the plain band on Belle's left ring finger. "Wait, did you actually marry the creature?"

Belle bit her lip. At least he hadn't taken the ring concealing a tracking device within it. Maureen had been scant on the details of how the ring worked, but Belle hoped being locked in the cargo hold wouldn't block its signal. She'd hadn't been so lucky with her brass knuckles. As soon as the Ringmaster discovered them concealed in her pockets, he'd taken them away.

The Ringmaster scoffed. "Maybe I should ask Madam Wyerstone to delay her revenge. I'm sure your offspring would fetch a hefty price for admission."

Belle shook her head. "You're delusional. You call yourself a Ringmaster, but you don't have a circus any more. Now you're Delphine's lapdog, at least until you fail her again. How many times are you going to go crawling back to her?"

The Ringmaster leaned in, his hot breath far too close to Belle's ear. "I'll keep going back to her as many times as I can if it means I get my revenge. You ruined me." His rough hands grabbed her by the chin, pulling her forward until they were nose to nose. "I'm going to thoroughly enjoy this. She's going to break your Beast, then break you."

Beast growled, pulling against his restraints. The bandages on his face were slipping, revealing feral rage in his honey-colored eyes.

The Ringmaster cocked his brow. "I see you're still a bit of a monster, but you're all bark and no bite."

"It's not my bite you need to worry about." Beast's voice was low and deadly quiet. "Don't you remember your last encounter with Belle?"

All the color drained from the Ringmaster's face as he spurted indignantly. Huffing, he retreated to the other side of the cargo hold. He balled his fists, glaring balefully at them both.

Loud banging sounded from the outside of the hatch. "Open up!" More frantic knocks punctuated Captain Charity's muffled voice.

From within the airship, the hum of an engine turning out drowned out the rest of the captain's words.

An intercom turned on with a whine, and a woman's voice cut through the static. "Are you done yet? Delphine's waiting. And that loon is trying to break down the hatch."

Belle furrowed her brows. There was something familiar about the irritated woman's voice.

Beast leaned back, catching her eye. "The chancellor's secretary," he mouthed.

The Ringmaster dashed over to the call button on the wall, his red coat billowing out behind him. He cleared his throat before answering, "Yes, I'm on my way. You can let Delphine know both targets have been acquired."

"You can tell her yourself. I'm done being a secretary." The intercom clicked off with a snap.

The Ringmaster swore violently under his breath as the airship began its ascent. He stormed out of the cargo hold and the door sealed shut behind him.

Belle strained against her chains, but they didn't budge. She stopped when Beast coughed. "Did they hurt you?"

"A little. I feel weaker than I'd like to be." Beast struggled to turn his head to look at Belle. "They could have skipped the chains. I don't think I can move far on my own."

"I couldn't protect you at the lab. I've made a mess of things charging ahead and now we're in more danger." Her lips quivered.

Beast shook his head. "You didn't do this. Did they hurt you?"

"I'm fine. More upset about these chains than anything else." Belle attempted to rotate her ankle, hoping for relief against the ill-fitting anklet. "I never thought I'd be wearing one of these again."

Beast sighed. "I still can't figure out how they knew when to break in. I tried to listen to everything when I was awake, but I only briefly saw the *Curiosity* crew before they drugged me."

"Apparently, there was a listening device planted in the room with us back at the lab. Delphine's been listening for some time." Belle tensed as she realized she'd need to be careful with anything else she told him. For all they knew, Delphine could be listening right now.

Beast's chuckles drowned her worried thoughts out.

"What's so funny?" Belle tilted her head.

"I bet we gave her quite the earful in the lab." With a mischievous glint in his eyes, Beast added, "I wish I could have done more than talk with you."

Heat rose on Belle's cheeks. "Beast!"

"Well, it's true." He shrugged before his gaze softened. "I never thought I'd see you again. When I woke up aboard the airship, I thought it was over for me. I didn't know if they'd killed you."

"I was always going to come for you." Belle wished she could tell him about the tracking device planted on her. Instead, she said, "I also found a listening device in our bedroom. It was rigged to explode. Our room is in shambles, but the rest of the cottage is fine."

All mirth disappeared from Beast's countenance. His voice shook as he said, "Then I'm even more relieved to see you."

"Me, too." Belle winced as the airship took a sharp turn. When the movement settled, she added, "I might have called out Delphine over the listening device before it blew up."

"That's my girl. We'll rebuild our room when we get out of this. Maybe get a proper bed this time?"

Thoughts of Damek's condition kept Belle's smile from reaching her eyes as she replied. "I'd like that."

"I wish I could hold you," Beast complained, weakly struggling against his restraints. "I've missed your touch."

"I've missed yours." Belle's gaze dropped. It was getting harder to not tell him everything that had transpired. The guilt settled in her gut like a heavy weight. "I thought I would never see you again, too."

"You'll have to tell me someday how you found me here." Beast shifted to look at her. "Not that I'm complaining."

"I will. Let's just focus on getting out of here. For all we know, Delphine or the others are listening in."

"Agreed."

The silence stretched between them. Belle had so much to tell Beast, but with the possibility of being overheard, she was conflicted. Being more cautious would be the wise choice, but she feared not being able to have another chance to talk to him.

As if sensing her distress, Beast said, "We'll get through this."

"Yes, we will." Belle set her jaw.

Deciding she could carefully distract them both from their predicament, Belle told Beast about her plans for the library's opening. It was surreal talking about something so mundane as organizing shelves in their situation, but she was doing her best to stay away from crucial information like Damek's damage in the explosion and anything that might give away her tracker ring.

Eventually, Beast pointed out that she'd need to sleep, or their chances of survival would be in jeopardy.

"Between the two of us, more depends on you." Beast's shoulders slumped. "I wish it wasn't so."

With that, Belle finally gave herself permission to doze. It was not an easy task, sleeping in an uncomfortable seat while chained, but eventually, exhaustion won.

Hours later, Belle and Beast were startled awake.

Over the intercom, the Ringmaster's voice echoed in the cargo hold. "Rise and shine. We're here."

Belle's stomach dropped. She had hoped that the *Figment* would have caught up with them midair before they reached their final destination. Maybe the airship had been sabotaged?

After a tumultuous landing, Belle felt thoroughly rattled. When at last the airship stopped shaking, she whispered, "Beast? Are you okay?"

Beast grunted. "I could be better, but I feel like it's about to get much worse. You?"

The outer hatch groaned and creaked as it unlocked.

Belle narrowed her eyes. "Same."

The hatch opened, revealing Delphine wearing a green hooded cloak, flanked by a pack of snarling Hounds.

"Looks like you came for me after all." Delphine smirked. "Probably not the way you envisioned, though."

CHAPTER THIRTY-THREE

Belle wrinkled her nose at the cloying floral perfume clinging to Delphine as she entered the cargo hold, her long-sleeve green dress and matching cloak billowing behind her. The sickly sweet scent was as overpowering as the rank, hot breath of the Hounds.

The Ringmaster smoothed his red coat and adjusted his blond braid before bounding toward Delphine and her creatures. "I've got both of them, as promised. I told you if we took Beast, she'd be quick to follow."

Belle wished she could knock the toothy grin off the Ringmaster's face. Her handcuffs and anklet bit into her skin as she tensed.

Delphine regarded the sniveling man with a cold gaze. Close behind her, the canines bared their teeth at Beast and growled. "Yes, very good, pet. Now be a good boy and mind the Hounds."

The Ringmaster grimaced as he pressed the controls on his new black cane. The orbs on the Hounds' collars turned a brighter shade of crimson as the creatures stood still at attention and ceased their snarling.

Beast grunted as he weakly pulled against the restraints

strapping him to his crude medical bed. "What do you want with Belle? I'm the creation that got away, not her."

Raising her thin golden brows, Delphine pressed a manicured finger to her lips as if to shush him.

The door to the interior of the airship opened with a hiss. Ms. Palmer stood in the doorway, no longer appearing as the demure, meek secretary Belle remembered in Maureen's lab. Instead, she wore green leather trousers with a matching vest over an ivory blouse. Aviator goggles were pushed on top of her head. With a pinched expression, she nodded at Delphine.

"I don't have to fly with him again, do I?" Ms. Palmer asked, cutting her eyes at the Ringmaster as he brandished his cane at the Hounds, his finger hovering over the shock button.

Shaking her head, Delphine chuckled. "No. Were you followed?"

Ms. Palmer shrugged. "No, the skies were clear."

"Very curious." Delphine pursed her lips. Snapping her fingers at the Ringmaster, she gestured to Belle and Beast. "Let's bring my guests into the manor while we wait for the cavalry to arrive. I need time for my plans to come to fruition."

Belle flinched as Delphine approached her, looking down at her. "You're nothing special, yet you've managed to foil my plans so far. I'm going to amend that today. You'll be of use to me yet."

Scowling, Belle shook her head. "I very much doubt that."

Belle's eyes adjusted to the bright mid-morning sun as she was pulled out of the airship by ether-laced chains. The Ringmaster had tethered her to Beast's wheeled bed, keeping his gloved hand on the ether-laced chain. He brandished his cane with his other hand as he barked orders at the Hounds tailing her.

Ahead, Delphine walked arm in arm with Ms. Palmer along the cobblestone path, their heads tilted close together as they conversed. Straining to listen, Belle hoped she'd glean some information, but their voices were too low. All she could hear was the panting of the creatures and Beast groaning every time the wheels of his bed hit a bump. The Hound, who was easily distracted by squirrels and birds running into the dense forest, wasn't the most reliable guide as he pushed Beast.

The huge birch trees along the overgrown path swayed in the breeze as the Ringmaster pulled Belle's chain once more. Lost in thought, she stumbled while trying to recall why the trees seemed so eerily familiar. Her eyes widened when realization hit her: these woods were the same place where she'd met Beast. Somewhere within this forest was the former campground of the Circus Illume.

Eventually, the path came to a clearing, and they passed a dilapidated greenhouse with several planes of glass replaced by boards. Wild greenery grew out of the cracks and snaked around the greenhouse's metal frame.

Beast snorted. "It looks like it didn't take long for this place to fall apart without me."

"You tended the gardens here?" Belle asked, earning a growl from the Hound on her left.

"Yes."

The Ringmaster snarled as he snapped Belle's chain. "That's enough out of both of you. You're not here for chatter."

"Quiet," Delphine called. "We're almost there. Then we can properly deal with our guests."

A sprawling stone manor that must have been the picture of elegance before the ravages of time took their toll came into view as they passed the greenhouse. Roses in unnatural violet hues grew wildly around its perimeter and ivy snaked around the copper pipes, running the height of the building. A tower jutted out of the steepled roof with an array antenna haphazardly attached to its side. On the far side of the manor, an enormous generator emitted puffs of steam, shrouding the grounds in a haze.

"Bring them to the lab. I've got work to do." Delphine's cloak swished behind her as she opened the manor's heavy front door.

Delphine's lab was nothing like Maureen's. While the mayor's lab had the feel of a cozy library with machinery in it, Delphine's was a strange array of esoteric bottled elixirs, animal skulls altered by ether-radiation, and white marble sculptures of women's torsos. Dramatic chandeliers bathed everything in electric light, casting strange shadows in the corners of the room. A heady floral scent wasn't enough to mask the fetid smell of decay permeating the lab.

Long tables with alchemical experiments in various stages surrounded an examination table in the center of the lab. Across the room, an ornate floral dressing screen walled off a sitting area featuring an emerald fainting couch and an end table covered with glass vials with droplets of colorful residue left from whatever elixir had once filled them.

"Strap her to the examination table and park his bed over here." Delphine pointed at a machine similar to the one in Maureen's lab except the elixir hooked up to it shimmered silver-blue.

With a grunt, the Ringmaster did as she asked while the Hounds stood guard.

When he finished, Delphine dismissed her lackeys with a wave of her hand. "Ms. Palmer, keep your eyes open for the *Figment*. There's no way that Maureen isn't coming for these two." She smirked. "This is like the automaton all over again, but this time, I'm ready for her."

Belle's stomach churned. She struggled against her restraints quietly, but it was no use; the ether-laced chains didn't budge.

"Happy to be of service." Ms. Palmer left the room, shooting the Ringmaster a disgusted look.

"What would you have me do, mistress?" the Ringmaster simpered.

Delphine rolled her eyes. "Go tend to the Hounds. I'm sure they need grooming after the flight."

The saccharine smile on the Ringmaster's face fell as he bowed clumsily. "Right away." With a flick of his cane, the pack followed him out of the lab.

"You must be feeling confident if you're sending your guard dogs away." Beast glowered.

Delphine scoffed. "I've nothing to fear from either of you. These ether-chains are expertly made. Neither of you are going anywhere."

"We can stop this now. No one has to get hurt." Belle attempted to sit up, but the restraints were too strong, even for her.

Delphine raised her perfectly arched brows. "It's too late for that." She threw back her cloak and peeled off one of her elbow-length green gloves. The golden veins crisscrossing her skin looked far more severe than when Belle had glimpsed them at the Exhibition Hall. "My time is running short. I need a cure before this worsens. It's already spread so much."

"Then let Maureen help you! What do you need with us?" Belle furrowed her brows.

Delphine flicked Belle's nose. "You are bait. Maureen and that damned pirate of hers won't resist the chance to play savior while rescuing you." Her lips curved into a cruel smile as she pointed at Beast. "And he is the catalyst, the key to my cure. I can feel it in my bones. I need to undo whatever damage Maureen has done to my work and study his transformation."

Belle squinted at the markings on the other woman. "What happened? Do you have ether-poisoning?"

Delphine's eyes flashed with contempt. "This is no mere ether-poisoning. That would be child's play to fix." She scowled and flexed a prosthetic arm concealed by her other glove. "No, this results from years of work gone to waste from a simple miscalculation. It's already cost me an arm."

"You did this to yourself," Beast muttered.

"Perhaps I should remove your vocal cords while I'm at it. You don't need to speak to be of use to me." Delphine rubbed her chin.

"What good will studying Beast's transformation do?" Belle stalled for time as her mind raced. They needed a plan. Where was the *Figment*?

Delphine preened. "I want to change the building blocks of human anatomy. I've always pushed the limits on ether research, first using it to spark life where it hadn't existed before in an automaton. The Hounds were a mere stepping stone to Beast, my first successful transformation of a human into something wholly new. I'm going to cheat death and aging. Why shouldn't I continue inventing thirty, forty, one hundred years from now? Think about all the experience I will have.”

“But what is the point?” Belle narrowed her eyes.

Delphine leaned over her, her nose practically brushing against Belle’s. The scent of florals mingling with decay was overwhelming. “Power. Something you’ve never had, and never will. Now, I’ve a Beast to restore.”

Delphine strode toward Beast and the machines behind him.

“Wait!” Belle called out. “Take me instead!”

Delphine glanced over her shoulder at Belle, studying her from head to toe. Disdain filled her voice as she asked, “What would I want with you? There’s nothing interesting about you, save your size and strength.”

Belle gulped, taking a steadying breath. “Maureen cured me of my severe ether-poisoning. There’s something unique about my blood. She said as much when she helped me. It ended up being key to Beast’s cure.”

Folding her arms, Delphine pursed her lips. “Go on, I’m listening.”

“If you want a cure, start with me. Let Beast go, and you can have all the blood you need from me. Just free him.” Belle feebly turned her wrist over, wincing as her restraints chafed against her, and exposed the bottom of her arm to the predatory gaze of Delphine.

“Belle! What are you doing?” Beast groaned as he twisted against his restraints.

“Saving you.” Belle gritted her teeth. Beast meant well, but she wished he’d go back to being silent long enough for her to stall. She knew this was an awful plan, but her options were limited.

“That is a lovely thought. Though I have to wonder about your motives.” The other woman crossed the room to examine Belle’s hand, tapping the plain band on her finger. She narrowed her eyes and pursed her lips. “Oh, but what’s this?”

Belle's heart was pounding as she struggled to concoct a lie while Delphine was preoccupied with the ring which concealed the tracking device. Thinking became more difficult due to the prolonged exposure to ether-laced chains that clouded her judgment and weakened her strength. "Just a simple piece of jewelry, that's all."

In a fluid motion, Delphine slipped the band off Belle's finger and raised her brows while scrutinizing the ring as a jeweler might, turning it between her fingers. "Looks like Maureen's handiwork to me. Let me guess, she installed a tracking device within the ring?"

Belle's eyes widened. "No, why would—"

Using a manicured fingernail, Delphine pried open the tiny panel on the bottom of the ring to reveal its delicate circuitry. "As I thought. No matter." She placed the jewelry on her own finger.

"What?" Belle gasped.

"If I had more time, I'd amplify the signal. I'm surprised Maureen isn't here yet with her favorite pirate." Delphine scowled before her expression softened into a calm smile. "But I'm certain they're on the way. I'm counting on it."

Gulping, Belle's voice shook as she asked, "What are you going to do?"

"Nothing you should concern yourself with." Delphine brushed Belle's hair back, tucking the loose strands behind her ears. "I accept your generous offer of blood. Perhaps you are correct and it'll provide insight into my cure. But first, I have work to do."

"What? I thought we had a deal." Belle watched in open-mouthed horror as Delphine returned to Beast and inserted an IV into his arm.

Delphine chuckled as she turned on the machine. The silver blue elixir hooked to it glittered and swirled ominously under the low lighting. She raised her voice over the machine's pneumatic hisses and creaking gears as it warmed up. "You vastly underestimated the situation. This is my domain."

Beast roared, thrashing as the elixir entered his bloodstream. The restraints barely kept him strapped to the bed. His bandages ripped and tufts of silver fur stuck out between the tattered gauze. However, his transformation was not progressing as his creator planned. His teeth were still too long and sharp, but he had no muzzle and his build was considerably less bearlike than before his cure.

"Looks like you're resisting the change. I can fix that." Delphine frowned as she turned the dial on the machine, upping the dosage.

A sliver of hope bloomed in Belle's chest. Perhaps the cure Maureen had given him provided some resistance? She prayed if they escaped this place that the mayor could undo the damage, provided that Beast could survive a second transformation.

"It'll be good to have you back in your form." Delphine caressed the machine as she adjusted its knobs.

"You can't do this." The ether-laced shackles burned Belle's skin as she wrenched against them. The chains rattled but failed to break.

"I've already done it." Delphine sighed happily. "I love it when my plans come together."

A thunderous boom sounded from outside, shaking the whole lab. The transformation machine beeped shrilly as one of its dials lit up and blinked orange.

Belle shuddered. She hoped the boom was a sign of rescue, but it'd be for naught if the building collapsed on them.

"Right on time, though that blast was more than I had calculated," Delphine muttered as she strode across the room to press the red call button on the wall. "Ms. Palmer, report."

A second boom shook the lab, rattling vials and bottled elixirs on the shelves. Beast groaned as the machine ceased pumping elixir, its light switching from orange to crimson.

Ms. Palmer's voice shook over the intercom system, her words punctuated by static pops. "We're under attack!"

Delphine rolled her eyes. "We planned for this. Use the anti-airship device. I showed you how to use it!"

"The cannon's been—" Crackling static and a terrible racket drowned out her words.

A vein on Delphine's forehead throbbed. "The cannon has been what?"

"They disabled it! Oh no, they're circling around again. I've never seen an airship fly like that!" Static hissed over the intercom, echoing in the lab.

From her chained position, Belle smiled, grateful for Captain Charity's unorthodox approach to airship piracy.

Delphine slammed the call button. "Status?"

The intercom clicked off.

"If I want something done right, I'd better do it myself. Or make a henchman do it." Delphine shook her head and flipped a switch labeled "Kennel" mounted on the wall next to the call button. After pressing the button once more, she said, "Ringmaster? Bring the Hounds to the lab."

"They're riled up from the blasts. Are you sure this is wise?" The Ringmaster's voice was subdued.

"Question me again and I'll feed you to my pets. Move. Now." Delphine gritted her teeth.

"Right away, ma'am." The intercom abruptly clicked off.

Delphine pointed at Belle and Beast. "Stay put. Not that you can go anywhere, but you know. Details." With that, she left the lab, her green dress billowing behind her as she slammed the door shut.

Belle pulled as hard as she could against her restraints to no avail. Panting, she leaned back against the stiff leather bed. "Beast! Are you hurt?"

"Yes." Beast growled, his voice thick from the transformation. "I never wanted to go back to being a creature. It feels off, though. Something's changed."

"Maybe Maureen's cure is making you resistant?" Belle looked around the lab, searching for anything to break out of her bonds. All of Delphine's equipment and tools were out of reach.

"I just hope we escape, and Maureen can fix this," Beast replied. "At least my memories are intact this time."

Belle's stomach dropped. She hadn't considered the effects of Delphine's elixir. To this day, Beast'd had no memory of his life before his first transformation. "Are you sure you're going to be okay?"

"I'll get through this. I can't lose you." His low voice was quiet.

"You won't lose me." Belle tugged on her chains, willing them to loosen. "Any chance you can break out of your restraints? Mine won't budge."

Beast grunted and let out a painful yelp. His bandaged arms drooped uselessly at his sides. "No, I'm still too weak and sore. All these elixirs going through me can't be helping."

"We'll be fine." Belle tensed as outside the lab the sound of paws tapping against the wooden floor and the Ringmaster barking orders grew closer. For the first time, she wished that her circus act had been escaping instead of feats of strength so she could contort out of her shackles.

The door opened with a bang as the Ringmaster entered the lab wielding his cane. Six Hounds followed him inside, making the musty room feel hot and crowded.

"This is delicious. There's nowhere for you to go, and your precious Beast is turning back into his namesake." The Ringmaster's eyes glittered as he leered at Belle. "Delphine promised that after she's through with you, I can have you back to do with as I see fit. I'm looking forward to your next act."

"I'll die before I do anything for you again." Belle clenched her fists, her nails biting into the flesh of her palms.

"That can be arranged," the Ringmaster sneered. "It makes no difference to me. Either way, I win."

At a smaller explosion outside the manor, the Hounds huddled together, growling low and panting.

"What is it now?" the Ringmaster spat.

Hope filled Belle as footsteps approached along with the sound of another small explosion.

"Please let that be help," Beast muttered, his eyes squeezed shut.

"Even if it is, we will outnumber those two fools," the Ringmaster scoffed. "They'll never last against all these Hounds and Delphine's contingencies."

"Was the anti-airship weapon a contingency? Because I think they made it past that." Belle set her jaw.

The Ringmaster shook his head. "It's no matter, Delphine will —"

"Get her ass handed to her on a silver platter." Captain Charity stood in the lab's doorway, brandishing her lit electric saber. Unfamiliar goggles covered her eyes and her copper hair was wild, curlier than ever.

Maureen stood by the captain's side, wearing goggles and looking as if Captain Charity had chosen her wardrobe. She donned a leather corset and knee-high black boots with an indigo shirt. A bandoleer holding two round metal objects crisscrossed her torso. Her right hand held a brass rectangular device and her left hand carried a universal screwdriver.

"Get them." The Ringmaster pressed the button on his cane. The orbs on the creatures' collars turned crimson.

The Hounds' ears went flat as they stalked toward Maureen and Captain Charity.

"Poor choice." Maureen tsked and pressed the button on her device.

Belle squeezed her eyes shut, unwilling to watch her friends get mauled.

Everything went quiet as the animals ceased growling. There was a sharp whistle, and immediately, the Hounds and Beast howled in unison.

Belle opened her eyes. The Ringmaster frantically pressed buttons on his polished black cane. Sweat dotted his forehead as he looked between the Hounds and Captain Charity's crackling electric saber. "Move, dogs!"

Captain Charity grabbed the universal screwdriver from Maureen before sprinting across the room, her sword pointed at the flummoxed Ringmaster. The mayor stood in the lab's entrance, staring down the Ringmaster as she kept her finger on her device's button.

When the captain reached Belle, she sheathed her saber, turning off its electricity with a click. Captain Charity leaned over the examination table, frowning at the lock on the straps as she twisted the handle of the screwdriver, changing its tip into a lockpick.

"Looks like it's a pin and tumbler lock, but I've seen worse." Captain Charity inserted the tool, and the screwdriver's internal motor hummed as it automatically rotated and adjusted to each of the pins.

"I've never been happier to see you both." Belle wanted to say more, but it was impossible to focus as the howling reached a crescendo.

Captain Charity looked up, her red-rimmed eyes shining brightly as she blinked back tears. "Thank the Maker you're both still alive. We thought we'd lost you when Maureen's signal tracker stopped working."

Wishing she could cover her ears, Belle grimaced as the howling grew louder. "I thought we were doomed."

"She can't escape!" The Ringmaster's face turned purple as he charged at Captain Charity. The split cane became two smaller shock sticks that sparked from his frenzied movements.

"You again?" Captain Charity unsheathed her sword, blocking the shock stick as the automated tool continued to pick the locks on its own.

The captain parried each of the Ringmaster's clumsy swings, her electric saber singeing his mustache. Despite the dire circumstances, Belle bit her lip to keep from laughing.

Belle's amusement turned to alarm as Maureen entered her field of vision, freeing the panicked Hounds from their collars with her own pick, while her left hand held the noise machine.

Beast howled and thrashed against his restraints.

As soon as the lock clicked open, Belle bolted off the examination table, grabbing the screwdriver as she went, and praying she'd remember how to use it.

Belle laid a comforting hand on Beast's bandaged shoulder while she set up the lockpick. He shuddered under her touch.

"I know it hurts. I'm getting you out of here." Belle eyed the mostly full bag of elixir and the IV connected to Beast while the screwdriver unlocked his restraints. "And I'm sorry for this." She attempted to delicately pull the IV but ultimately had to yank it out.

Beast growled, snapping his eyes open, but his gaze softened as his honey-colored, distinctly human eyes met hers. Fur poked through the bandages and his canines were longer, but the transformation was far from complete.

"Still with me?" Belle waited with bated breath as his lock opened.

"Always with you," Beast rasped, panting.

"Good." Belle leaned down and kissed his forehead as Maureen stopped pressing the button.

Beast's breathing slowed as he reached for her hand and weakly squeezed it.

"It's over." Captain Charity advanced on the Ringmaster,

slashed with a wide arcing swing of her blade, and cleaved his shock sticks in two.

The Hounds looked on, dazed. A few bared their teeth as their eyes settled on the Ringmaster.

Captain Charity leaned forward, sheathing her saber as he scrambled backward. "Start running."

The Ringmaster's eyes widened as the growling and drooling canines circled him. He shrieked as he fled. The creatures chased after him, bloodlust in their eyes.

Captain Charity straightened. "Well, that should buy us some time. How is everyone?"

"Could be better," Belle answered, smiling at her friends, "But we're glad to see you."

"I'm a bear-man again," Beast complained as Belle helped him sit up. He looked at the mayor. "Can you fix me?"

Maureen's eyes widened. "I'm sure I can." She crossed the room, struggling under the weight of her gear. "Let's get you out of here. Belle, do you think you can push Beast's bed? I don't think he should walk yet. I'll examine him on the *Figment* once Damek finally lands."

Belle's jaw dropped. "Damek is piloting alone? How is he firing?"

Maureen's eyes sparkled. "I built him a friend. The other automaton needs work, but right now, they're a great shot. The rest of the systems will have to come later."

Belle blinked, shaking her head at the surreal turn of events.

"Damek made a convincing argument that he doesn't want to be alone." Captain Charity shrugged. "He said everyone else has someone, so why not him?"

"I-I see. Good for Damek." Belle was stunned. How long had Maureen been keeping this project a secret?

"And fantastic for me. I have a gunner now!" Captain Charity beamed. "At this rate, I'll have a full crew."

"Yes, but you're not going back to pirating after this." Maureen furrowed her brows.

"Yes, dear." Captain Charity kissed her fiancée's cheek.

"Should we get going? Beast needs attention right away and—"

Belle's words died on her lips as the Hounds howled again. The Ringmaster's screams faded in the hallway.

"What was that?" Beast craned his head to look.

"I don't know, but we need to move. Something feels wrong." Maureen strode to the door, halting as Delphine entered the room carrying a long, metal staff that ended in a wickedly curved blade. Inside the curve of the blade, an emerald orb crackled with malicious electric energy.

Delphine pointed the blade at Maureen's neck. Her signature gloves were off, revealing the sickly golden veins on her arm. "You think you're so clever, don't you? As if I hadn't already anticipated your every move. Pathetic, really."

Captain Charity unsheathed her electric saber. "Get away from her. Or do you want to lose another limb?"

"One step closer, and she's gone." Her golden prosthetic arm shone green, reflecting the orb's light as she pointed at the captain. "Turn off your sword and throw it to the ground."

"Don't do it!" Maureen pleaded.

Smirking, Delphine pressed the blade closer to Maureen's neck. The electricity around the orb sparked. The air smelled of burnt ozone.

Captain Charity shut off her saber and threw her weapon on the floor. "Don't do this. You loved her once, didn't you? Doesn't your shared past mean anything?"

Delphine scoffed. "What about our past? We had plans for the automaton we built out of our dreams, blood, and sweat. You two stole my future. I want my automaton back. You both owe me."

"I owe you nothing," Maureen spat. "How many years did you manipulate me into helping you with your experiments? I always cared about you, but all you wanted was to push the limits of science for your twisted reasons. You always grabbed too much."

"I'll take what I want. Why should I settle? After the automaton was built, you turned into a coward. We could have revolutionized human evolution and put an automaton workforce to building our inventions. Every country would have given us whatever we desired. But no, you had to play politician for a bunch of misfits." Delphine sneered. "You could have had it all."

"I already have it all." Maureen winced as the blade nicked her skin. "Let me help you. You've hurt yourself. It's not too late to turn this around."

"It was too late years ago. Get against the wall over there with your precious girlfriend. I'm going to enjoy this." With her free hand, Delphine pointed at the far wall before removing Maureen's bandoleer. "And you can leave your bombs here. No tricks."

Maureen glowered before she joined Captain Charity against the wall across the room. "Darling is my fiancée."

"Whatever. I'll have to think of something especially creative for you two when I'm finished here," Delphine mused as she traced her fingers along the alchemy symbols engraved into her metal staff.

Belle inched closer to Beast, bending to whisper, "I love you."

Beast tilted his head. "I love you, too, but why——"

Belle pressed a finger to his lips as she positioned herself next to the elixir machine. "Let them go!" Her voice was stronger than she felt. She clenched her fists to keep her hands from trembling.

"What now?" Delphine scowled as she faced Belle.

"For someone who's supposed to be a genius, you forgot something." Belle lifted her chin. "Beast's transformation didn't work."

"What's that supposed to mean?" Delphine brandished her staff as she stalked closer.

"If you need a cure, I'm your best hope. Let them go." Belle grabbed Beast's IV. The needle remained connected to the undamaged hose.

"You wouldn't dare." Delphine glared. "You could lose yourself entirely."

"Last warning." Belle's pulse thrummed as she stared down the other woman.

"I'll never let anything or anyone go. Your empty threat won't save anyone." A flicker of concern passed over Delphine's face. "Now put down that needle. The last thing I need is a contaminated blood sample."

"Then you should have let my friends go." Belle jabbed the IV into her arm and turned on the elixir machine. Pain seared through her as the shimmering blue elixir entered her veins.

CHAPTER THIRTY-FOUR

"Belle!" Beast's anguished cry rang out in the lab, his voice weak. He crumpled back against the examination table, unable to lift himself despite his unlocked restraints.

Screams ripped from Belle's throat as the elixir burned through her veins. She desperately wanted to tear the IV out of her arm, but she couldn't let Delphine have her blood for a cure. Not with her friends' and Beast's lives on the line.

Even as it felt like her flesh was being melted and expanded from the inside out, Belle fought to focus her thoughts on remembering who she was, praying she wouldn't lose herself to this transformation.

She hoped Maureen could fix the consequences of her rash decision.

If they all escaped the lab.

"Stop that at once!" Delphine stepped forward, her bladed staff's emerald orb crackling and growing brighter as she aimed for Belle's heart. A mechanical cylinder below the orb whirred, its humming growing louder.

Stopping was a tempting idea, but it was too late. Belle doubled over, gritting her teeth as a fresh wave of pain wracked her. Using

Beast's table to right herself, she gripped the edge with her free hand, glaring at Delphine.

Captain Charity threw herself against Delphine's body as she fired the staff. A sound like thunder boomed, shaking vials in the room as a bolt of green electricity shot from the orb like an arrow.

The bolt struck a marble bust high on a shelf, charring the statue's torso.

With a fluid movement, Delphine swung her staff, landing a blow on Captain Charity's back and knocking her to the stone floor.

Delphine shook her head, tossing her golden hair as she recharged her weapon with a click. "Fool. You've only delayed the inevitable."

"No!" Maureen lunged at Delphine, dropping her tools. She tugged on the staff with one hand while attempting to pry the other woman's grip loose with her other hand.

With a grunt, the captain pushed herself off the floor and joined Maureen. Shouting filled the room as all three women fought for control of the humming staff. Delphine kept them at bay, neither of the other women able to wrench the weapon free.

"Why are you so freakishly strong?" Captain Charity yelled as she struggled to maintain her grip.

There was a sickening crunch as Belle's bones grew and twisted, her flesh stretching to cover her changing form. Her clothing ripped as she stumbled, kicking off her constrictive boots as her feet widened into paws. Dark fur sprouted from her body and her nails grew into razor-sharp claws.

The taste of copper filled her mouth as her canines sharpened, biting into her still-growing mouth. With another agonizing crunch, her nose flattened and stretched.

For a moment, the world went black as the sensations overwhelmed her.

Finally, the shifting stopped.

When she opened her eyes, everything was in sharp focus, as if enhanced.

There was a stabbing sensation in her arm. Fumbling with her claws, she ripped the IV out.

Her body felt foreign to her.

Who was she?

What was she?

Confused by her disjointed thoughts, she looked around the strange, eclectic room. The scent of harsh chemicals brewing over low-burning fires overpowered her senses. Rotten decay mingled with florals, making her queasy. With clumsy steps, she stumbled against a hard surface.

"What have you done?" A woman with golden hair shrieked as she held onto a staff, the other two women unable to break her iron grip.

Get the woman in green, a distant part of her mind whispered. Hackles raised, she growled.

"Belle, are you still with me?" a low, gentle voice asked. Rough linen brushed against her paw.

She looked down to see a bandaged man reaching for her. Familiar honey-gold eyes met her puzzled gaze.

Belle. She was Belle, and her Beast was beside her. Her memories came back in a rush: sharing apples by her campfire, running from the circus, dancing in the cottage, and all their heated touches late at night, full of the promise of the future they longed for.

"I'm still me." Her voice felt wrong, too thick and gravelly.

Across the room, Delphine wrenched her staff free from Captain Charity and Maureen, knocking them to the ground. She brandished her weapon, sending emerald sparks flying with each movement. "Who's next? It's nearly charged," she taunted.

Maureen and Captain Charity clung to each other.

Instinct took over. Belle charged at Delphine, the tattered remains of her clothes falling off as she crossed the room too quickly for the other woman to react.

With a roar, Belle ripped the staff from Delphine's shockingly strong hold and threw the weapon to the ground, cracking the orb. Its light immediately dimmed, though the cylinder still whirred.

Stomping with all her might, Belle smashed the staff's handle, ending the humming.

Delphine gulped, backing away from her slowly. "Don't be hasty.

I can reverse this. You don't want to be trapped like this forever, do you?"

Belle wrinkled her nose as she could smell the other woman's pungent fear.

Towering over the other woman, Belle snarled. "All this time, you could have changed Beast back?" She huffed. "After Maureen worked for months to undo the damage you caused him?"

"I had no reason to turn him back." Delphine shrugged.

"It's over." Maureen approached, her wide eyes on Belle.

"Maker's moldy knickers, you turned yourself into a bear-woman," Captain Charity muttered under her breath. Louder, she said, "Delphine, you've run out of options. Let us go."

"I wouldn't say I'm completely out of options." Delphine smirked.

Seeing red, Belle swiped her paws at the other woman, but only met air.

Faster than what should be humanly possible, Delphine sidestepped out of Belle's range and ducked down, scooping Maureen's dog-whistle device off the floor. She pressed the button.

The noise was piercing. Belle roared, covering her ears. From his prone position, Beast's pained growls rose.

Delphine grinned triumphantly as she fled the room, device in hand.

Captain Charity and Maureen shouted something in their direction, but Belle couldn't hear them. During the chaos, the captain had retrieved her electric saber. The pair raced out of the room.

As the shrill noise of the device grew faint, Belle stumbled over to Beast's side. Beneath his loose bandages, his eyes were closed.

"Beast?"

"Belle, what did you do to yourself?" He opened his eyes.

"Whatever I could to protect you." Belle's heart ached as she answered. "But it wasn't enough. Delphine escaped."

Beast craned his neck, his bandages slipping with the movement. "I thought I heard Maureen and Captain Charity in here. Or did I imagine it?"

Belle grimaced as she helped Beast sit up. "They were here, but they went after Delphine."

In the hall, there was a crash, then a shout, followed by baying and growls.

Belle's nostrils flared as the scent of the Hounds rushing past the lab hit her. "I'll come back for you. Stay safe."

She lumbered toward the exit with an unsteady gait. Outside of the lab, the growls grew quiet. All she could hear was the low hum of the lab equipment and Beast's labored breathing. The astringent odor of elixirs brewing in the lab muddled her senses, deepening her unease.

With Delphine on the run and no sign of Captain Charity or Maureen, the abrupt silence was unsettling. Where had everyone disappeared to?

A frantic commotion in the lab startled Belle out of her musings. She turned to see Beast clumsily climbing off the examination table, knocking over the elixir machine.

"Belle, wait!" Beast shakily stood, his bandages slipping.

Shaking her head, Belle trudged to his side. "You should lie down. You're not in any state to move, let alone wander through this creepy manor."

Beast huffed as he leaned against the table, his legs wobbling. "You're one to talk after injecting yourself with Delphine's elixir. It's lucky that you have your memory intact."

"I'll be fine." Belle furrowed her brows as she stared at Beast. There seemed to be less fur poking out between his bandages than she remembered. Was it her imagination, or was his frame changing shape? "You can barely stand. Let me help you lie back down."

Beast shook his head. "I don't think Delphine's elixir is taking the way she'd hoped."

Before Belle could protest, Beast tore the tattered remains of the bandages covering his upper body. His skin glowed brightly, like ether reacting. As the light faded, he shifted from the bearlike shape she'd known to a much more human frame. His silvery fur vanished, revealing scarred, pale skin.

Beast was a man.

Wild silver-white hair streaked with black strands brushed the top of his broad shoulders. Dark brows with flecks of white hair framed his warm, honey-colored eyes. His mouth formed an "o" while he studied his strong, calloused hands.

"Beast?" Belle's mouth went dry.

Scar tissue covering his muscular chest and arms drew her gaze. Belle wanted nothing more than to trace his old wounds and soothe his past hurts. Reaching forward, she stopped short of touching him when she remembered her wicked claws.

Beast laughed, revealing his canines were still long and sharp. "I don't believe it! Did Delphine accidentally cure me?"

Belle tilted her head. "How? You transformed back into a creature while connected to her machine." She tapped her muzzle. "Look what her elixir did to me."

"I know." Beast's voice grew quiet as he placed his hand on her muzzle. "Maybe something in Maureen's cure reacted with Delphine's elixir?"

"We can ask Maureen when I find her." Belle placed her paw over Beast's hand. "Please stay here. We don't know what the elixirs mixing did to you."

"Don't ask me to leave you. I can't do that." Beast gave her a rueful smile. "Besides, it might not be safe here. From what little I remember from my time here, Delphine moved about the grounds in a way that seemed unreal. The way she'd appear and disappear at will was alarming."

"Couldn't that be because you were newly transformed and disoriented?" Belle frowned.

"Maybe? It wouldn't surprise me if she had hidden tunnels all over this place. Look what she did with her lab." Beast nodded at the chandeliers. "She has a flair for the dramatic."

Belle sighed. "Fair point. I still think you shouldn't be up, though."

"I know, but I'll be fine. Trust me."

With his free hand, Beast traced her jawline, sending delicious shivers down her back. She closed her eyes, enjoying the warmth of his touch.

In the distance, there was shouting, followed by high-pitched whines.

Heart pounding, Belle opened her eyes and met Beast's determined gaze.

"Let's find Maureen and the captain." His mouth set in a grim line.

"You're going to go after them like that?" Belle pointedly stared at the bandages barely staying in place around his waist and legs. She tried in vain not to think about how the softness around his stomach looked perfect for curling up against.

Beast bit his lip as he sheepishly looked down. "I have little choice. I guess if all else fails, maybe I can be a distraction?"

"That's one way to look at it." Belle snorted before gesturing to the doorway. "Shall we?"

"One last thing." Beast pressed his soft lips against Belle's muzzle. "I know you're trying to save us, but please don't be so reckless. Let's get through this together. I couldn't bear the thought of life without you."

Belle's chest tightened. She wished she could promise to be more careful, but she couldn't stand the thought of lying now. Instead, she replied, "Let's find our friends and get out of here."

Belle wished she'd been paying more attention to her surroundings when they'd been taken prisoner. She and Beast finally made it out of the winding corridor and found themselves in an expansive open foyer that rose several stories. Treacherous stairs with no handrails spiraled all the way to the ceiling.

The circular room looked identical on all sides, with plain doors spaced evenly around the perimeter. There was no discernible exit. The marble floor's pattern of runes offered no clues, only further mysteries, as two scorch marks marred the otherwise pristine floor.

A wooden door across the room burst open. Captain Charity dashed into the foyer, wielding her electric saber. Maureen closely followed her, gripping her universal screwdriver and fleeing a pack of Hounds giving chase.

"Wrong door!" The mayor shouted. "And I'm out of bombs!"

"I'll hold them off. Try another door!" The captain yelled back.

"Too late!" Maureen gritted her teeth.

Soon Captain Charity and Maureen were in the center of the room, back-to-back and surrounded by confused Hounds. The canines' ears were flat as they whined, circling their prey. They seemed to pay neither Belle nor Beast any attention.

"Why aren't they attacking?" Beast asked.

"No collars." Belle's eyes narrowed. "But something made them run."

A sizzling crack sounded from the open door. The Ringmaster brandished an electric whip. "Quit your useless whining. Fetch." He cracked his whip again, sending sparks flying.

Whimpering, the pack drew closer to Maureen and Captain Charity.

The Ringmaster stalked closer, raising his whip. "Now." He struck the closest one, singeing its fur as it howled piously.

All the creatures panicked as they scrambled into the foyer.

"Fine, I'll do it myself." The Ringmaster stepped forward, only to be blocked by the Hounds running in circles and snapping. "Out of my way!"

Everything became a blur of sparks and fur as chaos erupted in the foyer.

"Stay back," Belle whispered to Beast before charging into the fray.

She was thankful the frightened animals didn't leap to attack her, but their frenzied movements made it impossible to reach her friends. She shoved past the pack, growling at them when they snipped at her.

Intimidated, the canines backed off, their tails tucked between their legs as they retreated against the wall.

At last, Belle reached Captain Charity and Maureen. "Are you either of you hurt?" she asked as she anxiously looked the pair over.

Maureen shook her head. "We're fine. What about you?"

Before Belle could answer, Captain Charity asked, "Where's Beast?"

"He's right over—" Belle's stomach dropped as she spotted the

Ringmaster chasing Beast up the stairs, the cracks of his whip close to striking distance.

"I'll get Beast. You two find a way out." Belle sprinted on all fours to the stairs.

Paws made climbing the narrow stairs even more challenging. Belle stumbled several times in her ascent, but at last, she caught up to the Ringmaster.

With a roar, she swiped at his red coat, shredding the material.

The Ringmaster cried out and dropped his whip. As soon as it fell, its electricity shut off. Before he could recover, Belle kicked the weapon over the edge of the stairs.

She gulped when she looked down. They were up at least two stories. With her paws, her footing was not confident. She backed closer to the outer wall.

"Beast, are you okay?" she asked, keeping her eyes locked onto the Ringmaster.

"Don't worry about me. Stop him." Beast sounded out of breath but confident.

"That's the creature?" The Ringmaster's jaw dropped.

"That's my Beast." Belle towered over the Ringmaster, snarling as she pushed him closer to the edge of the stairs. "And you're going to leave. Understood?"

His blond mustache twitched as he gulped. "Perfectly."

"Good." Belle scooped the Ringmaster around his waist and placed him on the steps behind her. "Get out of my sight."

She watched the Ringmaster begin his descent before turning her attention to Beast. He was crouched against the wall panting. Fresh scratches and bruises dotted his chest.

"You're hurt." Belle lumbered to his side, placing her paw carefully on his shoulder.

"I'll be fine." Beast touched her paw lightly. His eyes widened. "Belle, look out!"

Stabbing pain shot up Belle's back, radiating from just below her left shoulder blade.

Behind her, the Ringmaster cackled. "As if you were going to win. Please!"

Roaring, Belle swayed as she tried to steady herself.

The Ringmaster's smile faded as barking Hounds bolted up the stairs.

"Stay back!" The Ringmaster balled his fists.

Belle found her footing and planted herself in front of Beast.

"No!" The Ringmaster stepped back as the pack rushed him. He slipped and fell over the edge of the stairs.

Against her better judgment, Belle tried to reach for him but missed.

The Ringmaster screamed the whole way down, landing in a sickening thud.

The Hounds dashed down the stairs, snarling at the broken body before scattering.

"Can we leave now?" Bile rose in Belle's throat as she looked down at the vile man's crumpled form. Unable to stomach the view, she turned to check on Beast.

He was gone.

There was a sliver of an opening in the section of stone wall against which Beast had been resting that wasn't there before. Behind the hidden door, Delphine smirked before the passage sealed shut, completely invisible again.

With an anguished roar, Belle slammed her paw against the wall.

CHAPTER THIRTY-FIVE

"He's not in the lab." Captain Charity's voice echoed in the cavernous room as she entered the foyer, pointedly not looking at the floor. "Are you finished yet?"

"Almost!" Maureen called as she knelt next to Belle. Her med pack and the late Ringmaster's bloody knife lay on the step next to her. The mayor had grumbled about stitching on the stairs, but Belle didn't want to budge from the sealed passageway.

Belle's heart sank. She was relieved that Delphine hadn't dragged Beast back to the lab, but she hated not knowing where he was.

"This is going to sting," Maureen warned as she opened an antiseptic vial.

"Please, hurry." The strong scent of the medicine made Belle's eyes water as she stared at the deceptively plain stone wall. If only the Ringmaster had listened to her, Beast would still be here and the former circus tycoon wouldn't be a broken corpse lying on the cold foyer floor.

"I'm going as fast as I can while keeping you safe. It's a small wonder the wound isn't deeper. Hold still."

Belle hissed as the antiseptic stung and clenched her jaw as Maureen stitched.

Captain Charity bounded up the stairs, gasping when her gaze landed on Belle's back. "Oh, that looks nasty. Should you be moving?"

"I'll be fine." Belle stifled a yelp as the stitches were pulled taught.

As Maureen applied bandages, she said, "I suppose this is the part where I'm supposed to tell you to let us find Beast while you find somewhere safe to wait, but you're probably not going to listen, are you?"

"Not a chance." Belle winced as she straightened. The wound throbbed painfully, but she'd live. "Thank you for patching me up."

"You're welcome. Try to be careful, though. We don't know how stable your transformation is." Maureen pursed her lips as she watched Belle over her octagonal glasses. "You could wait. We radioed Chancellor Elmstone during our flight. Backup should be on the way."

"Since when has the chancellor ever done anything helpful for us?" Belle scoffed. "If it were the captain missing, what would you do?"

Maureen sighed. "I'd be tearing the building down stone by stone."

Belle looked back at the sealed wall. "I wish you still had bombs."

"Me too." The mayor shook her head as she repacked her medical bag.

Captain Charity cleared her throat. "Do we have a plan? It looks like the Hounds have scattered. Poor things are curled up in the corridors. At least we shouldn't have to worry about them for now."

Belle stood shakily, balancing one paw on the wall as she found her footing. With her other paw, she pointed up. "Delphine mentioned back at the lab something about sending Ms. Palmer to a tower. Maybe she knows something?"

Worry lines creased Maureen's forehead. "Can you climb all that?"

Belle let go of the wall and squared her shoulders. "I have to."

After a strenuous climb on all fours, Belle panted as she squeezed through the opening to the landing at the top of the stairs. The small room was devoid of any decoration or furniture save flickering gas lamps in dusty sconces.

Maureen and Captain Charity crowded around the lone door in the room, arguing quietly with each other.

"It's probably a trap. You need to get back." Maureen held up her universal screwdriver. "Besides, I'm the one with a pick."

"I can pick it just as easily as you can." Captain Charity's voice was heated. "Don't you think we need your brains more if it's rigged?"

Padding across the floor, Belle nudged past the couple. "I adore you both, but we're wasting time."

Before either woman could protest, she clumsily pulled down on the door handle, bracing herself for a shock, or worse. No explosions came as the door creaked open. A pitch-black hallway stretched before them.

Captain Charity rubbed the back of her neck. "At least we don't have to pick the lock."

"That was reckless." Maureen glared as she pushed forward. "The unlocked door makes me more nervous than any trap. Let us lead the way."

Belle wanted to argue, but the others were already making their way through the hallway.

Grumbling under her breath as she pushed through the door, Belle reluctantly followed. She felt a pang of guilt for letting her friends go first, but she knew it was the wiser choice as her bearlike frame slowed her movements in the cramped passage.

Much farther ahead than Belle cared for, her friends' silhouettes were barely visible as they stood in the open doorway at the end of the hall. They stepped through the entrance and the door slammed shut behind them with an ominous series of clicks.

"Wait!" Belle struggled to move faster, growling as her shoulders scraped against the rough wall.

At last, she finally reached the door, pushing it with the full weight of her body. The door wouldn't budge. With every ounce of strength, she leaned into the door. Sounds of scuffling, shouts, and an alarming snap spurred her to act faster. When brute force failed to do anything other than make her shoulders sore, she clumsily ran her claw around the edge of the door, hoping for an opening. No such luck.

She slumped against the door. Had she really come so far to be stopped by a mere door?

Almost of its own volition, the series of clicks resumed and the door swung open. Warily, Belle stood. She knew this was certainly a trap, and yet a tiny ray of hope refused to be extinguished as she ventured into the eerily quiet room. Her stomach dropped as her eyes adjusted to the dim lighting. She couldn't see Captain Charity or Maureen.

In the center of the room, machinery, vaguely humanoid skulls, and rows of elixirs crowded onto tables pushed together in a U-shape surrounded Delphine. Beast's eyes were closed as he reclined on a raised cot.

Belle's blood froze as she realized Beast wasn't strapped down. What had Delphine done to him? The rise and fall of his chest as he breathed gave her a small measure of comfort but did nothing to slow her pounding heart.

Behind the lab setup, Ms. Palmer hunched over a control panel next to a window, muttering as she sent frightened glances toward Delphine. Next to the controls on a shelf, empty mugs and a radio balanced precariously.

"I was wondering if you were going to come." Delphine's thin lips stretched into a wide grin as she looked up from her work. Sweat dotted her skin, ruining her makeup and making her dark gold veins visible in splotches. "Looks like my calculations were correct after all."

"Let him go." Belle emitted a low growl. "Where are my friends?"

Delphine swept her arm, the long, green sleeves of her gown billowing as she pointed at the far side of the room. "Over there, where they can't interfere with my plans."

Bile rose in Belle's throat as she turned to look.

Ether-laced chains shackled Captain Charity and Maureen together to a stone pillar. Crimson orbs glowed in their collars. The captain's saber lay dormant on the floor in front of them. Both women were conscious and scowling at Delphine.

"Careful, Belle. She probably has the whole room trapped." Maureen coughed. Fresh scratches marred her face, and her glasses were askew.

"Are you hurt?" Belle padded toward her chained friends, keeping Delphine in her line of sight.

"Only our pride," Captain Charity said breezily, despite the purple bruises darkening on her left cheek. Her fingers were closed, as if concealing an object.

A tiny spark of hope bloomed in Belle's chest. Perhaps the captain had the lockpick?

"Stop there." Delphine held up a blood-red orb on a golden chain and dangled it between her slender fingers. "One more step and they'll be in for the last shock of their lives."

Belle barred her teeth. "You won't get away with this. The Ringmaster is dead. The Hounds aren't in your control anymore."

Delphine shrugged. "The Ringmaster was never that useful. All talk and disappointing results. Perhaps I should have experimented on him instead of making him an errand boy." She tutted. "As for the Hounds, that's only a temporary setback. I can always make more. But first, I have my most important work to complete."

Rage filled Belle as Delphine turned, adding a shimmering blue elixir to an all too familiar machine next to Beast. Wordlessly, Belle crept closer. If she could catch the madwoman with her back turned, maybe she'd get them all out of here alive.

Suddenly Belle's paw connected with a hidden pressure plate. An electric fence buzzed to life, surrounding the miniature lab. The current singed the tip of her muzzle. She howled as she retreated a few steps back.

"Not so fast. You sit tight while I'm working. The fence comes down when I say so. I'll get to you next." Delphine wagged her finger at Belle, the chained orb bobbing with the movement.

Chest tightening, Belle watched in wide-eyed fear as Delphine leaned over Beast.

"Now, where were we?" Delphine crooned as she swept his hair out of his face.

Beast's hand shot up as he lunged for Delphine's orb. His movements were clumsy as he stumbled off the cot, but his hand wrapped around the jewel. Tugging it free, he threw the orb to the ground and stomped on it with a scream.

Belle winced as she remembered his feet were bare.

The electric fence shut off with a weak hum.

"You've ruined everything!" Delphine shrieked, holding her hands like claws as she turned on Beast.

He glared. "Good." His skin paled as his balance slipped. He barely caught the edge of the cot as he swayed on the spot.

Belle bounded toward Delphine, pulse pounding. "Get away from him!"

"No!" Delphine held up a vial of a noxious black liquid. "Any movement from you and I'll kill him myself. Getting a new subject will be a pain, but I'll never let you have him back."

"Don't let her take me," Beast whispered before his eyes fluttered closed. He slumped forward, his fall broken by Delphine as she caught him in her arms.

"Beast!" Belle watched in agony as Delphine laid him on the ground.

Across the room, there was a metallic clatter.

"Now what?" Delphine screamed, her face turning scarlet.

Captain Charity and Maureen, freed from their shackles, flanked the cowering Ms. Palmer. The mayor clutched the lockpick while the captain held her electric saber to Ms. Palmer's throat.

"It's finished." Maureen reached her hand toward Delphine. "Let me help you find a cure. You've been unwell for such a long time."

"Never!" Delphine scoffed. "This is just another scheme of yours."

Belle had enough. She rushed forward and knocked Delphine away from Beast's prone body. The black vial shattered on the ground, hissing as it spilled on the floor.

Delphine groaned as she landed next to the table full of elixirs.

"You're done," Belle growled as she stalked closer.

"I'll never be done." With a triumphant smirk, Delphine swiped a golden flask off the table.

Belle halted, staring at the flask warily. She wouldn't put it past the other woman to have acid or something equally dangerous on hand.

"Don't do it!" Ms. Palmer screamed. "You haven't tested it!" More quietly, she sobbed, "Please. Let them help you."

"You're just as spineless as she was," Delphine sneered as she downed the flask. Her words died on her lips as her body convulsed. A scream ripped from her throat as her bones shifted.

Unwilling to watch Delphine's transformation unfold, Belle hurried to Beast's side. His breathing was much too shallow.

"Beast?" Belle gently lifted him into her arms.

His eyes fluttered open weakly. "You're here. Are we safe?"

"I think so."

Dreading what she'd see, Belle looked up.

Clutching her chest, Delphine staggered into her vials, blindly grabbing potions and drinking them as her form continued to change. At last, her body settled into her familiar shape.

"I've done it." Delphine smiled radiantly as she whispered. Her golden veins were no longer visible on her alabaster skin. Her eyes closed, and she collapsed to the floor.

"Delphine!" Ms. Palmer's anguished cry rang out.

As Captain Charity lowered her sword, Ms. Palmer and Maureen rushed to Delphine's side.

Crouching down, Maureen checked the fallen woman's pulse. After several moments passed, she sighed. "She's dead."

"You should have listened." Ms. Palmer shook her head, tears streaming down her face as she knelt next to Delphine.

The radio crackled on. A gruff voice called, "This is the Nuzaran National Armada. We have you surrounded, Delphine Wyerstone."

Captain Charity rolled her eyes as she mouthed, "Useless."

The captain pressed the call button. "This is Captain Charity. I'm here with Mayor Dawkins. Delphine has been dealt with, but please tell the chancellor's people to come clean up the mess. We're exhausted here."

"It's over?" the voice asked, muffled by static.

"Almost," Captain Charity replied as she watched Belle hold Beast against her chest.

CHAPTER THIRTY-SIX

Maureen fretted as she redressed Belle's bandages in the *Figment's* med bay. "Between you and Beast, I'm not sure which one of you I need to wrap in something protective."

"Beast. Definitely Beast." Belle narrowed her eyes as Beast reclined on the cot next to her pallet, wrapped in a well-loved quilt. "I can't believe you dove at Delphine while drugged."

Beast pointed at Belle and raised his dark brows. "That's funny coming from you after what you did with her elixir."

"Fine, we're even," Belle huffed.

"Fair enough." Beast's dazzling smile faded as he attempted to tug his loose shirt tighter. All his former clothes were far too big on him, but nothing else on the airship fit, leaving him with plunging necklines. His clothes were almost all made of lightweight material, as anything heavier used to cause him to overheat. "Can I have another blanket? These clothes are doing nothing for me."

After putting away the medical kit, Maureen retrieved a blanket from an overhead cabinet. "I'm grateful everything worked out, but please, take it easy for a while. Both of you."

Belle grimaced as she curled up on her pallet. Without the

adrenaline rush from immediate danger, her whole body ached. "I won't be moving around much at all, trust me."

"Good. No more injecting yourself with strange elixirs." Maureen tutted as she took her pulse. "It's going to be messy sorting out what Delphine's concoction did to you."

Belle lifted her head up. "But you can undo it, right?"

Maureen pursed her lips. "I think so, but without knowing how her elixir interacted with your ether-poisoning cure, it's going to be a lot trickier. I think it's a good sign that your memory is intact. But —"

"Are these your friends?" A bubbly voice cut in, every other word punctuated by the whirring of motors and solenoids. Gears groaned and heavy, uneven footsteps tapped against the floor.

Damek entered the med bay with another automaton who looked like a half-finished prototype made of a hodgepodge of various metals and spare parts.

"Yes, but you really should sit. You're not fully operational yet!" Damek's eyes flashed orange as the other automaton stumbled. His mechanical arms clanged as he caught her by her waist.

"I've been wanting to meet your friends since you told me about them! It motivated me to keep my aim steady during my first airship battle." The automaton's bright eyes lit green.

"And *last* airship battle." Maureen coughed and cleared her throat.

The automaton's face plates scrunched together in a frown. "That's not what the captain said."

Damek elbowed his friend. "Belle, Beast, this is Hope. She's the best shot I've ever witnessed."

Hope grinned, loosening the bolts holding together her jaw. "So nice to finally meet you. Damek told me all about you two." Her eyes rapidly changed colors, cycling between green, blue, and amber as she looked from Belle to Beast. "I thought you said the man was the furry one?"

"Beast got better. I had an incident." Belle couldn't help smiling at the automaton's curious nature. "Hope's a beautiful name. Thank you for coming to our rescue."

"You're welcome!" Hope bounced on her heels, earning another concerned look from Damek as her knee joints creaked. "I chose it because Maureen kept saying it while she was working on me. My creator said it so many times that I thought it was my name." With a perfect imitation of Maureen's voice, she said, *"I hope this works. I hope we're not too late. I hope this isn't a terrible plan."*

The mayor rubbed the back of her neck. "We should let Belle and Beast recover until takeoff." She sighed as she checked her pocket watch. "I'm sure the chancellor will want to check in before then. Last I heard, they're still cleaning up."

Maureen nodded at Belle and Beast. "If you two need anything, hit the call button."

"Will do." Beast snuggled into his blankets and yawned.

Belle hummed in agreement.

After Maureen left, Belle and Beast rested in silence. Assuming he had fallen asleep, Belle stared at the ceiling, willing her mind to quiet down. Her body was so sore, but her thoughts raced as she considered Maureen's unfinished sentence about undoing Delphine's elixir.

There was a rustling sound from Beast's cot as he sat up and brushed his hair out of his face. "You're thinking so loud I can almost hear your thoughts. What's the matter?"

Belle sat up, her mouth going dry at the sight before her. Beast's blanket slid down, and the deep cut of his shirt left little to the imagination. With tremendous effort, she forced herself to look him in the face, which did nothing to quell her new line of thought as she took in his tender gaze and parted lips.

"Belle?"

Shaking her head, she slumped her shoulders. "I hate that I'm stuck like this when you're finally cured. We can't catch a break."

Beast reached his hand across the narrow gap between his cot and Belle's pallet to hold her paw. "I'm just happy we're together. I bet Maureen will be able to cure you when we're back."

"I hope so." Belle gloomily extended her claws, careful to avoid Beast's hand. "How did you ever do anything with these? Sorting books at the library is going to be a nightmare."

"Lots of practice that I'm hoping you won't have to experience." Beast rubbed circles on the pads of her paw. "I'll help you with the books until Maureen figures out a solution for you. You're not alone."

Eyes watering, Belle whispered, "Thank you."

"You're welcome. Let's get some rest. I can't wait to go home with you." Beast squeezed her paw, and soon they both drifted off.

Unfortunately, going home was not a straightforward affair. After an arduous flight, all Belle wanted to do was go straight back to their cottage. She did not expect to see the mayor's secretary waiting for them at the airship docks.

Wringing his hands, Mr. Cadwell explained to Belle and Beast that the contractors had discovered the fire damage was more extensive than previously thought, and repairs were still underway.

Maureen took the news in stride. "You two can stay with us. It makes sense to keep you in town while I work on your cure, anyway."

Belle sniffled, carefully wiping back her tears. "Thank you so much."

The hazy summer days passed by in a blur as Belle and Beast settled into their new routine. Maureen ran tests, poured through Delphine's journals, and tried different elixir combinations on Belle with varying degrees of success, though none eradicated her beastly form. The most successful of the batch gave Belle a little more dexterity in her paws, making it marginally easier to hold silverware and read books.

"I'll figure this out. I swear it." Maureen clenched her fists. She'd already cured the rounded-up Hounds that the chancellor had insisted on sending to Duchollow for rehabilitation.

"Thank you." Belle's friend's determination touched her deeply, though despair was hard to resist.

On good days, Belle ventured out to the library after Beast returned from their cottage to tend to his garden. They left together under the cover of darkness to avoid the stares of the townspeople. Though the citizens of Duchollow had once been used to Beast's bear-like form, Belle didn't want to deal with their shocked reactions at her appearance.

During their library visits, Beast kept Belle entertained with updates about the cottage's repairs and his garden. There was a sparkle in his eye when he talked about their home and that warmed her heart.

As the weeks passed, though, it was increasingly difficult for Belle to keep her spirits up.

One night in the library, she sighed as she fumbled re-shelving another book.

"Let me get that." Beast placed his hand on her back.

Belle swallowed as she watched his powerful thighs as he bent down to pick up the book. Captain Charity had done an excellent job of helping him find clothes that set off his assets.

"All better." Beast straightened, then frowned as he looked at Belle. "What's the matter? The book isn't damaged."

Belle shook her head. "It's not that." She looked down, feigning interest in the pattern of the ornate rug. "Do you think I'll ever be human again? I'm beginning to think I'm stuck like this."

Beast tucked his hand underneath Belle's muzzle, gently guiding her to look at him. "I know this is hard. Remember how long it took for me to be cured? I'm sure Maureen will find the answer soon enough."

"I know. I'm so tired of waiting."

"I'll wait as long as it takes." Beast kissed the side of Belle's muzzle.

The library door opened with a loud bang. Maureen entered looking frazzled, her glasses askew. "I think I've found the answer! Can you come back to the lab?"

Belle and Beast stared as the mayor approached.

"Really?" Belle's knees suddenly felt weak and she leaned against Beast.

Maureen nodded vigorously. "Between Delphine's journal and my own notes, I've got it." She looked at Beast. "I'll need you, too. Grab your things and let's go."

The long table at the lab was set up with a complex arrangement of colorful vials alongside the contraption she had used to cure Beast. Belle was not looking forward to having the wolfish mask over her face again, but the hopeful atmosphere in the lab renewed her confidence.

"I just need a vial of Beast's blood again. My supply ran out," Maureen said as she lowered the flames beneath a shimmering flask full of viscous fluid. "Cracking Delphine's code took longer than I thought. She was paranoid until the end, writing false information between bits of truth. But she had an emergency cure drafted in her notes."

"What makes you sure it'll work this time?" Beast asked as the mayor finished drawing his blood.

"Days ago, I tested it on a sample of Belle's blood. It was completely human when I was finished. I've replicated the process twice since then." Maureen added the vial to the elixir, watching the shimmering liquid shift from gold to a deep purple. She poured in another vial, and it became silver.

"Ready?" Maureen donned her goggles.

"As ready as I'll ever be," Belle sat down in the examination chair and braced herself against the armrests.

Beast kissed the top of Belle's head. "I'll be right here with you."

Belle blacked out several times as the elixir burned its way through her veins. Screams ripped from her throat as her body thrashed and her bones shifted.

At last, her agony ended.

There was a pneumatic hiss as the wolfish mask and arm shackles released with a series of clicks.

Belle blinked as her eyes adjusted. Her aching muscles felt too tight. Lifting her arms to stretch, she did a double take as she saw her fingers, not claws, for the first time in weeks.

"It worked." The crushing weight of despair finally lifted, making Belle giddy as she wiggled her fingers.

"Yes!" Maureen pumped her fist in the air. "Let me get a mirror."

"You're back." Beast leaned down, tucking Belle's hair behind her ears. "How do you feel?"

Instead of answering, Belle's gaze lingered on his lips. "Almost better. There's something missing."

"I can help with that."

Beast delicately brushed his lips against Belle's. Not content with a small peck, she laced her fingers through his hair to pull him closer, earning a chuckle from him as he deepened the kiss. Warmth grew in Belle's stomach as she arched into him.

Neither of them heard Maureen return, nor did they hear her set the mirror down on the table before quietly leaving.

The plaza in the center of Duchollow was lit by strings of warm light. Garlands of violets swayed in the breeze. There was a hint of fall in the crisp night air. Belle smoothed down the skirt of her midnight blue gown as she waited for Beast, content with people-watching as guests chatted and danced to the festive melody played by two violinists accompanied by a pianist.

The music swelled, carrying over the crowds' delighted cheers as Maureen and Captain Charity entered the dance floor, both beaming and wearing identical wedding bands on their intertwined fingers.

Captain Charity pressed her lips to Maureen's hand as the band switched to a romantic waltz. The captain's dreamy white gown twirled magnificently as Maureen spun her. The mayor's matching white suit was equally stunning.

Belle smiled as she watched her friends, though the chime of the grand clock tower announcing the top of the hour dampened her enthusiasm. Where was Beast? He'd mentioned a last-minute errand, but she thought he'd be here by now.

Fidgeting with her rose necklace, Belle sighed. It seemed she and Beast couldn't catch a break since she'd made a full recovery. The library was open six days a week, and she spent most of her time training new librarians as the patrons increased exponentially every day. Beast was occupied with his garden during the harvest season.

Worst of all, renovations to their cottage were taking far longer than the contractors had estimated. Living at Maureen and Captain Charity's afforded them little time alone.

A gentle tap on her bare shoulder startled Belle out of her musings. She turned to see Beast dressed in a well-tailored suit. He'd trimmed his scruff and tied his long hair back with a ribbon that coordinated with her gown.

Beast's voice rumbled pleasantly in her ear as he leaned in. "Sorry to keep you waiting. Work ran late, then getting ready took longer than I thought."

"I was worried about you." Belle kissed him on the cheek. "Are you okay?"

"Better now." A mischievous glint appeared in Beast's honey-colored eyes as he looked her over. "You look amazing. Now I'm doubly sorry for keeping you waiting."

He traced Belle's rose necklace with his finger, letting it brush against her collarbone. He grinned wickedly when she shivered at his touch.

"The necklace looks good with your dress."

"Thank you." Belle blushed. "I'm glad I can wear it again."

Applause from the other guests caught their attention. Maureen dipped Captain Charity dramatically, both radiating with joy. The band began another waltz and their guests flocked to join in.

"Shall we?" Beast offered his hand.

Belle slipped her hand into his. "I thought you'd never ask. I'd love to."

"Good answer." Beast kept his hand at the small of her back as he led her to the dance floor.

Belle happily leaned into Beast's embrace as the waltz transitioned to a more upbeat tune. At the end of the song, he mimicked Maureen, dipping Belle low, and she giggled as he helped her back up.

Her laughter died on her lips as Beast pulled her close.

"Want to get out of here early? I don't think anyone will miss us." His breath tickled against her ear.

Belle's eyes sparkled. "I suppose if anyone asks, we can say we wanted to check on Cinders."

While Belle and Beast had volunteered to watch the cat while their friends went on their honeymoon, Belle privately felt she and Beast might almost be more impatient for time alone than the newlyweds.

Beast hummed in agreement. "Good idea. Let's go wish the happy couple a wonderful honeymoon."

They found Maureen and Captain Charity sitting at a table with Hope, Damek, and a bemused Mr. Cadwell, who was trying to explain the concept of dancing to the automatons to the newlyweds' amusement.

"But why do they move their limbs like that?" Hope asked, waving her mechanical limbs in the air. Her repairs were complete, though her movements were still disjointed.

Damek shook his head. "The problem is you're applying logic to the human's behavior. It's all part of their nonsensical courtship rituals."

Mr. Cadwell rubbed his temples before standing. "I need a drink before I answer any more questions."

"Ooh, what kind of drink?" Hope stood, wobbling, until Damek leaped to his feet to steady her.

The secretary let out a long, suffering sigh. "Follow me."

Mr. Cadwell nodded politely to Belle and Beast as he left the table, the two automatons following closely behind him.

Maureen waved to Belle and Beast, wiping away tears of laughter with her free hand. "Come join us!"

"Actually, we were coming to say goodnight." Belle fidgeted with her necklace, suddenly feeling shy.

"Heading out already?" Captain Charity raised her eyebrows. "I can't imagine why."

Belle blushed, rubbing the back of her neck, but laughed when Beast guffawed.

"You've caught us." He shrugged.

"We wanted to say congratulations again. We're so happy for you two." Belle came around the table and hugged her friends tightly.

"Thank you, dear." Maureen's eyes misted. "It's wonderful to see you two so happy as well."

Beast put his arm around Belle's waist. "Thank you for everything you've both done for us. We'll treat you to dinner after you're back. I hope you have a fantastic honeymoon."

"And don't worry about anything. Everything will be taken care of here. We'll keep Cinders company," Belle promised.

Beast and Captain Charity exchanged knowing glances. Before Belle could ask what was going on, Maureen and the captain waved them off.

"Goodbye!" Maureen and the captain hugged them both again before Beast led Belle away from the reception.

To Belle's surprise, they did not go straight to Town Hall. Instead, Beast took her down a side street to Maureen's truck.

"What are you doing?" Belle asked.

"I have a surprise for you." Though the lighting was dim, Belle could hear the smile in his voice. "Maureen said we could borrow her truck. She's spent the last few weeks teaching me how to drive while you were at the library. Mr. Cadwell's taking her and the captain to the airship dock tomorrow."

Belle tilted her head. "But where are we going?"

Beast beamed. "Home."

"What do you mean?"

"Mr. Cadwell is going to watch Cinders instead, at his request. He mentioned something about finally enjoying some peace for a few days, though I don't think the automatons are on board with that idea."

Belle threw her arms around Beast. "Finally!"

As they pulled up to their cottage, Belle's eyes widened. There was a trail of lanterns leading to the back of their property.

"More surprises?" Belle teased as Beast helped her out of the borrowed automobile.

Beast pressed a chaste kiss to her fingers. "You're not tired of them, are you?"

Belle shook her head.

She snuggled against Beast as he guided her toward the greenhouse. Though the temperature outside had rapidly cooled, inside the warmly lit greenhouse, red roses were in full bloom. Soft music played on a radio next to the cozy sofa. Belle recognized it as the song they had slow danced to the first time Beast cooked for her.

"What's all this? It's gorgeous," Belle breathed.

"I wanted to make our first night back special." He pointed to the sofa. "Have a seat?"

Belle nodded, careful not to crinkle her skirts as she sat.

When Beast didn't immediately sit down, she furrowed her brows. "Aren't you going to sit, too?"

"In a moment." Beast removed an ornate carved box from his breast pocket. He knelt and turned the brass gear on its outer lid. Inside the box, gears turned, and the lid opened, revealing the most beautiful ring Belle had ever seen. The ring featured a diamond nestled between two red crystal roses. Its band resembled a stem shaped into a circle. It matched her necklace perfectly.

"I can't imagine spending my life with anyone else but you. Belle, will you marry me?" Beast's eyes shimmered with emotion.

Belle stood up and then knelt next to Beast, throwing her arms around his neck and kissing him soundly. "Yes! A thousand times, yes!"

The force of her embrace nearly knocked them over. Beast barely caught her before they lost their balance.

"I appreciate your enthusiasm," he teased as he placed the ring on her finger. "May I always bring you such joy. I love you."

"I love you, too." Belle admired the perfect fit of the ring.

"Can you handle being married to a beast?" He raised his brows, smirking.

Belle ran her fingers along the line of his jaw. Despite

conducting an extensive investigation at Delphine's manor, no clues had been found regarding Beast's origin or identity. The prevailing theory was he had once been her gardener. He had taken the news in stride. Later, he confided to Belle that he liked the way she said his name, so there was no reason to change it.

"I think I can manage."

Beast took her into his arms, rubbing small circles on her lower back. "I have no family name," he reminded her.

"We'll make our own."

Beast kissed her again, igniting a spark in Belle.

When they parted, she tapped his lips lightly.

"Beast?"

"Yes?"

"Take me home."

Beast placed a lingering kiss on her knuckles.

"Nothing would make me happier."

Inside their cottage, rose petals led to their newly renovated bedroom. An iron-wrought canopy bed was in the center of the room. Ethereal, gauzy curtains hung from its frame and the mattress was covered by inviting soft white blankets. It looked incredibly comfortable, but that was the last thing on Belle's mind as Beast carried her carefully to the bed and set her down as if she were the most precious thing in the world.

His lips met hers in a hungry kiss, as if he'd been waiting forever for this moment. Belle kissed him back with the same intensity, heat flooding her body as his hands tenderly traced her curves.

Arching her back, she moaned into his mouth.

Beast's breathing was ragged when he came up for air. He kissed down her neck, eliciting gasps from her before he moved to the end of the bed, leaving Belle bereft.

At her pout, he chuckled. "Patience. I'll make it worth the wait."

He kissed the faded scars on her ankle before pushing her skirt back as he placed heated kisses up her legs. Beast's idea of patience had Belle grabbing the blankets with her fists and crying out as his scruff rubbed against her inner thighs. When his lips finally returned to hers, she returned his kiss eagerly. It wasn't long before their clothes were in a crumpled pile on the floor as they became one.

Much later, Belle nestled into Beast's side and sighed happily.

He kissed her forehead. "Better?"

"So much better." She pointed to her ring. "How did you manage this surprise?"

Beast grinned. "Maureen helped me find the jeweler. It's the same place she bought Captain Charity's ring. The captain gifted me the materials. She said they were relics from her pirating days."

Belle covered her mouth as she laughed. "I'll have to thank them when they're back." She laced her fingers with his.

"Do you want a big wedding like theirs?"

She shook her head. "Their ceremony was beautiful, but I'd prefer something small. Let's elope and celebrate with our friends."

Beast brought their joined hands to his lips. "Sounds perfect to me."

As they drifted off, Belle dreamed of their future. She couldn't wait to spend her days working at the library, helping Beast with his garden, and visiting their friends in town. They'd found their home together at last.

ACKNOWLEDGMENTS

This book would not have been possible without the support of the original serial readers. So many of you were the first to ask me when Forsaken Beauty and the Etherbeast would be available as a book. Thank you so much for your encouragement!

Thank you so much to my team of beta readers who assisted me with the monumental task of taking an epic length serial and reworking it into novel form. Thank you so much for your thoughtful feedback, attention to detail, and most of all, your time.

I feel incredibly blessed that I had two amazing editors, Jeanne De Vita and Kristi O'Meara, work on this book. Jeanne, your enthusiasm, patience with my dangling modifiers, and teaching have made an enormous impact on me. I have learned so much from you and I'm in constant awe of your abilities. Kristi, your insights helped me see my work in a whole new light and I will be forever grateful for your suggestions.

Thank you so much to my proofreaders, Jeanne De Vita, Kristi O'Meara, and Stephanie Fung, for the invaluable gift of your time!

Besides formatting the book, Michael Lee also designed my gorgeous website, set up my newsletter, created graphics, and answered approximately a billion of my questions with incredible patience and humor. Without his extensive expertise, I would be completely and utterly lost. Thank you for helping make my writing dreams come true!

I will never forget how much my family has supported me throughout this journey. They are my biggest cheerleaders, always there to listen and make sure I have enough iced coffees for writing. My family gave me the confidence to go after my dreams, even when I doubted my readiness. Thank you for being understanding when I needed to retreat to my office or the library to work on particularly difficult sections. I love you all dearly.

ABOUT THE AUTHOR

Kelsey Josephson is a steampunk enthusiast and a sci-fi fantasy author from the Midwest. She is a member of the Science Fiction and Fantasy Writers Association (SFWA) and the Alliance of Independent Authors (ALLi). She has a deep love for Universal Monster movies, all things related to Nikola Tesla, and iced coffee.

Keep up to date by subscribing to Kelsey's newsletter.

Find out more at www.kelseyjosephson.com

instagram.com/authorkelseyjosephson

facebook.com/authorkelseyjosephson

tiktok.com/@authorkelseyjosephson

bookbub.com/authors/kelsey-josephson

amazon.com/stores/Kelsey-Josephson/author/B0882KCTRZ